A two-time ⸻ ⸻ of the ⸻ itish ⸻ ⸻ Mark
C⸻ ⸻ ⸻ ⸻ mining communities of South
Derbyshire and studied Economic History at Leeds before
becoming a journalist. Now a screenwriter for BBC television
drama, he has also run an independent record company,
managed rock bands, and worked on a production line and
as an engineer's 'mate'. He is the author of the celebrated
The Dark Age, The Age of Misrule and *Kingdom of the Serpent*
trilogies. *The Swords of Albion* novels, featuring Will Swyfte,
were inspired in part by a mysterious portrait discovered at
Corpus Christi College, Cambridge, which may be the
only surviving depiction of the playwright and alleged spy,
Christopher Marlowe. It is inscribed with the motto *Quod me
nutrit me destruit* – 'That which nourishes me destroys me'.

Mark Chadbourn lives in a forest in the Midlands. To find out
more about him and his writing, visit www.jackofravens.com.

D0550576

Also by Mark Chadbourn

THE DARK AGE:
THE DEVIL IN GREEN
THE QUEEN OF SINISTER
THE HOUNDS OF AVALON

THE AGE OF MISRULE:
WORLD'S END
DARKEST HOUR
ALWAYS FOREVER

KINGDOM OF THE SERPENT:
JACK OF RAVENS
THE BURNING MAN
DESTROYER OF WORLDS

LORD OF SILENCE

THE SWORDS OF ALBION:
THE SWORD OF ALBION
THE SCAR-CROW MEN
THE DEVIL'S LOOKING GLASS

THE
SCAR-CROW
MEN

MARK CHADBOURN

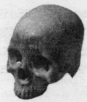

BANTAM BOOKS
LONDON · TORONTO · SYDNEY · AUCKLAND · JOHANNESBURG

TRANSWORLD PUBLISHERS
61–63 Uxbridge Road, London W5 5SA
A Random House Group Company
www.transworldbooks.co.uk

THE SCAR-CROW MEN
A BANTAM BOOK: 9780553820232

First published in Great Britain
in 2011 by Bantam Press
an imprint of Transworld Publishers
Bantam edition published 2012

A CIP catalogue record for this book
is available from the British Library.

Addresses for Random House Group Ltd companies outside the UK
can be found at: www.randomhouse.co.uk
The Random House Group Ltd Reg. No. 954009

The Random House Group Ltd supports The Forest Stewardship
Council (FSC®), the leading international forest-certification organization.
Our books carrying the FSC label are printed on FSC®-certified paper. FSC
is the only forest-certification scheme endorsed by the leading environmental
organizations, including Greenpeace. Our paper procurement policy
can be found at www.randomhouse.co.uk/environment.

Typeset in 11/14pt Bembo by
Kestrel Data, Exeter, Devon.
Printed and bound by
CPI Group (UK) Ltd, Croydon, CR0 4YY.

2 4 6 8 10 9 7 5 3 1

For Elizabeth, Betsy, Joe and Eve

PROLOGUE

PAST THE CANDLEWICK STREET PLAGUE PIT THEY RACE, BY THE
red crosses blooming on doors like spring poppies, and the
words *God have mercy* daubed on house after house. Breath
burning in their chests, they stumble and fall in the night-
dark alleys only to haul themselves up on shaking legs to run
again.

They are not consumed by terror of the sickness that has
left London sweating in a feverish vision of its own demise,
with florid images of blackened skin and blood haunting every
thought. It is fear of what lies at their backs, sweeping through
the filthy streets, caught in the glow of candles, like moths,
eyes blazing with fierce passions. The ones who have footsteps
like whispers, whose passing is a cold breath on the back of the
neck.

'Do not look behind. Do not slow,' Christopher Marlowe
yells to his companion.

His desperation rings off the wattle walls that press in on
either side. In the heat of the late spring night, dark patches of
sweat stain his grey doublet. His short Dutch cloak has been
torn by a nail and his flat-top hat lost several streets back.

Marlowe is a playwright, one of the most famous in

7

England, but he has other work, secret, dirty and dangerous. In intermittent shafts of moonlight, Marlowe's face appears too pale, his features etched with a profound sadness that is surprising in a man still in his twenties. His eyes are dark against his almost translucent skin, the clipped black beard and moustache as wispy as the first face hair of a boy.

Beside him, Jack Wainwright is like a Kentish oak. Though almost ten years older than his companion, with a beard streaked with grey, he could easily shoulder a full beer barrel at the Mermaid Tavern on Cheapside. The whites of his eyes show clearly beneath his heavy brows. Scared, he ignores Marlowe's order and glances back.

Lights dance in the dark, drawing closer.

'We could hide and take them by surprise,' Wainwright says with a wavering voice that contains no enthusiasm. Under his working clothes, a loose coat over a shirt belted with cord, his sweat is cold.

'Would you take that risk? You are strong, but you are not a fighting man. And I, God help me, can do damage only with a quill,' Marlowe gasps. At the crossroads, he pauses, tries to steady his pounding heart, takes his bearings and then moves on.

Careering into the middle of a street near ankle-deep in dung, the two men skid to a halt a hand's-breadth from stamping hooves and creaking wheels. Eyeing them from beneath the brim of his battered hat, the driver spits an oath through the filthy cloth tied tightly across his mouth. He cracks his whip and urges the lumbering horse on. It is the death-cart. In the back, the wrapped bodies are stacked like cordwood, leaking fluids on to the roadway with every jerk and rattle. For a moment, Marlowe and Wainwright stare after the wagon as it disappears into the night.

With a rough shove, the older man urges his companion on. 'We shall not outrun them.'

'No. It is too late for us now,' the playwright mutters under his breath. 'Perhaps it was always too late.'

The route between the filthy hovels is as black as pitch, but Kit has run it many times to avoid the constables and beadles, the drunken cutpurses and the low men to whom he owes money. Continuing west, they pass the open shutter of a cellar crammed to bursting with the poor, huddled in the dark in the reek of their own sweat. Pale faces glance up from the gloom, eyes wide with hopelessness.

Marlowe picks a path through a maze of stables and stores until he sees the spire of St Paul's silhouetted against the night sky. The cathedral would be open for sinners to find sanctuary. He urges Wainwright on.

'We can bolt the door,' he says, clapping a hand on his fellow's shoulder. 'Pile the pews against it.' Although he knows it will do little good.

The fugitives tumble into the candlelit cathedral and slam the heavy door behind them. The echoes rumble like thunder through the cavernous interior of the grand old building. Their breath ragged, they inhale the ghost of incense. With trembling fingers, they draw the bolts lightning-fast, a moment before something crashes against the oak with the force of a carriage. The two men are hurled across the worn flagstones, the impact knocking the wind out of them. Whatever is outside continues to pound the door with a steady, deafening rhythm.

Thoom. Thoom. Thoom. A funeral drum.

The blood hammers so loud in his head, Marlowe can barely think, but after a moment he gathers himself. 'Quick! Help me!' he calls. Wiping the moisture from his brow, he scrambles to his feet and runs to the nearest pew. It is too heavy for him to lift alone, but Wainwright grasps his end and raises it effortlessly. The two men haul it across the door, and then return for two more.

''Twill not delay them long,' Wainwright shouts above the booming echoes. His face is red, his sweat vinegar-sharp in the air.

'It will buy us a moment or two. That is all I need.' Fighting back his queasy dread, Marlowe, followed by Wainwright, runs down the nave's great length. The locals call it Paul's Walk and it is nearly six hundred feet long, making the cathedral the third-longest in Europe, so the clergy boast. Past the scars of the destruction inflicted by Old Henry's dissolution and the Chantries Acts they race, under the vaulted roof and past the triforium which gives the cathedral a grandeur that makes Kit wish he was a Christian with a God who would listen to his pleas. He fixes his attention on the stained glass of the great rose window at the east end, hoping to see a glimmer of dawn, although he knows in his heart there is still a good half-hour to go.

In the sanctified interior, Jack Wainwright has calmed a little, though he winces at every crash against the door. 'What were they doing in that house? Did we really see that . . . that terrible thing?' he asks, kneading his hands. Marlowe knows his companion hopes for a denial. When none comes, Wainwright crosses himself and blinks away tears of dread.

'Put it out of your mind. We have little time left to us. Spend it on whatever pleasant thoughts you can summon.' Distracted, Marlowe continues to search along the nave.

'Pleasant thoughts!' Wainwright exclaims, lifting his hat to run his fingers through sweat-plastered hair.

Marlowe tries to ignore the sour taste of failure. He recalls the hope he felt as he readied himself for the mission at sunset, but as in all his dealings with the Enemy he had also prepared himself for the worst. Now it is a matter of make-do and hope once again. Against his hip, the sack weighs heavily. Will its contents be enough to turn the tide of events?

As the crashes against the great oak door grow louder, he glances back and knows it will not hold much longer.

Grasping a candlestick, the playwright drives the shadows back until he finds the object of his search in the north aisle of the choir. A wooden plaque has been fastened to a pillar to mark the grave of Sir Francis Walsingham. A rush of memories surprises Marlowe with their intensity. Though there had never been any love lost between him and England's former spymaster, he still thinks the funeral was a sad end to a powerful man.

He recalls standing at that same spot three years ago amid the tight knot of men: Will, Burghley, a handful of others, heads bowed, faces solemn. Candlelight and shadows, the sweet smell of incense, the muttered prayers of the priest rustling all around. The Queen, whom the great man had served so well, was noticeably absent. There had been none of the pomp and ceremony that usually greeted the passing of such a dignitary, no cathedral draped in black, no procession of the curious public to see the interment. The funeral was at night, out of sight of the masses, as if it was a guilty secret to be quickly hidden away. They blamed the quiet affair on the huge debts that hung over Walsingham at his death, but Marlowe knows the truth.

The flickering candle drips hot balls of wax on to the plaque with its banal Latin inscription outlining what is public knowledge of the spymaster's life. The playwright laughs bitterly at the volumes of truth that have been omitted.

Dropping to his knees, he finds the unmarked stone slab beside the final resting place of his former master's son-in-law, Sir Philip Sidney. He sees that the other great men buried in the cathedral have towering alabaster monuments, but Walsingham's grave is as he lived his life, unobtrusive, a shadow, easily missed.

From the sack tied to his side, Marlowe draws a pot of ink and, with his quill, begins to deface the tomb.

In the beginning was the Word, he writes.

Wainwright squats beside him, babbling, 'Why are we here? Why do you do this?'

The pounding on the door suddenly ceases. The silence that follows is somehow worse.

'Is there nothing that can save us?' the big man pleads. 'I could turn myself to God and pray for forgiveness.'

'If you feel there is some good in it, then do it.' Kit's tone is warm and he hopes it will comfort, but he sees a shadow cross his companion's face and knows he has accepted the suggestion too readily. Wainwright begins to shake until Marlowe puts a steadying hand on his shoulder.

'We should go our separate ways. That at least gives one of us a fighting chance,' the playwright urges in a quiet, calm voice.

Wainwright nods. 'I have no regrets, Master Marlowe. I have done good work for the Queen and our country, though I have not always been a good man.'

'I have no regrets, either. What will be, will be.'

The harsh grating of bolts being slowly drawn echoes along the vast nave. Yet there is no one near the door. Marlowe and Wainwright spring to their feet and shake hands before racing back along the nave, Wainwright to the north door, Marlowe to the south. Crouching behind a stone pillar, the playwright can just make out the vague form of his colleague in the gloom on the far side of the cathedral.

The west doors crash open. The pews fall aside as if they are autumn leaves. Footsteps echo off the flags. Whispery voices chill the blood.

Marlowe knows he should run, but he has to see. Keeping to the shadows around the pillar, he watches the pools of candle-light along the nave. Grey shapes flit around the edges of the illumination. Then, after a moment, one of them walks into full view, stands and looks around.

Naked to the waist, his skin has the colour of bone, his cadaverous head shaved and marked with blue and black concentric circles. Black rings line his staring eyes as he searches the shadows of the cathedral. Leather belts criss-cross his chest to secure the axe and sword on his back. His name is Xanthus.

Ice water sluices through Marlowe, and recognition.

In the candlelight, a cruel smile plays on the lips of the new arrival, and he takes from a pouch at his hip a silver box large enough to contain a pair of shoes. It is ornately carved. Marlowe thinks he glimpses a death's-head on its lid before Xanthus places the box on the flagstones and flips it open.

Run, the voice in the playwright's head insists, but he is in thrall to the curious sight. Why a box? What does it contain?

For a moment the only sound is the wind whistling through the open doors. Then a faint rustling begins. Marlowe spies movement at the edge of the dark interior of the box, one small shape wriggling, then another, then three. And from its depths streams a swarm of black spiders, each one as big as a man's hand. Too many for the size of the box, it seems.

A gasp comes from the other side of the cathedral. *Wainwright, you fool*, the younger man thinks.

Xanthus' lips pull back from small, pearly teeth, he glances into the shadows where the man hides and in a black tide the spiders wash towards the unseen spy. A moment later a cry of

13

agony echoes up to the vaulted roof and Wainwright staggers into the candlelight, tearing at his skin. The creatures are all over him, biting. The pale figure only watches and grins.

Marlowe clasps a hand to his mouth in horror. He sees raw flesh on his companion's face, and blood flowing freely to pool around the man's shoes. Screams fill the vast space of the cathedral. However much Wainwright rips at the spiders, he cannot stop the agony. Wet bone gleams on the doomed man's head, and the back of his hands.

The screams subside. He staggers like a man in his cups, and falls to his knees, still slapping at his skin weakly. And when he pitches forward on to the cold stone, the creatures still feed.

Covering his face, Marlowe tries to drive the hideous vision from his mind.

This is only the start, he thinks.

Gripping the cold iron ring, the playwright throws open the south door and bolts into the warm night. His laboured breathing echoes off the walls of the houses, punctuated by the beat of his Spanish leather shoes on the dried mud. The thunder of blood in his head destroys all thoughts, and it is only when he is racing south through the winding streets towards Blackfriars that he realizes fortune is with him; but not with poor Wainwright.

He forces aside a tide of regret and grief and guilt. Will always told him he would never thrive as a spy because he felt too keenly. Now he understands that the past no longer matters, nor do his failings and dashed hopes. Only the future is important, and the slim chance that he can do something to avert the coming tragedy.

After a few moments the playwright hears his pursuers on the trail once more. Time is short.

Marlowe reaches the muddy banks of the slow-moving

Thames, black under the dark sky, and he thinks of the River Styx. He smells wet wood and vegetation, and hears the symphonic creaks of straining ropes on the boats moored along the river's edge. Across the water is his own personal heaven: Bankside, and the gardens surrounding the Swan Theatre and the Rose, and the stews and dives where he can be the man he wants to be, away from the scrutiny and demands of powerful people.

Fearing he is too late, the playwright searches along the sticky path between Blackfriars and Baynard's Castle. But then he hears the stamp of hooves and follows the sound to find a young man dozing beside his horse, swathed in a brown woollen cloak. Kit studies the sleeper briefly, seeing the clear skin and slender frame and innocence, and suddenly he feels so very old. Gently, he shakes the young man awake.

'Tom? Thank you for coming, but there is now a need for urgency,' the spy says.

Tom rises, stretching. He is taller than Marlowe, his eyes as grey as the winter sky, his hair blond, falling over his ears and to the nape of his neck. 'I thought you would not come. What is your wish? The horse?' he asks sleepily. He doesn't notice the playwright's dishevelled state.

'That is for you, to get as far away from here as you can, and quickly.' Marlowe looks on his young friend with affection, and a rising sadness, and he tries to keep the edge of fear out of his voice.

A howl echoes only a few streets away. The playwright cannot be sure if it was made by a beast or something that had the shape of a man. *The Enemy can never be considered men*, he thinks with a pang of bitterness. *They have no compassion, no joy or love.*

From the sack at his side, Marlowe pulls a thick sheaf of papers, tied with string and sealed with red wax. 'Tom,

15

listen to me. You must deliver this to my good friend Will Swyfte.'

'England's greatest spy?'

Marlowe smiles wryly. 'Yes, that is indeed how he is known. But first, and quickly, I must write a note to accompany the work.' He retrieves his quill and the pot of ink.

A troubled thought distracts him and he peers deep into Tom's face, searching for familiar signs, knowing it is not enough. Then he puts one hand at the back of the young man's neck and pulls him into a deep kiss. When he breaks away, he stares into Tom's eyes; it is still not enough, but he has to hope.

'What is wrong?' Tom asks. 'You are not yourself.'

Marlowe laughs at that.

Hearing his pursuers closing in upon their position, his hand trembles as he grips the quill. Too much is at stake, and he dare not write plainly. But too obscure and Will will not understand his warning. In the end, he can only trust in his friend's intellect.

I fear this may be our last communication, my dear, trusted friend. The truth lies within. But seek the source of the lies without, he scrawls. *Trust no one.* He underlines this last.

Quickly, he folds the letter and slides it under the string before handing the complete bundle to Tom. By this time, the young man is alarmed by his friend's actions. He senses their finality.

'You will come with me?' Tom asks. 'My horse will carry two a short distance.'

'There is nothing I would like more than to ride away with you, good Tom, and recapture those honeyed moments that made me so happy. But I fear it would mean your death. Now, be away, and fast.' Marlowe hears the faintest tremor in his voice, but he hides it quickly, seals it with a smile.

16

He kisses Tom again, and turns to the boats so his young friend will not linger. He allows himself one quick glance back when he hears the hoofbeats drawing away, and a moment of sadness too, and then he scrabbles to free the mooring rope of the nearest waterman's vessel.

Whispers roll along the river bank. Shadows emerge from an alley.

Lurching into the cold shallows, Marlowe feels the mud sucking at his shoes as he launches the boat into the current and drags himself on board. Loud splashing erupts behind him, but the current takes Marlowe away just quickly enough. Shadows flit along the water's edge, keeping pace.

Ahead, the first gleam of dawn lights the horizon. The playwright looks to the bank and sees the grey forms melt back into the darkened streets.

Marlowe feels no relief. He lies back in the boat, letting the current take him where it will. This life is already over for him, he knows that. There is no escape.

Somewhere a killer lurks in plain sight, with a plan that threatens to engulf England in a rising tide of darkness. He listens to the water sloughing past the boat and hears in it the whispers that have haunted him since he made the first shocking discovery. Two words repeated in a rhythmic chant.

The end, the end.

The end.

CHAPTER ONE

THE MAN, DANGEROUS AND CONTROLLED, WAS MOVING
through what felt like a dream, with devils and wolves, cats
and dragons, dolls and jesters on every side. Fantastical faces
peered at him from the growing shadows, gloved hands rising
to mouths in surprise or intrigue or desire.

An excited chatter of anticipation buzzed through the
upper gallery of the Rose Theatre that evening. Amid the
heady atmosphere of timber, fresh plaster, perfume and sweat,
the masked guests parted to allow the man through, their
whispered comments following wherever he went: '*Spy . . .
spy . . . England's greatest spy.*'

The evening's entertainment was yet to begin, but the Rose
was already full. The carriages and horses had been arriving in
a steady stream under the late afternoon sun that cast Bankside's
green fields and dusty roads in a warm, golden haze. The
women had alighted, their flat-fronted bodices and divided
overskirts in popinjay blue, or sunset orange, or lusty-gallant
red, the celebratory colours sending a message of defiance in
dark times. The men wore quilted doublets and flamboyant
white ruffs, peasecod bellies, jerkins in cloth of silver and
half-compass cloaks. Their colours were more muted, greens

and blacks and browns, but the sumptuous velvet and silk embroidered with gleaming gold spoke of that same defiance. The court of Queen Elizabeth, in all its glory, would not be bowed.

The spy, Will Swyfte, was a storm cloud amid the summery festivities, unmasked, dressed all in black, quilted doublet embroidered with silver, a jerkin of fine Spanish leather and a cloak. His black hair reached to the nape of his neck, his moustache and chin-hair trimmed that very day. His eyes too appeared black. He quietly cursed the ornate masks that hid the faces of the good men and women of England as they hung over the wooden rails of the upper galleries. He couldn't see the eyes with any clarity, and certainly couldn't identify any threat that might lurk there. And threat there was aplenty, all around London.

Underneath the musk of the crowd, the man caught the fragrant whiff of the numerous concoctions of herbs carried to ward off the terrible death. It was a pleasant change from the sickeningly sweet stink of rot that hung over the city like a permanent autumn fog.

Pausing at the rail, the spy peered down the well of the theatre to the yard in front of the stage. The audience was lit by the dying rays of the sun falling through the central, open area of the thatched roof. The black-garbed man studied the red-brick and timber frame of the many-sided theatre, noting the best vantage points, the escape routes, the places where a life could be taken without drawing too much attention. Even in that crowded, confined space throbbing with noise, death could wait patiently for an opportunity.

'Still no sign of Master Marlowe.' It was Nathaniel Colt, the spy's assistant, also unmasked. Eyes bright and inquisitive, he was smaller and younger than his master, slim and wiry, with a thin, tufty beard and moustache that made him appear younger still. 'I would have thought he'd rather lose his writing hand than miss his own first night.'

'Kit is a mercurial soul. He very rarely takes the path one would expect. Though I have not seen him for several days now, I have never known him to miss the opportunity for applause.'

Or not to pass on the vital secrets he promised three days ago, Will thought. The playwright's hastily scrawled message had implied news of great importance, and a great threat too.

'Why pass on information here?' Nathaniel pressed. 'Why tonight? What could be so important that it could not be conveyed within the safe walls of one of the palaces, or at his own residence, or in one of the many vile and disgusting establishments you and Master Marlowe enjoy?'

The older man had already considered all those questions. 'I will ask Kit when he arrives. In the meantime, Nat, enjoy this fine entertainment that he and Master Henslowe have provided for us.'

With a shrug, the assistant returned his attention to the stage. 'There is still some novelty to be found in these theatres, I suppose,' he muttered. 'When Master Henslowe built the Rose six years ago, I doubted his good sense. The Bankside inn-yards had always provided a serviceable venue for plays.'

'Master Henslowe is sharp as a pin when it comes to matters of gold.' Will leaned on the rail, continuing to search the audience for any sign of danger: a hand raised too fast here, a man skulking away from his companions there. He knew his instincts were rarely wrong. He could feel some unseen threat lurking in the theatre. But where? He turned again to Nat. 'He bought this land for a song, here on the marshy river borders. And the theatre is close to the many earthy attractions of Europe's greatest city, the brothels and the bear-baiting arenas, the inns and gaming dens. There is always an audience to hand.'

'Then he must be doubly pleased that Master Marlowe insisted his first night be held here, for an audience of the court only. With the theatres all closed by order of the Lord Mayor because of this damnable sickness, Master Henslowe's purse must be crying for mercy.'

'The aristocracy are starved of good entertainment in these plague-days and for a new Marlowe they will clearly travel even unto the jaws of death.'

Will's eye was caught by a subtle nod of the head at the rear of the gallery, where the lamps had just been lit. John Carpenter waited, scowling. His fingers unconsciously leapt to the hair that hid the jagged scar running down the left side of his face, the bear that had attacked him in Muscovy never forgotten.

Pushing his way through the audience, Will nodded to his fellow agent. 'Anything?'

Carpenter grunted. 'I do not understand why we take such measures. Who in their right mind would strike in such a crowded place?'

'An attack here would send a message to the Queen and the Privy Council that nowhere is safe.' Will looked out across the masked audience filling the upper gallery. Though he was half hidden by shadows, one cat-masked woman in emerald bodice and skirts turned to look at him directly. Even with the disguise, Will recognized Grace, the young woman he had been charged to protect and the sister of his own missing love. 'Kit's message implied a mounting danger. We take no risks.'

Carpenter shook his head with frustration. 'The Queen

is safe and sound in Nonsuch. A few popinjays make poor targets.'

'You have somewhere better to be?' Will gave a wry smile. 'With pretty Alice Dalingridge, perhaps?'

The scarred man looked away, his cheeks colouring. 'Who do you fear? The Spanish? Papists? Or our true Enemy? The Unseelie Court have not been active for many months.'

'Which is when they are at their most dangerous.' In his mind's eye, Will saw white faces and churchyard eyes emerging from the night-mist on a lonely moor. Those foul creatures still haunted the dreams of England, and, he feared, always would.

Further along the upper gallery, the good men and women of the court surged back from an area beneath one of the lamps. Angry shouts rose up.

'Come!' Drawing his blade, Will raced along the outer wall of the gallery. Carpenter remained close at his heels.

The two men found their ally, Robert, Earl of Launceston, pressed against the plaster, three swordpoints at his neck. His unnaturally pale face loomed out of the shadows like a ghost, the absence of colour in his grey woollen cloak and doublet only adding to his macabre appearance.

His three opponents eyed the two newly arrived men, contemptuous smiles creeping on to their lips. 'England's greatest spy,' the leader sneered.

Will recognized the wiry, red-headed man: Tobias Strangewayes, the most prominent of the new band of spies the Earl of Essex had established to rival the traditional secret service. He was a proficient swordsman, but he had a hot temper that meant he would never be a master with the rapier.

'Leave him be,' Carpenter growled.

When the scarred spy made to advance, Will held him back

with an outstretched arm, although they shared an equal contempt for Strangewayes and his men. In a court now riven with
factions, Essex's rival group served only to distract attention
from the true threats facing England. 'Now, now, John. There
are only three of them. Why, that is no challenge for Robert.'

'Perhaps another time.' Launceston's voice was as devoid of
emotion as his face. 'A little aid would not go amiss at this
moment.'

Strangewayes' eyes were black slits. 'I warned your man that if
he spoke to me again there would be a reckoning. Your master
may tolerate his unnatural tastes, but I do not have to.' He drew
the tip of his rapier in a circle a finger's-width from Launceston's
neck.

'You profess a moral stance, yet act like a rogue. Would
you spill the blood of an unarmed man here, in full view of
women? Even spies like you must abide by the law.' Frustrated
that he was dealing with this conflict instead of searching for
the real threat, Will's voice hardened and he levelled his rapier
at the red-headed man.

'I can beat you in a fair fight, Swyfte.' Strangewayes
moistened his lips, but Will could see the uncertainty in his
darting eyes.

'Leave Launceston alone.' Carpenter took another step
forward. 'He is a better man than you.'

'Better than I?' The rival spy gave a mocking laugh. 'Better
at killing innocents, and wallowing in their final suffering. He
is a devil, with no morals, who deserves to be removed from
this life.'

'We are all devils in our own way, Master Strangewayes,
and you prove it by passing such harsh judgement on a fellow
man, with no evidence, only hearsay and old wives' gossip,'
Will said.

24

His attention was caught by a flash of ostentatious white brocade and lace as a man in a ram's mask swaggered from the audience. 'Your day has passed, Master Swyfte,' the man boomed. He removed his mask to reveal himself as Robert Devereux, Earl of Essex, in his own estimation the most handsome man at court. 'Your master, Sir Robert Cecil, is proving a poor defender of the realm and a most unfortunate replacement for the sadly missed Sir Francis Walsingham. His spies . . . your companions, sir! . . . have failed time and again to win an advantage for England in Spain, and in Flanders.'

'Your analysis, as ever, is passionately voiced, sir,' Will said with a bow, 'though I fear not all the details of our great successes have been brought to your attention.'

With a fixed smile, Essex held Will's gaze for a long moment, searching for any hint of the disrespect he knew was there. 'You would do well to study Tobias here, Master Swyfte. He is the future,' he said with a hearty laugh, clapping his red-headed favourite on the shoulder.

Strangewayes grinned.

Will could feel Carpenter and Launceston bristle beside him. 'I have always said Master Strangewayes is a lesson to us all.'

Sensing that his authority was close to being undermined, Essex grunted. Flashing Will a guarded look, he replaced his mask and strode back into the audience.

The black-garbed spy stepped past Carpenter, and with a flourish brought his blade under Strangewayes' sword, flicking it away from Launceston. 'If you wish to fight, then let's have at it.'

Uneasy now he had lost the upper hand, the rival spy glanced around and saw the rows of masked faces turned towards him. Slowly, he lowered his sword, then sheathed it. 'My master was correct. Your time has passed, Master Swyfte,' he sniffed, pretending he was bored with the confrontation. 'England no longer needs you. And if you do not see the truth in that statement now, you soon will. Come, lads.' He turned on his heel and pushed through the audience with his two men close behind.

Will sheathed his sword. 'You have a knack of finding trouble in the most unlikely places, Robert.'

'Is this what it has come to?' Unable to contain his bitterness, Carpenter stalked around them, his fists bunched. 'We fight among ourselves while England slowly falls around us?'

'These are dark days, indeed. And they could grow quickly darker if we do not uncover the threat that may lie within these walls.' Will held a hand out to the Earl. 'Robert, there is still no sign of Kit?'

'The doormen say Marlowe paid a brief visit earlier this day, wearing a hood to hide his identity. He stayed only a short while, and gave new directions to the players before departing.' Launceston's voice was so quiet it was barely audible under the buzzing of the audience.

Will felt a deep foreboding. 'Speak to the players,' he ordered. 'Find what Kit did here this day and why he left in such a hurry. Quickly, now!'

CHAPTER TWO

'IF YOU SEE CHRISTOPHER MARLOWE ANYWHERE IN THIS theatre, or hear a whisper of his voice, you come to us. Do you understand?' Carpenter growled. He shook the nodding stagehand roughly for good measure and flung the lad to one side. The youth scrambled away backstage, casting fearful glances at the two spies.

'The playwright is not here. I can feel it in my bones,' Launceston said in his whispery voice, looking across the sunlit audience in the yard from the shadows at the side of the stage.

'He is probably drunk in some stew or other and we, as always, are wasting our time,' Carpenter grumbled, itching the scars that marred his face.

A black-haired young woman in a plain white mask stepped lightly up. Plucking off her disguise, she laughed, her sharp blue eyes gleaming. 'Why are you always so gloomy, Master Carpenter?' she teased, folding her hands behind her back and leaning forward so her nose was only a hand's-width from the spy.

'Alice, I am working,' the scarred man began, a light smile rising to his lips unbidden. He still found the sensation un-familiar, yet pleasing.

'This is an evening for entertainment, not swords and scowls. Do you like my dress?' The young woman showed off her pale green bodice and skirt. It was plain compared to the lavish dresses of the other women, but it was all a kitchen maid could afford.

'It is beautiful, as are you, but you must return to your friends.'

With a theatrical sigh, the young woman twirled around, casting one teasing look at her love over her shoulder before replacing her mask and disappearing into the crowd.

Carpenter watched Alice go, unable to believe that a woman so warm and generous could have any affection for a man like him. If pressed, he would admit that he did not deserve her. But she was with him nonetheless.

Realizing Launceston was studying him, the spy scowled and said, 'What are you looking at, you elf-skinned giglet?'

'It is difficult to be certain, but it would appear to be a love-sick jolt-head,' the Earl replied dispassionately.

Waving an irritated hand at his companion, Carpenter turned backstage, but the pallid man grabbed him by the shoulder. 'You will get yourself killed, and the girl. The business of spies demands dedication and concentration. There is no place in it for a woman.'

Carpenter threw off the hand. 'Then it is good that I am about to leave this miserable profession,' he snapped.

'Leave?'

'It is my intention to marry Alice.'

'And do what? Become a chandler, or a draper, or sell eggs in the market? You are spoiled for the life that others lead.'

'We deserve our chance at happiness, like any other man or woman,' said Carpenter, jabbing a finger at his friend.

Launceston remained unsettlingly calm. 'You are not like other men. How many have slit a throat, skewered a heart, hanged, strangled, eviscerated, and lopped off limbs? How many—'

'Be still.' The scarred man seethed, long-held resentments bubbling to the surface until he could contain them no longer. 'For five years now, I have tried to hold your demons in check. That hellish fever! When I see the light in your eyes, my heart is crushed with despair, for I know that I will soon be dragging you away from some drunken man, or some doxy, or a lady of the court even. Boys. Priests. Merchants. Sailors. When your dagger is gripped so that your knuckles are white, I know the madness is upon you.'

'I know.' His pale face blank, the Earl glanced around, half listening.

'I have seen blood . . . so much innocent blood.' The bleak memories tumbled over themselves. 'That poor girl near the Tower. That butcher . . .' The scarred man shook his head. 'I could not tell him from his wares.'

With mounting desperation, Carpenter saw Launceston eyeing another stagehand dragging a box towards the tiring house, and knew his companion saw only the pulse of blood in the artery, the shape of the skull in the cheekbones, the gleam of organs revealed to air.

'But they all lived, John. You saved them all. And you have saved me,' the Earl murmured.

Carpenter felt desolate. Out of friendship, he had stepped in to keep Launceston from destroying himself without realizing the true price he would have to pay. That act had consumed his life, his every thought; watching, cautioning, knowing that if he ever failed, his conscience would be scarred by the death of an innocent. Launceston's burden had become his burden, and he could bear it no more. *Yet, God help me, I have to. For if not me, who?*

The Earl continued to watch the stagehand, unaware of his friend's turmoil.

So much sacrifice and it was not even noticed. His rage now gone, Carpenter could not meet Launceston's eye. 'No more, Robert. I am spent.'

'Then what is to become of me?'

Carpenter heard no emotion in the Earl's voice, no regret or self-pity, only a baffled child trying to make sense of a parent's decision. With an exhausted sigh, he replied, 'You will find a way, Robert. All that I have done has taken its toll on me, but it is meaningless to you. You are broken inside. You need no one. You survive. The rest of us . . . we need friends, warmth, love.'

'It means a great deal to me,' the sallow man said in the same neutral tone he used when choosing wine or beer with his meal.

The spy looked his companion in the eye, and gave a weary smile and nod. 'Of course. Now, let us find answers and put Will's mind at rest.'

Slipping backstage to the tiring house, the two men found the players putting on their make-up and costumes. One man wore ram's horns, his eyes ringed in black beneath cruel eyebrows. 'You,' Carpenter demanded, pointing. 'What are you?'

'The devil. Mephistophilis,' the ferociously made-up man stuttered. 'Who are you?'

'Quiet, you common-kissing bum-bailey.' Carpenter grabbed the devil by the undershirt. 'I would know about the man who puts words in your mouth.'

'Kit Marlowe?'

'The same. He was here earlier?'

The player nodded, futilely looking for support from his fellows.

Launceston leaned in to the unsettled man and whispered in his ear, 'What are you hiding from us?'

'Nothing, truly. Master Marlowe was eager to make some final changes, that is all. It is not unusual. He places great weight upon small detail. But . . . but he was not himself.'

'How so?'

'He slipped into the Rose in cloak and hood and revealed his presence to us only at the last.'

Launceston and Carpenter exchanged a look. 'What small details did he attend to?' the scarred agent asked. 'Show us.'

Reluctantly, the player led the two spies to the side of the stage. Keeping out of sight of the audience in the yard, the man in the devil's costume indicated a magic circle painted in red on the stage. 'Master Marlowe insisted on changes to yon design. New symbols etched around the outside of the circle. The marks already there served their purpose, in my opinion, but who can divine the mind of a great man like Christopher Marlowe?'

The Earl studied the markings. 'The playwright came here in a manner that suggests he did not want to draw attention to himself,' the pale-faced spy mused. 'Yet all he did was alter a few scribblings on the boards? Do you take us for fools?'

The player recoiled from Launceston's unwavering stare. 'No, please stay your hand! I cannot pretend to look into his mind. Never had I seen him in such a mood. When I encountered him backstage, I took such fright. His eyes were wide with terror, his face so drained of blood he looked like a ghost. As if he feared the devil himself was at his back.'

31

CHAPTER THREE

'WHERE ARE YOU, COZ? WHAT THREAT DID YOU UNCOVER?' WILL
muttered, unable to throw off his black mood of foreboding.
From the wooden rail, he watched the garishly dressed players
step on to the stage from the wings. The final golden sunlight
of that May day shafted through the opening in the thatched
roof, and he could smell the rose gardens that gave the theatre
its name, and hear the evening birdsong in the awed silence.

In the shadowed upper galleries and in the sunlit yard, the
audience stood rapt, unreadable behind their masks. Standing
in the sunbeam centre-stage, a fat man with a bushy white
beard and long white hair threw his arms wide and began to
declaim in a dreamlike cadence. Will drifted with the words.

> *'Whereby whole cities have escap'd the plague,*
> *And thousand desperate maladies been cur'd?*
> *Yet art thou still but Faustus, and a man.*
> *Couldst thou make men to live eternally,*
> *Or, being dead, raise them to life again . . .'*

In the warmth of the evening, Will's thoughts moved back
in time, inexorably, to his love, Jenny, stolen from him that

hot summer day as she made her way across the cornfield on the edge of the Forest of Arden. There one moment, gone the next. Taken by the eternal Enemy, the Unseelie Court, before his very eyes, to a fate the spy could barely bring himself to consider. His hand unconsciously went to Jenny's locket which he always wore next to his skin, a symbol of his hope that one day he could put the terrible mystery to rest – for good or ill – and find some kind of peace.

Nathaniel appeared at Will's elbow, gripped by the scene on stage where a grotesque devil towered over the protagonist Faustus. Men surreptitiously crossed themselves, women averted their gaze. The plague had made everyone more fearful of hell's torments. Another of the perverse tortures in which Kit revelled, Will mused: promise the great and the good entertainment, and then make them afraid for their mortal souls.

'*The Tragical History of Doctor Faustus*. This is a troubling play,' Nathaniel noted. 'Men selling their souls to the devil. Is this truly a subject for entertainment? I have never seen the like before. It could drive women mad. And men too, for that matter.'

Will watched the heavily bearded Faustus stalk the stage, demonstrating his arrogance to the audience. 'Kit always has something of import to say in his work. I fear this one may be more personal than his others, however.' Will had been concerned about his friend's state of mind in recent days. The work they did had been eating away at Marlowe for years, but in the last few weeks the playwright had been taking time away from the people he knew. Though all writers were prone to black moods, Kit's spirits had never been darker.

'These players are not as good as Edward Alleyn's Men. They bark their lines as if they hail fellow sots outside a stew,' Nathaniel commented dismissively.

33

Will listened to the colourfully attired player boom his lines to reach the back of the audience. 'There are few players of quality left in London with the plague rampant and the theatres closed,' he said. 'Alleyn has taken Lord Strange's Men and some players from the Admiral's Men on a tour of the country to make ends meet. Kit must make do with the dregs.'

Glancing around, Nathaniel hissed a warning. Will followed his assistant's nod to where the audience was being parted by three men, two without masks, the third wearing the face of an angel. Gowned in black velvet, the man removed the mask with a flourish to reveal the face of the spymaster Sir Robert Cecil, a small, hunchbacked man with intense, dark eyes that held a sly intelligence. With him were Robert Rowland, tall and slender with a face like an unmade bed who oversaw the secret service's complex files, and Sinclair, a saturnine former mercenary who never left Cecil's side. A head's-height above his companions and with the broad shoulders of country stock, Sinclair glared at Will.

The agent cursed under his breath, frustrated at this unwelcome distraction from the threat he sensed near to hand.

'Fitting, no?' Cecil indicated the angel mask and then gestured to the devil on the stage. 'Come.'

With a speed and strength that belied his disability, the spymaster pushed his way through the audience to the rear of the gallery where they could talk without being overheard. The Queen teased Cecil with the nickname Little Elf, but Will knew the man's sharp mind had helped him maintain power at court ever since his father, Lord Burghley, had installed him as secretary of state after Sir Francis Walsingham's death. Clasping his hands behind his back, the short man stood with all the gravity of someone possessed of an ambition that far exceeded his stature.

'I have news of some import that may impact upon your work in the near future, Master Swyfte. Intelligence comes to us from France. Henri de Navarre is close to converting to Catholicism, encouraged by Gabrielle, his whore, the Duchesse de Beaufort et Verneuil,' Cecil announced, his head cocked back in a supercilious manner.

'A Catholic!' Rowland exclaimed, plucking at his eggshell-blue and yellow doublet in distress. 'Are we to be isolated completely?' His high-crowned hat only drew attention to his long, crumpled face.

Cecil paid his file-keeper no heed, but said dismissively, 'Her Majesty will resent it, but religion only matters insomuch as it drives politics.'

'Yet it still has the capacity to draw fresh blood,' Will noted a little more sharply than he intended.

Cecil fixed a mistrustful eye on his agent. Will resisted the urge to respond. The Little Elf was more concerned with his own advancement at court than with the men who risked life and limb for him, and often seemed to suspect his charges more than the enemies they faced.

'It was English troops and a fortune from our coffers that helped Henri win his kingdom. This is betrayal,' Rowland continued, his cheeks flushed with passion.

'It could work in our favour,' Will mused. 'Henri de Navarre is clever. Such a move would shift the balance of power in the Catholic League, and he could prove a strong, friendly rival to curtail the ambitions of Philip of Spain.'

Rowland stopped wringing his hands at Will's assurance, and bowed his head in reflection. But Sinclair loomed over the smaller man's shoulder and growled, 'Still, we are beset from many quarters. The situation in Ireland is a concern.'

Cecil nodded, his gaze raised to the rafters a hand's-width

above Sinclair's head. 'Hugh O'Neill cannot be trusted. He professes loyalty to the Crown, but he builds his own power slowly. He will be trouble, mark my words. And the people of Ireland already hate us. But where are the results I need, Master Swyfte? Should I dispose of all the spies I have and find a better crew?'

Will took a moment to contain his ire, and then said calmly, 'Some men complain of poor resources and little support, Sir Robert. Others that they have been abandoned in the midst of dangerous waters. It is hard to spy when you feel you stand alone.'

'You know I must keep a close eye on our coffers, sir. The Earl of Essex continually looks for ways by which he may criticize the work we do, and he has already spoken to the Queen about our profligacy. We must all cut our cloth accordingly in these difficult times.' The Little Elf gave a patronizing smile which fell away quickly when he caught sight of his gleaming rival, clad all in white, with a smirking Tobias Strangewayes at his side.

'Damn him,' Cecil whispered. 'What mischief is he planning now?'

'Essex seeks to undermine our work at every turn,' Sinclair growled, glowering at the two men. 'In these times no one can be trusted. We are beset by enemies on all sides. Across Europe, in the towns and villages of England and, yes, even in the court itself. There are spies everywhere, spreading lies and deceit. Where once this great land was filled with bravery, there is now only sweat, and doubt, and fear.'

And we cannot even trust our own masters any more, Will thought bitterly. His relationship with the old spymaster, Walsingham, had always been tense, but now it seemed like a golden age.

'Are you enjoying Kit's work?' he asked. He cupped his

hand to his ear, pretending to listen to the players' words. 'It tells of a man surrounded by devils.'

Cecil's eyes flashed. 'Do not speak to me of Marlowe. He can no longer be trusted.'

Will fought to control a flush of anger. 'Kit has always been a faithful servant,' he said as calmly as he could.

'He is consumed by his weaknesses. Drink. Gold. And the unnatural desires he takes no pains to conceal. He has passed his point of usefulness.' Beside Cecil, Sinclair nodded his agreement. Rowland looked away, pretending to be intrigued by the play.

The loud declaiming of the players rose up from the stage below.

> *'Then fear not, Faustus, to be resolute,*
> *And try the utmost magic can perform.'*

The words were followed by the clatter of iron and wood to signify thunder.

Will studied Cecil to see if this was another barb to prick a response. His master's face gave nothing away. 'I know Kit has been reporting to the Privy Council every day,' he said. 'Is the council to proceed with the charge of blasphemy?'

The secretary looked around the sea of colourful masks, either ignoring the spy or seeking some platitude that would deflect Will's question.

Laced with fear, a cry rang out from the stage.

Cecil, Sinclair and Rowland all started, and jerked their heads towards the rail. The scream soared higher and was then swamped by a rising tide of panic from the audience. All around the gallery, the crowd surged forward to get a better view of what lay below.

'What is happening?' Rowland exclaimed. Sinclair had already disappeared into the mass of bodies.

'No player ever acted that well,' Will shouted above the clamour.

Leaving Cecil behind, the spy shouldered his way to the rail and peered down the well of the theatre. The day's light was fading rapidly, the sky turning cerulean, and all around the yard and stage, lanterns now glowed a soft gold. The flickering light illuminated the pale faces peering down from the packed upper tiers, which were cloaked in dense shadow.

In the yard, a wave of bodies crashed towards the doors that had been locked to prevent curious commoners wandering in from the plague-ravaged city. Screams and cries became one constant shriek. A man in a harlequin mask shouldered his way through those ahead of him, regardless of status or gender. A woman with a now-tangled mane of grey hair hooked her fingers and raked and spat like a frightened cat. The surging mob crushed a lady-in-waiting against one of the timbers. An elderly man as thin as a sapling disappeared beneath the trampling feet. Across the yard, the masks came off. Will saw terror in the features of some, confusion in others. The cause of the tumult was not clear.

Nathaniel arrived at his side.

'Nat, there will be disaster here.' Will watched the infection of fear spread across the audience. 'Find Master Henslowe or one of his associates. The doors must be opened immediately.'

In the upper gallery, bodies pressing forward to witness what was transpiring below pinned Will against the rail. Fighting his way to the stairs would take too long, he knew. With a jab of his elbows, he dragged himself out of the mass and up on to the rail, where he balanced on the balls of his feet. Pointing at him, a woman cried out in alarm. From his precarious position, he had a brief impression of the dizzying drop into the pit of heaving bodies below.

Glancing back across the sea of heads in the upper gallery, he accepted the truth: there was no way to go but down.

Steeling himself, the spy made a graceful pivot and grasped one of the rose carvings on the timber column. His cloak billowed in the updraught from the hot yard. Knuckles white, he clung on to the carving, praying that Henslowe's carpenters had done a masterful job. Blood pumped in his head. Will allowed himself one look down into the depths, and then felt around for a foothold on the carving below.

His leather shoe slipped on the polished wood, and caught, just. The drop pulled at him.

Then, through the cacophony of screams below, a single cry rang out clear: 'The devil is here! The devil!'

CHAPTER FOUR

WILL SWUNG DOWN THE TIMBER POST FROM CARVING TO carving and dropped the final few feet to the now-deserted yard in front of the Rose's stage. On it, a knot of players huddled in fear. Leaping up to them, the spy grabbed the huge-bellied, white-bearded man who played the lead role, Faustus, and shook him alert.

'What caused this outcry?' Will demanded in a cold, authoritarian tone.

In the stage's lantern light, the make-up that made the player's features stand out to the upper galleries transformed him into a grotesque – white skin, red lips and cheeks, dark rings around his eyes.

'The devil—' the player croaked, barely audible above the shouting audience crowding towards the doors.

With his fist gripping the neck of the costume, Will shook the man roughly once more. 'No superstition. Keep a clear head. What was seen?'

A young, smooth-cheeked man stepped forward, his hair tied back ready for the wig that would transform him into the spirit of the beautiful Helen of Troy. 'I saw it,' he declared in a clear voice that belied the terror in his eyes. He indicated the magic circle inscribed on the boards, surrounded by anagrams of Jehovah's names, astrological symbols and ancient sigils. 'When Faustus completed his incantation to summon the devil Mephistophilis, in the presence of Lucifer, a second devil did appear. But this was no man! He . . . it! . . . wore no make-up!'

Faustus gripped his head, reeling. 'The devil was summoned here this night to torment us for speaking his name, and making a mockery of his dark majesty!'

'There are devils aplenty in this world to worry me first before I turn my attention to Hob. Now, good lad, which way?' Will glanced around the empty yard.

The young player pointed backstage.

Faustus caught Will's arm. 'He will take your soul,' he said in a tremulous voice.

'If I still have one to give.' Drawing his rapier, Will jumped back to the mortar floor and slipped along the side of the stage to a small cluttered area with a space for the players to await their cue, heavy with the smells of paint, chalk and make-up. Timber frames, winches, painted scenery, and the artefacts used to make sound effects looked strange and unsettling in the half-light.

Watching the shadows for signs of movement, Will edged beyond the backstage jumble. He found himself in a walkway leading past the tiring house to a series of small chambers used for storage or recreation, places where the players would game with dice or cards while waiting for their moment on the boards. The backstage area was still. Yet he noticed it was unaccountably colder than the rest of the hot, crowded theatre, and an unpleasant smell hung in the air. Brimstone.

If this is a trick, it is designed well to tug at our fears, he thought.

He glanced into the first room on his left. The stub of a single candle guttered on the floor in the far corner, its flickering light revealing row upon row of costumes in emerald and crimson and sapphire, as well-made as the finest court clothes to cope with the wear and tear of multiple performances. A pair of intricately constructed wings of goose feathers hung from the ceiling, like an invisible angel taking flight.

A whisper rustled somewhere ahead in the gloom of the walkway, the words unclear.

Will's breath caught in his throat. With a fluid movement, he stepped into the costume room just as a shadowy presence emerged from a room three doors ahead. He remained still, his breathing measured, the tip of his sword resting on the floor so it made no noise when he moved.

Soft footsteps came to a halt, and Will pictured whoever was there waiting outside the room. He heard a low growl, like one of the beasts in the Queen's menagerie.

From that inhuman sound, Will tried to imagine what stood in the walkway, but nothing came to mind that made any sense to him. *The devil*, the player had said, gripped with fear of whatever he had witnessed. Will remained calm, despite the pull of age-old superstitions. He had faced many men, and many things, that had been called devils and he had held them all to account.

The rumbling sound ebbed and flowed. The echoes suggested the intruder was turning his head, looking up and down the walkway.

The spy tightened his grip on the hilt of his sword, his muscles taut. The blood pulsed in his head, the familiar rhythm of his life, the music of impending death.

After a moment, the footsteps padded away. Will waited a few heartbeats and then stepped out into the shadowy walkway. He glimpsed a figure disappearing around the edge of the backstage, too indistinct in the gloom to tell if it was devil or man. Silently, he followed, keeping close to the wall, and low.

When he turned along the rear of the stage, he came up hard. The figure waited for him. Instinctively, Will swept his sword up ready for a fight before he had even registered the identity of his opponent.

It was Jenny. His long-lost love.

The spy reeled from the shock. Long-dammed emotions flooded up, his incomprehension washed away by the plangent yearning of all those desperate years without her, followed immediately by a pure joy that he was seeing her again, not a hazy, half-formed memory, but Jenny, really and truly there. He lowered his rapier, his lips silently forming her name.

She looked exactly as she had done the last time he saw her all those years ago, when she had disappeared from his life, in full view, in that Warwickshire cornfield on that hot summer day. When she had walked out of life and into mystery. Still wearing the same blue dress, the colour of forget-me-nots. Her hair still a lustrous hazel, tumbling across her shoulders, her features pale and delicate yet filled with strength of character and intelligence.

Questions flashed through Will's mind, each one dying in the heat of her glorious return.

'Jenny,' he murmured. The word fell close to him with the dull resonance of a pebble dropped on wood.

The woman held out a hand to him, and he wanted to feel her fingers in his more than anything in the world; it was all he had thought of, for years, since that awful day.

Sheathing his rapier, Will stepped towards his love, unable to take his gaze from her face. All around him, the world fell into shadow until there was only the moon of her presence, drawing him in.

43

Jenny's face remained still and calm. Will watched her lips for the familiar ghost of a wry smile, but it was not there.

'Speak to me,' he whispered.

And then Will looked deep into his love's eyes. They were as black as coal from lash to lash, not the green eyes of his Jenny; devoid of any of her warmth, empty of all her love and her compassion. These were the eyes of a devil. In them, Will saw his own pale, desperate face reflected, and he realized he had been tricked. But there was no time to feel the bitterness of hope dashed, or the anger of the cruel blow that had been struck at him. The hands of Jenny-that-was-not-Jenny clamped on the sides of his head and pulled him in until those black eyes were the only thing he could see. His vision swam, and any thought he had of fighting free was washed away. With barely a murmur of protest, he tumbled into deep waters that were beyond his understanding.

He stands under the cold eye of the full moon. Pearly mist drifts across the silver grass of a meadow, the swirling snowy tufts parting to reveal a sable slash of woodland in the distance. Glancing up the slope of the grassland, Will sees a scarecrow silhouetted against the white orb of the moon, its angular form topped by a wide-brimmed hat. He thinks that this chiaroscuro world is not England, perhaps Scotland, or the Low Countries, though he does not know why he feels that.

The scarecrow troubles him, oddly. Will has passed many like it, rough figures made from a timber frame and straw-stuffed old clothes, but this one feels like something more. It feels, he decides with a note of mounting dread, like the judge of all his life.

In a dreamlike state, the spy draws closer to the stick figure. The shadow thrown by the brim of the hat cloaks the face. Though his heart pounds wildly with dread, he cannot look away. The dirty undershirt is tied at the waist by a piece of cord, the hem flapping in the night breeze. Straw hands poke out from the sleeves of the outstretched arms. Obliquely, Will thinks it looks like a crucifixion under the cruel judgement of the god of the fields. These feelings, this experience, are not his, he knows.

Though every fibre tells him to turn away, Will has to see. He peers into the dark beneath the hat's brim. A pair of staring eyes gaze back, wide with terror. But there is no mouth, and it cannot voice the agonies of its dreadful existence. The spy finds those eyes chillingly familiar, and with mounting horror he feels that he is looking at his good friend Kit Marlowe, trapped there.

Pleading for help.

Reeling backwards, his heart pounding fit to burst, the spy whirls to see he is not alone. Moving steadily out of the drifting mist across the meadow are indistinct figures, like shadows on a moonlit pond: five, ten, more. As the strangers take on more substance, he feels a palpable sense of threat. Their clothes echo the cut of long-gone times, bucklers, belts and breeches all glistening with mildew as if buried long underground. They draw nearer.

The Unseelie Court, the great supernatural Enemy who used to torment all England, stealing babies from cribs and luring unwary travellers to their underhill homes.

One of the figures clutches a staff. He is of indiscernible age, his cheeks hollow, dark rings under his icy eyes. The skulls of small rodents and birds have been braided into his long, straggly gold and grey hair. Green robes marked with strange symbols in a gold filigree are caught in the moonlight.

Will remembers his first glimpse of this strange being, on a warm night deep on lonely, haunted Dartmoor. Deortha is the Unseelie Court's equivalent of Elizabeth's adviser Dr Dee, a keeper of secret knowledge, perhaps a black magician, Will cannot be sure. But dangerous, certainly, as are all the Enemy. The figures want him dead for what he has discovered here; for what he is about to discover.

Turning, the spy runs. Terror strips his wits bare. Careering down the meadow, he plunges into the mist, glancing back to see the shimmering figures loping hard on his trail. There is no escape, he thinks. They will never stop now he has seen.

The world shifts around him, the grassland folding in on itself, and Will is now racing through a dark place, stone walls, low ceiling, the throb of a hammer on an anvil beating out the rhythm of his heart. Screams ring in the distance, throats torn in agony. The suffocating heat of a furnace sears his flesh. It is hell, it is hell, and he is trapped.

The spy runs into a wide chamber where a brazier burns with a dull, red light. And there horror floods through him as he sees . . . he sees—

Convulsively ejected from his vision, Will fought back a flood of nausea and staggered against the wall. The dream-scene in the meadow burned into his mind.

The scarecrow, alive yet not. That hellish underground. What had he seen?

Standing still in the gloom, *Jenny* observed him with those cold, black eyes, a perversion of the woman he loved. Sickened by the sight, he felt his disorientation slowly turn to anger. Will could recall the touch of her hand, and her lips, he could remember the exact note of his feelings the last time they lay together on the edge of the Forest of Arden, all as if it were yesterday. He could only imagine what lay behind the mask of the face he saw in front of him.

'What was the meaning of the vision?' he spat.

Jenny continued to watch him, as if her silence were answer enough.

'Was it intended for me? Why do you appear in the form of Jenny?' He staggered forward, drawing his rapier. 'What are you, truly?'

Caught in the grip of those terrible eyes, Will's head swam

and his vision blurred. When his sight cleared, he saw the figure in front of him falling into shadow, or perhaps it was as if the dark was rising up like a flood tide. In mounting desperation, he thrust with his sword, but the blade met no resistance.

As the sharp brimstone odour faded, Will found himself alone in the backstage walkway. Caught up in a whirlpool of confused feelings, he raced along behind the stage, calling out Jenny's name. He knew it was not his love, yet he could not bear to lose her again.

But it was too late. She was gone.

CHAPTER FIVE

ON HIS KNEES, NATHANIEL FORCED HIS WAY AMONG THE FEET of the heaving audience. Boots cracked against his head, his back, his hips, stamped on his fingers. Just when he thought he would have the life crushed from him, he scrambled out and lurched up against the plaster at the rear of the upper gallery, sucking in a huge gulp of breath. Struggling bodies hurled him back and forth, as if he was caught in the wash of a stormy sea.

Clawing his way to the stairs, the young assistant was struck by the roar of mayhem rising up from the lower levels. *What could terrify them so?* With plague, impending war, famine among the poor and bodies piling high in the streets, he would not be surprised if the devil really did walk the streets of London.

Nathaniel threw himself down the timber steps two at a time. Bodies slammed him against the walls, spun him round, crushed him so that he could not draw air into his lungs. Panic gripped him, but Will had given him a job to do. At the foot of the stairs a dense mass of people were crushed around the door, their cries ringing so loudly it made his ears ache. Against the wall, three women and a man slumped like rag dolls, eyes shut, but still the press continued.

How was he supposed to open the doors when he couldn't get near them? His master seemed to take perverse delight in giving him impossible tasks.

Nathaniel yelled for calm until his throat was raw, but the shouts and curses drowned his voice. Red-faced men sputtered or roared, eyes swelling with fear, the women caught up with the furious flow. Pressed against the wall near him, one woman in a corn-coloured dress grew white, her eyes fluttering shut.

A youth with a tuft of brown hair, one of Henslowe's stage-hands, juddered to a halt behind Nathaniel.

'Help me!' Nathaniel urged, throwing himself into the press of bodies. Dragging one man back, he shouldered two others to the side, ignoring their furious protests. Battered and buffeted, Will Swyfte's assistant fought until there was space for the stagehand to join him. They each grasped an arm of the unconscious woman and hauled her along the wall and out on to the stairs.

Once he had seen the woman still breathed, Nat shouted, 'We must open the doors or there will be deaths aplenty.'

'I have the key, but there is no room to use it,' the stagehand yelled in reply, glancing back towards the crush.

Nat gripped his shoulders and demanded, 'There are more ways out of here? A stage door?'

'Beyond that.' The youth waved a hand at the heaving crowd.

Nathaniel grew anxious at the pounding of feet above his head. The audience in the upper galleries was surging towards the crush. An idea struck him. 'The windows?'

'You will break your neck if you attempt to climb from that height.' The stagehand hunched over the prostrate woman, fanning her with his hands.

'Nothing valuable, then.' Nat snatched the key from the

youth and drove himself back up the stairs, squeezing past the first trickle of what would soon become a deluge.

Dragging himself into the corridor that circled the perimeter of the first gallery, Nathaniel put his head down and kept close to the wall. Small, diamond-pane windows glittered along the Rose's fourteen sides, the only source of natural light in the theatre's gloomy interior beyond the central well above the stage and yard. Pressing his face against the glass, he peered out across the darkening landscape. It was a drop of about thirty feet to the chalk and stone path that circled the theatre. Horses grazed on the surrounding grassy common land, and beyond the remnants of the old rose garden that gave the theatre its name was a small orchard sprawling towards the grey, slow-moving river. The young assistant saw he was on the wrong side of the building to where he needed to be.

Fighting his way around the first-floor gallery, he found the going became easier as the flow of audience members slowed. At the third window, he glimpsed the silhouettes of the stews, inns and rough houses of Bankside. Candles were being lit in the windows. Near to the theatre was an old, thatched, timber-framed cottage that Henslowe had established as a brothel for his players and guests.

Nathaniel wondered if he could leap the gulf to the roof, decided it was madness, and continued to the front of the theatre where he found the window above the entrance. He threw it open. The cool late spring air swept in, laced with woodsmoke from the house fires and the stink of rotting refuse.

Below was a small thatched porch over the entrance, flimsy and easy to miss. The spiralling cries of distress carved through his doubts. He climbed into the window space. With a whispered prayer, he allowed himself one glance down to mark his course, then he gripped the window frame and dropped.

The small porch shattered, showering straw and shards of wood around the theatre's entrance. Nathaniel slammed into the chalk and stone walkway. Winded and seeing stars, he shook the fog from his head. *No broken bones.* The porch had slowed his descent just enough.

An unfamiliar woman loomed over him. Her hair was flame-red and she wore a bodice and skirt of black taffeta and gold. When he looked into her green eyes, Nathaniel felt he was a mouse before a cat, but she was sophisticated, definitely not one of the Bankside whores.

'Let me help,' she said with a hint of an Irish accent. She offered her hand.

As Nathaniel limped to his feet, he was enveloped by the sweet scent of her perfume. 'Who are you?' he asked.

'A friend.' The Irish woman took the key from his hand.

'I am always wary of friends who announce themselves as such.' The clamour on the other side of the door almost drowned Nathaniel's words.

'You are right to be cautious, for terrible deeds are planned this night.' The stranger's green eyes flashed towards him as she slipped the key into the hole.

'What do you know?' Nat asked, concerned.

'That before this night is out, the Rose Theatre will be the scene of a murder.' The woman turned the key. 'And that the victim will be England's greatest spy, Will Swyfte.'

CHAPTER SIX

WILL WAS SLAMMED AGAINST THE PLASTER WALL OF THE
walkway outside the tiring house before he even realized he
was no longer alone. His head throbbed from the impact,
jarring the last vestiges of his thoughts of Jenny. Before he
could recover, strong hands grasped his shoulders and thrust
him into the dressing room. He fell, sprawling across the hard
mortar floor. Shattered bottles drove shards of glass into his
flesh and drenched him in wine.

Ignoring the pain, he rolled on to his haunches, whirling
towards the doorway. Looming out of the darkened walkway
was a crimson face with black-ringed eyes and horns. It took
only a moment for Will to see it was a mask, not the devil
returned to destroy him but a man, as tall as Will and wrapped
in a black woollen cloak. To his back, he had affixed the angel
wings that had been suspended in the storage rooms. Silver
glinted in the light of the single candle on the floor in one
corner. The spy saw it was a blade gripped in his opponent's
right hand, not a cut-throat's knife but one lovingly crafted
for ritual purposes, with a slight curve to the tip, and a cleft
for cutting ligaments. Black symbols had been inscribed into
the steel.

The attacker lunged like a raven falling on a dead rabbit, thrusting the knife towards Will's neck. Still shaky from his vision, he sluggishly pulled aside. The blade missed him by a finger's-width, gouging a furrow in the wall plaster.

Will lashed out at his attacker's groin. When the masked man danced away, the spy found a moment to leap to his feet.

'You are confused,' Will mocked. 'A devil or an angel?' He couldn't see any sign of the masked man's true identity, or guess the purpose of the attack.

From the yard in front of the stage came relieved chatter and the hearty laughter that is heard only after the release of fear. The audience was creeping back inside. The theatre manager loudly directed the throng to their positions, promising wonders to come.

Lunging forward, the knife-wielding foe drove Will back against the wall, and with a strength as demonic as his appearance, crushed the breath out of him. Gradually, the attacker increased the pressure. Fire burned in Will's chest.

'Will? Are you here?' Nathaniel's voice echoed along the walkway.

Distracted, the devil-masked attacker flinched. Will head-butted his opponent, smashing the mask from the top edge to just above the painted, grimacing mouth. As the man threw himself back, clutching at his crumbling disguise, Will glimpsed wild eyes filled with fury. He lashed out, trying to knock the mask away. It slid off further, revealing a hint of a familiar face, but before Will could fathom the man's identity, he stumbled back, dragging the mask into place.

'Will!' Nathaniel's concerned voice rang out closer.

'Show yourself. I would know what name to carve upon your gravestone,' Will growled, drawing his rapier.

Closing the rift in his mask with his left hand, the murderous foe bolted from the room.

Will pursued the man into the walkway, ignoring Nathaniel's surprised cry. The angel wings shimmered in the half-light, creating the illusion that the devil-masked man was flying just above the mortar floor.

Ahead, excited chatter filled the passage. A group of five players in garish make-up and wigs hurried back to their rooms from the front of the stage, eager to return to their performance. The masked attacker darted in front of them into a corridor to his left. Barely noticing his drawn rapier, the players swarmed around Will. Roughly, the agent thrust them to one side. Turning left, he was confronted by a large door hanging open.

Will raced out into a small area of hard-packed chalk where the wagons were unloaded. The sweet-apple scent of horse dung filled the air.

Night had fallen, hiding whatever path the devil-masked man had taken from the Rose. In the distance, the lights of Bankside gleamed. Clouds obscured the moon, and the wind took away any sound of disappearing feet.

A breathless Nathaniel arrived at Will's side. 'Thank God you are alive,' he gasped. The young man was flushed and his clothes were dishevelled from fighting his way through the milling crowd.

'I was caught up in the business of devils and angels, Nat,' Will responded, trying to make light. His heart ached with memories of Jenny, close enough to touch yet as far away as ever. His thoughts spun with the echoes of his vision, tinged with dread by the still-clear sight of the living scarecrow.

'You were the intended victim this night.' Nathaniel stepped in front of Will, his expression grave.

'How so?' Will asked.

Before his assistant could reply, a breathless Carpenter and Launceston raced out of the theatre door. The spy could see in the scarred man's face that something was very wrong. 'What is it?' Will demanded.

Unsure how to reply, Carpenter's gaze flickered to his emotionless companion for support. 'Word has just reached us from Deptford,' he stuttered. 'A body has been found. Murdered.'

A silent scream of despair tore through Will's head. He knew what was to come an instant before Carpenter spoke again.

'Christopher Marlowe is dead.'

CHAPTER SEVEN

'THEY'RE KILLING ALL THE DOGS. WON'T BE A HOUND LEFT IN all London soon,' Henry Cressy muttered, flicking his whip to urge the death-cart horse into Candlewick Street. On the seat beside Cressy, Thomas Bailey tied his scarf tighter around his young, pockmarked face. In the summer heat, the first load of the day reeked even worse than usual after the bodies had been left in their houses overnight.

'The Lord Mayor says the hounds disperse the plague,' Thomas said. 'Though in the Cross-Keys, they are now taking bets on which will die out first – men or curs.'

'God punishes us for our indiscretions, but he will never see his creations gone.' The carter, broad-shouldered and round of belly, still stank of the beer he had been drinking all night. After a moment's drunken reflection, he added thoughtfully, 'Although the plague's pace has not slowed. Indeed, it grows faster. Entire streets are now empty around the Tower.'

'I heard tell they are running out of men to watch the houses to make sure the poor, sickened souls do not leave, and now they are hiring boys and women. And the aldermen have called for yet another death-cart to ply this grisly trade.'

'As long as I get my eight pennies a day, and my free beer, I care little.' Cressy hunched forward, gripping the reins in his chubby fingers as he peered along the quiet street. The carters and merchants had found other routes to take them away from the vicinity of the plague pits.

To his right, Thomas eyed the constant, sinuous movement in the early morning shadows next to the walls of the timber-framed houses. Rats everywhere, filling the space that the tradesmen had vacated. The vermin had never had so much food to feast upon.

The wheels rattled across the ruts as Cressy guided the creaking cart towards the plot among the row of houses. It had once been a garden, but now the youth could see only brown earth. A black cloud of cawing crows enveloped the site, rising to the blue sky in a thunder of wings when the cart came to a halt. Tails lashing, the sleek rats scurried around the edge of the yawning pit.

'Nearly full now,' Cressy grunted, heaving his large frame from the seat. 'The Lord Mayor's men will need to find another plot to dig, if they can. Not much left in this here city.'

Even through his scarf, Thomas choked at the stench. His eyes watering, he levered himself from the cart while the older man ambled to the edge of the pit. A moment later, Cressy's strangled cry rang out. At first, the youth thought the carter had tumbled into the grave, but with a hand clutched to his mouth, the fat man was staggering backwards, his gaze fixed on the dark hole.

Thomas ran past the stumbling man, slowing as he neared the pit.

What horrors has he seen?

Peering into the stinking grave, the youth thought his heart would stop. The shroud-wrapped bodies had moved. Blackened faces stared up at him, the stained linen torn away from the

57

heads. Thomas remembered laying the corpses flat, but now they were in a jumble, some leaning against the muddy walls of the pit as if they had tried to climb out, others upended or sprawling in seeping piles.

Were the dead angry at their plight? Could they no longer rest in peace?

The youth crossed himself and whispered, 'In God's name, what monstrous thing has happened here?'

CHAPTER EIGHT

A SHAFT OF SUNLIGHT BLAZED THROUGH THE DIAMOND–PANE window on to the blanket-covered body. Around the head, the rough woollen shroud was stained brown, and more blood had spattered the dry rushes on the floor. A thick-set man in a shabby doublet tore bunches of fresh-picked rosemary, thyme and mint in a futile attempt to disguise the foul smells, but the corpse of Christopher Marlowe had lain in that cramped, hot room for a day and a half.

Will could not take his eyes off the dirty blanket, that simple, pathetic image telling him everything he feared about Marlowe's life and his own future. He felt the loss more acutely than he would ever have imagined.

It was mid-morning on 1 June. Standing at the back of the chamber, which contained only a bed, a bench and a trestle, the spy eyed the sixteen men of the inquest jury crowding around him. They pressed scented kerchiefs to their noses, intermittently coughing and gagging, their eyes watering. Will identified the two Deptford bakers, George Halfpenny and Henry Dabyns, florid and sweating, and Robert Miller, who kept Brook Mill on the road between Deptford and Greenwich, a serious, ascetic man. Others were unknown to him, gentlemen and yeomen, mostly local, landholders and wharf owners.

Will had pushed aside all thoughts of the haunting vision of Jenny at the Rose and the baffling attack upon him. News of Kit's death had struck him like the wash of an icy winter tide. For most of the night and the next day, he had been numb. His friend was gone. That was all that mattered.

Unable to contain himself any longer, a tall, thin man with silver hair opened the window and wafted the fresh air inside. Through the casement, Will now had a clear view of the sun-drenched garden of the lodging house of Mrs Eleanor Bull, ablaze with colour, the silver of sea lavender, the crimson of roses, the blue of forget-me-nots, with a row of unruly yews at the far end. The ringing calls of the merchants travelling along Deptford Strand drifted in, accompanied by the rumble of wheels and the neighs of the old nags that pulled their carts. In the distance Will could just hear the shouted orders of the men working in the great shipyards that sprawled along the Thames.

His attention returned to the black-robed man who faced the jury alongside the body. Wearing a gold medallion of office on a blue sash, William Danby was the coroner to the royal household, a gaunt man in his late sixties, who looked like he would be at home with the many bodies he encountered in his work. Will was surprised to see him in charge of Marlowe's inquest; Danby would not normally trouble himself with what most would consider such a minor death.

When Danby pointed at the corpse, his thick-set assistant pulled back the blanket. With a sharp exhalation, the jury recoiled as one. Crusted blood and brains created a caul across Kit's face. As the assistant measured the wound, Will covered his eyes for a moment, trying to focus on the detail of the

60

murder as if it were some stranger that lay before him.

Could the playwright truly have died as the result of an argument over money, as everyone claimed? A tragic death, but meaningless? The spy could not believe that.

In the corner next to Danby stood the accused, Ingram Frizer, sullen, with heavy features and prematurely greying hair, a man of business with a penchant for speculating in property and tricking the naive out of their cash. His head had been bound with bloodstained rags to cover several wounds. As Will looked deep into Frizer's face, he felt the spark of a slow-burning anger. Had the torch of a sensitive, passionate, talented soul really been extinguished by this man?

Standing alongside the accused were two other sullen men who had been present when Kit had died: Nicholas Skeres, at thirty a year older than Marlowe, lanky and shabbily dressed, a moneylender with a reputation even shadier than Frizer's; and Robert Poley. Will knew him. Their eyes met briefly before the other man looked away. Strong and fit, he wore clothes of a finer cut and held his chin at an angle that suggested he required respect.

Poley was a spy.

For many years, the older man had worked for Will's former master, Sir Francis Walsingham, yet he had also been a leading player in the criminal underworld of London. Like Marlowe, he played both sides. Unlike Marlowe, Poley enjoyed his work. Will had heard tell he was a master poisoner, as well as an informer and troublemaker among the Catholic plotters.

'And what have you found?' Danby said, in a deep, rumbling tone.

His assistant re-covered the body and stood up. 'The dagger entered just above the right eye and pierced the brain, sir. One single stroke is all I see.'

'Master Frizer. Step forward and give your account.' Danby gestured towards the space in front of the jury.

Frizer shuffled forward, his hand springing to the painful wounds on his head. 'The four of us met here at the house at about ten o'clock that day to discuss our business. We took lunch together and afterwards walked in the garden,' he began in a low, wavering voice, his gaze darting across the faces of the jury. 'At about six o'clock that evening, we came in and had our supper. Master Marlowe was tired and lay down.' Frizer indicated the bed in the corner. 'The three of us sat on the bench in a row, playing tables. I sat in the centre.' He pointed to the backgammon board, the counters still in position, the dice rolled to a six. 'Master Marlowe was in an irritable frame of mind. We argued about the sum of pence owed to Widow Bull for our food and drink that day. The reckoning was a small matter, but Master Marlowe became increasingly incensed and we exchanged malicious words. In anger, he leapt towards me, and with Master Skeres and Master Poley on either side, I could in no way take flight.

'Master Marlowe snatched my own dagger from my sheath and struck me two blows with it.' His hand went to his head wounds again and he winced. 'I thought I would die. Master Marlowe was possessed with a terrible rage, and I could do nothing to protect myself but wrest the dagger from his hand. I struck out, unthinking, and the knife went in above his eye. He died instantly.'

Danby waited for the scribe to finish noting Frizer's account before he said in a commanding voice, 'It is to your honour that you neither fled nor withdrew yourself, and this is a matter which must be considered by the jury.'

'Because I struck in defence of my own person, sir, and not to harm Master Marlowe. I would not. He was my friend.' The accused gave a deep bow. Will could see the man's hands were shaking so badly he had to clasp the one with the other.

The spy watched Frizer's face for any hint of a lie. If he couldn't prove that he had struck in defence of his own life, the accused would face death. Will accepted that the bandaged man must have been completely sure of his position not to flee the scene of the crime, or at least sure of the outcome of the inquest. But the coroner was experienced, and his reputation was strong. He had held the post for more than four years, with another fifty years of legal work behind him since he began his studies at the Inns of Court. He would not have been open to bribery, nor would he have ignored the slightest fact that threw the evidence into doubt.

Will listened carefully to the testimonies of Poley and Skeres. They both backed Frizer's account, as would be expected. After only a brief deliberation by the jury, Danby formally announced the result: 'That said Ingram Frizer had killed Christopher Marlowe in the defence and saving of his own life.'

Coughing and spluttering, the jury filed out of the hot chamber, glad to be away from the stench. Will allowed himself one last look at the form under the blanket, choosing to remember one night of joyful, drunken conversation in the Bull at Bishopsgate rather than the misery that had latterly haunted Kit. Stung with grief, Will bid his friend a silent farewell and then stormed into the flower-filled garden in search of answers.

Frizer, Skeres and Poley were already slipping around the side of the house, flashing concerned glances in Will's direction. *They flee troubling questions – the very sign of guilt*, he thought with mounting anger.

'Hold,' the spy called. 'I would have words with you three.'

Before Will could break into a run, Tobias Strangewayes stepped on to the path from the shade of a sweet-scented lilac. 'Stay your hand, Swyfte. There will be no trouble here,' the red-headed rival spy insisted.

Enraged, Will thrust Essex's man to one side. 'No one will stop me reaching the truth, least of all you.'

Spinning round, Strangewayes drew his rapier and leapt back into Will's path. 'I was warned that you would lose control of your wits when you witnessed your friend's pitiful end. Then it falls to me to restrain the man who was – once – England's greatest spy.'

'Is this more of the petty jostling for power that your master plays with my master,' Will blazed, snatching out his own blade, 'or are you too involved in Kit's death?'

Steel clashed.

'The Queen will see she can no longer place her trust in Cecil's men when they disrupt an inquest into the tawdry murder of an atheist,' Strangewayes said, grinning.

Will saw red. Slashing to the right, he almost knocked Strangewayes' blade from his grip. As Essex's man struggled to bring his rapier up to parry, Will slashed to left and right in quick succession and then thrust his sword through his opponent's defences. The tip of the rapier stabbed into the man's doublet over his breast. The rival spy looked scared, unsure if Will would follow through.

Before the answer came, Will was knocked roughly to one side. Strong arms clasped him in a bear-hug that forced him to lower his blade. Strangewayes danced backwards, flushed with relief.

'Calm yourself now, or Sir Robert will have one less spy in his employ,' a voice hissed in Will's ear. It was Sinclair, Cecil's towering bodyguard. Beside him, dressed in a black, old-fashioned velvet gown, the archivist Robert Rowland shifted from foot to foot and looked as if he would rather be anywhere but there. His crumpled face was the only one that showed a hint of sadness at that morning's grim events.

Seething, Will saw the moment had passed. Frizer, Skeres and Poley had already departed. The spy ceased his struggles until Sinclair released his grip, and then threw off the former mercenary. Will rounded on the three men. 'Something is rotten here,' he said, pointing a finger at the gathered group, 'and I will not rest until I discover who truly killed Kit Marlowe, and why. And when I uncover the names of those involved, the reckoning will be in blood.'

Storming away, Will fought to contain the tide of anger that threatened to engulf him. As he shielded his eyes against the sun, he noticed Danby watching him, the coroner's saturnine features a pool of darkness in the bright garden. His head held at an aloof angle, the dour man came over and gave a curt bow. 'I am aware of your reputation, Master Swyfte. You have served the Queen and our country honourably.'

'And I am aware of your reputation, sir. But I have some matters of concern about this inquest,' Will replied in as calm a voice as he could muster.

Danby's eyes narrowed, but he continued to smile politely. 'Master Marlowe was your friend, was he not?'

'We shared good times together.'

'The verdict has been reached, Master Swyfte. There is no going back from it.' Danby shook his head in an attempt at sadness that did not ring true.

Fighting back another surge of anger, Will took a step towards the other man. 'There is more to the evidence,' he stressed.

Unused to being questioned, the coroner flinched. 'But you

heard the evidence, sir. There is no doubt Master Frizer acted in defence of his own person.'

'Except that Master Poley is a spy, known to me and to Kit. Two of the men in that room were spies, and I would wager there may well have been more.' Will's hand unconsciously went to his rapier but he snapped his fingers shut at the last moment, and hid them behind his back.

'You suggest this is a matter of subterfuge, then? Some business of spies? Plots and conspiracies?' Danby gave a sly smile that only made Will's anger burn hotter.

'I suggest only that there is more to this than meets the eye, as there always is in the world I inhabit.' The pulse of blood in Will's head drowned out the song of a thrush and the soft music of the breeze in the elms. His vision closed in until all he could see was the coroner's supercilious expression.

'That is not enough, Master Swyfte. In matters of law, only facts can be considered, not suppositions.' Danby gave a shrug and began to walk towards the path back to Deptford Strand and his waiting coach. 'The matter is closed. Master Marlowe's body will be consigned to the earth this afternoon.'

Will recoiled. 'So soon? No pomp or ceremony?' Marlowe's fame as a playwright would have excited the interest of many. Even in the desperate atmosphere of the plague-ridden city there should at least have been an adequate announcement so the crowds could gather, not to mention an invitation to dignitaries, a procession and a full service.

'He is just a man,' the coroner said.

Will was stung by Danby's dismissive tone, adding insult to the raw emotion he already felt at his friend's passing. Kit was being discarded by the authorities, despite his years of sacrifice and service to the Crown.

'This is to do with the accusations of atheism?' Will grabbed

66

the coroner's shoulder. Danby recoiled at the outrageous lack of respect. The spy didn't care.

'I would not know. I do not make these decisions. I only investigate—'

'You answer to the people who make such decisions. In the circles in which you move you are privy to knowledge that is denied to the rest of us.'

Scared, Danby backed away a step.

'Who took the decision to bury Kit without ceremony?' Will pressed.

'I cannot say.'

'You do not know? Or you refuse to tell me?'

'I . . . I . . .' the coroner stuttered, his eyes darting.

'Tell me,' Will snapped.

A tremor crossed Danby's face, the muscles twitching as if they could not decide which expression to sport. To Will's astonishment, the coroner broke into a broad grin and then began to laugh. At first it was just a chuckle, but it rapidly transformed into a breathless bark. Yet Will could hear no humour in that sound and the coroner's eyes were still scared and flecked with tears. A shadow of confusion crossed the man's face as if he couldn't understand his own strange response, and then, still laughing, he turned and almost ran across the garden to the path.

Will had never seen anything like it before. The Queen's foremost coroner had acted like a madman, caught up in inappropriate emotions beyond his control. Was it fear of discovery? Fear of his masters? A passing lunacy?

Concerned, the spy made his way across the now-deserted garden. Before he reached the path, he glimpsed movement, high up on the lodging house. Spinning round, he looked up, shielding his eyes against the sun's glare. Not even a bird flapped on the brown tiles, but Will was convinced he had caught sight of something large hunched on the edge of the roof, watching his passage.

Something inhuman.

CHAPTER NINE

THE FUNERAL PROCESSION ARRIVED AT DEPTFORD GREEN TO A chorus of hungry gulls sweeping low overhead. While the coffin rested at the lychgate, a young man stepped up to Will, glancing around, a sack clutched to his side. The spy recognized the red, tear-stained face.

'Tom, I am sorry we meet again under these circumstances. We have both lost a good friend.' Will went to shake the hand of Marlowe's companion, but the man was racked by a silent, juddering sob of grief.

When he had recovered, Tom thrust the sack into Will's hands. 'Kit bid me give you this,' he hissed. 'I have spent two days searching for you, but you are hard to find.'

'By design,' the spy replied.

'The last I saw of Kit, on the banks of the river near Baynard's Castle at dawn, he . . . he was not in the best of humour. He feared for himself . . . feared that to be with me would bring about my death. I should . . . I should have known. Helped.' The young man swallowed noisily.

'Do not punish yourself. We can never know what is to be.'

In one tearful look, Tom communicated more than words could ever express and then he hurried away along the street.

Puzzled, Will peered into the sack. A sheaf of dog-eared papers lay at the bottom. He shrugged, and found his attention drawn back to the coffin as the pall-bearers shouldered it once more.

'Will?' In her black mourning dress, Grace gently touched his sleeve, her eyes still red from crying. 'We both loved Kit. He was a kind and gentle man, for all his troubles. But now I worry for you. His death has burned into your heart, and I can see you change by the moment. Do not let it harden you.'

Although her face was flushed with grief, Will could see elements of her sister, Jenny, in her stance, and once again he was transported back to that summer's day when his love was cruelly snatched from his life. He put the thought from his mind.

'Kit deserves justice,' he responded, his expression grim. 'I do not believe he received it at the inquest this morning, and this poor excuse for a funeral only adds insult. He deserved better. If those who used him while he was alive cannot find it within them to give him justice, then that duty falls to me. And I will seek it out in a much harsher manner than they ever would.'

The procession wound its way into the graveyard. The parish church of St Nicholas was solid and unremarkable. The final resting place of one of England's greatest playwrights was an unmarked grave near the church's north tower, and there a small group of men waited. Will was puzzled to see Thomas Walsingham, the second cousin of Sir Francis, stylish in black and gold, his lithe, powerful build that of a fencer. How could he have arrived from his home in Chislehurst so quickly, when the funeral had been announced only that morning? Will wondered.

He knew Thomas, a year older than the playwright, and

wealthy, had been one of Marlowe's patrons. He had also been a longstanding friend of Kit's through their service in the spy network, and Kit had been staying on and off at Thomas' house for most of the last month.

Walsingham nodded to Will and gave a sad smile.

As they gathered around the hastily dug grave, Will left Grace to be comforted by Nathaniel and joined Carpenter and Launceston.

'There are too many spies in this affair for my liking,' he whispered to the other two men. 'Poley, who was there at Kit's death. Now Walsingham.'

Launceston stared deep into the hole as though he were considering jumping in. 'We are a loathsome breed. Worse than snakes,' he replied in a bloodless tone.

Once the funeral was over, Will sent Carpenter and Launceston on their way and then paused by the grave to throw in a handful of the rich Deptford soil. Thomas Walsingham broke away from the small group of Marlowe's acquaintances to join him.

'This is a harsh accident,' the patron said as he stared at the cheap coffin.

'An accident? You believe it is so?' Will replied in a cold voice.

'Ingram Frizer did not mean to strike the killing blow. I have spoken to him at length, beyond the evidence he gave at the inquest. Poor Kit was like a wild thing, driven momentarily mad by the pressures of his double life.'

'That seems like an easy answer.'

'Frizer would not lie to me.'

'You know him well?'

'I am his master.'

Will flashed a look towards Walsingham, but the man's

expression was emotionless, his gaze fixed on the grave. The spy felt cold at the revelation of yet another hidden connection. 'Do you know what business they gathered here in Deptford to discuss?'

Walsingham folded his hands behind his back and raised his face to the sun. 'Not in the detail. Frizer told me it was mundane matters, of loans and debts, and some dealings in the unpleasant world they were all forced to inhabit. Nothing of import. This is more about Kit's state of mind than what transpired in that room.' His tone was reasonable, but something about it did not ring true to Will.

'I have my doubts.'

'Oh?' The other man glanced at him askance.

'Come. We are all taught to accept nothing is ever as it appears in our world.' Will paced around the grave to face the other man across the dark hole.

'True. But it is wise never to delve beneath the surface too publicly,' Walsingham said with a dismissive shrug. 'None of us knows who can be trusted. And that is worse now than it ever was when my cousin Sir Francis was spymaster. His poor replacement, Sir Robert Cecil, has ambitions, as does his rival, the Earl of Essex. Why, I would not be surprised if there were a civil war. Fought quietly and behind the scenes, in the manner of spies, of course.'

'And which side would you be on?' Will asked with a cold smile.

Walsingham's own smile was a mask. 'I am loyal to the Queen, as always.'

'Perhaps the war has already begun.' Will glanced towards the gravediggers waiting impatiently to fill in the hole.

'Spies die all the time. No one cares.' The other man plucked a piece of lint off his fine doublet. 'Their work is all that is important, and it is noted in files and stored away, paid for in blood and often forgotten before the blood is dry. Do you not find that our work is all like one of Kit's plays?'

'How so?'

'Declamatory statements, blood and thunder, words and images.' Walsingham threw an arm into the air as if he were on stage. 'Then the play ends and the audience goes home and life continues, and all that went before is forgotten. Do we pretend to ourselves that what we do has some meaning, when it is really just entertainment?'

Will pointed into the grave. 'In entertainment, men do not end there.'

'True. But Kit, like all who love art, knew that there is more to this world than the games we set for ourselves. We lose sight of what truly matters.'

'Spoken like an educated man. Some do not have the luxury of such reflection, when their life is a daily struggle to stay one step ahead of the reaper,' Will replied.

Walsingham laughed. 'You have me there, Master Swyfte. I am fortunate, I know that. Still, I would think you miss the easy certainties of the time when Sir Francis oversaw these great affairs.'

'He is gone, and we have all moved on. There is nothing to be gained by looking back.' Will felt a brief pang at the irony of his statement.

'There are some who may not agree with you. Sir Francis' grave was defaced only the other day.' The other man pursed his lips to show his distaste.

'Oh? When?'

'On the night before Kit's death. Who would do such a thing?'

The question was rhetorical, but Will's thoughts raced.

Who would deface the grave of Sir Francis Walsingham, and several years after his death? Someone who knew him and the work he did, perhaps? That was a small group.

'I must return home to Chislehurst,' Walsingham continued. 'Important matters call to me, and a clear head is required. This business saddens me, though. I will miss Kit greatly.' He walked around the grave to shake Will's hand. 'I know he was important to you too. Kit always spoke of his good friend warmly. Do not let his death lie on you. He is in a better place now, and finally at peace.'

Will watched him walk through the gravestones to where his companions waited by the lychgate. Walsingham clapped his fellows across the shoulders as if he were on a jaunt to the nearest inn. There was no sign of the grief he professed.

'Will?' Grace questioned, taking his arm.

'I would have one moment alone with Kit and then I will join you,' Will replied gently. Her eyes moist, the woman nodded and made her way towards the lychgate.

A sudden breeze brought with it the stink of the Isle of Dogs and the sound of hammers from the shipyards. Will felt eyes upon him again. The gravediggers were already collecting their shovels and inspecting the pile of soil.

'Leave me alone,' Will snapped, looking into the dark hole in the ground. His grief felt like a rock on his back, his impotent anger a fire in his heart. As he tried to make sense of all that had happened, a faint movement in the heavy shadow along the church's western wall caught his eye. A figure was watching the grave from beyond two ancient yews, carefully positioned to avoid being seen.

Slipping away from the graveside, Will circled the church along the eastern wall. Darting around the back of the squat stone building, he approached the watcher from behind. It was a woman in mourning dress, and from her flame-red hair he guessed it was the one Nathaniel had encountered outside the Rose.

Will approached silently until he was close enough to prevent her fleeing and then he said, 'Do not be shy. If you wish to pay your respects, come closer.'

The woman let out a small cry and whirled, pressing herself back against the corbelled flint wall of the church. Her eyes flashed with recognition when she saw who had startled her.

'You know me?' The agent stepped closer so she could not slip by him.

'Will Swyfte. England's greatest spy. Who does not know you?' Will heard clear Gaelic notes in her voice, but he couldn't read the emotion behind her words. She raised her chin defiantly and brushed a stray wisp of hair from her pale forehead.

'And yet you appear to know more than most. Like the time and place of my intended death.' He leaned in close so their faces were only a hand's-width apart. He could smell her heady fragrance, the notes of orange and cloves.

'I came to the theatre to warn you. Would you have preferred I made no attempt to save your life?' The woman seemed unthreatened by his forthright behaviour.

Will stared deep into her eyes, but couldn't see any deception. She held his gaze with confidence; there was no pretence of coyness. He realized she was used to sustaining the attention of men. 'You must think highly of me if you would go out of your way to save me,' he said.

'You think highly of yourself,' she sniffed. 'I would have done it for anyone.'

'A charitable woman. How charitable would that be?'

'My charity is only dispensed to needful cases. I sense you

are never in want, Master Swyfte.' Her shoulders relaxed against the hard wall, and a faint smile flickered on her lips.

'We all find ourselves at a loss from time to time.'

She cocked her head wryly as if she saw something in his face that he hadn't realized was there. 'Then I would suggest you work on your swordplay in the privacy of your room, Master Swyfte,' she breathed. 'I hear you are regularly called upon to use your weapon, and it would not do to be found lacking in that area. Self-improvement is a virtue.'

Will grew tired of the game and said firmly, 'Perhaps we should leave discussion of virtue to a later time. Will you give me your name?'

'Margaret Penteney,' she replied, so confidently that Will was convinced it was a lie.

'You are here tending the grave of a family member perhaps?'

'My business is my own, Master Swyfte.'

The spy took a step back. 'Of course. But I am concerned for your safety. A woman abroad in Bankside, outside a theatre at night? That is not a safe place. Does your father or husband allow you to put yourself in such danger?'

'You should thank me for so endangering myself to try to help you.'

'And it is a happy accident that I am in a position to thank you, here in Deptford, so far from London,' Will said sardonically.

'We are not to know God's plan, Master Swyfte.'

'Not God's, no. However, the plots and plans of men are of great interest to me. And women. How did you uncover the threat against my life?' He allowed a hard tone to enter his voice, but the flame-haired woman still did not flinch.

'I see and hear many things in my business.'

'Which is?'

'Will?' Grace was standing at the corner of the tower with a hurt expression. She looked from Will to the woman who stood so close, they could have been involved in a lovers' tryst.

'Return to the graveside, Grace. I will be back soon,' he said with a sharpness that he instantly regretted.

With a cold expression, Grace held Margaret's gaze for a moment. The Irish woman gave her a smile that Will only ever saw women share among themselves; it circumscribed a position of strength.

Once Grace had gone, Will hardened. 'Now. Your business.'

With a skip in her step, the flame-haired woman moved away from the wall into the warm sun. 'I am a wife and I tend my home well, Master Swyfte. I only meant that as I go about my chores I keep my eyes and ears open to the gossip of my neighbours.'

'And one of your neighbours threatened to kill me?' Will mocked. The woman still gave no sign of lying, but he didn't believe her. He had started to accept that she was as skilled at deceit as he was.

Will was puzzled to see her come to a sudden halt and the blood drain from her face. 'I am innocent,' she said in a whispery voice. The spy realized her widening eyes were looking past him to the yews.

A figure stood in the stark interplay of shadow and sunlight beneath the swaying trees, framed by ragged gravestones. The spy's stomach knotted when he saw it was Jenny, followed by a moment of excruciating dislocation when he realized it wasn't Jenny at all. Those same black, hateful eyes fell upon him as they had in the Rose Theatre.

Will sensed Margaret hurry away, but his attention was locked on the cruel imitation. He felt a sudden attraction, a

77

part of him desperately trying to make up for the years of grief and yearning. But another part of him was repulsed, and the point where the two sides met left him sickened.

'Is this it, then? I have my own devil now to torment me?' the spy whispered to himself.

Drawing his rapier, Will ran into the dense copse of yews only to find that whatever had waited there was gone. Only a wisp of brimstone remained in the air to show it had ever been. But he could feel its black eyes on him even then, and a deep, chilling dread that was so tightly wound around him he was afraid it would never leave.

Will already understood what Marlowe was describing in the play he had half heard the other night at the Rose: to want and never gain was a special and very personal hell.

CHAPTER TEN

REACHING THE TOP OF THE ROPE, WILL HAULED HIMSELF SOUND-
lessly over the battlements into the shadows of the walkway
overlooking the western road out of London. Crouching, he
peered along the wall to where the guard leaned against his
pike under the glow of a gently swaying lantern. The man's
head nodded, and the spy heard the drone of juddering snores.

Easing the rope up, Will tested the grapnel was secure
and then lowered himself down into the deserted Palace of
Whitehall. He would have found it easier to gain access by
hammering on the eastern gate to rouse the guards, but he
didn't want anyone to know he'd been there.

Slipping through the dark among the jumble of stone and
timber-framed palace buildings, Will felt that he had spent
the last two days trying to navigate sandbanks in the fog. He
glimpsed meaning among the shifting strands of devils and
murder and knife-wielding masked men, but it disappeared
before he could tack a course towards it. One beacon remained
clear, though: the Unseelie Court.

*The scarecrow staring with Marlowe's eyes. The pale figures pursu-
ing him with lethal intent.*

The empty palace with its ringing halls and blank windows

was the wrong place to contemplate the stuff of nightmares. Even though the Queen and the court had long since fled London to escape the plague, Will felt he was being watched.

Creeping to the edge of a large cobbled courtyard, he let his eyes rise up the tall tower that stood at its centre. At the very top of the Lantern Tower, as it had always been known for no good reason that he could see, a faint green glow rolled and folded, like the lights people said they often glimpsed in the northern skies.

Will felt his stomach knot and an ache rise deep in the back of his head. The sole occupant of that tower burned so fiercely not even stone walls could contain her power.

Always alert, four steely-eyed guards in helmet and cuirass walked the courtyard, hands only an inch from pike or musket. The tower itself was filled with lethal traps, many newly installed, but it was the unseen defences that were the most deadly, Will knew. The court's former alchemist, Dr John Dee, had ensured nothing could get in and the prisoner could never get out, for if that were to happen England would fall.

England's guilty secret.

Few people knew the tower's secret, only Her Majesty and a handful of her most trusted men. But Will had learned the truth, and it had eaten away at him for five years now.

Her protectors slaughtered, the immaculate, terrifying Queen of the Unseelie Court had been stolen in an act of grand betrayal during a convocation to discuss peace in the generations-long struggle between men and their supernatural foe. An uneasy truce was no use to a nation caught between the twin poles of fear and ambition, and Queen Elizabeth and her advisers had realized her forbidding counterpart could become the fulcrum of Dr Dee's magical defences, a shield that could keep the great Enemy at bay for evermore.

Watching the green light wash out, Will imagined the Fay Queen sitting in her cell, seething, plotting, waiting for the moment when her imprisonment would end and a new reign of terror could be unleashed upon the land.

Dread and grief intermingling, the spy's mind flashed back to a small hamlet not far from Stratford, beside the green, green Avon, where he had stood next to Kit Marlowe in front of a dense wall of briar reaching up higher than his head. Some of the twining growth was as thick as his arm, the thorns as sharp as knives. It had not been there the day before.

'I am ready,' the playwright had said, holding his chin up defiantly.

Will had glimpsed the fear in the young man's eyes and nodded. 'I am sure you are. But it is one thing to learn about the Unseelie Court in the safety of the Palace of Whitehall and another to meet them in the pale, grave-tainted flesh.'

Marlowe swung the axe above his head and began to hack through the dense vegetation. What sounded like a muffled scream echoed through the briar with each blow. 'They will not scare me,' the young man replied.

Will hoped Sir Francis Walsingham and his strange, mad aide, Dr Dee, were correct and Marlowe was ready for his first encounter with the supernatural foe. He had seen other men destroyed by their first brush with the nightmarish force. 'Remember,' he said gently, 'the mind rebels against the slightest contact with those foul creatures. They are beyond all reasoning, the source of all fear, the secret behind all the most blood-chilling stories told on a winter's night since the days of your ancestors.'

'I know,' Kit gasped, sweat dripping as he hacked. 'There is some quality to them that can drive a man mad. But I am prepared.'

In the centre of the briar wall, the two men heard the muffled screams more clearly. Marlowe blanched, pointing. Arms stretched wide, a man hung in the twisting strands, his eyes wide with terror. Only when he stepped closer did Will see that the briar was driven through the man's flesh, through his very body, piercing one cheek, or one side, or one leg, and bursting out of the other. Small thorny twists had stitched his lips together so that however much he wanted to express his agony, he could not cry out.

'What do we do?' Marlowe whispered, sickened.

'There is nothing we can do. The Unseelie Court have turned cruelty into a fine art.' With a soothing smile, Will stepped forward and plunged his dagger into the poor soul's heart.

Marlowe crumpled for a moment, but when he had recovered, he hacked through the remaining briar with angry determination. On the other side, the two men saw a quaint thatched cottage with whitewashed walls and a trail of woodsmoke rising from the chimney. A young woman stood by the door, pretty but heavy-set in the manner of country girls. She smiled at the new arrivals and brushed down her corn-coloured skirts.

But Will and Kit couldn't tear their gaze away from the figure who stood beside her. Tall, with long brown hair, sallow skin and doublet and breeches of grey, he looked back with fierce contempt almost masked by a supercilious smile. Will felt his stomach churn, and he saw the blood trickling from his companion's nose. Marlowe was shaking and Will placed a hand on his friend's shoulder to steady him. 'Be resolute,' he whispered.

The playwright nodded, drawing his rapier. The two men advanced on the pale being, but they had barely covered half the distance to the cottage when the Fay leaned in to whisper in the woman's ear.

'No,' Will shouted, breaking into a run.

A shadow crossed the woman's face. The supernatural being gave a cruel smile and in the blink of an eye he was gone.

When the two men reached the woman, she was humming a pleasant song and rocking gently from side to side. 'Did you meet my husband?' she asked in a musical voice. 'He has been punished for kissing that harlot Rose Culpepper.'

'You called that thing in?' Will asked, unable to hide his sadness at the pain the woman had inflicted upon herself and her love in her hurt.

She nodded and beckoned. 'Come indoors and see my beautiful baby. He sleeps so quietly.'

Marlowe looked full of dread.

The two men followed the good wife into the warm, smoky interior. She went straight to a crib near the hearth. 'My boy, my Daniel,' she said with love.

In the crib was a twisted briar mockery of a baby, blackened and covered in thorns, but it writhed as its mother cooed over it. Sickened, Marlowe turned away.

'That is a beautiful child, indeed,' Will said. 'Now, my friend would like to see your garden, while I attend to a matter here.'

The woman smiled, but her eyes showed little sanity left. Hesitantly, Kit led her outdoors, casting troubled glances at his companion.

Once they had gone, Will snatched the changeling from the crib. It spat and lashed out tiny, thorny hands. He hurled it on to the fire where it cried like a real baby before it was consumed by the flames.

Barely had the last screech died away when Will heard Marlowe shouting. He rushed out into the small herb garden, only to see his friend hunched over the bank of the rushing spring river that curled past the cottage.

'She threw herself in,' Kit gasped, reeling.

'Though her mind was destroyed, a part of her knew the truth. That is why we fight the foul Unseelie Court. They prise open the weaknesses in the human heart and destroy from within. They have done this since man first walked England's green land and they will try to do it until judgement day if we are not vigilant.'

After a long silence, Marlowe said quietly, 'And I will stand by your side, God help me. Though my life be corrupted by dread from this moment on, I do what I must for my fellow man.'

Proud but sad, Will had clapped his friend on the shoulder and led him back to their horses with the promise of a night of wine to dull the memories, but they both knew Kit's life was changed for ever.

Will flashed back to the moonlit courtyard, his heart heavy with grief at his friend's passing. That day in Stratford their friendship had been forged, for they had shared an experience, however terrible, that set them apart from their fellow men. Despite Will's fears, Marlowe had survived and grown to be an effective spy. A good man, a sad man, and now he was gone.

What part, if any, had the Unseelie Court played in his friend's demise?

Looking to the top of the Lantern Tower, Will whispered, 'Kit will be avenged. And if I find your pale hands stained in his blood, you will pay a thousandfold. I vow this now.'

CHAPTER ELEVEN

'WHO KILLED CHRISTOPHER MARLOWE?' CARPENTER ASKED IN a low voice. The guttering candle in the centre of the beer-stained trestle illuminated the unease in his features.

Enveloped in the shadows that engulfed the rest of the small, hot, low-ceilinged room, Will and Launceston leaned in to the dying flame.

'We have a few suspects,' Will mused, his mood as dark as when he had left the Palace of Whitehall. 'Frizer, the one who stood accused at the inquest. Poley, his associate, a man we all know is capable of anything.' He paused, damping down his anger. 'Or even Thomas Walsingham, Kit's patron. There were always rumours that their relationship was more than just business, but who knows? I saw little sign of grief in him. Yet Kit's young friend Tom said Marlowe was gripped with a fear for his own life that very same morning. Would he then proceed to a meeting with the men he was afraid would kill him?'

'When your attacker's devil-mask slipped at the Rose, you say you thought you knew the face beneath?' Carpenter enquired.

''Twas a glimpse. The merest suggestion of recognition. I would not say more than that.'

'Hrrrm,' the Earl said thoughtfully. 'One spy dead, another attacked. But what part does this devil of yours play? This vision you had of the Unseelie Court?'

Will listened to the sound of energetic lovemaking reverberating through the ceiling from the room of one of Liz Longshanks' doxies. The bedroom at the top of the Bankside stew, and his favourite comely companions, pulled at him, but instead he was there, sequestered in the private room at the back where the rich merchants drank before indulging their carnal desires. 'I have thought about this a great deal, and I have come to believe that it was a warning.'

'From whom?' Launceston breathed.

'Kit Marlowe. He knew nothing of conjuring devils. All he conjured was words. I have no idea how he could have brought that . . . that thing,' the spy flinched at a painful vision of Jenny, black eyes gleaming, 'into existence on the stage.'

'There are plenty in the government and the court who considered him devilish for his outspoken views,' the white-faced man continued.

'The vision felt like it was a portent, perhaps, or some kind of guidance, though it had the feel of a dream. Fractured. Symbolic. Off-kilter.'

'Then what use is it?' Carpenter sniffed.

Frustrated, Will reflected for a moment, then plucked a new candle from the mantelpiece and lit it with the dying flame of the old. The shadows in the room fled to the corners. From under his stool, he pulled the coarse sack young Tom had given him at the funeral, and tipped the sheaf of papers on to the table. Carpenter leaned past him to read the title scrawled on the front in Marlowe's familiar flourish.

'*The Tragical History of Doctor Faustus*. Why, it is only the play Marlowe presented at the Rose the other evening,' the scar-faced man snorted. He went to a pewter tray on a stool in the corner and poured himself a goblet of malmsey wine.

With deft fingers, Will plucked the folded letter from under the string around the bundle. 'Kit was keen that I received this work, and he has never given me one of his plays before.' Holding the letter close to the candle, he scanned it quickly. The words had been written at speed, scrawled feverishly and at times blotted where the ink hadn't dried before the letter was folded.

I fear this may be our last communication, my dear, trusted friend. The truth lies within. But seek the source of the lies without. Trust no one.

By the time Will had read the note, Carpenter was once again at his shoulder, his brow now furrowed. 'Trust no one? This sounds to me very like a plot.'

'That explains why Kit was not at his first night. He was in hiding.' Will got up and went to the tray to pour himself some wine. He placed one foot upon a stool and sipped his drink, brooding.

Launceston drew his long, white fingers over the sheaf, stopping to tap on the wax that sealed the string. 'A secret message, then. A warning,' the Earl suggested in his whispery voice.

'Trust no one,' Carpenter repeated. 'He states the obvious, for once. Damn this world we inhabit. Everyone keeps secrets, separate lives. We know little even of those we depend upon.'

'As in life,' Will said with a shrug.

Carpenter drained his drink in one go and slammed the goblet down on the trestle. 'We expend all our energies keeping secrets from each other,' he snarled, wiping his mouth with the back of his hand. 'What would our old master Sir Francis have said? Since his death, our world has fallen into darkness, and we all march on the short road to hell.'

Will became aware of Launceston scrutinizing him. He had come to believe the Earl was acutely sensitive to the emotions of others because he couldn't feel or understand his own. 'What is it, Robert?' he asked, taking a sip of his wine.

The Earl spread the fingers of both hands on the trestle before him. 'I am thinking about the Irish woman you encountered in the churchyard, the one who spoke to your assistant at the Rose. She knows of the plot, somehow. You did not recognize her?'

'He has forgotten more women who have graced his bed than you or I have ever encountered,' Carpenter muttered.

'She is not familiar, though I will pay strict attention if she crosses my path again. Perhaps she is a friend of Kit's.' He returned his gaze to the letter. *The truth lies within*. The playwright always chose his words with precision.

Launceston was thinking the same, Will could see. 'If Marlowe could have written clearly, he would, but he was afraid his message would be intercepted,' the Earl noted, tapping one scrupulously clean fingernail on the table. 'And so, perhaps, he hid clues to what he knew within the words of his own play? *The truth lies within* would suggest that approach.'

'Perhaps.' As Will swigged his wine, he was struck by a revelation. 'At the graveside, Kit's patron told me that Sir Francis Walsingham's grave at St Paul's had been defaced. It puzzled me at the time. Who would do such a thing? But now I wonder . . . Tom met Kit at the river, not far from the cathedral.'

Carpenter leaned in, eager. 'Marlowe could have left another message. He would have known such an act would reach our ears eventually.'

'I think I should see the grave for myself, on the morrow,' Will said, pouring himself another goblet of the sweet wine.

'And while I busy myself with that task, I have a job for the two of you. Kit had a bolt-hole that few knew of, a small room in Alexander Marcheford's lodging house not far from the Rose. Go there and find any information he might have left that would explain his death.'

'But what is the plot?' Carpenter hammered a fist on the trestle, his voice cracking with dismay. 'To kill a pair of spies? Why go to such lengths? We kill ourselves sooner or later,' he added with bitterness.

'Trust no one, Kit said, and so we should not speak of this outside this room.' Will tapped one finger on the table. 'The court is already riven with factions. There are plots and counter-plots aplenty. In that unruly atmosphere, there is space for a greater plot to flourish, unseen by those charged with looking out for such dangers.'

'The Unseelie Court plays a long game.' Unblinking, the Earl watched the wavering flame, his pale skin even whiter in the light. 'With so many of us distracted by threats within and without, this is a good time to strike.'

'Nothing here makes sense! So many strands, yet we cannot weave them into any cloth. And meanwhile our fate approaches like the tide.' Carpenter ran a hand through his long hair, his mood darkening by the moment. 'What is happening to England?' he added, his voice falling to a mutter. 'Since the Armada was defeated, we have been cursed with bad luck. Walsingham dead so soon after his greatest victory. Dee exiled to the north. Spain regaining its strength and still scheming, along with most of the other nations of Europe. Papists plotting our Queen's death within our own shores. And now this plague, eating its way through the heart of our country. We have never been at a lower ebb. Where will it end?'

'They say the Fair Folk are masters of bad luck.' Launceston's emotionless voice added an eerie weight to his words. 'The Enemy that has tormented us for so long was always good at souring milk and breaking apart man and wife and destroying friendships by driving a wedge into the cracks caused by human weakness. Perhaps they are the invisible hand behind all our misery.'

Will was struck by the Earl's words. Breaking the seal on the play, he flicked through the papers. No additions to the text leapt out at him, but he knew Kit would be more subtle than that.

Settling into his chair, with his boots on the table, he began to read the work while Carpenter and Launceston drank and dozed. Will was soon engrossed in the hubristic story of the scholar, Faustus, who had reached the limits of his studies and decided to devote himself to magic to continue his intellectual growth. Summoning the devil Mephistophilis, he makes a pact with Lucifer: twenty-four years of life on earth with the devil as his servant, and then he must give up his soul. The ending remained ambiguous: no evidence was found of Faustus' fate, though the implication was that Lucifer had taken him to eternal damnation.

As he came to the end amid Carpenter's growling snores, Will reflected on the content. His friend's stories, like those of many writers, had more than one meaning, and what lay on the surface was not always the most important. Kit had spoken many times about how there was little difference between his work as a writer and his work as a spy – both roles required a convincing liar – and he had been sure it was one of the reasons he excelled at both, to his own self-loathing. There was a great deal in the story of Faustus that would have applied to Marlowe too, Will decided. One statement by Mephistophilis, describing hell, struck him particularly:

Hell hath no limits, nor is circumscribed,
In one self place, but where we are is hell,
And where hell is there must we ever be.
And to be short, when all the world dissolves,
And every creature shall be purified,
All places shall be hell that is not heaven.

Hell is in the minds of everyone, Mephistophilis appeared to be saying, and not a physical location. *We make our own hells,* Will thought, *or have them thrust upon us.* He considered the thing that had taken the form of Jenny and wondered if he would see it again.

The sheaf of papers was Marlowe's original script, covered with blottings, scribblings, annotation and rings of dried wine. Some sections had been obliterated with furious strokes of the quill, and new lines written nearby. Mephistophilis' description of hell was one of them, and Will wondered if Kit had changed it only recently, as matters came to light. If there were clues hidden within, it would take time to decipher them, and if he knew his friend's mercurial mind, some clues might well be hidden in the symbolic nature of the text and the meaning might never be fully understood.

The truth lies within, but seek the source of the lies without.

What did Marlowe mean by the last part of his infuriatingly cryptic advice? Frustrated, Will retied the string.

A sharp knock at the door made all three of them jerk alert. Launceston was at the entrance in a flash, his knife ready. 'Who goes?' he growled.

'Will? Are you in there?'

The pale-faced man relaxed. 'Your assistant.'

At Will's nod, the Earl opened the door and a breathless Nathaniel darted in. 'I have run all the way from the river,' he gasped. 'I did as you asked, and spent the evening with the watermen listening to the gossip from the city.' He doubled up, one hand on his knee, as he caught his breath. 'You were right to fear poor Kit's death was not the end of it. One of Sir Robert Cecil's advisers came across the water in such a state I thought he would pull out his hair in a fit. He demanded a horse to ride to Nonsuch immediately to tell your master the news.'

'Which is?' Will asked, growing cold.

'Another spy has been murdered, and in a manner that would give a grown man nightmares.'

CHAPTER TWELVE

WITH THREE SWIFT STROKES, WILL POUNDED THE HILT OF HIS rapier on the broad, iron-studded door of the deadhouse. Those sturdy stone walls had housed unclaimed bodies, and those waiting to be claimed, for centuries. Fidgeting, Carpenter cast unsettled glances along the night-dark Bread Street towards St Mary-Le-Bow churchyard. Intermittently, the scarred man pressed a scented kerchief against his nose to keep out the reek of decay which was stronger than usual on that warm night. His gaze eventually alighted on Launceston, immobile on the edge of the circle of light cast by the lantern over the door. The Earl's pale skin glowed white in the flickering illumination.

'Let us hope no watchman chooses this moment to deliver a corpse they have stumbled across in the street,' Carpenter muttered. 'They already believe the deadhouse to be haunted by its silent inhabitants.'

Launceston raised one eyebrow at his sullen companion, but gave no sign that he was offended.

'No more bickering this night,' Will cautioned. 'You two are like an old married couple.'

Will would have had both his companions silent from the moment the three of them left Liz Longshanks' stew, but the men had spent the entire journey across the river into London arguing about Carpenter's woman.

As he waited for an answer to his knock, there at death's door, he thought of poor Kit once more. Will recalled the last time he had sat with his friend in the Mermaid, drinking beer beside the fire in the small private back room. 'We have been the best of friends for many years now,' Kit had said, his tone maudlin. He was hunched over his earthen pot with its silver handle and lid, staring into the murky depths of his ale. 'Perhaps you are my only true friend.'

'This business of ours does not make for easy friendships, Kit,' Will replied. 'But it is what it is, and we have to make the best of what we have.'

'I think I am spent. You . . . you have your Jenny to keep you searching. Your quest for answers. But I have nothing. A few pennies here and there. Is that any reward for the sacrifices we make? The loss of all things that make life worth living? When I entered the halls of Cambridge I thought my days would be spent in writing and thought and joy. Not this.'

Will clapped his friend on the shoulder. 'You are having a black day, that is all.'

Marlowe shook his head, slopping beer drunkenly as he raised his pot to his lips. 'Events were set in motion that night we first met, and I fear they are now coming to a head.'

'Kit, I do not like to see you this way. Let me get you back to your lodgings . . . or at least to that bawdy-house filled with boys that you love so much.'

Kit pushed Will's hand away. 'We understand each other, you and I.' He looked at Will with raw emotion. 'Despite all the applause that follows *England's greatest spy*, I know that behind it is a tormented man, lonely and lost and at odds with the world in which he has found himself. And you know the truth of my life in the same way. Men like us need our friends, otherwise we are adrift in a stormy sea.' Marlowe pushed back his stool and lurched to his feet. 'Know that you have been a good friend to me, Will, and I hope that one day I can be the same to you.'

Grabbing his cloak, Kit had staggered out into the night, throwing off all Will's attempts to draw him back to the fireside. At the time, Will had put that dark mood down to the drink and the regular melancholy of the writer, but now the note of finality in his friend's words troubled him. Had Kit foreseen his own death? And had Will ignored those warnings? Had he failed his friend when Kit needed him most? If so, he was a poor friend indeed.

After a moment, shuffling footsteps approached from the other side of the deadhouse door. It swung open with a juddering creak to reveal the mortuary assistant, his beard unkempt, his eyes heavy-lidded. He wore only a filthy shirt and a pair of equally stained hose, the feet a dark brown. His breath had the vinegary stink of ale. His slow, drunken gaze lay on the three arrivals before he looked around for a body.

'We have no deposit for you,' Will said with authority. 'We are here to see a body. A man, brought in this day.'

The assistant moved his stupid eyes from Will to Carpenter and then to Launceston. After he had taken in their fine clothes, he grunted and nodded, shuffling back the way he had come.

'I think he means us to follow,' Launceston sniffed.

In the cool entrance hall, dirty sheets lay on the worn flagstones alongside a pile of splintered boards used for transporting the bodies. Two lanterns glowed on opposing walls. The assistant took one of them and, holding it aloft, lit the way down a flight of wide stone steps. At the foot, a large cellar was divided into four rooms by arches, the stone walls black with moisture, glistening in the wavering light of candles. In each vault, large, worn trestles stood in rows. The body of a woman rested on one, her skin white and pockmarked, her neck broken. Her clothes were poor and filthy. A whore, Will guessed. A gutter ran across the centre of the stone flags where the blood and bodily fluids could be sluiced.

'As cold as the grave,' Carpenter growled uneasily, unconsciously rubbing his pink scar.

'And as foul-smelling as the Fleet,' his leader responded. 'But we are all used to the stink of death by now.'

Launceston hummed a jolly tune.

The mortuary assistant led them to the farthest vault, where a heavily bloodstained shroud was draped over a body on a trestle. 'This one?' he grunted.

'Leave us,' Will said. 'We would be alone with our brother in this sad hour.'

'I wouldn't be lifting the sheet,' the assistant grunted, turning and shuffling back up the steps.

'We should not be here,' Carpenter said, a hand to his mouth. He took a step away from the trestle. 'Why put ourselves at even greater risk of the plague?'

'The Lord Mayor and the Aldermen have decreed that no plague victims should find their way into the deadhouse. They are dispatched directly to the pits for burial.' Will eyed the rusty stains that covered the entire length of the sheet.

'This business reeks of the Unseelie Court,' the scar-faced man spat. 'Whenever there is something that stinks of churchyards and night terrors, they are not far behind.'

'They have been silent in recent times but they circle us like wolves, ready to fall upon us when we display the merest sign of weakness,' the Earl agreed.

Will took the edge of the sheet and hesitated, thinking

of Kit beneath the filthy blanket on the floor of Mrs Bull's lodging house.

'You know the bastards are skilled at finding weaknesses and exploiting them. They see our greatest desires, our basest yearnings, and they twist them and draw them out until we follow like fools.' Launceston's right hand trembled in anticipation as he watched his leader holding the sheet corner.

'Get on with it, then,' Carpenter snapped, flashing a glance towards the shape under the shroud. 'If these remains can tell us aught of this mystery, let us look and be away.'

The Earl leaned over the trestle as if trying to see through the sheet. 'You are abnormally squeamish, John. You are no stranger to death.'

'Not in this form. Some deaths come naturally. Others are necessary. But this . . .' Carpenter choked on his words as he pointed to the sodden sheet. 'This is an abomination.'

'Let us see.' Will steeled himself and stripped back the shroud.

Carpenter recoiled, covering his mouth in horror.

Launceston still hovered over the trestle, bemused. 'I think that is Gavell,' he muttered.

The corpse was almost unrecognizable as the man who gambled away his meagre earnings in the inns of Bankside. Where two brown eyes had been were now black holes. The straw-coloured hair still stood up in tufts on the head, but the skin of the face, neck and torso had been carefully removed to reveal the oozing, red musculature beneath.

'Why, this is the work of a master,' the Earl breathed. He hovered for a long moment, seemingly oblivious to the meaty smell coming off the body. In a slow examination, he moved around the torso, his nose a hand's-width from the flesh. 'See here, and here,' he whispered. 'The merest knife cuts. The skin has been removed with great skill. This is no butcher's work.' His brow furrowed and he looked up. 'The curious knife you described, the one wielded by your masked attacker. Could it have been designed for this?' He waved a hand across the sticky corpse.

'I would say', Will mused, 'that it would have been perfectly designed for this task.' He had a sudden vision of himself lying upon the trestle.

'What is the point?' Carpenter's voice was almost a shriek. 'Kill a man and be done with it, but why take time to flay him, unless you have lost your wits?'

'Why, indeed?' Will rubbed his thumb and forefinger thoughtfully on his chin-hair. He felt a wave of compassion. Gavell was by no description a good man, but he deserved a better ending than this.

'Wait, what is this?' the Earl mused. He indicated black streaks smudged across several areas of the raw flesh. Examining them for a moment, he shook his head and moved on. Finally he stood back, his breath short. 'This may simply be a work of art, like one of Marlowe's plays. The same attention to detail. The same loving care.'

Will stared into Gavell's empty eye sockets for a long moment, allowing the detail of the murder to settle on him, and then he said, 'No. Two spies dead. An attempt on the life of a third. I cannot believe that it is by chance. Turn the body over.'

'God's wounds!' Carpenter cursed. 'Leave the poor sod be.'

'If this is a plot, we must divine its nature from whatever we have to hand,' Will stressed. 'Turn him over.'

Muttering oaths under his breath, the scar-faced man kept his eyes averted as he gripped the sticky shoulders. Launceston took the ankles without a second thought, and together they eased the body off the puddle of congealing blood with a low, sucking sound. Carpenter grimaced.

Gavell's grisly remains clunked face down on to the trestle. Will pointed to a mark carved into the muscle of the dead man's back: a circle, bisected at the compass points with short lines, and with a square at its centre.

'From this we can surmise that Gavell was not simply dispatched because of the work he did,' he said. 'This is not a crude murder. There is thought and meaning in this design.'

'But what does it mean?' the Earl asked.

Circling the trestle slowly, Will ignored the question and reflected on the matter at hand. 'Is someone attempting to kill the spies of England, one by one?' he said thoughtfully. 'And if so, to what purpose? Our lives already have little value and we are easily replaced.'

'Because of what we know?' Carpenter suggested.

'And what do we know?' Will paused as a notion struck him. 'We know a matter of the greatest importance: the existence of the Unseelie Court. It is a secret held only by the Queen herself, the Privy Council, and we spies under the command of Sir Robert Cecil. It is considered too terrible to be discussed beyond that small group. Even Essex has not been allowed to tell his men, which must leave him greatly aggrieved, for his spies can never be effective without that knowledge.' Pondering, Will began to walk around the table once more.

'Yes.' Launceston's eyes were like lamps in the half-light. 'For if all the spies who knew of the Enemy were killed, who could ever stop them?'

Coming to a halt, Will leaned against the damp stone wall and folded his arms. 'Which raises one other troubling matter. Everyone in England recognizes the work I do as a spy. But who knew Gavell participated in these dark arts?'

99

Will took another look at the raw, red body. 'I am rapidly coming to the conclusion that we should heed Master Marlowe in these matters,' he said quietly, 'and seek a solution ourselves. Our lives may depend on it.'

'Surely you do not suspect Cecil?' Carpenter exclaimed. 'Or any in our greater circle?' He turned his back on the corpse and looked towards the steps, as if planning his exit.

'I suspect everyone until I have proof otherwise,' Will replied. 'There is too much that is unknown here, and little that makes sense with the information we have to hand. I would learn more first.'

A loud booming resonated from the deadhouse door above them. Will raised a hand to quiet the other two.

'A watchman delivering a body,' Carpenter whispered. 'Or a beadle.'

At the top of the steps, the deadhouse door creaked open. A loud voice echoed, demanding entry.

'That is no watchman,' the Earl said quietly.

Other raised voices were followed by a cry that could only have come from the mortuary assistant.

'Quickly.' Flinging the shroud back over the corpse, Will whirled a pointing finger towards a haphazard pile of boards and unused trestles in a large alcove beside the steps. As they darted towards the hiding place, there was another cry and a clatter. The drunken assistant slid down the steps and sprawled on the flagstones, where he lay in a stupor, moaning gently.

The three spies eased themselves behind the trestles and boards and ducked low, finding positions where they could look out into the shadowy mortuary. They'd barely settled into place when the pounding of boots down the stone steps heralded the arrival of five men, their rapiers drawn. The intruders all wore tall-crowned, flat-topped black hats and black cloaks that reached down to their ankles. Will strained to see their faces, but they kept the brims of their hats pulled down. They paused at the foot of the steps and scanned the cellar before the leader said in a gruff voice, 'Empty. Go.'

With well-drilled speed and efficiency, the other four men responded to the order, fanning out across the mortuary to examine the bodies on the trestles. Uneasy, Will wondered if they were part of the militia. Certainly, the leader stood with an air of authority as he watched his men move quickly around the underground room.

A low, short whistle came from the man who had found Gavell's body under the sheet. The leader marched over to inspect the corpse and gave a nod of approval. With busy hands, the four other men wrapped the seeping body in the shroud and then, on a count of three, lifted it on to their shoulders.

Will, Carpenter and Launceston exchanged suspicious glances. Gavell's remains belonged to his family. This theft went against the very laws of the land; no authority would have sanctioned such an act.

The men marched towards the steps, the leader following behind like a mourner. As he neared the hiding place, the glare of a candle lit his face under the brim of his hat. His eyes were the colour of steel, his cheeks pockmarked, and he sported a well-trimmed black beard. Will knew he had seen that face before, perhaps somewhere among the personal guards of one of the nobles at court, but he could not recall exactly.

The mortuary assistant moaned loudly as the intruders passed with Gavell's body, and he struggled to raise himself up on his arms. The leader of the black-cloaked men stooped down to grab the drunken assistant's filthy shirt at the neck, and with a rough movement hauled the bleary-eyed face up.

'If anyone asks what happened to the body of the flayed man, you do not know,' the steely-eyed man growled. 'If you speak of this, you will quickly find yourself one of your own customers. Do you understand?'

His eyes wide with fear, the assistant nodded.

The leader of the intruders flung the man back down on the flagstones, and waved a hand at his waiting men. 'Get him out to the cart and away, quickly. Like the last one,' he ordered in a low, gravelly voice. 'No trace must remain.'

The men lurched up the steps with the sticky, cloth-wrapped body, and after a glance around the vaults the leader followed, casting one final, brief look at the mortuary assistant. In that stare, Will read the man's thoughts: he considered killing the drunken sot, but knew it would raise even greater questions. A missing body could be explained away. A murdered mortuary assistant would have consequences.

When the deadhouse door boomed shut behind the intruders, the drunken man released a pathetic whimper and scrambled up the steps, no doubt to lose himself in more beer. The three spies eased themselves out from their hiding place and stood in troubled silence for a moment.

'What does this mean?' Carpenter asked quietly. 'He said, *Like the last one.*'

'Another murder, then,' Launceston mused. 'Hidden before we heard of it. But who was the victim?'

'Someone at court is covering the bloody trail,' Will replied, his expression grave. 'This plot reaches further than we ever imagined – to the heart of England itself.'

CHAPTER THIRTEEN

CUPPING HIS HAND AROUND THE CANDLE FLAME, OSWYN Hasard strode through the silent chambers of the sleeping Nonsuch Palace. The glow flared under the brim of his tall-crowned hat, lighting the steel in his eyes. Though it had been three hours' hard riding from London, the stink of the deadhouse still clung to the black-cloaked man. The flayed body had been weighted with stones and dumped in the river to feed the fishes, like the other two, and his men had been sent to their beds, their lips sealed. With still an hour to dawn, the night had been a success.

Whispered voices reached his ears as he neared the oak-panelled chamber overlooking the palace gardens. Glimpsing the faint glow of a candle, he moistened his thumb and forefinger and extinguished the flame of his own light, slowing as he reached the door, which stood ajar. Peering through the crack, he saw his master, Lord Derby, in huddled conversation around a stubby candle with the Earl of Essex. The two men could not have been less alike: Essex, strong, handsome and filled with the vigour of youth, aglow in his white doublet and cloak; Derby, heavy-set in his black gown, broken-veined cheeks the colour of ham above his wiry grey beard. The darkness appeared to press in tightly around the two figures.

'Why should I trust you?' Essex was asking, eyeing the other man suspiciously.

'I have your best interests at heart, as always,' Derby responded firmly. 'The Queen's Little Elf has become troublesome within the Privy Council, guiding Her Majesty away from the light and into the shadows. *He* can no longer be trusted.'

The Earl's eyes gleamed. *Exactly what he wants to hear,* Hasard thought.

'Cecil's power is based in part upon his network of spies. If they were constrained . . . relieved of their influence . . . crushed . . . there would be an opportunity for your own band of spies to gain ascendance,' Derby continued in a whisper, 'and the Queen would have no choice but to anoint you as her true favourite at court.'

Essex tugged at his beard, already imagining the power he might wield. 'And what do you gain from seeing Cecil cut down to his true size?'

'There are a few of us in the Privy Council, at court, in positions of authority, who are distressed at the path England has taken since the glorious defeat of the Spanish navy. At that moment we were on the cusp of a golden age. Power. Control of trade. Influence.' Derby's eyes flashed. 'All that opportunity has slipped through our fingers. We are beset on every side by enemies, including the one we fear most.'

Essex nodded gravely.

'I do what I do for England,' Derby continued. 'There is no personal gain.'

'Noble motives,' the Earl replied with a nod. 'At first I feared this was some plot to dethrone Elizabeth. If that were true, I would have been forced to move against you. As it is . . .' He paused thoughtfully. 'Cecil's spies must be removed from the game in the first instance, and then . . . we shall see.'

With undue eagerness, Derby grasped the other man's hand and pumped it. 'You have made the right choice,' he said. 'Those who do not stand with us are against us.'

Essex nodded, smiled and made to remove his hand, but Derby held fast. Hasard felt a ripple of unease. Wide-eyed and grinning, the older man leaned forward, a soft, breathy laugh escaping his gritted teeth. With his thumb, he began to stroke the back of the Earl's hand. The caress was not a suggestion of intimacy, Hasard could tell, but it was still breathtakingly inappropriate. His master looked as if he had lost his wits.

Unsettled, Essex tore his hand free, muttered a goodbye and hurried away. Hasard pressed himself back into the shadows so he would not be seen.

When the Earl had disappeared into the dark along the corridor, the cloaked man slipped into the oak-panelled chamber. With a sly smile, Derby nodded, once more the man Hasard recognized. 'All is well,' the newcomer said, still uneasy. His master was a man of propriety, restrained, sophisticated, aloof. He had never behaved in such a manner before.

'Good,' Derby replied, beckoning his assistant closer to the candle flame. 'Our plans move apace. We now pull the strings of the Earl of Essex. In thrall to his ambition, he will do all that we wish.'

But who pulls your strings? Hasard wondered.

'Our numbers grow by the week,' Derby continued, rubbing his hands eagerly. 'Our influence reaches into all parts of the government, and soon, very soon, we will be ready to make our move. For now, I have more work for you and your men.'

'Another body to dispose of?'

'Not yet. I fear Cecil's spies are becoming aware. We must act quicker than we intended. Harry them at every turn. Seek out Swyfte – he is the most dangerous when roused. But his men, too, must be driven off course. Go to Bankside first, where they waste their days and nights in the stews and inns and gaming halls. Search all London. Do not allow them to rest for a moment. Capture them, if you can. Kill them, if you must. They are a threat to England's future prosperity.'

'Very well.' Hasard bowed.

'I will send someone to help you.'

'Who?'

'You will not see him, but he will be there.' Derby looked past his assistant to the door where Danby the coroner had entered silently, with another, hooded man who clutched four fat candles to his chest. Hasard was disturbed to see a long trail of spittle hanging from the corner of the coroner's mouth.

'Go now, Master Hasard, and help us usher in a new age for England.' Derby waved his hand to dismiss his assistant.

Hasard left, unnerved by the fire he saw burning in Danby's eyes. As he passed the two new arrivals, he looked into the deep hood and was shocked to see the face of a devil. Only when he had stepped out of the door did he realize it was a mask, fiery red, with a jagged crack running across it.

Hurrying into the palace's dark, Hasard discerned the faint words of Derby as he greeted the two other men: 'Now we must listen carefully to the whispers of our masters in the shadows.'

CHAPTER FOURTEEN

CARPENTER LISTENED TO THE TERRIFIED WHIMPERINGS, BUT HIS mind was elsewhere. A dark foreboding had gripped him from the moment he left the deadhouse and even the light of day could not dispel it.

On the other side of the cramped room tucked away in the rafters of a timber-framed Bankside house, Launceston pressed his dagger to the neck of the kneeling landlord, his other hand dragging the man's head back by his greasy hair. The landlord looked like a bullfrog, eyes bulging with fear above a flat, broad nose and fat lips, his filthy linen undershirt barely concealing his large belly and badly worn breeches.

Christopher Marlowe's secret lodgings had been torn apart, the bed upended, loose boards ripped up to reveal the mouse droppings and straw beneath; the small table lay upturned, the chair in pieces. Shards of plaster had been torn from the walls in a search for hiding places and now lay in heaps everywhere. White dust coated all the surfaces, whipped into whirls by the breeze from the open door so that it appeared to be snowing in the shaft of sunlight breaking through the little window.

'Who did this?' the pallid man demanded as if he were asking the time of day.

'Four men!' his prisoner gulped. 'They came in the night three days ago!'

'And you have not yet cleaned and relet these premises? I have never known a landlord to leave a room sitting empty.' The Earl surveyed the room's detritus for anything important that he might have missed.

'I was afraid. In case they came back.' Spittle sprayed from the fat man's mouth.

The room was barely ten foot square, cheap in an area where all rooms cost little rent, but it would have served Marlowe's purpose, Carpenter knew. Few would have come looking for the famous playwright there among the cutpurses, and apprentices, and poor field labourers.

'What did they look like?' Launceston pressed.

'I did not see their faces. When they forced their way in, I hid in my room until they had done their business,' the terrified man babbled.

'Rogues? Or gentlemen?' Carpenter sifted through a bundle of papers scattered across the boards. It was the remnants of an unfinished play in Marlowe's spidery scrawl. Nothing of importance, he thought.

The landlord rolled his wide eyes towards the scar-faced man. 'Not rogues. I saw fine clothes.'

Carpenter glanced over in time to see Launceston's dagger wavering over the pulsing artery in the landlord's neck. The Earl had the familiar hungry gleam in his eye.

'Robert,' Carpenter cautioned. His voice was understated, but the pale man knew the meaning by now. Reluctantly, the Earl removed the blade and thrust the landlord roughly across the boards.

The fat man clutched his hands together and insisted, 'I speak the truth! Marlowe only wrote his plays here. He kept nothing of value.'

'Then why would gentlemen be searching his room?' Carpenter continued.

The landlord gaped stupidly. Knowing any more questions would be futile, the scarred spy grabbed the neck of the landlord's shirt and dragged him to the open door. A loud crashing echoed as the man half fell, half threw himself down the winding stairs.

Carpenter kicked the door shut. 'Our suspicions are proving correct. Marlowe's room searched on the night of his death. Sweeping up any filthy trail left in the wake of a murder. And no lone killer, either. A plot, then.'

Launceston's hand was trembling as he sheathed his dagger. 'Marlowe offended many people in his short life. But this smacks of careful planning and authority.'

The scar-faced man crossed to the small window and peered out over the thatch and clay tiles of the Bankside rooftops towards the river. 'This is not good weather for any of us. Yet I cannot see a pattern here. In Marlowe's murder the culprit is known, and no attempt was made to hide the body or the crime. But the attack on Will at the Rose was a different matter, as was the brutality inflicted on Gavell.'

'If the Unseelie Court truly is eliminating spies who know of them, one by one, there may well be no pattern,' the Earl mused. 'Any means of dispatch would suffice.'

'But this is a conspiracy of madness.' Carpenter watched the men at work in the fields and dreamed of another life. 'Men at court working alongside our traditional Enemy? That is like lambs lying down with wolves.'

He had a sense of the world closing in around him. It was

bad enough that his only real friend was Launceston, who appeared to have no human feelings and lived only for killing.

'Hurrm,' the Earl grunted at his back.

'What is it?' Carpenter snapped.

'The room has been torn apart. Whoever did it must have believed that Marlowe had information which could be of use to us.' The pale-faced man continued to turn slowly, studying every aspect of his surroundings. 'What did our playwright discover?'

Carpenter righted a stool and sat on it. 'We might have got more information from the landlord if you hadn't been overcome by your feverish desire to draw blood,' he growled irritably.

'And do you think it is pleasant for me to listen to your whining morning, noon and night?' Kneeling, the Earl began to examine the upended table.

'And that is the thanks I get? Where would you be without me? Your head on a pike at the bridge gates, I would wager.' The surly Carpenter kicked a goblet across the room in anger. 'What now? Are you ignoring me?'

Launceston traced his pale fingers across the tabletop and then righted it. With the back of his hand, he brushed off the dirt and then grabbed a fistful of plaster dust, spraying it across the wood. Carpenter watched him curiously. Leaning close to the surface, the Earl gently blew the surplus dust away. He studied what remained behind for a moment and then said, 'Here.'

The scar-faced man came over and saw, first of all, an out-line in white where the dust had filled the grooves carved by a knife. It formed a circle with a square within it, the same symbol that they had both witnessed at the deadhouse, carved into the back of the spy Gavell.

110

'Marlowe knew of Gavell's murderer,' Carpenter said in a quiet, thoughtful voice.

'Or he must have known this sign had some special significance.' The Earl drew a finger around the outline. 'I would say he carved it here one night, while ruminating over the meaning of what he had discovered.'

'There.' Carpenter pointed to letters carved into the wood near the symbol.

Launceston threw more plaster dust on the surface to make the words clearer. 'Clement. Makepiece. Swyfte. Marlowe. Gavell. Shipwash. Pennebrygg. And here, further down, Devereux, with a question mark.'

'Robert Devereux? The Earl of Essex?'

'Perhaps. The family is old, with many branches.'

Carpenter's eyes widened. 'All spies. Swyfte, Marlowe, Gavell — in order. If this is a list of victims, then those poor bastards Clement and Makepiece are already dead. I have not seen either of them in recent weeks.'

'Nor I.'

'We must warn Shipwash and Pennebrygg—'

Launceston held up a hand to silence his companion. 'Think clearly, you droning codpiece. Why are *these* spies listed out of all our fellow liars, cheats and murderers? How would Marlowe know these names in advance of the murders being committed, or some of them, at least?'

A noise at the door brought a flash of steel. In an instant, the two men were either side of the entrance, silent, poised, glinting daggers at the ready. At Carpenter's nod, Launceston tore open the door and dragged in a figure in a grey-hooded cloak, poised on the threshold.

With a cry, the stranger turned, throwing off her hood, to reveal black hair and a pale, pretty face. 'Wait. It is I.'

'Alice? What are you doing here?' Carpenter said, shocked. His eyes flickered towards the Earl, who studied the woman icily. Though the face gave nothing away, the scarred spy could read every critical thought in his companion's head. 'You should not be here,' he continued, flushing.

When Alice drew closer, Carpenter saw deep concern in her features. 'I went to the stew you frequent,' she whispered with only a hint of embarrassment, 'and Will Swyfte's man directed me here. I was lucky to catch him before he left to meet his master.'

'Enough prattle. Speak your message and then be off,' Launceston snapped.

Carpenter glared at his companion.

'In the kitchens last night, one of the other girls said that she'd heard a rumour that all Kit Marlowe's closest friends were to be questioned, on the orders of the Privy Council,' the woman said, clasping her hands together. 'They fear Master Marlowe has infected you all with his atheist views. John, you know what that means. The Tower . . .' Her voice tailed away, unspoken fears of torture and execution clear in her face.

'Rumours,' the Earl snorted.

'I understand your doubts,' Alice continued. 'There is fear and suspicion throughout the court these days, but I could take no risk. And when I arrived here in Bankside, I saw strange men everywhere, questioning apprentices and merchants, stopping carts. John, they are watching this very house. Four men across the street—'

'What? And you still came here?' Carpenter exclaimed, worried now.

'For you.' Concerned, the woman pressed her palms together as though she were praying for his soul. 'Oh,' she said, puzzled, her hand going to her nose. When she examined her

112

finger, a droplet of blood glistened. 'I feel unwell . . . an ache in my belly . . .'

'Now see what you have done,' the Earl hissed.

Easing open the door, Carpenter stepped to the top of the dusty wooden stairs. He could feel the familiar sensations himself now as his body rebelled against the presence of something unnatural: the dull thump deep in his head, the churning in the pit of his stomach, as if he had eaten sour apples. 'Not now,' he muttered, the panic rising, 'with Alice here. Please God, let it not be so.'

His hands trembling, the spy squatted on the top step and tried to peer around the turn in the stairs. From below came the faint creak of a foot upon a step. The rest of the house was still.

Carpenter glanced back into the room where a baffled Alice waited. He felt his chest tighten.

His head was filled with a sound like a dagger drawn across glass. It was only a man slowly climbing the stairs, the spy told himself. Mere flesh that could be torn with a blade. A life that could be extinguished without another thought.

Another long, low creak.

Carpenter gripped the banister until his knuckles turned white. 'Just a man,' he breathed, readying his dagger.

The soft tread continued up the stairs.

Carpenter felt the pressure in his head grow until he thought he would faint. Blood trickled on to his upper lip. Desperation gripped him and he leaned out over the banister to try to see what was coming, although he knew, God help him, and he could deny it no longer.

A grey shadow fell across the cracked plaster of the wall.

Turning, Carpenter waved his hand frantically at Alice and Launceston, but they only stood like statues. In frustration, he almost cried out. But what could they do? His gaze was drawn back by the terrible pull of that rising shadow. A drop of his blood spattered on the boards.

All he could think was: *It should not be here, not now, in Bankside in broad daylight.*

For a moment the spy thought he saw two shadows, the one on the wall and the thing that cast it. The figure climbing the stairs took on more substance, as if it was emerging from autumn mist. Carpenter glimpsed bloodless skin, a head marked with black and blue interconnecting circles. It wore a black cloak with a hood thrown back, that swirled around it like a storm cloud. Rooted, the spy felt the ringing in his head grow so loud he thought his skull would burst.

As though it could sense Carpenter's presence, the thing turned its head slowly up to him. The pale figure's gaze fell upon the scar-faced spy like a shroud. Thin, pale lips pulled back from yellowing teeth in what could have been a wolfish grin, or a predatory snarl, but meant the same thing.

Tearing himself out of his frozen state, the scarred man threw himself back into the room, slamming the door and dragging the bed in front of it. 'Robert, help me,' he pleaded pitifully, looking around the small chamber. 'Help Alice.'

Launceston only stared blankly.

'John, what is wrong? Have they come for you?' the woman cried, running to grasp his arms.

Carpenter pushed her away. 'Robert, please. I need your help. Take her . . . take her,' his eyes fell upon the small window, the only way out of the room, 'out and across the roof. It is our only hope.'

Troubled by her love's desperate tone, the woman began to protest. Carpenter grabbed her shoulders and begged, 'Alice, you must trust me. If you see what is beyond that door, you may never sleep again. You may lose your wits, or your life. Go now, and do not look back.'

'What about you?'

'I will hold off our Enemy as long as I can.' The spy looked to the Earl and at first thought he was not going to help. But then Launceston gave a curt nod and beckoned for the woman to join him as he threw open the window and looked out into the bright morning.

Carpenter drew his rapier, prepared to die. At the Rose Theatre, he had dismissed the Earl's warning that he would be the death of Alice, but now he was terrified he had brought about that very tragedy.

Footsteps approached the door.

'What is out there?' the woman whispered, growing pale.

'Go,' Carpenter yelled, throwing more broken furniture towards the door with his free hand.

Levering himself into the small window, Launceston wriggled out and pulled himself up on to the eaves. A moment later, he leaned back in, upside down, and grasped Alice's arm. She shrieked as he manhandled her to the window.

'This is not a time for niceties,' the pale man said. 'Do not struggle or I will drop you to your death.'

The footsteps had come to a halt and there was a faint rustling sound on the other side of the door. In the room, the quality of light dimmed, and even the slightest sound became strangely distorted.

Half wondering if he had doomed his love to a different kind of fate, Carpenter held her gaze for a moment until she was dragged up to the roof. He felt a flood of relief.

A crash shocked him alert. The door was being driven into the bed frame, and then again, pushing the obstacle away. His blade levelled, he backed to the window.

'Get out here, you gleeking canker-blossom,' Launceston bellowed at his back. 'Or do you wish to die to prove your love?'

Sheathing his rapier, the spy clambered into the window space. As the door crashed open, he felt like he was peering into an open grave, but then the Earl grabbed his cloak and almost dragged him out of the window. Carpenter had a vision of his death from two quarters: from the thing in the room, or the plummet to a muddy yard where hens ran clucking. But then he was clutching for the eaves and trying to kick away from the window ledge.

The spy felt something cold and dry grab his ankle. He kicked back furiously and gave a tight grin when he met resistance. Nails dug into his flesh and inexorably he began to be pulled back inside.

The ghastly face of Launceston appeared upside-down in front of him.

'Go,' Carpenter gasped. 'You have a chance to get away.'

'And leave you here?' the Earl replied, holding on tight.

Carpenter felt as if he would be torn in two. His leg was afire with agony as the talons continued to tear at him, but he knew the thing in the room was only taunting him; it could tear his entire limb off in an instant if it chose. Realizing he had only a moment to save himself, the spy gave himself to his companion's grip and freed one hand so he could draw his rapier. Leaning down, he rammed the blade through the open window. He was met with a satisfying roar of pain and his leg came free.

Launceston dragged Carpenter roughly over the eaves and on to the creaking tiles. Alice cowered further along the roof. 'Hurry,' the scarred spy gasped. 'It will be after us in a moment. How can it move so freely? What has happened to our defences?'

'It is worse than that,' the Earl said, helping his friend to his feet. He pointed down to the street where men in black cloaks and hats were running towards the house.

'The world has gone mad,' Carpenter muttered.

Precariously, he edged along the tiles behind the Earl. It was hot in the morning sun and the breeze caught the scent of the fields and woods to the south. Taking Alice's hand, he whispered, 'Do not look back, whatever happens.'

'John, I do not want you to live in this world any longer,' the woman replied tearfully.

The scarred spy cast an eye towards Launceston before replying. 'We shall talk of these matters later. But for now we must escape. I fear there is no longer a safe place for us anywhere in London.'

How far does this plot spread? Carpenter wondered as he listened to the cries of the men spreading across Bankside. He couldn't estimate the numbers, but he now knew there were more than the five they had encountered in the deadhouse.

'We have no choice now,' the Earl whispered as if he could read his companion's thoughts. 'We must run . . . hide.'

Glancing back, Carpenter saw a hooked, white hand reaching over the eaves.

'Where do we go from here?' Alice asked, terrified.

He nodded towards a thatched cottage next to the lodging house. 'We jump.'

Before the woman could protest, Carpenter gripped her hand tightly and propelled her towards the edge of the roof.

CHAPTER FIFTEEN

'KEEP WATCH? FOR WHOM?' BAFFLED, NATHANIEL EXAMINED the wash of faces streaming along the nave of St Paul's. Gentlemen displayed the fine silk linings of their cloaks and cutpurses slyly eyed the gullible and the rich. Merchants and lawyers ambled with clients, servants swapped gossip and usurers barked for trade. The din echoed up to the cathedral's vaulted roof, tongues from across Europe colliding with accents from all England, Scotland and Ireland. Deals were negotiated, bargains made, crimes and conspiracies planned and meetings held. Despite the threat of the plague, Paul's Walk was busier than any nearby street.

'Watch for anyone watching me,' Will replied under his breath. He kept his head down, trying to lose himself in the throng. Every sense buzzed. He edged through the press of bodies, the sweet smell of incense mingling with the sour sweat of the herd. Here and there, bright afternoon sun slanting through the stained-glass windows threw rainbows across the honey-coloured stone, small points of beauty in the middle of confusion.

Will located Sir Francis Walsingham's final resting place with ease. Many had forgotten the location, but that sad, understated funeral had been burned into his memory as the point when everything changed.

As the old spymaster's second cousin, Thomas, had hinted at Kit's funeral, the lettering stood out on the unmarked stone flag that lay above the grave, despite the numerous feet that had trudged across it in the days since it had been penned. Squatting beside the steady flow of passers-by, the spy read what had been clearly scrawled in desperation: *In the beginning was the Word.*

Under *beginning* and *Word* had been drawn a tiny circle with a line through it: Marlowe's private signature for his closest friend, a message for Will's eyes only. A code? The line came from the Gospel of John and continued: *And the Word was with God, and the Word was God.*

What had Marlowe been trying to tell him, and what was the relevance of the double signature of bisected circles? Had Kit meant to highlight the two words – *beginning* and *Word*?

'Will?' Nathaniel hissed in warning. Half standing, Will peered through the stream of people to see three stern-faced men moving purposefully through the crowd towards the grave, their gaze fixed on Nathaniel.

'Come,' the spy whispered. Keeping low, he weaved through the crowd with Nat close behind him. When they reached the great east door, he glanced back and saw the glowering men had caught sight of him. Now in no doubt as to their intention, Will watched them thrusting their way through the bodies in his direction.

'Who are they?' the young assistant said with a note of concern. 'More cuckolded husbands seeking recompense?'

'Would that they were. Run, Nat. I fear it would not do to encounter those three now.'

The churchyard was just as crowded as the nave. Men haggled

for business, raising their voices to drown out the preachers bellowing their prophecies of the End-Times to small clutches of the devout. As he ran past, Will snatched a handful of the cheap, sensational pamphlets from one of the sellers and flung them up into the air. The fluttering sheets only added to the confusion, as the cursing seller scrambled to gather them up.

The two men raised angry cries from all quarters as they shouldered their way through the throng. Glancing back, Will saw the three pursuers had now drawn their rapiers.

'Stop them!' one of the men yelled. 'Thieves!'

A brave soul dressed in a flamboyant, expensive cloak stepped forward to apprehend the fugitives. Before he could utter a sound, Will had knocked him flat with one punch. But others were already moving in to answer the call.

'This does not bode well,' the assistant said, glancing around uneasily.

'Nat, where is your sense of adventure?' Will unsheathed his sword as he ran, flashing it back and forth to clear a path.

'I left it in the box where I keep my wish for an early grave,' the young man gasped, trying to keep up with his master.

Will came to a halt at the line of carts and horses trundling along the rutted street. On the other side was the jumbled sprawl of houses and filthy alleys south of Maiden Lane where he knew they would be able to lose themselves if they gained a little distance.

Glancing around for a likely opportunity, he saw heads turned suddenly away from the street, man after man cross-ing himself and muttering prayers. Even before he smelled the sickening spoiled-eggs stench, he knew what was coming.

As the death-cart trundled into view, Nathaniel too tried to turn away, but Will grabbed him and said, 'This is no time to be worrying about your mortal soul, my friend. If we are fortunate there will be time enough to make amends to God.'

Grabbing the assistant by the scruff, the spy hauled him into the flow of carts. The angry calls of the carters cracking their whips and yanking on the reins to steady their horses drowned out Nathaniel's protestations.

'Not a moment to lose, Nat,' Will said, eyeing the three men who had just broken through the confusion to reach the cathedral gates. He dragged the young man down the centre of the street in between the rows of carts. They came to the death-cart where the driver and his assistant sat on the bench with their heads bowed, their drawn faces scarred by the things they had been forced to witness. In the back, the corpses were piled high, tightly wrapped in stained sheets.

As Will ducked by, he flicked the tip of his rapier into the horse's flank.

The beast reared up, whinnying in shock. Up too went the cart, the bodies tumbling like sacks of grain into the road, the driver and assistant both flung from their bench. The horse close behind also reared to avoid the grisly cargo dumped in its path, and within a moment beasts all around were skittering wildly, the carters fighting to keep them under control as their wagons swerved and ground to a halt. Along the edges of the street, men and women were shouting and calling to others to come and see the spectacle.

Will kept a tight grip on Nathaniel, dragging him under a cart to the other side of the street. He allowed himself one glance back to see the three pursuers caught up in the crush, before squeezing through the raucous mob and away into the quiet alleys beyond.

Racing along a convoluted path among the houses, he finally brought Nathaniel to a halt beside an old beer barrel where a dog sheltered from the day's heat. A pall of smoke hung over the still alleys from the fires smouldering outside many of the homes. The Lord Mayor had directed that all refuse should be burned three times a week to help limit the spread of the plague. No one wandered these streets. Most of the traders' premises were shut and the familiar cry of 'What do ye lack?' had been silenced. Used to the constant din of London, the thunder of hammers on anvils, the booming of the workshops, the shouting and singing and fighting and streets near-packed from wall to wall with people and animals, Will found the scene unaccountably eerie. London held its breath so death would not notice it.

Hands on his knees, Nathaniel sucked in gulps of air. 'Who were those men?' he gasped.

Will continued to search the smoke-clogged alley for any sign of pursuit. He knew that from now on he would never be able to rest. 'Someone would prefer that the murder of Kit Marlowe remain a closed book,' he replied. Had Thomas Walsingham mentioned the defaced grave at the playwright's funeral to draw him into the open? Will wondered. Or had some other dark power decided that spies could no longer roam free in London? Step by step, they were being whittled back.

'Nat, I have work for you, if you can bear to be in this foul, disease-ridden city a moment longer,' the spy began.

The assistant eyed his master suspiciously, wondering what was to come next.

'In his letter, Kit said: *The truth lies within. But seek the source of the lies without.* The first sentence clearly implies he had hidden a message within the play he sent me. The second . . .' Will raised one finger as he turned over his conclusion to be sure it was correct. '*The lies* refers to the story. A fiction. What Kit meant was that we should look in the world around us for the origin of his story of Faustus. If I am correct that will point us in the direction of the answers we need.'

'There were some plays from abroad about Faust, yes?' The words were muffled as the assistant covered his mouth and nose to keep out the death-stench.

'Perhaps. Perhaps there is more to it than that. And I want you to find the answer for me. There are scholars who know these things in London. Seek them out.' Will clapped a hand on the young man's shoulder.

'And you? If even the great and famous Will Swyfte can be hunted in the streets of London I would think you would want to find a safe bolt-hole.'

'Of course not, Nat. That is exactly what they would expect me to do.' Though his eyes glittered like ice, Will grinned. 'First, I go to find John and Robert at our agreed meeting place to share what we all have discovered. And then I ride to the very source of this danger and these lies – Nonsuch Palace.'

CHAPTER SIXTEEN

'WHO MURDERED MY FRIEND?' WILL DEMANDED, BURSTING into the candlelit chamber with the big mercenary Sinclair at his heels, blood streaming from his nose.

Roaring, the bodyguard lunged for the spy until his master, Sir Robert Cecil, flapped a diffident hand to halt him in his tracks. 'Leave him. Master Swyfte is searching for a length of rope to hang himself,' the spymaster said.

Reluctantly, Sinclair retreated, closing the door as he went, but his parting glance left Will in no doubt that retribution was already being planned.

Like its owner, the chamber was filled with shadows that hid a multitude of unpleasant secrets. Plain walnut panelling contained the gloom that pressed in against the single candle in the centre of a large table swamped with papers. There was a chair, a bench and two stools, but no other comforts. Cold, grey ashes cascaded out of a Kentish stone fireplace on the far wall. Despite the heat of the summer night, it was not warm.

Will had expected some resistance when he crossed the moonlit hunting grounds on the last leg of his three-hour ride from London. But as he rode down the sweeping lane to the turreted gatehouse, all was peaceful. Old Henry's legacy, the grand brick and stone lodge, sprawled beyond, candles gleaming in the windows. The guards allowed him into the inner court without a second glance and the only jarring note was the stark gallows erected to execute any member of the court displaying signs of the plague. Death was the great leveller. Even a royal heart was afflicted with fear of the end.

As the spy made his way through the thrum of servants to Cecil's chamber on the second floor of the western wing, he found the familiar rhythms of court life troublingly incongruous. The palace appeared untouched by the tensions unfolding in the city.

His ermine-fringed black gown flapping, Cecil went to the window and opened it a little, then stood with his back to Will looking out over the hunting grounds. 'It is too warm in here. Summer comes up hard, and the beekeepers say it will be hot.'

'I have no interest in the passing of the seasons. I want—'

'I know what you want,' the spymaster snapped, half turning to fix a cold eye on his agent. 'You waste your time and your breath. What is one death compared to the two thousand victims of the plague this month alone in London?'

'All deaths are not equal.' Leaning across the large table, the spy pointed an accusatory finger at his master. 'Christopher Marlowe was a loyal servant to the Queen, and to England. He sacrificed his pleasures and all his potential to do your work, and the work of your predecessor, Sir Francis. And the fame he achieved for his writing will echo down the years—'

'Pfft. What use are writers?' Cecil waved a hand as if swatting a fly.

'Nevertheless, he deserves more than this lack of concern I find at every turn.' Will took a breath to steady himself. 'I would know who ordered his death. And why.'

Clasping his hands behind his back, the spymaster held

his head at an aloof angle, but made sure he kept the table between himself and his visitor. 'Marlowe had few friends,' he said scornfully. 'He was barely trustworthy. Time and again the powers of this office were required to save him from punishment. Theft. Deception. The propagation of his unseemly religious views. His inappropriate liaisons with young men. The stabbings and the beatings caused by his vile temper. And on, and on.'

'Marlowe had his troubles. He was not at peace with the work we do.' Will clenched his fists on the tabletop, his knuckles growing white.

'There is no great plot here. No mystery. No wider danger,' the spymaster stated. 'Nor is there any meaning to your *friend*'s death. It was as sordid and empty as anything else in his wasted life.'

'The man who killed Kit works for Thomas Walsingham. You may be aware of that name,' the spy pressed.

Cecil flashed a glare at Will's impudence. 'And one of the other men there, Skeres, works for Essex,' he responded sharply.

This new information wrong-footed Will. He had been right: spies everywhere, secret connections, a web in which Marlowe had been caught.

Cecil could see Will's thoughts play out. 'I repeat, no plot. There were spies present because that is our world. There are spies everywhere. That is rather the point, is it not?'

Will scrutinized the spymaster for a flicker of guilt that would suggest complicity in the murder. 'When he was not working, Kit took pains never to associate with spies. He was always a man of great taste.' Will's voice dripped acid. 'Which suggests to me that the meeting in Widow Bull's house in Deptford concerned our work, in some form or other.'

126

'Do you think I would not know of such a meeting if it was our business?'

'I think you would not tell me.'

Cecil's cheeks flushed with mounting anger. 'Marlowe was not in good spirits recently. His temper was short. He acted in an erratic manner. And he was becoming more voluble in expressing his heretical views. The pamphlets were beginning to chide him for his atheism. He could not keep his mouth shut. These are the actions of a man whose wits were abandoning him. In the end, he lost control and paid the price. Nothing more.'

'It sounds as though his end was a happy one for you and the Privy Council. Words against religion could have incited the population at this time of calamity when the people need God more than ever.'

Cecil slapped the palm of his hand down hard on the table. 'Now you accuse me.'

'I merely state a fact.'

Leaning across the table, the spymaster spat, 'Marlowe was an irritation. And one that was being contained. He was reporting daily to the Privy Council to answer the claims made against him, and give his assurances that he would not continue to make incendiary statements. No charges had been brought, but it was only a matter of time.'

'Kit was no traitor.' In a rush of anger, Will swept a goblet from the edge of the table with the back of his hand. Cecil leapt back as if he had been scalded.

'So you say,' the spymaster growled. His gaze flickered towards the closed door beyond which Sinclair waited. 'In this time of permanent war, when the Unseelie Court circles constantly, ready to strike, and Spain unleashes plot after plot, what other word would you use to describe one of

127

our own citizens who sets out to undermine the established order?'

'The Unseelie Court have already struck!' Will began to round the table. Fearful, Cecil hurried around to the other side. 'I witnessed their involvement in a vision,' the spy continued, 'but more importantly, my men have seen the Enemy working alongside a group of English plotters. Men of authority, it would seem by their actions, who have attacked me and my allies.'

'You are mad!'

Will watched the spymaster's eyes, still unsure if he had any connection to the wider plot. ''Tis true. Even while we fight among ourselves, our true Enemy unveils a grand plot that could threaten the Queen's own life and all of England. This is not a time for secrets—'

'No.' Turning away, Cecil waved a hand to silence Will.

'You must go to the Privy Council—'

'No!' The spymaster whirled back, eyes wide and fearful. Will was struck by the intense reaction. 'Your grief has swept your wits away. You see plots where there are none. The Unseelie Court working with Englishmen! Listen to yourself.'

Will's anger abated. He scrutinized Cecil again, his trembling hands, his slippery gaze, his too-strong denials. Stepping back from the table, Will folded his hands behind his back. 'Our defences are crumbling,' he said with as much calm as he could muster. 'The ones Dr Dee put in place all those years ago. The ones that have kept our Queen and country safe from the supernatural foe that has preyed upon us since the Flood.'

The spymaster snorted.

'The Unseelie Court whittle us away one piece at a time.' Will held Cecil's gaze. 'Soon there will be only the heart of those defences, the one who resides atop the Lantern Tower at the Palace of Whitehall.'

Shock burst in Cecil's face and he turned away so he would not reveal any more of his inner thoughts. 'I do not know what you mean,' he said.

'I think you do. They will not relent while we keep their monarch in chains,' the spy continued.

'You think we can bargain with them?' Cecil roared, his face now red with rage. He caught himself, stabbing a thin finger towards Will. 'You should not know these things. You cannot be trusted—'

'Who can?' Will snapped. 'Spies are being murdered, Gavell, the most recent—'

'A rumour, thankfully untrue.'

'I saw the body myself.'

Cecil hammered a fist on the table. 'There was no body in the deadhouse. I sent my own men to investigate.'

'Because it was removed, by those parties unknown that have allied themselves with our own true Enemy. A grand lie in the making, to keep us sweet until it is too late. Where are Clement and Makepiece?'

In the spymaster's hesitation, Will saw that the Little Elf also feared the two spies were dead, as suggested by the list of names Launceston and Carpenter had discovered at Marlowe's lodgings.

'Drunk in some inn or other, I would expect,' the hunch-backed man lied.

Will leapt around the table to grab Cecil by the gown, thrusting his face close. 'Are you one of the traitors who have betrayed us? Or is it Essex and his own band of spies, and you see some advantage to yourself in letting him play his game?' Will shook the spymaster roughly. 'Who had Kit killed? Tell me!'

'You have gone too far!' the spymaster shouted. 'Sinclair!'

The door crashed open and the towering mercenary stalked in, glowering. Instantly he drew his rapier, growling like an animal as he advanced. In the red mist of his own anger, Will pushed Cecil aside and went for his own sword. Then, struck by how quickly his simmering rage had burned out of control, he fought to contain himself, allowing his hand to fall impotently to his side.

'Take Master Swyfte to his chamber and hold him there,' the spymaster ordered, leaning on the table to calm himself. He cast an accusatory eye on Will and said under his breath, 'I allow you some small leeway for the madness your grief has caused, but you have much to answer for. Do you think you can speak secrets vital to England's security without conse-quence? You will be taken before the Privy Council tomorrow to answer the accusations against you.'

'What accusations?' Will growled. 'That I speak the truth?'

'That Marlowe has infected you with his atheism.'

'You wish to silence me.' Will's cold, unwavering gaze brought an involuntary shudder from the spymaster. 'What, then? The Tower? My head on a spike at London Bridge?'

'Take him.' Cecil turned away from that awful stare.

Sinclair grabbed Will and propelled him towards the door.

'This is not the end of this matter,' Will said icily, with no further regard for his own well-being. 'Kit's death will be avenged. And all who stand in my way, whoever they might be, whatever position they hold, will pay.'

CHAPTER SEVENTEEN

THE THUNDEROUS KNOCKING HAD AN INSISTENT EDGE. WILL opened the door to find an unsettled Nathaniel, who pushed his way into the chamber without waiting to be invited. From the shadows in the corridor, a solitary pikeman watched, as he had from the moment Sinclair had bustled the spy into his quarters.

'I thought I was going to be locked out of the palace. They questioned me at the gatehouse for near an hour,' Nathaniel said, taking off his cap and running a hand through his hair. 'What has happened? Is the Queen's life under threat?'

Will closed the door and guided his assistant towards the table where a meagre portion of bread and cheese and some wine had been placed by a servant. He was not in the Tower yet, so the spymaster had to treat him with a modicum of dignity. 'The Queen is well, but it appears Sir Robert has taken my warnings to heart. Some small good may come from this night.' He carved himself a piece of cheese and spiked it with his knife. He sighed. 'I fear I have let my mouth run away with me.'

Nathaniel eyed his master askance as he removed his cloak. 'You speak those words as if they are somehow new to you.'

'This time there may be more at stake than hurt feelings. In anger, I revealed a secret I have carried with me for several years. A secret that goes to the very heart of England and the Queen's security – and, in truth, what it means to be an Englishman and how we perceive ourselves in the world.' The spy made to eat the cheese, stared at it for a moment and then tossed the knife and morsel on to the table. 'And I, God help me, must defend the ideal, knowing the darkness and violence that lies behind it. Am I then as tarnished?'

'You are too hard on yourself, as always.'

Smiling at the young man's loyalty, Will poured Nathaniel a goblet of malmsey wine. The assistant, who rarely drank to excess, took the offering hesitantly.

'There are plots upon plots unfolding all around us, Nat, and we can no longer trust all that we once held close. You must be on your guard,' Will said, his face serious.

'Is this why you are held prisoner?'

Will poured himself some wine and rested one foot on a stool as he drank. 'It takes more than one guard to hold me prisoner.'

'Ah, yes, I forget myself,' the assistant said. 'England's greatest spy. The great Will Swyfte towers above all normal men.' His gaze fell on the sheaf of papers set on the table in a pool of candlelight. 'You have been reading Kit's play.'

Will traced his fingers across the surface of the wine-stained first page. 'Kit was a greater man than even his most ardent supporters believed,' he said. 'There are deep messages in this play, about our propensity for pride, certainly, but also the lengths we will go to to fulfil our own personal quests, even when we know to do so will damage us or those around us.' Though Will knew Marlowe was writing about himself, the play was unsettlingly apt for his own situation; he could no more give up on his search for Jenny than Faustus could walk away from his deal with the Devil. He found a page and read, almost to himself,

'Why this is hell, nor am I out of it.
Think'st thou that I, who saw the face of God,
And tasted the eternal joys of heaven,
Am not tormented with ten thousand hells
In being depriv'd of everlasting bliss?'

'Unlike you, I am a God-fearing man,' Nathaniel sniffed, 'and I do not like all this talk of devils and hell. Remember: speak his name and you will summon him.'

'You are a fortunate man, Nat, for you have found your own private heaven in employment with me,' Will said, lightly.

Nathaniel snorted.

Will tapped his finger on the papers. 'But in his cleverness, Kit has hidden messages here on two levels. The one in symbolic form, in the themes of the play, and that will be hard to decipher without knowing the author's intent. But look here for the other.'

On a line halfway down the page, Will pointed to a letter O with a barely visible dot beneath it. He flicked on two pages and let his finger trail down the lines until he located a W marked with another dot. Three pages on, another highlighted letter appeared.

'A code,' Nathaniel said.

'A cipher, to be exact. A code involves the substitution of words or phrases, a cipher the substitution of letters.' Will pointed to a page where he had copied out marked letters – E, T, M, I, T, O, W, R, W, E. 'I have not yet collected all Kit's

133

hidden marks, but even then I will not be able to understand the meaning.'

'The cipher is too hard to break?'

Moving the quill and ink pot to one side, Will sat on the stool and found a clean page. 'Kit always used what is known as a Vigenère Square,' he said. 'Vigenère was a French diplomat who studied the codes and ciphers of the great masters Alberti, Trithemius and Porta and then developed their work into his own system. It is remarkably strong because it uses not one but twenty-six separate cipher alphabets to conceal a message.'

Will took the quill, dipped it in the pot of ink and proceeded to draw a grid of twenty-six by twenty-six squares. Above the grid, he inscribed the alphabet, and then numbered each row from one to twenty-six down the side. 'This is the plaintext,' he said, pointing to the alphabet at the top, 'where we choose the letters we want to encrypt.'

Along the first row of the grid, he then wrote the alphabet beginning with B and adding A in the twenty-sixth box. On the second row, he began the alphabet with C, adding A in the twenty-fifth box, and B in the final one.

'The system continues, shifting the letters one space to the left on each line,' he explained. 'Then it is a matter of using a new row of the grid to encrypt each new letter of the message you wish to send.'

Nathaniel puzzled over the Vigenère Square for a moment and then concluded, 'But how does the one receiving the message know which rows have been used? You have twenty-six different choices for every letter. It would take a lifetime to determine the true choices from the multitude available.'

'Nat, you are cleverer than you appear,' Will said with a warm smile.

Nathaniel gave a dismissive shrug.

'The hidden message can only be understood with the use of a keyword, known to both the sender and the receiver,' Will continued. 'Pay attention now, for even the cleverest may stumble here.'

'Speak slowly, master, for I am but a thick-headed country boy, and not someone who keeps the wheels of your complicated life spinning,' Nathaniel said archly. He sipped his wine in a studiedly aloof manner.

'Let us say the keyword is BLACK, and our message begins, *Marlowe says.*' Will wrote the message and then above the first five letters wrote BLACK, and the same over the second five. 'We repeat the keyword across the entire message. Then we take our Vigenère Square. See, the first row begins with B. That means the first letter of our message must be encrypted with this row.'

He traced his finger along the plaintext alphabet above the grid until he found the M of *Marlowe* and continued down to the first line to find the letter N. 'N is the first letter of our coded message. Then we proceed to the row beginning with L, then A, then C and so on until the entire message has been encrypted.'

Leaning in, Nathaniel thought for a moment before circling the keyword with the tip of his index finger. 'And you are about to tell me Master Marlowe uses a different keyword for every message, and you have no knowledge of the current one.'

'Remember, Nat, before you outgrow your boots, a little intellect is like a little gunpowder – enough to blow your hands off, but not enough to achieve anything worthwhile.' Will poured himself another goblet of wine, realizing how much he valued the company of his assistant. He had taken it for granted for a long while, as he had so many other things in his life.

Tearing off a chunk of bread, Nathaniel chewed on it lazily. 'I am warmed by the knowledge that you always have my best interests at heart, and I am duly chastened,' he replied in a tone that dripped acid. 'Why, if I got ideas above my station, I might demand a higher wage and then I would be beset by the problem of how to spend my earnings, instead of bare survival.'

With some of the tension relieved, Will returned his attention to Marlowe's play and the secretly marked letters. He could try to guess the keyword, but he knew it would be a futile exercise; Kit would never have chosen anything obvious. But the fact that he had sent Will the annotated play in the first place indicated that he expected Will to break the cipher.

The defacement of Walsingham's grave was part of the puzzle, Will was sure. *In the beginning was the Word.* The easiest answer was that the keyword was God. *And the Word was with God, and the Word was God.* But it was too short to create an effective cipher, and Marlowe always revelled in double meanings; the one on the surface meant one thing, but the one beneath was more important, more profound. The answer lay there somewhere. Why that biblical quotation? Why Walsingham's grave? The clues and hints had been sent through different channels so they would not all be intercepted, each one only beginning to make sense when they were viewed as part of the whole. There were still pieces missing, but Will was convinced he was drawing closer to the solution.

'This puzzle will not be solved without a great deal of thought,' he mused. 'Nat, you appear troubled by your own discoveries. Tell me what you found out about the origin of Kit's play.'

Suddenly weary, Nathaniel leaned back and sighed. 'I spoke to scholars aplenty, labouring away in their dusty rooms. I did not rest. And now I rather wish that you had not given me this task.' The assistant steadied himself with a gulp of wine. 'I am told Master Marlowe's story of Doctor Faustus is based upon a much older one of a man who sold his soul to dark powers for knowledge. This is detailed in Latin pamphlets that have been preserved for many years. There was also another fiction, in German, based upon this legend and published six years ago, and some feel Master Marlowe may have had a translation and used this as the basis for his play.'

'A story circulating for years, told and retold . . . That is not the answer I needed, Nat.'

'There are many elements of Master Marlowe's play that are not apparent in the original story,' the assistant continued. 'It is believed that he also drew upon another tale, one that is founded in truth. You have heard of Wykenham?'

'I know of children's fairy stories. A village of ghosts. Empty houses where the living dare not walk.'

'Ghosts! Would that that were the only horror.' Nathaniel grew animated, his eyes widening. 'Yes, that is the story they tell in the inns and markets to frighten the gullible, but the truth is worse. Wykenham is in Norfolk, a hamlet not far from the coast. Secluded. Little more than one street of pretty houses and a church. Empty houses, yes. Empty houses now.' Nathaniel eyed Will suspiciously to see if the spy knew more than he was saying. 'I heard tell that the truth was hidden by Sir Francis Walsingham, God rest his soul, to keep the peace in Norfolk, and farther abroad, I would wager.'

'If that is true, Nat, I have not heard it. Sir Francis ensured a great many things were kept secret for the security of the realm, and it is certain he would not have shared them with me unless I needed to know.' Intrigued by the unfolding story, Will leaned across the table. Shadows cast by the candle distorted his features and Nathaniel briefly trembled.

137

'This business concerns one Griffin Devereux, a distant cousin of the Earl of Essex.'

Will hadn't heard the name at court and his brow creased in doubt.

'You will not have heard of him, for, with Essex's complicity, Sir Francis spread untruths and rumours and false information until all who might have known the truth doubted the existence of Griffin Devereux. Even Essex denies him. Even Devereux's own father denies he exists,' Nathaniel stressed.

Will thought for a moment. Was this the man Kit had identified in the name scratched into the table in his lodgings – not Essex, but his cousin? 'What did he do to deserve this treatment?'

'Why, he set himself up as Faustus. I do not know if he had experience of those Latin pamphlets, or those books that Dr Dee kept under lock and key at the Palace of Whitehall and in his library in Mortlake, which the mob destroyed all those years ago, but Devereux had occult knowledge. He spoke to devils.' The assistant laid the palms of his hands flat on the tabletop, steadying himself. 'He bartered with them, and tried to control them. And on a November night four years ago, he travelled from his home to Norfolk to complete his bargain with Lucifer. They say the storm that swept in from the sea was the worst in living memory. Thunder so loud it made a man deaf, and rain like stones. Lightning shattered the steeple at Wykenham where Devereux was completing his incantation, unbeknown to the good people of the hamlet.'

Will smiled.

'What?'

'These stories always have these atmospherics. Would it be as good a tale if it happened on a summer's day?'

'I was told!'

'I do not doubt you, Nat. But I take nothing at face value. People embellish these tellings to help them understand, or to cover up their own fears.' Will pressed his fingers together and peered over the tips at the frightened young man.

'Perhaps you are right,' Nathaniel accepted, running a trembling hand through his hair. 'For if Devereux had completed his foul act on a summer's day, without the Devil whispering in his ear . . . If it had been Devereux and nothing more, it would have been too much for any man to bear, for then it might mean that we are all capable of such things.'

'Go on, Nat.'

'I will tell it as I was told, and leave it to you to judge the truth of it,' the assistant replied, his unease bringing a crack to his voice. 'Devereux called down the Devil to Wykenham, but Old Hob demanded more than the paltry offerings Devereux had brought with him. His incantation failed. He was forced to swallow the Devil whole, and with the thing inside him he went out into the night and killed every living soul in that place. He slit the throats of children in their beds, dashed in the heads of babies with a rock, set fire to farmers' wives as they ran screaming from their homes, put out eyes, pulled out lights, hacked and cut and slaughtered all who moved like they were animals in the field. And when he was done, not a single man, woman or child lived in Wykenham. He had murdered the entire hamlet.'

'What happened to him?' Will still could not mask his disbelief.

'He was found the next day, naked, in the churchyard, covered with the blood of his victims, wearing a hat of skin. His wits had been driven from him, and the Devil lived inside him.' Crossing himself, Nathaniel bowed his head.

'There was no trial? No execution?'

'No. Sir Francis, Essex and the Queen herself felt the truth would cause even more damage. We were facing uprisings within and invasion from Spain without. Better to shut Devereux away and pretend he never existed. Then it would be as if the things he did had never taken place either.'

'If Sir Francis destroyed all signs that this happened, how does your informant know?' Will pressed.

Nathaniel took another sip of wine and closed his eyes for a moment as he drove the terrifying visions from his mind. 'A vicar from an adjoining parish was there on the day Devereux was found,' he replied in a small voice. 'He wrote a pamphlet. When it was published, all copies were seized and destroyed, and the vicar silenced. *Most* were destroyed. One or two found their way out, as these things do, and they are now kept in the libraries of scholars and debated at length, in secret to avoid the attention of your own kind.'

Will still wasn't sure he believed the story. It sounded to him like a blood and thunder tale for a dark night, but if there was truth in it, it would certainly be the kind of thing that intrigued Marlowe. 'And you say they let such a monster live? How? Where?'

'Why, in London.'

Will laughed. 'Where in London could such a man be kept without everyone knowing?'

'In Bedlam, of course.'

CHAPTER EIGHTEEN

MURMURING A FEARFUL PRAYER, GRACE WAS GRIPPED BY THE vision of death she spied through the crack in the Queen's bedchamber door. Elizabeth lay rigid on the sheets, skin a waxy white and smallpox-scarred, cheeks hollow, tufts of greasy grey hair sprouting among the bald patches. Her Majesty's wide eyes stared blankly at the ceiling.

On the brink of raising the alarm, Grace released her own tightly held breath when she noticed the faint rise and fall of the monarch's chest. Without her red wig and make-up, Elizabeth looked much older than her sixty years, frail and withered and a far cry from the warrior queen who had told the world only five years ago that she had the heart of a king. The strain of maintaining power in the face of multiple threats to her rule had taken a terrible toll.

Relieved, the lady-in-waiting gathered up her dark grey overskirt and pulled away from the door, only to be caught by the sight of a shadow moving across the bedchamber. It had been so still within the room she had not known anyone else was present.

It was Elinor Makepiece, one of the six maids of honour who tended to the monarch most closely. Although the woman had dressed herself in pretty pale green, she could do little to disguise her plain looks and heavy features, or her unruly thick brown hair. Yet her manner was always pleasant. All the Queen's other ladies had tongues like knives, but Elinor had offered many kindnesses when Grace first began her service in the royal household.

Her thoughts flashed to Will, who had helped secure the post for her, she knew, though he had denied it. He still treated her like the girl she was when they first met, at the cottage in the Forest of Arden, as he came courting her elder sister, Jenny. In frustration, she absently tugged at the blue ribbon holding back her chestnut ringlets, then glanced down at her slender frame. Could he not see she was a woman now? She had curbed her impulsiveness, a little at least, yet still he was blind to her charms. All he did was try to shield her from the work he did, and make light whenever she questioned him about serious matters.

Her simmering annoyance faded as she watched Elinor. At that hour, the older woman should have been hurriedly tidying the Queen's make-up and removing the bowl of water she had used for her ablutions, Grace knew, but instead she moved with a puzzling lethargy. No maid of honour would ever dawdle in Elizabeth's presence while she lay in bed. The other ladies of the bedchamber had already departed.

Grace was transfixed by Elinor's steady, purposeful steps, a cloth slowly folded here, an ornament brushed by fingers there, but no movement that could disturb Her Majesty in her half-sleep. To the younger woman, it seemed almost as if the maid of honour was circling Elizabeth, waiting for a moment to draw closer.

When the Queen's eyes flickered, the other woman made her move. Like a snake, she darted low near Her Majesty's pillow, her head turned away so Grace couldn't tell what was being said. The younger woman was gripped by the oddness of the scene: against all convention, Elinor, rigid, looking away, speaking without being spoken to, and speaking at length.

The Queen appeared to be asleep, even as she responded.

After a long moment, the maid of honour stood up and Grace retreated from the door so she would not be seen. Hurrying across the Privy Chamber and out, she put on a bright smile to deflect the stern glance of the Gentleman Usher, but the incident continued to trouble her.

As she made her way to her chamber, she heard a faint commotion on the ground floor. Creeping down the echoing stone steps to the entrance hall, she saw an unfamiliar woman in a scarlet cloak ordering the servants to bring in her belongings. In the candlelight, Grace couldn't see the woman's face in the depths of her hood. All around her, the servants worked incessantly, carrying her possessions and preparing a room.

Grace caught the arm of one of the serving girls, still sleepy-eyed from being woken. 'Who is that?' she asked.

'It is the Lady Shevington. Wife of the Viscount Shevington,' the girl said with a country burr.

Grace's puzzled expression brought a shy smile from the serving girl. 'No one knew he had taken a wife,' she whispered behind her hand. 'He has not been seen at court for many months since he took up the Queen's business in Ireland.'

Grace knew that meant Viscount Shevington was most likely a spy, reporting back on the tensions as the English attempted to secure control of Ulster, but news from that part of the world was always thin and frequently distorted.

'Where is Viscount Shevington?' she asked.

The serving girl flashed a glance at the woman in red. 'Still in Ireland, Lady Margaret says. He will be joining her shortly to report back to the Queen.'

As the serving girl hurried about her business, Lady Margaret threw back her hood, revealing hair that was only a few shades darker than her cloak. It was the woman Grace had seen pressed against Will by the church in Deptford during Kit Marlowe's funeral.

The lady-in-waiting felt a flush of anger tinged with jealousy. She hated feeling that way and left quickly, but she couldn't stop herself wondering why the woman had come, what she wanted.

Back in her chamber, Grace threw the window open and leaned out into the warm summery night. As she looked around the inner ward below, she was caught by a curious sight. A man lowered himself by rope from a window and quickly found the dark at the foot of the walls. Shocked, she realized it was Will. He crept in the direction of the gatehouse.

As Grace began to wonder what secret business engaged her friend's attention, the thought died suddenly. She thought she glimpsed more movement a few paces behind him, a blur as if it were only mist; or a ghost. Will was oblivious to his silent companion. She lost sight of the pursuer in the shadows, if it had even been there, but she couldn't shake off the chill it left in her.

CHAPTER NINETEEN

BEDLAM.

The screams rang out into the still dawn air, even through stone walls as thick as a man's arm. His grim face shadowed in the depths of his hood, Will Swyfte hid in the lea of the hospital wall, making sure his arrival had not been witnessed.

With each passing moment, he felt his sense of foreboding grow stronger. Where were the Unseelie Court? Like ghosts, the Enemy were defined by the subtle patterns of terror they drew in the world, the trail of blood and ruined lives, but those otherworldly predators remained unsettlingly elusive. Though he could feel their eyes upon him, the tug of their subtle manipulations, he could not understand why they had not yet shown their hand.

Eyeing the feared Hospital of St Mary of Bethlehem, Will saw only a crumbling wreck, like those inside. Moss and sprouting grass and sickly twirls of elder had turned the roof green. Panes were cracked or missing and the gaps filled with mildewed wood, the glass too dirty to see out or in. Open sewers flanked Bedlam so that the air was always heavy with the stink of excrement. In the courtyard in front of the hospital, yellow grass grew among the broken cobbles and the cracked flags, and when it rained a stagnant pond grew like a moat to keep out the world.

Will knew that on Bishopsgate Street Without, just beyond the city wall, merchants travelling north to the villages or south into London often paused, thinking they had heard someone call their name, or a whisper from one of the passers-by, or some other voice rustling in the spaces among the rumble of cartwheels, the rat-tat of horses' hooves, and the back and forth of sellers and apprentices. When they realized the true origin of the sound, they moved on quickly, their heads bowed as if the mere act of hearing would infect them with the illnesses of Bedlam's inhabitants.

His black cloak billowing around him, the spy dashed across the open courtyard to the main door. Will had heard that the governors of Bridewell, who had inherited the management of Bedlam from the City of London, were more concerned with the cut-throats and thieves in the great prison than with the insane patients of the Hospital of St Mary of Bethlehem. No one cared about those lost souls. No one remembered them, or wanted to remember them.

It was the perfect place to keep a devil-haunted man who had slaughtered an entire village.

Hammering on the old, splintered door with the hilt of his dagger, the spy waited for long moments until he heard unhurried footsteps shuffle near from the other side. The door creaked open to reveal the Keeper. The face was not one Will recalled from his last visit five years ago, but the hospital's overseer was cut from the same cloth. It was not work for soft men, and his features carried the same marks of easy cruelty and quick brutality. Unkempt black hair, a beard that had not been trimmed in weeks, a filthy undershirt and brown jerkin, he could have been any rogue found in the more dangerous streets of the capital.

'I would speak with one of the patients,' Will said, keeping his head low so his face remained shrouded.

The Keeper hawked phlegm and spat. 'Too early. Later. Family?'

Will pulled a leather pouch from his black and silver doublet and waved it in front of the overseer so the coins jangled.

Lizard-tongue flicking out over his lips, the man's eyes sparkled. 'Who do you want to see?'

'One Griffin Devereux.'

The light died in the man's face, and his sullen gaze flitted around the deserted courtyard over the visitor's shoulder. 'Nobody here by that name.' Will found the lie so obvious he almost sighed at the Keeper's brazen stupidity.

'My time is short, my patience shorter. Take the money. Buy yourself a shave and a haircut. Some clean clothes. You may then be able to look in the mirror without retching.'

Growling, the man made to close the door.

Will kicked the heavy door so the sharp edge smashed into the Keeper's broken-veined face. Blood spattering from pulped lip and gouged nose, the man howled as if he was one of his own inmates. The spy dived in, driving his fist into the dazed face, and as the overseer went down backwards, arms windmilling, Will caught the neck of his filthy undershirt to lower him slowly to the cold flagstones.

Whipping out his dagger, he pressed the tip against the man's neck and leaned in so his face was close enough to smell the Keeper's beer-sour breath. A droplet of blood rose where steel met flesh. 'A good man has been murdered. My friends' lives hang by a thread. Do not cross me,' the hooded man hissed.

'You . . . you are Will Swyfte,' the Keeper gasped, his eyes glistening with tears of dread.

'Take me to Griffin Devereux or I will cut you into chunks and feed you to the dogs on Bishopsgate.'

Dragging the whimpering man to his feet, the spy thrust him across the gloomy entrance hall and towards the Abraham Ward. Pitiful cries echoed from behind the locked door. Will kept his dagger at the man's back as he fumbled through his jangling ring of iron keys and then they stepped into a long, dark hall that reeked of despair. Scattered with filthy straw, with cells on either side for the patients, the ward fell silent at first. But when the Keeper slammed the door and turned the key in the lock, the throat-torn screams echoed as one as if a great beast had been woken.

'How many patients?' Will asked, casting his gaze towards the clutching hands reaching through the barred windows of the cells. His nose wrinkled at the choking stench that rose up from the Great Vault, the hospital's overflowing cesspit beneath the ward.

'Twenty-one.' The Keeper's eyes flickered towards Will's blade. 'On the books.'

'And the one we are visiting?'

The Keeper shrugged, said nothing.

Some of the patients were kept in chains in their filthy, vermin-infested cells and allowed no contact, 'for the sake of their wits'. The calmer ones were free to roam around the Abraham Ward for a few hours a day. Some wore little more than rags.

'Poor wretches. Who pays for their keep?' Will enquired, his attention caught by one inmate who had the fresh, unmarked face of a child.

'Their parishes, or a family member, or a livery company,' the surly man grunted in reply.

'And who pays for our patient?'

Again the Keeper didn't respond. After a moment, he muttered, 'I ask what I think I can get, depending on how fine their companions are dressed. No less than ten shillings a quarter. Some here have wealth. Merchants. Men from the law courts. We have a fellow from the university at Cambridge. One has been here for twenty-five years, another for nigh on ten.'

The cacophony of the Abraham Ward ended with the slamming of a sturdy door. The sullen man led Will down a flight of stone steps to the hospital's vaulted brick cellars. The ever-present stink of the cesspit mingled with a smell of damp and age. The Keeper took a candle to guide them past rubble and puddles. Rats fled into the shadows before them.

At the western end of the cellars, a heavy door was set in the wall. Candlelight danced through the small, barred window.

'He has many visitors?' Will asked.

'Only one in all the time he has been here. An educated man with the face of a boy.' The gruff man looked Will up and down and added, 'Good clothes like you. A cloak with crimson lining. Gold in his purse.'

Kit.

Turning back to the door, the Keeper hesitated. He tried to moisten a mouth that had grown dry and sticky, his eyes flickering around as he fumbled with his keys. The candle flame threw wild shadows across the salt-encrusted brick.

'Leave me alone to speak with him,' the spy demanded.

'Gladly.'

'Raise the alarm and you will die. Keep your tongue still and you will get your coin.'

The man nodded, though Will could see the raw hatred in

his eyes at his treatment. As he found the right key, the Keeper added, 'Do not listen to his lies. He is the prince of lies.'

'I will weigh all his words.'

The Keeper snorted, clearly believing that Will had misunderstood the severity of his warning. 'I tell you this because I would not wish it upon any man. Not even you,' the man continued, his heavy-lidded gaze filled with loathing. 'He has a manner about him, friendly at first, but he worms his way into your skull, and soon you find yourself thinking things no God-fearing man would think. He can twist your thoughts with words alone, and make you do what he wants. Make you his puppet.'

'He committed the acts of which he is accused?'

'He is capable of them.'

'Why do you keep him here, away from the others?' Will glanced around the dank cellar.

The sweaty, overweight man bowed his head, his voice falling to a whisper. 'On his first night, I placed him on the Abraham Ward. He spent the night whispering to a wretch in the next cell, a merchant, who cried and wailed for hours. In the morning, he was silent. He had plucked out his own eyes.' The Keeper continued to stare at the door as if he feared it would suddenly fly open. 'Devereux will never leave here. He deserves to have his head on a pike at the crossroads within the walls, but that will never happen. He has powerful friends. Sometimes I think they fear death will not hold him, and he will return to seek vengeance on his tormentors.'

No sound came from the other side of the door. Will had the feeling that the cell's occupant was waiting too, listening to their breathing, his own breath caught in his chest as he anticipated a hand reaching out for the door handle.

Finally the Keeper stirred. He wrenched open the door and

stepped aside to allow Will to enter. There was a space a little longer than the length of a grown man's arm before a row of floor-to-ceiling iron bars. Beyond them was a cell larger than the ones that lay off the Abraham Ward, perhaps twelve foot square. Straw was scattered across the damp stone flags. Illumination came from a single stubby candle in a pewter holder placed on the floor against one wall. Rats rustled through the straw just beyond the circle of light, giving an impression that the cell was filled with many people.

The door closed behind Will with a boom.

CHAPTER TWENTY

GRIFFIN DEVEREUX STOOD IN THE CENTRE OF THE CELL, LOOKING over his right shoulder at Will, with a smile of pleasant, innocent warmth. Will had expected a monster, but he had the impression he was studying an eager-to-please child. Tall and slender, the inmate had a pale complexion, his eyebrows and short beard blond, but his head was shaven. He wore all black – shirt, doublet, breeches – with fine embroidery in gold; it was the dress of a nobleman, but the dark colour only made his skin appear translucent.

As Will looked closer, he saw a faint shabbiness to the smiling man's clothes, a touch of silvery mould, wear on the elbows and knees, hanging threads, from his time in the cell. Devereux's hands had the delicate bone structure of an artist, and he folded the long, thin fingers together in front of him in a manner that was both studied and relaxed.

'You honour me.' His voice was gentle, and in it Will heard a deep sadness.

'My name is Will Swyfte. I am a friend of Kit Marlowe, who visited you once.'

Devereux nodded. 'Poor Kit.'

'Why *poor Kit*?'

'His troubles weighed heavily on him. He longed for death. A release.'

'You knew all this from one meeting with him?'

'Kit and I met before, long ago. But I see many things that are not apparent to others. Kit, though, poor Kit, wore his misery clearly. He could not hide it. You know this.' His tone compassionate, the prisoner turned to face his visitor and gave a slow, sad nod.

Will attempted to get the measure of Devereux from his eyes, which were the colour of a winter sky over the moors. He expected to see deceit, cruelty, the kind of mask cultivated by men for whom violence was only a heartbeat away, but there was only heart-wrenching honest emotion.

'How is London?' Devereux said with touching hope. 'Bright and filled with life? Have the fashions changed? What song is popular in the taverns? Can you . . . can you sing it for me?' He caught himself, letting his head fall. 'No. I do not wish to hear your answers. It will only make this cell seem darker still, and the hours reach out longer than they do. Have you ever been imprisoned?'

'From time to time, but never for long.' Will glanced around the confines of the cell, accepting what it must be like to live in a world with such oppressive boundaries.

'Perhaps you understand, then, a little.' The prisoner took a step away from the bars, putting his head back and letting his eyelids flutter shut, imagining, the spy guessed, the city beyond the walls. 'Those who still have the luxury of freedom would think they would miss the conversations with their friends and family. The joys of a masque, or a feast.' The poor wretch shook his head slowly. 'I miss the sun on my face, in my garden on a May morning. The birdsong.' He traced the notes through the air with the fingers of his left hand. 'I miss

153

the sound of rain upon the glass. Such a little thing, but when I sit here and remember, I cannot halt the tears.'

Will shrugged. 'London is a vile place at the moment. The plague is here. There have been many deaths. The stink . . . the smoke of the burnings . . .'

Devereux smiled sadly. 'You do me a kindness, Master Swyfte, and I thank you for your compassion.'

'Why did Kit come to you?'

Lowering his head, Devereux held Will's gaze for a moment, his smile growing fixed, and then he turned his face away. 'He thought I could shine some light on the darkness of his existence.' He gave a faint, hollow laugh. 'Light. Here.'

'Kit wrote a play, about a man who sold his soul to the Devil for knowledge, ambition.' Heeding the Keeper's warning, the spy stood stock-still, his face revealing nothing of his inner thoughts.

Without meeting Will's eye, the prisoner extended a languid arm towards the shadows in the corner of the cell. 'The stories that surround my life provided colour for the background to his tale.'

'Just stories?' the spy pressed.

Devereux turned his back fully to Will, his head falling and his shoulders hunched. His quiet voice had the merest hint of despair. 'When men do not understand the hearts of their fellows, they invent fictions to make sense of the world. It is an easy comfort.'

'Did you teach Kit some of your magic?'

Facing the spy once more, Devereux laughed bitterly. 'There is no such thing.'

'An incantation, the ritual lines and words drawn upon a circle? To summon a devil, as his character did?' Will pressed.

With a step, Devereux disappeared fully into the shadows

154

in the far corner of the cell beyond the reach of the guttering candle flame. His voice floated back to the light. 'There is no magic, in any form. Only the dark of the human soul. We do the things we do, driven by devils that we alone create in our hearts and minds, and then we layer our blame upon them so we can sleep easily, or sleep at all.'

Will's eyes narrowed as he tried to see into the gloom. 'There is some truth in what you say, but not the whole truth. I have seen signs of what many would call magic. There are powers that are not rooted in this world.'

A long silence followed. Will thought he had offended Devereux, but then the prisoner stepped back into the candle-light. The spy was puzzled to see a subtle change had come over the other man. The muscles of his face had tautened in a different configuration, only very slightly, but it made him seem almost another person: his cheeks appeared hollow, his brows falling lower over his eyes, which had hardened a touch. Will could no longer see the simple emotions in them.

'How well did you know your friend?' The prisoner's voice was now much deeper, and had the country accent found in the villages of Norfolk. Devereux's hunched shoulders and slight stoop suggested a farm labourer rather than the elegant, educated man the spy had first encountered. Will searched the prisoner's face for any sign that this was a game, but Devereux appeared oblivious to any change.

'As well as any,' the spy replied.

With a grunt, the prisoner shuffled around, kicking up the straw. 'Not well at all, then.'

'Every man has hidden chambers where he keeps the private parts of himself safe from the harsh observance of the world. That is no great insight.'

'But it is in those chambers that the truth of a man lies. If

155

we cannot pass behind their closed doors, we can never know anyone.' Devereux flashed a surly glance.

Folding his arms, Will puzzled over what he was observing in the cell. 'And what did Kit hide from me that is important?' he asked.

'Places he's been, and people he's met, aye.' Devereux chewed on a nail thoughtfully. 'And his true nature.'

'What is that?'

'Ah, well, there's the thing. What is the true nature of any-thing?' The prisoner gave a little chuckle to himself.

Tiring of the back and forth, Will's voice grew hard. 'What is your true nature?'

'I'm a simple man,' the cell's occupant replied with a shrug.

Though his words hinted at deception, there was no sign Devereux was playing a game. This new character was so different, and the change so puzzling, that the spy could only assume that the prisoner was as mad as all the other men in the Abraham Ward, despite first appearances. Perhaps Devereux spoke the truth when he said he did not believe in magic, and the atrocity he had committed was nothing more than the action of someone who had completely lost his wits.

A thought struck Will and he asked, 'What is your name?'

'Samuel.'

'Not Griffin?'

After a long pause, Devereux replied, 'Griffin is here.'

'Where?' Will asked, his curiosity piqued.

The prisoner rapped his temple with irritation. 'Here!'

Mad indeed, Will thought. 'Which of you spoke to Kit Marlowe?' he asked in a kindly manner so as not to annoy the man further.

'Both of us.'

'And neither of you spoke to him of magic?'

Devereux made a circle with his forefinger and thumb, a sign the countryfolk used to ward off the evil eye or the attention of witches.

'Or devils?' Will continued.

'Do not speak of such things!' Crouching, the prisoner wrapped his arms around him and glanced furtively into the dark corners of the cell. 'If you say the Devil's name he will appear.'

'Tell me—'

'No! I will tell you nothing!' He thrust a hand towards Will as if he were wielding a knife. His face contorted in an animalistic grimace before he dropped his head, rocking gently.

Will weighed if it was worth questioning Devereux any more. Before he reached a conclusion, the man in the cell stood up suddenly. Another change had come over him. Now he held his head at a proud angle, and there was a touch of cruelty at the edge of his mouth. Whereas before he had exhibited the discomfort and rough edges of a labouring man, he now had the bearing of an aristocrat.

'You have a changeable nature,' Will said.

'We are all many things, Master Swyfte. Thinker, worker, lover, student.'

'Killer?'

'That too. And I would wager you know as much about it as I.' Tugging gently at his beard, Devereux gave a knowing smile.

Reflectively, the spy paced along the small space between the bars and the chamber wall. 'I would ask my question again, then,' he said. 'Why did Kit visit you?'

'For the same reason any stranger seeks out another. To learn. Although,' the prisoner added thoughtfully, 'Master Marlowe was not so much of a stranger.'

Will glanced at Devereux. 'When did you first meet Kit?'

'I met several of your associates before, Master Swyfte. Sadly, many of them are now, and recently, deceased.'

'You speak of spies.'

'That I do.'

'You were a spy?' Will came to a halt in front of Devereux, now eyeing the prisoner as he would a predator.

The cell's occupant tugged at his beard thoughtfully. 'After a fashion. In that I did the work of spying, on a particular occasion, at the behest of my distant cousin, the Earl of Essex, who in turn was charged by Sir Francis Walsingham. But it was not my employment as such. I agreed to aid my country, and was paid handsomely. It changed my life in a great many ways, for good and ill.'

The revelation that Devereux had been a spy had a queasy inevitability, Will felt. Their business burrowed into the flesh of life like ringworm, corrupting and destroying everything. His anger flared, but he was brought up sharp when he saw the prisoner observing him with a sly smile as if his inner thoughts were laid bare. 'And this was when you first met Kit?' the spy demanded.

'It was. He was a different man, then. He had hope, and his future lay ahead of him, long and bright. That changed, of course, as it did for all of us.'

'Tell me of this occasion on which you met Kit.'

Smiling, the prisoner clasped his hands together. 'You move too quickly, Master Swyfte,' he said with a shake of his head. 'Let us savour our time together. There are things I would speak of. I receive little news within these four walls, less entertainment, no joy. Allow me some simple pleasure.'

This incarnation of Devereux had a sly wit about him that the other two did not exhibit. Will tried to understand the origins of these characters; they were each undoubtedly Devereux, sharing many of the same mannerisms, yet each also definably different. Had the original Griffin Devereux been shattered by his experience in Norfolk into fragments of his true self, each with a life of its own? Was it some product of the magic he attempted? The curse of seeking to achieve forbidden wisdom?

Certainly, this third incarnation had the part of Devereux that was dangerous, black depths hidden beneath shifting surfaces.

'I hear you are a man forged by your own hardship,' the man said.

'We are all shaped by the obstacles we encounter in our life.' Leaning against the wall with studied nonchalance, Will folded his arms.

'Shaped, yes, but not made. Your experience created a new man. You are not the Will Swyfte you once were, I hear.'

'From Kit?'

'No.' Devereux paused playfully. 'I hear whispers that never reach the ears of most men.' Cocking his head to one side curiously, he appeared to be listening to those whispers there and then. 'A woman, hmm? Stolen from you. For a long time you hoped she was still alive, despite all evidence to the contrary, and now you are sure. But you still do not know where she is, or how you can reach her. You do not know if she is suffering at the hands of her captors, and that question torments you. Perhaps it destroys you a little with each passing day? Am I correct?'

Ignoring the question, Will responded, 'There is only one source that could have provided you with that information, and they are masters of lies.'

Devereux flicked the toe of his leather shoe towards an

inquisitive rat. It scurried away. 'Why, I thought that was the work carried out by you and your kind, Master Swyfte. Untruths. Deceit. Subterfuge. Are you saying I heard this talk from one of your own?'

'You twist words and thoughts deftly,' Will noted. 'You know of whom I speak.'

'The Unseelie Court.' The prisoner gave a faint, teasing smile. 'The ones who have tormented Englishmen since the Flood. Shadows on the edge of all we do, guiding us, shaping us, running us for sport. Slaughtering us. Stealing the babies from their cribs, and poisoning the cattle in the fields, as they crawl out from beneath their hills or lakes, or wander from the deep, dark forests, or dance like ghosts in the stone circles thrown up by the giants of long ago.' Devereux traced one long finger along his chin thoughtfully. 'Those?'

Refusing to play the man's game, Will waited patiently.

'But they have not been heard from for long months, Master Swyfte?'

'And that absence is as worrying as if they were here with us. More so. The Unseelie Court never leaves us, Master Devereux. If they are not actively destroying lives, then they are planning to do so.'

'Ah.' The prisoner's tone was mocking.

Will's voice hardened. 'Now, I have had my fill of your games. Kit Marlowe has been murdered. I will not rest until I find who was behind that crime, though I have to hunt down the highest in the land.'

'The highest in the land? The Queen herself?'

'I will follow the trail of blood to its source.' Will fought to keep the emotion out of his voice. 'I care not for my own safety. Justice for my friend is my sole motivation. You know more than you say. Speak now.'

160

'Or what? Where is the gain for me?' the prisoner replied, holding his head at a haughty angle.

Will's eyes narrowed. 'The gain? When I leave this foul-smelling cell you will still be alive.'

With snake-like speed, Devereux sprang close to the bars. Will stood his ground. Though the mercurial man's smile remained, his eyes darkened in response to the threat. The spy realized it was the first sign of honesty this incarnation had exhibited, the briefest glimpse of the true, chilling nature that hid deeply beneath layers of distraction.

'You think you could kill me?' the prisoner growled.

'You make a play of black magic, but a blade would loose your blood as it would that of any other man.'

Devereux searched the spy's face for a hint of weakness, and found none. 'But I have powerful friends.' His true nature slipped beneath the surface once more.

'I told you. In this instance, I care little for the powerful, and what they can and cannot do to me,' Will replied.

'You ride towards the edge of a cliff, Master Swyfte,' the prisoner cautioned, 'and I fear you do so wilfully.'

In anger, Will lunged, gripping Devereux's worn doublet and yanking him forward so hard his head crashed against the bars. The iron rang gently with the impact. With his left hand, the spy whipped out his dagger and pressed it against the other man's pale neck. 'If you cannot give me the answers I require, delve into yourself and pull out one of the shadows that can,' Will snarled, his forehead pressed against the cold iron bars so his eyes were only inches from Devereux's roving gaze.

'Do you really want me to do that, Master Swyfte?'

'I need information, Master Devereux, and I am in no mood to wait.'

161

'And you will accept the consequences?'

'In the work I do, the price is always high. Do what I ask.'

'Very well.' The man's head dropped as if he were in thought, but when he glanced up again, Will involuntarily flinched. Once again, Devereux's face had altered, this time substantially. The muscles pulled the mouth wider and down at the ends, the cheeks hollower; the eyes had retreated into pits of shadow, and when the candlelight caught them, Will saw the black pupils had expanded to cover the irises and most of the whites. There was nothing in them that was recognizably human.

CHAPTER TWENTY-ONE

DEVEREUX PULLED HIMSELF FREE FROM WILL'S GRIP AND RE-
treated to the centre of the cell where he squatted like an ape,
his breath deep and rumbling. For long, silent moments, his
head on one side, he levelled an unblinking gaze. Will felt as if
it was delving deep into his thoughts.

'Who are you?' he asked. He shivered. The room appeared
to have grown colder.

'Your friend called me Mephistophilis.' The squatting man's
voice was hoarse, strained and crackling like an old man's, the
words formed as if he was unused to speaking. Chilled, Will
felt it was as if some beast had slipped beneath Devereux's skin
and now wore his appearance like clothes.

'Is that your name?' he demanded.

'There is power in naming, and power in words. A word turns
something into what the word says it is, not what it is in essence.
That is a form of magic, is it not? To shape the world without by
a conscious thought within?' With a long thin finger, Devereux
traced an arc in the straw. He looked as if he was preparing to
pounce, desperate to tear Will limb from limb.

'I am angel or devil, whichever you choose to call me,' the
prisoner added.

'I could never imagine you an angel.'

The slow rumble of Devereux's breath was the only reply. Will could now see the cloud of his own breath.

'Then I will address you as Mephistophilis, if that is your wish,' the spy said, 'though I wonder if you are truly a devil, or some terrible part of Devereux himself, released from the depths of his mind by the atrocities he committed.'

'A good question. You must decide upon the answer for yourself.' Its black eyes did not blink.

'You came to Devereux after he murdered all those poor souls in Norfolk?'

'How could I not answer when the summons was so loud and clear?'

'And now you ride him like a mare.'

'I am always with him. Sometimes near, sometimes afar, but always there. To the end. And beyond. Once summoned, we cannot be dispatched until the deal is complete.'

Devereux continued to trace a pattern in the dirty straw with the tip of his index finger, but his intense gaze never left Will's face. *Still biding his time*, the spy thought. Waiting for him to take a step too close to the bars, to drop his knife or bare his neck. 'Then I know you, and I can weigh the value of your words,' Will said.

'Oh, you do not know me,' the crouching figure mocked. 'You will never know me.'

'Who killed Kit Marlowe?'

'He killed himself, through his actions.' The beast-like figure continued to breathe heavily, the rumbling echoes rolling around the cell.

Holding Devereux's gaze, Will rested a hand on the cold hilt of his rapier. 'So, we are to play games with words.'

'Words are nothing but games,' the prisoner growled.

'Kit came to you to learn an incantation for summoning a devil. Why?' the spy demanded.

'To aid you, his most beloved friend. Even in the face of his own death, he thought of you.'

Will knew Devereux's words were designed to sting, but that didn't lessen their impact. 'To guide me towards the one who has been killing England's spies, and the plot now unfolding. And his final act was a success, which I would imagine troubles you greatly. There would be no joy for you in a selfless act. But there is a greater mystery here than murder, and it involves the Unseelie Court. You have knowledge of the nature of that plot?'

'Before they wanted only their revenge for England's grand betrayal and the capture and imprisonment of their beloved Queen. Now their ambitions have grown.'

'How so?'

The beast smiled.

Will closed his fingers around his dagger, but kept it hidden from view for the moment. 'I see I am not to get answers out of this conversation. Perhaps it would be better if I finished it now, and ended your own miserable life in the process.'

'It is possible to learn without gaining answers. If you listen with care.'

'Clues, then. Hints.'

'Here is a hint, little man. This time you cannot stop the Unseelie Court until you find them. They are as close as a whisper and as far away as the stars. Close enough to step into the place you consider safest when the time is right. Sometimes you even look into their eyes and do not know.' Devereux gave a low, mocking laugh.

'I thank you. I will reflect on your *hint* at my leisure.' Will noticed the prisoner's breath did not cloud like his own, even though the temperature had fallen so steeply there was now the sparkle of hoar frost on the cell walls. 'And the murders of England's spies – it is by the hands of the Unseelie Court?' he added.

'It is by the hands of a man who serves the purpose of the Unseelie Court, although he may or may not be aware of that.'

'And they kill the spies who know of their existence, the soldiers in this long war, to hide their path.'

'Very clever, Master Swyfte. You have pieced together some parts of this great puzzle with no little skill. The very essence of the Unseelie Court's plot is that they become, once again, invisible and unknown,' the threatening figure replied. 'But a death is not always simply a death.'

'A riddle. I am told children and fools enjoy them.' When the spy took an unconscious step towards the bars, he saw Devereux's muscles tense. Quickly, he stepped back. 'So they have not been killed simply because they are spies. Their deaths serve another purpose for the Unseelie Court.'

'Three purposes, in fact. One: the murders mask the larger trail of those Good Neighbours. Two: they mask a smaller trail that may, perhaps, lead to the heart of their plot and the way to bring it all crashing down. And three . . .' Halfway between grin and snarl, Devereux's lips curled back from pointed teeth.

'Three?'

'The Fay, as they have been called and sometimes call themselves, destroy England's hard-won defences by degrees. Soon there will be nothing to keep them out in the night. And then . . .' The prisoner clapped his hands with dark delight.

Will shuddered. He pictured Gavell's flayed body in the deadhouse, the strange mark upon his back. Now he understood. The Unseelie Court were using the deaths of the spies in some ritual that would peel back the magical defences the court astrologer Dr Dee had put in place all those years ago. That was why Carpenter and Launceston had encountered that vile thing in Bankside in broad daylight. As the defences yielded, the Enemy would be able to move more freely, until they could strike with impunity anywhere, at any time, liberate their Queen . . . The spy had a terrifying flash of the beautiful, terrible Fay monarch walking free from the Lantern Tower at Whitehall, boiling with anger after years of imprisonment, fire and blood and destruction blooming in her footsteps like summer flowers.

'How many more murders before it all falls apart?' Will whispered.

'Three. Only three. Each life must be taken at the right time, in the right place.'

Will clenched his fist in defiance. 'Then we must stop more blood being spilled. I suppose you could not tell me the identity of the face behind the devil-mask?'

'In his appearance you already know his nature, and through nature one can divine a man.' The hunched prisoner levelled his gaze at a scurrying rat. It stopped in its tracks, held fast by the glare. After a moment, it fell on its side, dead. Devereux tossed it into a corner where it landed with a dull thud. 'I know many things, but I have little to gain by telling you,' he said, wiping his mouth with the back of his hand.

'You are scared of them, then. The Fay,' Will taunted, hiding his frustration.

The prisoner gave a broad, dark grin. 'Their agents dare not come near here,' he whispered.

'Who are their agents?' Will's eyes narrowed. He felt his anger grow at each of Devereux's new obfuscations and deceits.

'There is a play, performed in recent times at the Rose Theatre—'

167

'If it was staged in recent times, how do you know of it?' the spy interrupted sharply.

Devereux huddled even closer to the stinking, straw-covered floor and intoned in a low, resonant voice:

> 'Here, said they, is the Terror of the French
> The Scar-Crow that affrights our children so.
> Then broke I from the officers that led me,
> And with my nails digged stones out of the ground,
> To hurl at the beholders of my shame.
> My grisly countenance made others fly,
> None durst come near for fear of sudden death.'

'More riddles,' Will said scornfully. 'You waste my time.'

'Do I?' The prisoner began to crawl around the cell, flashing occasional glances back at him. 'There is a school that meets at night, wise men, artists, thinkers, and your good friend Kit was one of them. Yes, he had a secret life you never knew about. And they plot and they plan and they know more than you. And the writer of those words had heard of these agents, though he likely did not know the full truth, or he would have run screaming from his room and created no more fictions.'

Will laughed. 'These are *your* fictions.'

'Mine? No, all true.' Devereux pressed his hands together in a mockery of prayer. 'And here is another: if you would stop the agents you must find the Corpus-Scythe.'

'And what is that?'

'A tool, a weapon, a way for the Unseelie Court to control their puppets. For if the agents ever turned they could destroy all things, even the Fay.'

The spy listened to the cryptic comments Devereux made – *the Terror of the French, the school that meets at night* – and while they all hinted at a greater mystery, he felt only anger at the elusive nature of what he had been told.

Will stepped close to the bars.

The beast-like man turned suddenly, leaping like a cat towards the spy, mouth torn wide, spraying spittle and rat-blood. A rolling, ferocious snarl echoed off the brick walls. Will stood his ground, watching the prisoner rush towards him, hands like claws to tear out his throat.

At the very last, the spy stepped back. As both of Devereux's hands reached through the bars, Will grabbed the wrist of one with his left hand, and with his right drove his dagger through the protruding palm. He continued his thrust, forcing the blade through the palm of the hand he gripped and continuing upwards with all his weight behind it until he had both of the prisoner's hands impaled high over his head.

Roaring in agony, the creature realized he couldn't escape, but still he writhed and tore until the blood rushed down his arms.

Will pressed his face close, smelling his opponent's meaty breath. 'I care nothing for you, or your life,' he growled. 'I have no time for your games. I seek only revenge for my friend's death, and I will not be deflected.'

Those hideous black eyes loomed ever closer. 'I will tell you nothing,' Devereux snarled.

The spy twisted the knife.

Though he convulsed in pain, the possessed man remained silent, and when the agony passed he was eerily calm.

'Who are the Unseelie Court's agents?' Will asked, just as calm.

Defiant, Devereux held his gaze for a moment, and then replied, 'The Scar-Crow Men, and they are everywhere.'

'How do I know them?'

'You do not. They look like people you know, perhaps your own friends. But they are not. They are made of straw, or clay, or this, or that. You can trust no one. No one.'

Suddenly Will understood Kit's exhortation in the note that accompanied his play. *Trust no one.* And suddenly he glimpsed some of the meaning behind the vision the devil had given him in the Rose Theatre.

A faint smile told him that his opponent had revealed the information only to cause further distress, unease, perhaps fear, or despair.

The black eyes narrowed. 'Torture me all you will, but you harm only Devereux.'

'What are you?' Will asked with quiet intensity.

'You know. In the dark of the night, when you fear the worst there is of life, you know.'

The spy ripped out his dagger and the prisoner fell away from the bars, rolling back across the dirty straw to coil like a beast once more. 'I would tell you one more thing, given freely,' he said, 'for the more you progress into the heart of this thing, the more misery awaits you. And I would see you suffer.'

'Tell me,' Will said icily.

'All you seek springs from one event.' Devereux crawled forward to press his face against the bars, distorting his features monstrously as he peered at Will through the gap. 'Follow the marsh-lights back through time. Follow that small trail. You will find it for yourself.' His mouth split in a grin that was more hunger than humour, the teeth yellow and stained with blood.

'You think you drive me towards destruction. You do not,' the spy said with a dismissive wave of his hand.

'You are already on the road and you do not see it. But you

will. And soon.' Devereux looked just past Will's left shoulder and said, 'Ride him well, coz, when the time comes.'

The hairs prickled on the nape of Will's neck. Despite himself, he glanced back to see if the Keeper had entered the cell silently. There was no one behind him.

'You are no longer alone,' Devereux taunted. 'You have a companion now, always there, one step behind, guiding, whispering, waiting. Your own devil. For as your friend saved you, he also damned you.'

'This time your lies are too crude,' Will snorted.

'Your ending is already written, Master Swyfte, by the man you trusted most, and the final word is *damnation*.' Devereux's fat, shining tongue flicked out like a snake's. He still had not blinked.

'I choose my own ending,' Will stated emphatically.

As he left the cell, the door closed firmly behind him, he heard Devereux begin a keening wail, desolate and haunting like hungry birds over a lonely moor. It followed Will up to the Abraham Ward where the crazed patients watched him in eerie silence, their eyes oddly fixed a pace behind his back, and the sound only ended when he was out of the gloomy building and into the hot sun of the new day.

CHAPTER TWENTY-TWO

JENNY IS STILL ALIVE.

Grace woke with a start. She was still caught up in her dreams, visions of shadowy figures, and a man with a shimmering head like the moon, and, oddly, her sister Jenny calling to her across a vast expanse of water. Jenny, whom she had not seen since she was a girl, but who still seemed as young and vibrant as the day she disappeared, though her eyes were filled with desperation, and, perhaps, fear.

It was a silly thought, she told herself. Just a dream. Nothing more.

And as that notion faded, she was struck by another. She felt a chill run through her entire body.

She was not alone.

Rigid with fear, the young woman lay on her back on her hard bed. A shaft of moonlight fell through the window across the linen sheet lying loosely over her white nightgown. The rest of her chamber was in deep shadow, but she was convinced someone sat on the stool next to her bed.

Grace could sense the presence looming over her, and smell a hint of musk, but more troubling to her, she discerned a faint, wet smacking in the stillness of the room. Fighting back the rising panic, she strained to hear.

Lips, she thought. *The smacking of lips.*

Someone was eating.

The young woman shuddered. *Flee!* the voices in her head screamed. *Save yourself!* Her heart thundered, but she stayed calm, telling herself that if she made a sudden move the intruder could kill her before she was halfway across the chamber.

With an almost imperceptible movement, Grace eased her trembling hand through the dark to the small stool on the other side of the bed where she had left her comb and looking glass. Her fingers closed on the cool silver handle of the mirror and she brought it back up steadily.

The wet smacking sound now seemed as loud to her as a tolling bell.

Behind her fear, the young woman felt sickened. *What was it eating?*

Grace thought of lashing out with the mirror and then escaping in the confusion, but her curiosity was getting the better of her. She had to see. With a smooth, gentle movement, she eased the looking glass into the moonbeam and tilted it so the milky light reflected across her bed.

Her chest tight with apprehension, the young woman snapped her head round to see what was caught in the glimmer.

In her plain, grey nightgown, Elinor, the Queen's maid of honour, was hunched over like a bird of prey, talons curled. Her eyes were wide and white in the moonlight, her hair a wild, wispy mane.

Grace shrieked.

The older woman leapt to her feet, knocking over the stool,

and lurched out of the chamber with the door banging behind her.

Sitting up in her bed, Grace covered her face and tried to calm her racing heart. She told herself Elinor must have been sleepwalking, although every sign had suggested the maid of honour was wide awake. But the younger woman was troubled most by what she had seen her friend doing in that brief flash.

A lock of Grace's long, well-combed hair had been clamped between the maid of honour's thin lips. She felt the end of the strand, still wet with saliva.

Elinor had been eating her hair.

CHAPTER TWENTY-THREE

IN THE SWEET PLACES INHABITED BY THE UNSEELIE COURT, there is always music in the air, and beauty, and joy, and the haunting fragrance of honeysuckle. But not here. Fabian of the High Family wipes away a single tear searing his cheek and wonders how long he must endure the miseries of the cold human world. It is dark, the grand horizons obscured by stone walls, and echoing through them the thunderous rhythm of hammers upon anvils beating out the final days of man.

Fabian dreams of mirrors.

Selecting a long shin bone from the jumbled pile beside him, the doleful being proceeds to carve shapes and symbols in the yellow-white surface. Dressed in inky doublet and breeches, his hair black, his eyes too, Fabian reflects on the harsh decisions forced upon his people, known at times in the tongue of men as the Fay. And harsh they certainly are, for all poor mortals, that race which he admires so, and pities too. If only his brothers and sisters saw the Sons of Adam in the same light.

Sons of Adam. Fabian laughs at that. The stories they tell themselves! If only men knew the truth.

Finishing his carving, the black-garbed Fay takes the shin

175

bone and inserts it into a hole in a circular piece of stone cut from bedrock under the light of the full moon. Silver symbols glisten on the stone in the seething red light of a brazier. Fabian waves his slender fingers over the collection of objects scattered across the bench – the skull of a bird, a pink seashell taken from the beach at dawn, a five-bladed knife, a globe that throbs with an inner white light – and wonders which one to select next.

The booming of the hammers does not slow, and it never stops.

Two looking glasses stand in the gloom on the edge of the low-ceilinged chamber. The surface of one clouds and a dim light appears within it. When the surface clears, Fabian sees a spectral figure, tall and thin and dressed all in grey, his long hair a gleaming silver with a streak of black along the centre. Clinging to his arm is a hairless, ape-like creature with golden eyes. It stares too long, too hard.

'Lethe,' Fabian says in greeting, his attention still focused on his work. 'The Corpus-Scythe sings to me. I can hear the shape it wants to be. Soon now. Soon.'

The silver-haired being inscribes a circle in the air with his index finger, and laughs.

'Do not hurt them. They shine like stars, if only you could see it,' Fabian whispers, his voice almost lost to the din.

'Your pleadings are tiresome,' Lethe sighs. 'Whatever you have discovered in your unpickings, the fact remains that the race of men are the architects of their own destruction. Have you forgotten that our Queen is now held at the top of a tower in one of their palaces?' He clutches a hand to his mouth for a moment, fighting queasiness. His voice rising to a shriek, he continues, 'Our Queen, a prisoner. Alone, suffering, a victim of man's betrayal. The fuel for the very

176

defences that have locked us out of the land where we once sought our sport.'

The ape-thing places one paw upon its master's cheek to calm him.

'We will have our Queen back, Fabian. But that is only the start,' Lethe continues, his voice trembling with emotion.

Fabian chooses the five-bladed knife and affixes it to the stone with gold wire, muttering the ritual words under his breath as he does so.

'Then we are to proceed?' he asks when he has finished the next stage of his long, intricate task.

The silver-haired being claps his hands together with glee. The hairless ape-thing mimics its master. 'For the Fay, for the great, glorious Unseelie Court, a new age beckons. We step out from our sweet, shadowy homes into harsh light. This course has been thrust upon us, but we shall not flinch. We shall remain resolute. And soon, soon now, only one world shall exist. Our world.'

The second mirror clouds, then glows. Fabian glances up to see inscrutable Deortha, staff in hand, the skulls of mice and birds braided into his hair. Behind the conjuror, four candles flicker in the centre of a stone chamber, their flames reflected in a hundred golden-framed mirrors covering the walls. A black-robed man kneels in front of a wooden cross. Muttered prayers rustle out into the still room.

'*Da, quaesumus Dominus, ut in hora mortis nostrae Sacramentis refecti et culpis omnibus expiati, in sinum misericordiae tuae laeti suscipi mereamur.*'

The praying man wears a devil's mask on his face and the wings of an angel on his back. Deortha gives Lethe a cold smile and a deferential bow. 'Exaltus. We are to expect you soon?'

'Soon. I am eager to look out over my new realm.' Lethe

177

strokes slender fingers across the head of the golden-eyed creature. It mouths the same words as its master speaks. 'Your puppet dances to the tune we play?'

Deortha glances at the praying man. 'His weakness was easy to find, and even easier to prise apart. He has allowed his love of his God to unbalance his fragile wits, and now he sees his deity everywhere. Even here.'

The two Fay laugh. Fabian shakes his head sadly.

'And so he finds sanctity in the blood he spills,' the conjuror continues. 'He kills by our design. The victim, the time, the place. And with each life lost another part of England's defences crumbles. This land will be ours, as it once was.'

'And that is only the beginning,' Lethe says, his pet says. 'And our enemies know nothing?'

'They go about their business as if all was well with the world, these foolish men. And so we move quietly and steadily, drawing ever closer, and by the time we are seen it will be too late.'

'Soon, then,' Lethe whispers, the glass clouding around him. 'Soon.'

In the other mirror, Deortha turns to examine their puppet. His prayers complete, the man stands. Over his head, he raises the Gerlathing, the knife-that-severs-souls. The ritual blade glimmers in the reflected candlelight.

'Tell me, angels of the Lord,' the devil-masked man cries. 'Who dies next?'

And on and on the hammers clash upon the anvils, beating out the final days of man.

CHAPTER TWENTY-FOUR

THE STEADY CLANG OF IRON ON STONE SOUNDED TO WILL LIKE the remorseless proclamation of a funeral bell. He felt the vibrations run through his Spanish leather boots, up his black-clad legs and into the pit of his stomach as he crouched on Paul's Walk in the dark belly of the cathedral. His stomach responded with a queasy sensation that only added to his feeling that the world was out of kilter.

In the wavering light of the candle, Carpenter's scarred face glistened with a sheen of sweat. One blow with the iron rod along the join between the flagstones. Another.

Thoom. Thoom.

Along the nave, near the east door, Will could just make out Launceston standing guard in case anyone came to investigate the disturbance. The Earl was as grey and still as one of the statues of the saints that looked down from the alcoves along the north wall.

Crouching next to the candle to prevent the light reflecting through the stained-glass windows, Will watched Carpenter work. Chunks of stone were flying off the flag. Soon it would be possible to work the rod into the join and lift the paving.

'Defacing a monument to God's will. Disturbing the dead.

Grave-robbing. Perhaps they could even make a case for necromancy,' Carpenter growled, pausing to wipe his forehead with the back of his hand. 'I sometimes wonder if we can go any lower. But you always surprise me.'

'I see it as my life's work to provide you with new experiences, John,' Will replied. 'Besides, count yourself lucky. I am already wanted by the Privy Council after failing to present myself to them this morning, and they are not known for their moderation.'

When he had left Bedlam in the early morning sunlight, Will had made his way to the back room at the Cross Keys on Gracechurch Street where he had arranged to meet his two companions. Once the two men heard the information Will had gleaned from Griffin Devereux, they all agreed no more time could be wasted. The devil-masked murderer had to be found and stopped before the final defences fell.

Glancing around uneasily, Carpenter muttered, 'Since you mentioned those Unseelie Court bastards were close at hand . . . close enough to look us in the eyes . . . I see them in every shadow. Hell's teeth, I am like a child! Why don't they show themselves and I can plunge my steel into their guts?'

'Do not wish it upon yourself, John. The Enemy will strike soon enough.' Will eyed the dark areas of the cathedral, as uneasy as his companion. 'It is these Scar-Crow Men that trouble me more. Fay agents who can pass as human, or humans who have sided with the Enemy? I do not know how much of Devereux's words I can trust. But one thing is for sure, now we have to watch our own kind too.' He shook his head, concerned.

Carpenter grunted. 'We are alone, then. There is nowhere we can be sure we are safe.'

Will could not argue.

After a break, the scarred man continued with his work.

Thoom, thoom, thoom.

Will cursed himself for jumping at shadows all day. As he had slipped through the city gates after leaving Bedlam, two pikemen in shining steel helmets were chatting lazily in the sun, but another watched Will as if he had committed some crime. On Corn Hill, a man in an emerald-coloured cap with a band of black and white triangles paused suddenly in his walk to turn and stare at Will in an accusatory manner. Brought to a halt by a flock of sheep being driven to market, a lawyer in a black gown and carrying a purple-ribboned sheaf of papers had glowered at him. The wife of a wealthy merchant had watched him from the first floor of one of the large houses lining Cheapside. A gentleman in a furred compass cloak engaged in buying a mutton pie from one of the street sellers locked eyes with him for a long moment.

Imagination or truth? Had the Unseelie Court already all but won and no one yet knew?

Thoom, thoom, thoom.

Will was drawn from his reverie as Carpenter came to a halt. In the summer heat, sweat trickled down the scarred man's brow and soaked his doublet. The iron rod they had recovered from the cathedral tool store in the crypt was now jammed in the fractured joint between two flags. Gripping the top of the rod, the two men heaved together, and with a deep, resonant grinding the stone was levered free. Beneath was a layer of gravel and rubble that the masons had used to level the floor after the interment.

With the shovel they had also brought from the store, Will began to dig with determined strokes until the tool clanged against the stone that lay above the narrow burial vault. The spies paused, listening to the echoes roll out through the vast space. Along the nave, the ghostly figure of Launceston glanced back their way.

'If I am to lose my head for this, my dying breath will be a curse to damn you to hell,' Carpenter snarled.

'*Why this is hell, nor am I out of it,*' Will recalled, but there was a bitter note to the humour in his voice.

The scarred man only snorted, his gaze fixed on the stone covering now revealed. After a moment, he asked in a quiet voice, 'What possesses you to do this? None of us could call Sir Francis Walsingham friend, but surely he deserves better than to have his rest disturbed?'

Tossing the shovel aside, Will plucked up the iron rod. 'The dead are gone from this world. My concerns are for the living,' he muttered. He drove the rod into the dusty groove along the edge of the scratched covering. 'Why did Kit choose this grave to leave his message?'

'Because he knew the defacement of our former master's final resting place would eventually draw our attention,' Carpenter said with a shrug.

'That is one answer.' Drawing a deep breath, Will prepared to put his weight against the rod. 'Like all writers, Master Marlowe played tricks with words. In his hands, they often meant more than one thing at the same time. *In the beginning*, he wrote, here. A clue to the solution of the message he hid in his play, I am sure. The word. The keyword to his cipher. But I also feel he wanted us to look here for the beginning of this plot, or one beginning. There is usually more than one as events unfold.'

'Now you are starting to speak like him,' Carpenter sighed.

The spy pressed against the rod. As the stone lifted with a groan, such a foul stench rushed out that Will choked, and Carpenter turned away, covering his face. Gripping the edges of the heavy stone, the two men struggled to lower it on to the cathedral floor beside the gaping black hole. 'What is that monstrous reek?' the scarred man spluttered.

'Those are not the usual vapours that come off a body in a state of flux,' Will said, coughing. The acrid smell burned his nostrils and the back of his throat. 'And certainly not three years after the passing. It reminds me of the odours that used to emanate from Dr Dee's rooms at the Palace of Whitehall.'

Taking the candle, the spies tied kerchiefs across their faces and crawled to the edge of the hole. Inside lay a plain wooden coffin. With Carpenter gripping his ankles, Will lowered himself down and ripped off the lid of the box. The candle revealed the linen shroud that had been used to wrap the old spymaster's body, now stained from top to toe. Setting his jaw, the spy grasped the rotting shroud near the head and tugged until it tore free. The flickering light revealed a death's-head, the lower jaw hanging down so that it appeared that Walsingham was screaming his torment.

Carpenter let out a cry and then cursed loudly at his weakness. Dark holes stared where the eyes had been, the skin clinging to the bone like parchment, a mane of black hair still attached to the scalp.

'God's wounds,' the scarred man exclaimed. 'The colour of him!'

Walsingham's corpse was bright blue. Will gave another tug at the shroud and part of it came away in his hands. The edges looked like they had been burned, and beside the corpse there was a similar scorching in the wood of the coffin. In some places holes had appeared.

'What has happened to him?' Carpenter gasped, once his companion was safely back on the cathedral floor and well away from the burning smells rising from the burial vault.

'Poison.' The two spies started at Launceston's whispery pronouncement. He had come up silently behind them while they peered into the hole.

'I fear Robert is correct,' Will said, the candle flame dancing in his dark eyes. 'In the months before his death, when he was suffering fit after fit, his physician provided him with numerous concoctions. And as you know, despite all attempts to save Sir Francis' life, he deteriorated rapidly, almost as if the prescribed medicine was doing him more harm than good.'

'Then you think the physician murdered him?' Carpenter whispered, glancing towards the grave.

'Either that, or the concoctions were adulterated before they reached our master's lips,' Will replied.

Launceston tapped one white finger on his chin in thought. 'A subtle murder that would not draw attention to itself. Walsingham was the architect of our war against the Unseelie Court. With him gone there was a hole at the heart of our defences, and no obvious candidate to fill it.'

'The Enemy has planned this for three years?' Carpenter hissed incredulously.

'It was indeed the beginning of their slow unveiling of the plot,' Will replied. He stood up, cupping his hand around the candle flame to stop it going out. 'With our master gone, there was no one to protect Dr Dee, the other prime mover in the long struggle with our supernatural foe. You recall his advice was soon being ignored and then he was dispatched to Manchester to be warden of Christ's College.'

The Earl flicked a piece of rubble into the grave with the toe of his grey shoe. It landed with a soft thud. 'Dee was heart-broken to be dismissed so,' he said flatly. 'After guiding Her Majesty in her youth, and then giving his all to the security of the nation, it must have felt like betrayal to be sent away as though he were worthless.'

'That never made any sense,' Carpenter grunted. 'With Dee gone, who was supposed to ensure our magical defences would stay strong?'

'Our master's death left only chaos,' Will mused. 'Cecil and Essex jostling for the Queen's ear. No good advice getting through the whispers, deceits and rivalry. Only confusion. While we continued blithely with our lives, thinking all was well, the Unseelie Court silently set their plot in motion. In the shadows they moved their pieces into place, unnoticed, shifting ever closer to the heart of our nation. Now we stand on the brink of destruction and it may already be too late to raise the alarm.'

Will strode to the edge of the grave and held the candle over the hole. The blue, screaming face loomed up out of the dark.

CHAPTER TWENTY-FIVE

'TIME IS SHORT AND I MUST BE QUICK,' WILL SAID, PEERING FROM Nathaniel's chamber window over the sunlit palace grounds. 'You will have many questions, but for now all I can tell you is that we are surrounded by great danger.'

'Here, in Nonsuch?' Grace asked incredulously, her eyes still sleepy at that early hour.

'Especially here. Our Enemy has placed agents among us. People we once relied upon may now be working against us. No one can be trusted. Do you understand?'

Concerned now, Grace and Nathaniel nodded.

It was 4 June, three days since Kit had been laid in the ground. After their hard ride from London, Will, Launceston and Carpenter had slipped past the dozing guards into the still-sleeping palace. Speeding through the empty halls, Will had woken his assistant and the lady-in-waiting to warn them of what was unfolding.

'For now, I would that the two of you remain safe,' he continued. 'At the first sign of trouble, leave the palace.' He turned to Grace and added, 'Go with Nat, to the village where his father lives. I will meet you both there if I can. In the meantime, I have work for you.'

Alert now, the assistant ran a hand through his unruly hair. 'Tell me, I am ready.'

'Go to my chamber and retrieve Kit's play. My hope is that the cipher will reveal important information to help us to uncover the plot.' Will stepped away from the window when a girl collecting eggs for the morning meal glanced up as if she had heard something.

'You have broken the code?' Nathaniel asked.

Will smiled tightly. 'In the beginning was the word, and the word was *poison*.' He went to the chamber door and opened it a crack, peering out into the still corridor. Turning back to his worried friends, he added in a hushed voice, 'Now, return to your business and keep up the pretence of normal life. At all times, you must act as if you know nothing. Do not draw attention to yourselves. Keep safe.'

Easing into the sun-dappled corridor, Will found Carpenter and Launceston skulking at the top of the stairs where he had left them. The clatter of feet and the call of friendly voices told them the palace was rapidly waking.

'Visit Robert Rowland,' Will whispered. 'He was always a faithful servant to Sir Francis Walsingham, and as the keeper of the records of our business he will be able to locate what event united Kit and Griffin Devereux. Then perhaps we can get to the bottom of this matter before we end up at the bottom of a hole in the earth. And if the worst happens and I am taken, it will be down to you to bring a stop to this plot.'

'Two men against the Unseelie Court,' Carpenter laughed bitterly. 'And should we stop the Spanish at the same time, just for sport?'

'In your spare time, find who has been murdering the spies,' Will continued sardonically, clapping the Earl on the shoulder.

'Robert, I feel you have an understanding of the mind of the man who kills.'

Launceston nodded thoughtfully. 'He has strong tastes, certainly, and a fire that burns brightly in his mind. I will try to divine the way he thinks.'

Will shook the other men's hands in turn. 'We have been down in the ditches for a long while, but now is the time to stand and be men. To business, friends, and if that business involves blood, so be it.'

At the sound of two giggling maids climbing the creaking stairs, the three spies separated, Will striding purposefully towards Cecil's chamber. For once the spymaster's bodyguard, Sinclair, was not smoking sullenly outside the door, casting a murderous eye over anyone who dared approach his master's room. Without knocking, Will entered.

Cecil was leaning across a table scattered with charts of Ireland, sheaves of paper and the remnants of scrambled eggs and bread. He started when he saw Will, his eyes darting uneasily to the spy's rapier. 'What is the meaning of this intrusion?' he hissed.

'We must talk,' Will said in a grave voice.

'The time for talking is long gone. The Privy Council meets this morning to discuss your fate. Although, I would say, it was sealed the moment you decided not to honour them with your presence yesterday.'

'There is more at stake here than my fate, or yours, for that matter.' Seeing the window was open, Will went to close it so they would not be overheard. As the spy pulled it shut, the Little Elf darted around the table in an attempt to escape. Will was between him and the door in an instant, holding up one hand ready to push the frightened man back to the table if necessary.

'Lay a finger on me and your punishment will be great indeed,' Cecil said in a tremulous voice.

'You have already told me my fate is sealed, and it is not wise to confront a man who has nothing to lose.' Will calmed himself, snapping his fingers until his master retreated. 'We have had our differences, you and I,' he continued. 'You have little respect for me, or the work I have done – I do not know why. But we must put all that behind us. We are on the brink of disaster. While we have looked elsewhere, to Spain, and France, and Ireland, the Unseelie Court have been quietly circling us. Their plans have fallen into place, unnoticed, unsuspected, and now an attack is imminent. Indeed, they may already have won and we race around like a hen who has not yet realized her head has been removed.'

Regaining his composure, the spymaster strode back to the table, refusing to dignify Will with attention.

'I am still unsure if you are a part of this plot, but I am trusting my instinct, which has never failed me before,' the spy said. 'You are sly, manipulative, mendacious, and interested above all else in your own advancement, but I do not believe you would ever side with our greatest foe. True?'

Cecil flashed a sullen glare.

'Agents of the Enemy lurk within this court, perhaps people you yourself trust. They could turn on all of us, on the Queen herself, at any moment,' Will said. 'Our only hope is to strike like snakes and drive them out. This very day. I risk everything to be here, now, making this plea, and so should you, Sir Robert. Take control. Lead our resistance, and I will stand at your side. Her Majesty needs you. England needs you.'

His shoulders sagging, the spymaster rested both hands on the table and bowed his head. 'You will not judge me. Unlike you, I must fight for my own survival on a daily basis. There are men who move against me, and there always will be. This plot you mention . . .' He waved a hand in the air as if all he had heard was a trifle. 'If it distracts Essex, then all is well and good. But I have heard nothing of it, and I hear and see more than you.'

'You hear and see what you want.' Will's voice crackled with anger. 'You are distracted by your own ambitions while England falls around you. Failure to act will mean a defeat from which we can never, ever recover.'

'If I act as you say and we fail, or no one else joins this crusade of yours, then my power is weakened,' Cecil snapped. 'Better to wait until the path ahead is clear.'

'That will be too late.' Will felt a rising tide of hopelessness. 'I beseech you, heed me. There is still time to act. If we can find a few trusted allies—'

The hunchbacked man hammered a fist on the table, over-turning a pot of ink that flooded a black stain across one of his charts. 'You have been driven mad by your grief for Marlowe. You see plots where there are none, to give meaning to his death.'

Will drew himself up, his face stony. 'Very well. Then I must act alone, and you, God help you, must accept the consequences.'

The door burst open with a resounding crash. Twelve figures filed in, most of them black-gowned with black caps, their faces severe. Among the clutch, Will recognized Lord Derby of the Privy Council, Roger Cockayne, one of Cecil's advisers, and Danby the coroner, and one woman too: Elinor Makepiece, the Queen's maid of honour.

'What is the meaning of this?' the spymaster barked.

'Sir Robert, leave us, if you will,' Derby said in a low, stern voice.

190

After a moment's hesitation, the Little Elf scurried out of his own chamber with one uneasy backward glance at the door.

Coward, Will thought.

The spy looked along the row of faces, all of them unreadable, but the eyes glittered with a cold light. 'So now you step out of the shadows,' he began, his hand moving towards the hilt of his rapier.

In an instant, those implacable faces transformed as one into seething pits of fury. Mouths tore wide like those of wild beasts, teeth bared and spittle flying, and with a furious roar the men that had become beasts swooped down on Will Swyfte.

CHAPTER TWENTY-SIX

CLUTCHING TWO LARGE VOLUMES TO HIS CHEST, ROBERT Rowland, record-keeper to successive spymasters, entered his chamber with a bowed head as though he had a lifetime's problems balanced on his shoulders. The lines on his forehead were stark against his sallow skin, his face muscles sagging so he looked as if he had suffered a palsy.

Chests and towers of books, bundles of documents tied with black ribbons and dog-eared charts covered the floor of the cramped, dusty chamber. The stale air smelled of vinegary sweat, the rushes unchanged in days.

'Master Rowland. We feared we might miss you.' Almost hidden behind a pile of books and parchments on the trestle, Carpenter lounged in the record-keeper's chair. Launceston stood at the window, his back to the room, looking out over the inner ward.

In shock, Rowland cried out and dropped the two books.

'We offer our apologies for this intrusion,' came the Earl's monotone from the window. 'But matters are pressing, and politeness must wait its turn.'

'What do you want?' the record-keeper stuttered, gathering up the volumes and heaving them on to the only remaining space at the edge of the table. 'Did Secretary Cecil send you?'

Carpenter gave a faint smile, hidden quickly. 'Of course. Would we be here for any other reason?'

The Earl turned, tracing one finger through the silvery dust on a large volume. 'We seek to inspect the records of our former master, Sir Francis Walsingham, in particular those pertaining to the work carried out by Christopher Marlowe. Our interest lies in any task where he may have been accompanied by one Griffin Devereux. I understand accounts were kept of every matter of business carried out under instruction from Sir Francis?'

'They were.' Distracted, Rowland searched through a heap of parchments for a quill. 'Every piece of business conducted at home and on foreign soil. But you cannot inspect them.'

Carpenter jumped to his feet, knocking over a set of leathery books. Two silverfish scurried out from a spine. 'You would deny us?'

'I would deny you nothing, of course,' the record-keeper replied, unsettled by the scarred man's threatening demeanour. 'But I no longer have those records. They went missing on the day of Sir Francis' death.'

Launceston prowled around the table to take Rowland by the shoulders. 'Who took them?' he demanded.

'I do not know. I came to put them in order after the body had been interred and there was no sign of them. I could only imagine that Lord Burghley had ordered them to be removed for safe-keeping, but when I asked him, he had no knowledge of it.' Rowland pulled gently away from the Earl's grasp. 'I am sorry. I would help you if I could.'

Launceston exchanged a glance with Carpenter. 'Will was right. This plot has been in motion for years, and the track has been well covered.'

Raised voices echoed from the ground floor, punctuated by angry shouts and the cries of women. Exchanging a silent glance, Carpenter and Launceston bolted from the record-keeper's chamber. Outside the door, the two men ran straight into a concerned Nathaniel.

As they hurried along the corridor towards the source of the disturbance, the assistant slipped between the spies without meeting their gaze and hissed from the corner of his mouth, 'Will's chamber has been ransacked. Everything of value has been taken, including the play. I saw Roger Cockayne, one of Sir Robert Cecil's advisers, leaving with the sheaf of papers.'

'Damn them,' Carpenter growled. 'You must do whatever you can to retrieve that play. The information it contains could well be crucial, especially now.'

The raised voices rang off the stone walls. Inquisitive servants and curious ladies and gentlemen of the court streamed from chambers on either side, eager to discover what was causing the outcry.

'If you value your life you will not fail,' Launceston whispered.

'You do not need to threaten me,' Nathaniel replied. 'I am driven by my duty to Will, not fear.' The assistant slipped into the flow of curious people as they neared the top of the broad stone staircase that swept down into the entrance hall.

Standing at the back on tiptoes was Alice, her cheeks still flushed from the heat of the ovens, her apron white with dust from that morning's baking. Her face lit up when she saw the scarred spy. His own face fell.

Carpenter eased in beside his love and whispered, 'Alice, you must stay away from me from now on. I am a liability that will cost you your life.' Although he knew it was right to distance himself, he still felt heartsick and couldn't bring himself to look her in the face.

Yet when Alice turned her head slightly to whisper in his ear, her voice was defiant. 'I will do as I please. You may think yourself my master, but that is not the case. Yes, I will take care – I know the work you do is dangerous – but I survived my last brush with adventure, John, and I will survive the next. That is what love means.'

Afraid for her, Carpenter returned his attention to the commotion unfolding near the large, iron-studded door in the entrance hall. With Launceston beside him, he edged forward until he glimpsed a battered Will. Two of Essex's spies gripped his arms and the point of Strangewayes' rapier was pressed over his heart. Carpenter began to despair.

Hands clasped behind his back, the Earl of Essex strutted around his men, a faint smile playing on his lips. His eyes held a note of triumph as he gazed at the shorter, black-gowned figure of Cecil cowering on the edge of the group. For the first time the spymaster looked uneasy, if not frightened, Carpenter thought.

A defiant glint in his eye, Will stood proud and erect, his smile revealing no fear. 'I came here to warn of a plot against our Queen by our greatest enemy,' he announced. 'I will gladly go before the Privy Council to tell all that I know. We must be on our guard—'

Strangewayes cracked the hilt of his rapier into his rival's face, stunning Will for a moment. 'Enough of your lies!' the red-headed man spat. 'You will not wriggle out of this. Your past has caught up with you.'

Spattering blood on those nearby as he shook his head, Will reclaimed his wits. 'I do not lie,' he stated in a loud voice, 'and I will risk further punishment, even death, to tell the truth of what I have discovered. We are beset by enemies on all sides.'

The red-headed spy struck Will again with the hilt of his sword.

And then Carpenter noticed something that chilled him. All around, men with faces like whips were whispering in the ears of Essex and Cecil and most of the other Privy Councillors. Danby the coroner was there, passing comment, and Lord Derby, pink, broken-veined cheeks above his grey whiskers, moved among his fellows with a nod and a quiet word. Carpenter could think of only one thing.

Scar-Crow Men.

Shaping views. Infecting thoughts with sly words. Twisting the outcome to whatever would lead to victory for the Unseelie Court.

The scar-faced spy's heart began to pound. He glanced at Launceston and saw the grim-faced Earl was thinking the same. Carpenter began to suspect every face he looked into. How many agents were there? Who could be trusted?

A rush of urgent whispers swept through the crowd from the direction of the door leading to the palace's long eastern range. A wave of bowing heads followed.

Rustling a cloak of gold edged with ermine, the Queen stepped into the entrance hall accompanied by one of her maids of honour. Carpenter recognized the maid's plain looks and thick brown hair, but couldn't place her name. Elinor somebody or other, he thought. Elizabeth's face was a mask of white powder, but the scarred spy thought there was an odd cast to her features, a little dreamy as if she had only just woken.

'What is the meaning of this outcry?' the monarch demanded. Elinor stood unusually close to her mistress, her face turned towards the Queen's left ear.

'Your Majesty,' Will replied before any other could speak, 'I rode to Nonsuch this morning to warn of a plot against you, and against all of England.'

'A plot, Master Swyfte?' Elizabeth eyed the blood dripping from the spy's nose. 'Why is this the first I hear of this matter?'

'Because we do not seek to trouble Your Majesty with outrageous lies and calumnies,' Essex said with a flamboyant sweep of his arm. The monarch smiled at her most trusted courtier.

'Your Majesty, I implore you to listen to what I have to say,' Will pressed.

The Queen's eyes flashed at his impudence; one warning was all the spy would be allowed, Carpenter knew, and that only because he had been in Elizabeth's favour. 'Secretary of State,' she snapped. 'Master Swyfte is in your employ. What do you have to say?'

Cecil cast a dark glance towards the grinning Essex while he gathered his thoughts. Carpenter could almost see his master squirming as he struggled to find a way out of his predicament.

Here is your chance, at the last, Carpenter thought. *Stand up and offer your support for the man who has served you faithfully.*

'I have listened intently to the allegations of conspiracy made by this man,' the spymaster began in a clear voice, 'but I cannot say I find any truth in them.'

For a moment, Carpenter thought the Queen was about to dismiss the comment, but then he saw Elinor's lips move, only slightly, her words unheard. Elizabeth cocked her head to one side, a faint expression of bafflement springing to her face. She said in a quiet voice, 'What do you advise, my Little Elf?'

Cecil quickly extinguished the relief in his eyes and

feigned thoughtfulness, one finger to his chin. 'There is some suggestion of treason in Master Swyfte's actions, certainly, Your Majesty, though that would be a matter for the Privy Council to consider. And the earlier charge of atheism remains, of course. For those reasons, I feel the Tower may be the preferred option, while evidence is gathered and a case prepared.'

The Queen nodded.

Launceston stepped in close to Carpenter and whispered, 'All is well. We can free Will on the way to the Tower. There will be plenty of opportunities between Nonsuch and London for a cunning attack.'

For the first time that morning, Carpenter breathed a sigh of relief. There was still a chance to save something from the disaster that had unfolded with frightening speed.

Cockayne, the spymaster's adviser, had been edging closer while his master spoke and he suddenly darted forward to whisper in Cecil's ear. He was a small man, smaller even than the Little Elf, with a ruddy face and a shock of grey hair. Carpenter had seen him on the fringes of the secret service, but had never been wholly sure what he did.

The hunchbacked man listened intently for a moment and then announced, 'Your Majesty, please excuse me, but new evidence has just been brought to my attention. Master Swyfte has been overheard raving to merchants in Cheapside about necromancy and other even wilder tales. It is my advice that he has been afflicted with the mania and should be pitied and not condemned for his actions. To that end, he should be sent to Bedlam until the Privy Council can look into his case.'

'I hear your advice and it is good,' the Queen said. 'Dispatch

Master Swyfte to Bedlam immediately. And may God grant him peace from his suffering.'

Reeling, Carpenter looked to Launceston, but the Earl's face remained implacable. The Unseelie Court had won without a single weapon being drawn.

CHAPTER TWENTY-SEVEN

ALONG THE WINDING, NIGHT-SHROUDED ROAD LEADING TO THE Château de Pau, the trail of spectral carriages glowed with the lustre of pearl. Even the liveried horses and the coachmen, heads bowed, faces mercifully unseen, had the same misty luminescence, so that their appearances echoed the pale, glowing fish that lived in the deep cave pools of the nearby Pyrenees. Across the village clustering in the shadow of the castle, candles were extinguished and shutters closed so none would have to see what passed through their midst.

From a window atop the château's tallest tower, Henri de Navarre watched the procession with a grim face. Tanned and tall and dressed in his best clothes – a forest-green doublet studded with pearl buttons in the shape of the cross and a flamboyant white ruff – he carried himself with confidence, but he knew this night would test his abilities to the limit.

'They are ghost carriages!' Henri's loyal adviser, Maximilien de Béthune, duc de Sully, gasped. Raising a trembling arm to point, the black-gowned, balding former soldier stood transfixed next to his master. 'See, they appear from nowhere. The road is empty and then, suddenly, the carriages are there.'

'The Unseelie Court enjoy their shows of spectacle,' the

elegant ruler replied, drawing himself up straight and folding his hands behind his back. 'Breathe deeply, Maximilien, and hold fast. We have faced worse than this.'

'You still feel this is the correct course?' the adviser enquired.

'There is no other. Europe is as turbulent as ever, and we must chart a smooth course if we are to bring all of France together,' the tall, black-bearded man said in a soothing voice. 'We are close to our long-held aim. The Catholic League is in disarray, and Philip of Spain falters. We must hold fast for this final heave, however testing it may be.'

The carriages trundled on to the six-arched stone bridge across the Gave de Pau, the waters black under the star-sprinkled sky.

'Surely the Unseelie Court cannot be trusted as allies?' the black-garbed man said.

Henri laughed. 'None of our allies can be trusted. That is the way of this world, Maximilien. The Unseelie Court want what they want. We have our own aims. Somewhere there is common ground. But when they have served their purpose, we will drive them out.'

'You think you can manipulate them in that way? With all their power?'

'Elizabeth has succeeded in England. We can too.'

The battle-scarred adviser cast an eye towards his master. 'And this threat they hold over our heads, these Scar-Crow Men, has no part in your calculations?'

The King waved a dismissive hand and said with a hint of bravado, 'There are always threats, my friend. We deal with each one in turn, as we always have. Now, will you greet our guests and bring them to our table?'

His features etched with concern, Maximilien gave a bow

and strode from the chamber. Once the door had closed, Henri let his brave smile fall, lines of worry appearing on his strong face. Taking a deep, steadying breath, he left the chamber and descended the spiral stone steps to the grand hall. It was ablaze with candlelight, for he could not abide any shadows when confronted by those foul creatures.

Along the middle of the high, beamed chamber was an oaken table with a daringly constructed centrepiece, a representation of the château surrounded with peacock feathers, lavender, violets and other fragrant flowers picked from the gardens that afternoon. Beside it stood an enormous pie, the crust formed in the shape of a crown, gilt and silvered so it shone in the candlelight. It contained an entire salted stag, a goose, six chickens and a rabbit. The rich aroma of the cooked meats and gravy filled the air, with underlying notes of the subtle spices of northern Spain. That was only the appetizer. The kitchens had worked hard all day to prepare a feast grander than any enjoyed by the crowned heads of Europe.

It was all part of a play, Henri knew, but the Unseelie Court were at their least dangerous when they were flattered. For a moment, he surveyed the gold and silver platters, the sparkling goblets and jugs of blood-red wine until he was sure all was perfectly presented. On his way into the annexe, he paused before the large, gloomy portrait of François hanging over the great stone fireplace where fresh-cut logs crackled and spat. He bowed his head briefly, knowing the old King would understand. The path of the monarch was never easy.

From the adjoining chamber window, he watched the carriages draw up at the château's main entrance, but he pulled away before the occupants climbed out. After long, tense moments, Maximilien knocked and opened the door of the annexe. Putting on a warm smile, Henri stepped into the great hall.

With his very first glance across the assembled crowd, he felt a deep chill. Was he surveying a tableau arranged from the contents of a crypt? Bone-white, cadaverous faces were turned towards him, black-ringed, unblinking eyes staring. Nothing moved. The clothes were flamboyant, mirroring no current fashion but somehow capturing elements of the clothes worn by the King's ancestors across the centuries: voluminous shirts, bucklers, tied breeches and jerkins on the men, large skirts embroidered in odd designs and studded with pearls and white jewels on the women, their necklines plunging, their hair sculpted and dressed with more glittering jewels. Yet the scene was drained of colour. The clothes were grey, and there was an air of decay about them; they appeared to be dusted with mildew and were worn and scuffed with dirt as if they had lain long in the ground. To accompany that notion, the air was filled with the oppressive scent of clay.

Yet this vision passed in the blink of an eye so that Henri convinced himself it had been an illusion. Now the men all appeared handsome with square jaws and sharp cheekbones, their skin still pale but touched with a faint golden glow. The women had full lips, their thickly lashed eyes gleaming seductively. The clothes, however, remained the same grey, worn, strangely cut styles. Henri felt an odd queasiness at the juxtaposition of grave and voluptuous life, and as he looked around the faces he saw an unsettling hunger there, as if he were part of the coming feast.

'Welcome to my home, honoured guests,' he boomed, throwing his arms wide and laughing with studied joy.

One of the males rose from the foot of the table, stepping away from his place to approach the King with slow, languid steps. He sported long silver hair with a streak of black running down the centre, and was uncommonly tall and painfully thin, towering over Henri by a head, yet there was a graceful strength to his every movement. His eyes flashed emerald. Clinging to his arm was a hairless, ape-like creature with golden eyes. It stared at Henri too long, too hard. The Fay bowed, but undercut the show of respect with a faintly mocking smile.

'And we are honoured to be in the presence of such a formidable ruler as Henri de Navarre. News of your prowess has reached even to our distant homes,' the guest said with a slight sibilance. 'My name is Lethe. I am the most senior member of the High Family here this evening. Some of my brothers and sisters have accompanied me, but sadly not all. There is pressing business across this world that requires the attention of my other siblings.'

The King bowed in return, continuing to smile though his breath was tight in his chest. 'You have shown me great respect in bringing so many of your family here to my home,' he said.

'That only shows what great importance we place upon events now unfolding, and the value we see in having the great Henri de Navarre alongside,' the spokesman for the Unseelie Court replied.

You need me, the French monarch thought, *as I need you.*

With a knitting of his brow that suggested irritation, Lethe studied Henri closely as if he had read the King's thoughts, and then he swept an elegant arm towards his companions. 'Come. Let me introduce you to the other members of my family.'

The tall, thin man led the way to a beautiful woman who sat at his left hand, shining hazel hair tumbling around her bare shoulders. Her allure extended far beyond her appearance. Everything about her drew Henri's attention. She eyed the King with a look he had only ever seen in the brothels of

Paris, but then she shifted that very same glance to her brother. The tips of her fingers brushed Lethe's gently, the touch crackling like a summer storm with such passion that the French monarch was repulsed. 'Malantha is our ambassador to the court of King Philip of Spain,' the thin man said, holding his sister's gaze.

'You are a handsome man, King Henri. I look forward to enjoying your company,' she breathed.

The monarch found the clear suggestion in her words almost obscene, though he continued to smile politely. 'I am sure even a man of such devout ways as Philip finds you entrancing,' he said with a bow. Malantha and Lethe exchanged a knowing glance.

Sitting opposite the seductive woman was a man so grotesquely fat he occupied two places. His head was shaven, his piggy eyes peering out beneath a heavy brow, his nose squashed, his lips plump and broad. Thick rolls of flesh fell from his jowls to his shoulders and he was naked to the waist, so that he appeared to be carved out of wax. His huge, hairless belly glistened with sweat. He was as ugly as the other members of the Unseelie Court were decadently beautiful. His eyes brightened as they fell on Henri. 'You are a handsome man,' he said in a buttery voice. 'I heard the women were drawn to you, and now I see why.'

Chilled by the manner in which the fat man eyed him, Henri gave a curt bow.

'Brother Globelus enjoys many pleasures,' said Lethe, laughing. 'His hunger is never sated.'

The King hid the relief he felt at moving on to the fourth and final member of the High Family present, but his unease returned just as quickly when he found himself beside a man with long jet-black hair and a sallow complexion, his beard and moustache waxed into points. The stern figure's black eyes flashed with unconcealed hatred, but he would not let his gaze linger on Henri for even a moment. 'Lansing,' the Unseelie Court's spokesman said. There was an odd note in his voice that made the French monarch think even Lethe was unnerved by this brother. 'He speaks little, but sees all.'

The tall, thin man chose to ignore the other members of the Unseelie Court seated around the table and the ones watching with dark eyes from the far end of the great hall. Henri felt the tension in his chest ease when he could finally take his seat at the head of the table.

'Eat, then. Enjoy all that this house has to offer,' the monarch announced, pouring himself a large goblet of wine. But not one of the Unseelie Court made a move towards the food before them. They all continued to watch the King with those eerie, unblinking stares. Henri took a long draught to calm himself and then asked, 'How goes your business in England?'

'Well,' Malantha replied, her eyes on the King from under heavy lids. 'Our plans progress as we intended. Slowly but surely.'

Lansing spat on the rushes scattered across the floor. 'Blood will run like rivers and the smoke of the pyres will blacken the skies. And not before time.'

'We have more than one reason to crush them beneath our boots,' Lethe said, glancing around his brothers and sister. 'Cavillex will not be forgotten.'

Globelus waved a fat finger at the French monarch. 'You are not concerned that your ally will soon be destroyed? England has long offered you support, has it not?'

'I fear Elizabeth would not have been an ally for much longer anyway,' the French monarch replied. 'It is my desire to unite my country and to return to Paris to rule, but the Catholic

League have been obstructive. However, I plan to renounce Protestantism shortly. That will disarm my Catholic enemies abroad and console the Papist population at home, and I will be free to complete my plans.'

A ripple of laughter ran around the table. Flushing, Henri felt the humour was at his expense, directed at his belief that what he said was in any way important. 'Why take an interest in so small a country? I would have thought England beneath your notice,' he said in a sharp tone that he instantly regretted.

After a moment's silence, Malantha gave another of her shiver-inducing smiles and whispered, 'Our plans now extend far beyond England. In the peace of our homes, we were content to see your kind as,' she paused, searching for the correct word, 'entertainment. Our gentle sport was viewed too harshly by the people of that foul land, and they sought to harm us. Deceive us. When all we offered was kindness. We realized, sadly, that we could no longer ignore threats made against us.'

'The fields in which we played have become the fields in which we fight,' Lansing added, his words laced with cruelty.

Henri wished he did not have to deal with these creatures, nor did he want to bring harm to any God-fearing man or woman at home or abroad. When he saw Lethe studying him again, however, he drove the thoughts from his mind and said quickly, 'So France remains important in your plans?'

'England's defences slowly crumble,' Malantha replied, waving one hand in the air, 'and when they finally fall we must be prepared to move. France is perfectly sited for a speedy response.'

'We thank you for your offer of aid,' Lethe added, tracing one finger along the cleft in his smooth chin.

The French king poured himself another goblet of wine,

knowing he must never lose control of his abilities in front of the Unseelie Court but unable to refrain from drinking. 'I am glad to be of help,' he said, 'though I am sure your Scar-Crow Men would have *encouraged* my assistance had I not been forthcoming.' Once again he regretted speaking out of turn.

But this time the Unseelie Court only laughed. 'Who are these Scar-Crow Men?' Lethe said, sharing a glance with Malantha that he did not mind Henri seeing.

'If I knew that, my life would be much easier.' The King sipped his wine, the goblet hiding the contempt that played on his lips. 'I hear whispers . . . rumours. It is always difficult to pick truth from such things. But I fear it is not always wise to trust anyone, even those I have known all my life.'

'Why, you think we have agents everywhere, nudging you in the direction we require?' Globelus said, laughing silently so his entire frame shook.

'That cannot be,' Henri replied. 'For if it were true, you would not need to come here this night and everyone in Europe would be your puppets.'

A shadow crossed Globelus' face. Lansing scowled.

'And that tells me that if there are Scar-Crow Men, there must be some shortcomings in the plot.' The King took his knife and sliced an apple into quarters.

Malantha's smile grew wider, her full lips parting to reveal small, white teeth. 'A wise man would never make assumptions,' she said in a mellifluous tone. 'A knife will never be cannon, but it can still steal a life.' She clapped her hands twice. 'Now, enjoy your meats, Henri, and sup your wine, for life's pleasures pass quickly. For your kind. We will discuss our plans later, and draw up our treaty, and then, for a little while at least, Paris shall be ours. For now, the night has fallen and the moon is full. This is our time.'

At the end of the hall, two of the silent watchers drew fiddles from velvet sacks. Placing the instruments under their chins, they began to play a duelling melody, mournful at first. But gradually the tempo increased and the notes soared, summoning a sound that was both dark and exhilarating. Malantha rose and held out her hand for Lethe. Within a moment they were spinning around the room in each other's arms. Two by two, the other members of the Unseelie Court joined them, until the entire hall was a whirl of dancing and the furious fiddle music rang from the beams.

Henri sat alone at the table with his goblet of wine, the fine banquet spread out before him, untouched.

As they twirled by, Lethe bent Malantha back so that her lips were close to the King's ear. 'Trust no one,' she breathed.

CHAPTER TWENTY-EIGHT

GRACE'S HEART BEAT FAST AS SHE WATCHED THE QUEEN'S MEN from the window. In the inner ward, under the glaring red lamp of the setting sun, they marched in step, back and forth, back and forth, the tramp of their black leather shoes providing a relentless background rhythm to life at Nonsuch. A bloody crimson sash fell across their burnished cuirasses, and there was blood on their minds too.

With each passing day, the young woman found the atmosphere in the palace more unbearable: suspicion, fear and doubt wrapped around them all like a shroud.

Grace hurried along the corridor, avoiding the knots of advisers and Privy Councillors who had been huddling in quiet, intense conversation everywhere for the two weeks since Will had been hauled off to Bedlam. Talk of traitors operating within the court had unnerved everyone.

Carrying a jug of fresh water for the Queen's ablutions, Elinor approached. She nodded to Grace and gave a humourless smile, but her gaze was as sharp as a dagger. As Grace passed, she heard the maid of honour come to a halt and turn. *Watching me*, the young woman thought. *Spying.*

As she moved through the palace, Grace felt eyes upon her

everywhere. A serving girl pausing with a bowl of eggs. A Privy Councillor, crow-like in his black gown, watching her with implacable beady eyes. Two knights stopping their conversation to study her as she passed.

You will drive yourself mad with this worry, she repeated to herself.

Grace waited at the end of the corridor until Elinor's footsteps had faded away and then she opened the small door in the panelled wall and stepped into the tight-winding back stairs. At the foot, she listened to ensure the kitchen workers had left the area before crossing the flour-sprinkled kitchen annexe that still smelled sweetly of the honey cakes that had been prepared for that evening's meal.

Skipping to the door, she slipped out into the warm evening. A cloud of midges swirled in the sun's last rays. Breathing deeply to ease the tightness in her chest, she smelled the lavender from the formal gardens and the rosemary and mint planted in rows just outside the kitchen door.

Dressed in his best brown doublet embroidered with patterns of green ivy, Nathaniel waited near the orange-brick garden wall, still warm from the day's sun. He offered her a posy and bowed formally, his cheeks and large ears glowing a dull red. Grace laughed quietly and gave a small curtsy. Will's assistant played his part well, she thought.

'Good evening, Grace. Will you walk with me a while?' he asked in a clear voice that carried across the gardens.

'I will,' she replied, 'though I cannot be long. I still have work.'

Shoulder to shoulder, hands clasped behind their backs, they walked away from Nonsuch through the winding paths of the gardens, looking, as Grace had hoped, like two young lovers on a quiet romantic stroll. Once out of sight of the palace

211

behind a tall row of yews, they moved quickly through the gate in the wall into the deer park.

Nathaniel's face darkened as he offered Grace a hand over the large stones thrown across the rutted path that ran between two banks of nettles. 'We take a risk, even now,' he whispered.

'All is risk,' the young woman stated firmly. 'I hardly dare breathe in the palace for fear of a hand on my shoulder. There is talk that two of the boys from the stables and three kitchen workers have already been taken away for crimes unknown. If we are to help, we must act.'

'I do not disagree,' Nat said, 'but that does not make this any easier. Even two lovers out on a summer's eve is a cause for suspicion in this atmosphere.' He led the way along the line of the wall until they reached the edge of the palace grounds. 'I hoped to visit Will in Bedlam to see they were treating him well, but I was told the Keeper has orders to admit no one.'

'Nor is there any escape from that foul place. It is worse than Newgate,' Grace replied. She had vowed to shed no tears in public for the man she held so deeply in her affections, nor to offer even a word that would reveal any anxiety over his fate. That would not help. Only a clear head and a strong heart would be of use.

The bats were already flitting from their roosts in the dark woods that lay beyond the rolling grassland surrounding the palace. Steeling herself, Grace plucked up her skirts and ran, with Nathaniel close beside her, glancing back every few steps to see if they were being pursued. Even when they reached the shelter of the trees, the young woman still expected to hear cries of alarm at her back.

Ducking under the low-hanging branches, they avoided the thick banks of briar and progressed fifty paces into the cool, shadowy interior. Nathaniel brought them to a halt and gave a short, low whistle. After a moment it was answered away to their right. Stumbling in the growing gloom, they came to an old oak tree that five men linking hands could not have encompassed. As they looked around, two figures dropped from the branches as silently and stealthily as cats.

Carpenter pressed a finger to his lips as Launceston prowled the perimeter, one hand cupped to his ear as he peered into the dark beneath the trees. Their cloaks were smeared with mud and the green of tree bark from three days of living rough.

'Let me go to Bedlam to try to help Will,' Grace said, once they had exchanged curt greetings.

'What could a woman do?' the pallid spy sneered.

She raised her chin defiantly and fought to keep her voice steady. 'I would remind you, sir, who sits on the throne.' Ignoring the Earl's quizzically raised eyebrow, she continued, 'In the past, I have been reckless—'

'I recall risking life and limb in Spain trying to save your foolish life,' Carpenter snarled.

'I am not that same woman who strode blithely into danger following her heart. Wisdom has come to me, later than I might have hoped, but there it is. I will do anything in my power to aid Will in his hour of need, and to help save our Queen from this plot. Do not underestimate me, Master Carpenter.'

Shrugging, the spy flashed a smirk at Launceston which only made Grace angrier.

'Listen to her,' Nathaniel interjected. 'We all walk different paths, and we all have different parts to play in this business. Grace can help as much as any man.'

'As much?' Launceston said in a quiet, strong voice. 'Can she slit a throat? For this matter will come to blood in the end. There is no other way.'

Drawing his dagger, the Earl turned suddenly and peered into the dark. Leaves rustled in the breeze. Tense, they all grew still, but after a moment he returned his blade to its hiding place though his gaze continued to search the gloom.

'Robert and I will maintain our search in London for whoever has been killing our fellow spies,' Carpenter whispered. 'Once we have him, we should find out more about this plot. You do what you can here at Nonsuch.' He sighed. 'Though London is no place to be these days, with rumours of curses and magics and the corpses of plague victims moving of their own accord down in the pits.'

'How . . . how long do we have before they make a move on Will's life?' Grace ventured.

The scarred spy shook his head. 'Not so quick that it will look like the law is being circumvented. Not so long that he will prove a threat to the plotters.' He ran a weary hand through his long hair, revealing the ugly mass of pink tissue on the side of his face. 'Two spies, a fool and a woman against our Enemy,' he sighed. 'Kill us now and be done with it.'

Nathaniel bristled. Holding up a hand to calm him, Grace stepped close to the spy. 'It is time to stop complaining, Master Carpenter, and to accept that the four of us here are all we have. And we shall not be easily defeated, even if it costs my life.'

The scar-faced man eyed her curiously, struck by the passion in her voice.

'Who are the enemy?' Nathaniel snapped, still annoyed at being called a fool. 'The Spanish? Catholic agitators?'

Carpenter and Launceston exchanged a glance and weighed their words. After a moment, the Earl breathed, 'It does not matter which hands move the pieces in this game. The ones we must be concerned with at the moment are our own – our former allies, perhaps even our friends. We must be prepared to be betrayed on any side.'

'Can we trust each other?' Nathaniel pressed, his jaw set.

Before anyone could respond, their attention was caught by flickering lights moving far off among the trees; some were pale, some blazed red and gold like torches.

Nat caught the scarred spy's arm and hissed, 'Guards from the palace hunting for us.'

Carpenter's face drained of blood. He shook his head slowly.

'We must leave this place. Now,' Launceston snapped. 'We have little time.'

Breathlessly, they ran towards the edge of the woods, the lights closing on them.

'What are they?' Grace gasped, almost stumbling as she leapt over exposed roots. 'How do they move so fast?'

'No questions!' Carpenter snapped. 'Save your breath. And do not look back under any circumstances.'

On every side, the lights moved through the trees faster than any man could run. Grace's heart pounded with the rhythm of her feet.

As they closed on the edge of the woods, Launceston raised a hand to slow them, and then waved them behind a twisted old oak. Ahead, there was only a short run across the open grassland to what Grace told herself was the safety of the palace garden walls. A thin line of fiery light remained along the western horizon. Soon it would be dark.

Grace could see Launceston had heard something. His dagger drawn, the Earl stalked around the tree, keeping low. The young woman felt her heart would burst.

The lights glowed dangerously close.

A cry of alarm tore through the stillness. Spinning round, Grace saw one of the Earl of Essex's advisers standing beside a

215

tall elm tree, pointing at them. The lanky, ruddy-faced man's mouth hung wide and the jarring, high-pitched sound he was making was like iron on glass.

All around, the lights began to change direction. In an instant, Launceston had darted from the shelter of the oak and plunged his dagger into the neck of the pointing man. The shrieking ended with a sticky gurgle.

As Carpenter reached the Earl's side, Grace darted towards the two spies with Nathaniel close behind. But as she neared, she saw horror become etched in the scarred man's face as he glanced at the body of the adviser.

Turning suddenly, the spy held up his hands and shouted, 'Stay away! Do not look at the body! Do not look!' Carpenter bounded towards the woman. 'Run!' he shouted. 'Back to the palace, before they see your faces!'

Behind the spy, the lights swirled and drew near. In their faint glow, Grace thought she could now see shapes, like foxes, though larger, grey and indistinct, bounding sinuously among the trees towards them.

Turning, she lifted her skirts and ran towards the comforting candlelight of the palace. Nathaniel was by her side, urging her on.

At her back, she heard the pounding of the two spies' feet as they began to follow, but then the sound took a different direction and was accompanied by Carpenter's furious cursing and his companion's loud mockery. The two men were trying to draw the pursuers away, Grace realized.

Sacrificing themselves for me, she thought, her eyes stinging with tears.

A ferocious spitting and snarling erupted at her back, and she almost stumbled in terror. She had heard nothing like that sound before. Dimly amid the cacophony, Grace heard the two spies shouting in defiance.

Crashing through the gate in the garden wall, the young man held it open until they were both safely through and then slammed it shut. They ran on along the winding paths amid the perfume of night-scented stock, the terrible animal sounds dying down until only silence lay across the countryside.

Hidden in the dark by the palace walls, they came to a halt, leaning against the warm brick to catch their breath. Grace was crying silently, and she wiped her tears away with the back of her hand before Nathaniel saw. 'What . . . what was that?' she croaked. Her thoughts were like mercury, unable to make sense of what she had seen and heard.

The assistant took a deep breath and then said with a confidence that she knew was for her benefit, 'The enemy agents are accompanied by hunting dogs. That is how they discovered us so quickly.'

The woman found it easier to accept his explanation. She glanced back along the dark garden and asked in a quiet voice, 'Master Carpenter and the Earl of Launceston – are they alive or are they dead?'

CHAPTER TWENTY-NINE

THE LOW MOANS OF LOST SOULS DRIFTED LIKE THE WIND ACROSS frozen wastes. Bloodcurdling screams of agony punctuated the slow, constant exhalation of despair. In the eternal night of Bedlam there was no rest, nor easing of spiritual pain. No hope, no joy, no friendships, no love.

Pressed into the corner of his cramped cell on a thin covering of filthy straw, Will Swyfte listened, and waited. His time would come. In the midst of the enveloping misery, his vigilance was kept alive by the slow-burning fire of his anger. Despite the cold iron of the manacles that gripped his ankles, he would not give in, for Kit's sake, and the sake of all the others now at risk from the creeping plot of the Unseelie Court.

The choking stink of excrement filled the air from the overflowing vault beneath the madhouse. Across the entire floor of the Abraham Ward the straw heaved and rustled as scurrying rats searched for the meagre morsels of food dropped by the inmates. In the night, their high-pitched squeaking only added to the chorus of suffering. Sometimes the spy was sure he could hear another sound echoing deep in the background: the cries of Griffin Devereux rising up from the depths, as if the black magician somehow knew Will was now incarcerated in Bedlam too.

Purple bruises patchworked the spy's face and body and every joint ached from the ferocious beatings he had endured. The men Cecil had dispatched to escort Will to the hospital had treated him as they would any other traitor, with fists and feet and pricks of daggers, just for sport. But once the gates of the feared lock-up had clanged shut, the true pain had begun. Still seething from his treatment at Will's hands, the Keeper had found new sport in an inmate whose fame reached far beyond the walls of London.

'You raised yourself above me, and now you are beneath me. Indeed, beneath all men,' the key-holder had growled before launching the first of many assaults. Will had resisted, but, hampered by manacles and ropes, he could do little but soak up the pain until unconsciousness freed him from the agony.

With his eyes now used to the permanent half-light, he watched the stained door. The beatings would continue, but his time would come, and then there would be vengeance aplenty.

As his gaze fell away, Will thrust himself back against the damp stone wall in shock. He was not alone. Sitting in the corner opposite him was Jenny. She wore the same blue dress he recalled from the day she disappeared, but her pale skin was now mottled, her black eyes dark-ringed as though she were being consumed by sickness. She eyed him through a curtain of lank, dirty hair, her too-thin arms wrapped around her legs. In her face the spy saw none of the love he remembered. Instead there was coldness, and suspicion, and perhaps contempt, as if she would never forgive him for abandoning her.

Everything about her appearance was designed to hurt, and

even though Will knew that was the intent, he could not meet her gaze.

'And so Griffin Devereux was correct. I now have my own devil, like Faustus in Kit's play, to tempt me with sweet words and thereby condemn me to eternal suffering.' The spy laughed without humour. 'But you waste your time, creature of the dark – what do I call you? Mephistophilis, in honour of my friend? 'Twill suffice. For one, according to the words Kit wrote, it was Faustus who condemned himself. He opened the door. His devil only held it wide for the man to pass through. I will not make that mistake.' Will stretched out his legs to ease the ache from the manacles. 'And second, I do not believe in hell, or heaven for that matter. There is no hand of a loving God in the suffering I have witnessed in my life. And damnation is here with us, not waiting at the end of our lives. Men are the devils, inflicting pain upon their own for personal gain.'

'Your bitter thoughts will hollow out your soul.'

The spy was sickened by the voice. It had the gravelly, phlegm-tinged tones of an old man, yet it issued from the full lips that he had kissed those years ago on the edge of the Forest of Arden. 'Why go through these trials, if all is as you say?' the devil continued. 'If you believe this life is pointless, end it now and be done with it.'

Will kicked out at a rat which had been eyeing his bare feet. 'I see you would find pleasure in my passing, which only encourages me to grip tighter to life,' he replied.

'You think after the cruelties inflicted by the Unseelie Court that there is anything left of the Jenny you recall so fondly? You think she can return to a simple life in Warwickshire when she has been so spoiled?'

'Quiet!' the spy snarled. The chains clattered as he lunged

forward, but the manacles stopped him long before he got near the dark presence.

Mephistophilis gave only the faintest smile, but it was tinged with triumph. 'What will you do when you find her and she begs you to end her life? When you look into her eyes and see no love there, no hope, no softness? When you see only Bedlam, for ever?'

Will regained his composure, leaning back against the glistening stone even though the turmoil still raged inside him. 'I thank you,' the spy said in a calm voice. 'In harsh times, it is easy to lose your way and give in to hopelessness. But you have fanned the flames of my anger, and that will light my way in even the darkest night.'

Mephistophilis didn't move, its gaze heavy and unwavering. A fly crawled in the lank hair.

'So you have found your voice now,' the man continued. 'Will you explain the vision you showed me when we first met in the Rose Theatre?'

The devil shook its head with slow, deliberate moves. 'Knowledge or power is never given freely, and you have nothing to offer me. Your soul is already damned. I will torment you in this dark place through your few remaining days, and then I will take your life, and that small, misty thing that makes you who you are.'

'I have heard worse threats,' Will said blandly.

The rat returned, scurrying up to the form of Jenny. It sniffed at the skin of her foot and rolled over, dead.

'Here you sit, in the dark and the filth,' the devil whispered, 'a man who lives by his sword, now impotent. And while you rot away, death moves ever closer to the ones you love, and a shadow as dark and cold as the final night falls across your country. And still you see only a small part of the plot.'

'What do you mean?' Will's knuckles grew white where they gripped the rusty chain that held him fast.

'Your great foe has grown weary of the blows you have struck against it down the years.' The devil lowered its head slightly so the black eyes were almost invisible behind the wall of hair. 'A Queen stolen. Then a member of their ruling family slaughtered like a beast in the field. Every blow struck by each side contributing to a mounting spiral of agony. But now they have called, "Enough!"'

The spy studied the brooding demonic presence to try to pick any truth from the stream of lies. He sensed, however, that on this occasion Mephistophilis felt he could cause more damage by openness.

'Your Enemy sees there is nothing to gain from this carefully balanced war,' the devil continued. 'They have had their fill of the little irritations you pose. Away from the light of your attention, they weave their web, across this entire world. They stir great powers. They draw darkness up from the depths. They plot death and destruction on a scale only dreamed of by gods. War, plague, starvation – they pull these threads together, slowly but relentlessly, and by the time you see the shape of their thoughts it will be too late. Your kind are an infestation, in their eyes. A plague. And they will not rest until you have been eradicated.'

CHAPTER THIRTY

THEY'RE COMING.

Slipping out into the moonlit corridor, Nathaniel was sickened to realize that once again he had been tormented by the dream that had haunted him for nigh on five years. Ghastly, cruel faces looming out of the shadows. Under a full moon, grey, fluttering shapes pursuing him across a lonely moor. And a feeling of dread so great that upon waking he was left in a pool of sweat, his heart pounding. But this time the terrible things they had whispered to him were new and strange. Who was coming?

The way is beginning to open.

What way? Was he losing his wits?

The assistant had only closed his eyes for a while until the palace had drifted off into sleep and he could slip into Roger Cockayne's chamber and steal back the play. Laced with mockery, the echoes of the dream-words still rustled around his head.

As he entered the corridor in the western range, the young man paused. He heard a whisper of movement off in the dark towards the far end. Glancing around, he saw the only hiding place was in an alcove beside a large iron-studded chest underneath a gloomy portrait of Old Henry, the Queen's father. As he eased into the space and crouched down, pulling his cloak over him, he noticed several doors were silently opening.

Mouthing a silent prayer, he peeked out through a fold in his cloak. Five hooded figures skulked past, paying no attention to each other. What mischief would those creeping figures be planning at that time of night? he wondered. Who were they that they kept their faces hidden?

His suspicions mounting, he held his breath and waited.

Once he was sure the men had passed, Nat slipped out of his hiding place. Hoofbeats and the rattle of carriage wheels now echoed in the inner ward.

Through the window, the young man glimpsed a black coach stark in the moonlight. He saw it was adorned with peacock feathers, and so the property of someone high and mighty, perhaps a Privy Councillor. Unsure why, he felt a tingle of unease.

A cloaked and hooded man jumped down from the coach and held out his hand for a second passenger. A pale, slender hand extended from the shadows, a woman, Nat realized. As she stepped down to the cobbles, the assistant saw she too hid her identity in the depths of a hood.

A pikeman ambled up from the direction of the gatehouse, his burgonet and cuirass agleam in the pale light. The woman and her escort paused, their heads turned away from the approaching man.

Nathaniel felt an incomprehensible dread. As the pikeman stepped up, the escort whipped a gleaming dagger from the depths of his cloak and thrust it under the guard's chin and into his skull. Withdrawing his blade just as quickly, the hooded man stepped back to avoid the gush of crimson as the poor pikeman fell to the cobbles.

The young assistant clutched the wall in shock. The murder of a pikeman, in the open, within the palace ward? The like had never been heard of before.

On the brink of raising the alarm, Nathaniel froze when he saw shadows sweeping across the open space from the palace. More men, all cloaked and hooded, perhaps some of them the ones who had passed him earlier. He thought he counted ten at least, but they moved too quickly for him to be sure, collecting the body of the pikeman and carrying it out of sight towards the western range. The escort led the mysterious woman to the palace as if nothing had happened.

Nat's heart beat faster.

Silently, he ran back the way he had come. At the first set of stone steps, he began to creep down in search of the plotters, only to hear several soft treads rising from around the turn in the stairs. His breath caught in his chest. Dashing back into the corridor, he searched around, unsure where was the best place to hide.

As the footsteps neared, the young man pressed himself into a doorway, hoping the hooded figures would not pass by. Screwing his eyes tight shut, he prayed.

The footsteps emerged into the corridor and moved away from him. Peeking out, Nathaniel glimpsed the hooded figures with the woman among them gliding stealthily towards the Queen's throne room, where she oversaw the meetings of the Privy Council almost every day.

What could the plotters possibly want in that chamber? It would be empty at this time of night, and there was nowhere to hide; it contained only the throne, for the Privy Councillors always stood in Her Majesty's presence.

Stepping out from the doorway, Nathaniel resolved to follow. He had barely gone ten paces along the moonlit corridor when he realized his mistake. A single set of footsteps was approaching from the direction of the throne room. As he turned, he glimpsed a flurry of movement at the other end of the corridor; more plotters were drawing near.

Trapped.

Just as Nat thought his heart would burst in his chest, he felt a hand clamp across his mouth and he was dragged back into a chamber. The door whispered shut behind him and a woman's voice hissed in his ear, 'Make no sound.'

His body pressed against the wood panelling in the inky room, the assistant's eyes grew wide with terror. The footsteps approached. If the fingers had not been clamped so tight against his mouth, he was afraid he would have called out, but then the plotters passed by and he sagged with relief.

His saviour withdrew her hand.

'You,' he whispered, shocked.

In the gloom, the young man recognized the red-headed woman he had encountered outside the Rose Theatre. 'Lady . . . Shevington?' She too was cloaked and hooded, and for a moment he wondered if she was another of the plotters.

'Do you always lumber around at night like a wounded bull?' the Irish woman murmured as she opened the door a crack and peered out into the now-still corridor.

Nathaniel made to ask another question, but the woman pressed a finger to her lips to silence him and stepped out. With her cloak billowing around her, she ghosted through the shadows on the edge of the moonbeams towards the throne room. The assistant wanted to call out a warning – there would have been no time for the plotters to leave the chamber – but she was too far ahead.

Nat's thoughts were a ball of confusion. He no longer had any idea what was happening, nor why the Irish woman was prowling the palace at night. Conflicted, he caught up with Lady Shevington as she pressed her ear to the door, her brow furrowed. All was silent.

Gripped with horror, Nathaniel saw her reach for the handle, and though he lunged to stop her, she swung the door open.

The throne room was empty.

CHAPTER THIRTY-ONE

BLOOD SPATTERED INTO THE FILTHY, URINE-STINKING STRAW scattered across the floor of the Abraham Ward. Will slammed into the stone flags, and before he could dispel the ringing in his skull, he felt fire blaze in his ribs, his thighs, his arms, his chest. Cudgels rained down. Foot after foot lashed out. He felt new agony sear upon old, but the ropes binding his hands behind his back gave him no chance of escape.

Through the haze of pain he could hear a cacophony of shrieks, roars and catcalls, which sounded to him like feeding time at the Queen's menagerie at the Tower. A crowd of Bedlam's lost souls turned away from the display of violence, tearing at their greasy hair or pressing their hollow-cheeked faces into their filthy hands, fearing they would be next. The other inmates slumped in blank stupors in their dank cells, but still moaned with each blow struck.

The three burly men surrounding Will paused, hands on knees, breath wheezing into chests that were unused to such concerted exertion. Through one half-closed eye, the battered man could see that his tormentors were little more than cut-throats and rogues, giving up their time drinking cheap ale to take the Keeper's coin. Hair and beards unkempt, their doublets were worn and stained, the colours faded into muddy browns and greys, their jerkins mottled with the dirt of the street.

'You dance around me like maids at the maypole,' Will croaked through split lips, his swollen left cheek distorting his words.

Angered, a heavy-set roisterer with broken veins on his chapped cheeks snarled and stepped in to launch another kick. Will rolled out of the way, and the attacker stumbled off-balance, his scuffed leather shoe swinging in mid-air. Continuing his roll, the spy drove his legs up sharply into the back of the brutish man's supporting knee. With a surprised cry, the rogue crashed down. Drawing his knees together, Will rammed them against his attacker's jaw. There was a crack like a snapping branch and the lower part of the man's face skewed to one side. His agonized howl became a feeble whimper.

'One down, two to go,' Will muttered, his body numb from two weeks of beatings.

The remaining two attackers stared in shock for a moment and then assaulted Will with furious blows from their cudgels. One shattered on impact, so great was the force. 'He is a madman,' the wiry assailant said as he threw the broken weapon away. 'Bedlam is the right place for him.'

The spy gave in to the waves of pain, letting his thoughts find solace in the depths of his memory. It was a skill he had learned to master. This time he recalled Kit, and the first time they met, ten years ago on the second day of Christmas. Thick snow had blanketed the rooftops of Corpus Christi College in Cambridge, but the chill had spread deep into the hearts of the students who were being haunted by a series of mysterious events. Faces at windows. Locked doors mysteriously opening. Bodies washed up in the reed beds of the River Cam.

Marlowe had been one of those students, but unlike his peers he had been fearless, demanding answers, and that night he had encouraged two of his terror-stricken friends to follow a trail of inhuman footprints through the snow to the chapel.

'We do not give in to the dark beyond the fire. We do not give in to fear. We are men,' the budding playwright had called into the night.

Creeping into the incense-infused chapel, the three had been caught by a light around the altar. Kit had urged his two friends to investigate with him. The candle flames diminished. A low laugh rolled out, almost lost beneath the soughing of the wind. Unable to bear the fear any longer, one of the friends had turned and fled. As he reached the end of the choir, a whistle echoed, and the poor youth's head flew from his shoulders, rolling across the flags to look up at Marlowe from his feet.

The playwright was transfixed, but his other friend fled too. Kit found him a moment later, stock-still. In the lantern light, he saw with horror that white, fatty rivulets of flesh now ran down the student's face from beneath the hairline, his features a mess of drooping, unrecognizable skin as if he had melted. To Marlowe, Edmund looked like nothing more than the dripping candle in the lantern.

And that was when the thing that lurked there had revealed itself, pale and churchyard-thin like all its kind, black and blue concentric circles etched on its shaven head. Before it struck, Will burst into the chapel.

He remembered his greeting on that day: 'My name is William Swyfte and I am in the employ of Her Majesty. Some would call me ratcatcher, but the vermin I destroy are bigger and more malignant than any you would find in the kitchens of Corpus Christi, young student.'

Wielding his rapier, the spy barely held the thing at bay. But he was only biding his time. When the pale attacker lunged through his defences, Will showered it with the contents of one of Dr Dee's lethal pouches. The thing's agonized cries rang off the vaulted roof and in a peal of thunder and a burst of darkness it was gone.

Will had come to wonder if this was the same being Carpenter had described in Kit's lodging house in Bankside. Had the foul creature been stalking Marlowe ever since that night, trying to gain vengeance for what had later transpired? Was that the source of the haunted look that always lay deep in the playwright's eyes?

It was the start of it, and the end of it. Will had taken Kit from the college and overseen his induction into the spy network. Over weeks, the playwright had learned all the horrors of the Unseelie Court and the demands that would be made of him to combat them.

Through the pain, Will felt a deep blast of regret. Kit had been filled with so much life, so much potential, and the spy had been forced to watch it fade away over the years. All of Marlowe's miseries were Will's fault. He had recruited him into the life of spying. He had been responsible for him, for that innocence Will himself had lost, and however much he had tried to protect his friend on their dismal journey through the dark, he had ultimately failed. Kit was dead.

With a crash of the door that made the inmates scurry into the shadowy corners of the ward, the Keeper hurried in. Sweating in the heat of the June day, his glowering gaze briefly took in the fallen rogue and then he growled, 'Get that bastard back in his cell and make yourselves scarce. He has a visitor.'

Will forced a grin that sent blood running from his lips.

The two men snatched time for a few more kicks as the spy

231

was dragged through the straw back to his dank cell. Hurled against the far wall, he lay where he fell, laughing quietly to himself. The door slammed shut and the shrieking of the inmates reached a crescendo, drowning out the Keeper as he bellowed for silence.

The cool stone floor soothed the fire burning through every fibre of Will's body. Away from his captors, he accepted the waves of pain and let his thoughts wash on to the dark shores of his mind. He was only half aware when the door was opened once more and the Keeper said gruffly, 'Call when you want out.'

Will's eyelids flickered. As his gaze came into focus, he discerned a woman standing near the door, one hand sheltering the flame of a candle. Through his daze he was struck by the vibrant colour of her cloak, the blue of forget-me-nots, which reminded him of the dress Jenny was wearing on the day she disappeared. And then he felt sickened to realize that the colour now reminded him also of the devil that had taken his love's form. Even his last, pure memory was turning towards death and decay, he thought with bitterness.

The woman's hood was pulled low so that her face was lost to shadow.

'Grace,' the spy croaked. 'You should not be in this foul place.' He realized his mistake when the candlelight caught the visitor's growing smile. He saw a hardness to the shape of the lips that his young friend had never exhibited.

'The love-sick child was eager to visit the man of her dreams.' The musical notes of the Gaelic tongue rang in the honeyed voice. 'But I persuaded her to defer to a woman of experience.'

'Mistress Penteney,' Will noted. 'I have yet to decide if you are an angel or a devil. I have had my fill of the latter.'

'Lady Shevington actually.' Throwing back her hood with a flourish, she smiled at Will's puzzled expression. 'I apologize for my earlier deceit. I was not yet ready for you to know my true identity.'

'Viscount Shevington is in Ireland, carrying out the Queen's business.'

'Spying, you mean. Let us speak clearly.' Casting a narrow-eyed glance through the bars in the cell door, the Irish woman satisfied herself they were not being overheard. 'And I have been called both devil and angel in my time, but today, for you, I am undoubtedly a gift from heaven.'

Levering himself up on one elbow, the battered man struggled to form words through the dried blood on his puffed lips. 'And I apologize for not receiving you in a better condition. Although at least I am alive.'

'Not for much longer,' the woman sighed. 'The Privy Councillors have been directed to visit you here.'

'In Bedlam?'

'Your enemies will not risk you spreading dissent among your benighted countrymen out in the world of sane men, even for one moment. And so, for the first time, the Privy Council come to the accused, to this filthy, godforsaken hole. Why, it would be worth suffering this vile place for a while longer just to see those grey-bearded fools turning up their noses at the grime and the stink and the screams.'

Despite the pain, a wry smile crossed Will's lips. 'You have little love for our Queen's foremost advisers, my lady. Why, that would be considered traitorous in some quarters.'

'I am no daughter of this country. I do not need to bow my head and pretend.'

'What? Not even now that you have taken the hand and name of Viscount Shevington?' the spy said pointedly.

The Irish woman gave a sly smile in response. 'Ah, yes.'

With shaking arms, Will pushed himself up the cold stone wall until he was in a sitting position. 'Unless you were not his wife, of course,' he said in a light tone that continued the game they were playing. 'Unless, say, Viscount Shevington was dead, lost, perhaps, in one of the bogs of your homeland.'

'Who knows what may have transpired in the long weeks since I last saw my beloved husband? Certainly, if that were to be true, I would mourn him dearly.' The Irish woman set the candle down on the floor. 'As much as I enjoy this banter with so great a hero, Master Swyfte, time is short.'

Tipping his head back so he could study her from beneath his swollen eyelids, Will replied, 'I have all the time in the world, with only the rats, and my fellow inmates, and my friends with cudgels for company.'

'Alas, were that so. I have heard the decision of the Privy Council has already been made. You will be judged of sound mind and taken directly from this place to the Tower for execution.'

Will grew serious. 'You have heard?'

'I keep my eyes and ears open, Master Swyfte.'

'To learn that kind of information, you must keep them open in strange places. Bedchambers, perhaps.'

The woman did not flinch.

With the candlelight limning her flowing auburn hair, Will followed the line of the curls, considering their colour for the first time, the pale complexion, the flashing green eyes. 'I have heard tell of a spy operating in Tyrone,' he said thoughtfully. 'Some of my fellows who have had the pleasure of working in that green island call her Scarlet Mary. Her blade, they say, is as sharp as her tongue, and she is the equal of any man.'

The woman's face gave nothing away. 'I have heard those

234

tales too. I believe she is also known as Red Meg O'Shee. Spies are everywhere, Master Swyfte, but no one is ever the person they appear to be. Surely you must know that by now?'

'No more games, then,' he said, dabbing at the blood trickling from his lips. 'Why are you here?'

'To offer you aid.'

'Why? We do not know each other. And by all accounts Red Meg O'Shee would be more likely to slip a dagger between my ribs than reach out a helping hand.'

The Irish woman laughed, a hard and humourless sound. 'In other times that would indeed be the case. But this plot threatens all. Not just England. My country, and all of Europe, could go down in flames should the Unseelie Court have their way.'

In her warning, Will heard the echo of the taunts whispered by his own private devil in that very cell. A great plan unfolding. The world of men turning towards night.

'You are the very least of my concerns, Master Swyfte,' Red Meg continued, 'but a good man suggested you would make a formidable ally. That you understood the ways of our mutual Enemy better than anyone.'

'A good man?'

'The King of France, though not yet crowned as such.' The Irish woman shrugged. 'Only a matter of time.'

Will had heard the French monarch had taken many lovers, and from the glint in the Irish woman's eye the spy guessed she had been one. 'Henri? Our paths have never crossed,' he said.

'Nonetheless he knows of you, Master Swyfte, and the blow you struck against the Unseelie Court. All the crowned heads of Europe have heard of the unprecedented execution of one of the High Family, here, in England, after the failed Spanish invasion.' She flashed a surprisingly respectful glance at Will.

'I hear the Unseelie Court hate you, Master Swyfte, and not only for the murder of one of their kind; yes, and fear you too.'

Scarlet Mary prowled around the edge of the small cell, still keeping one eye on the door. Watching her graceful movements, Will tried to reconcile the brutal stories he had heard about the spy with the woman in front of him.

'But that is a conversation for another time. First we must get you out of this predicament.' The Irish woman gave an amused laugh seeing his disbelieving reaction to her words.

'A bribe may have got you into my cell but the Keeper will not be so accommodating, given the importance the Privy Council have placed upon my incarceration,' the spy replied. 'Or will you carry me away with the help of your angel wings?'

Red Meg lifted up her skirts, without the slightest embarrassment at revealing the shapely line of her legs. From the inner folds, she produced a woollen pouch.

Pressing one long finger to her lips, she gave a lop-sided smile and said, 'There is only one way out of Bedlam for you, Master Swyfte. You have to die.'

CHAPTER THIRTY-TWO

SHIELDING HIS EYES AGAINST THE JUNE SUN, SIR ROBERT CECIL clambered awkwardly down from the black carriage into the windswept yard of the Hospital of St Mary of Bethlehem. The cobbles still gleamed from the night's great storm that had torn tiles from the roofs of many of the houses he had passed on the journey from Nonsuch.

As the spymaster let his gaze wander over dismal Bedlam, he gritted his teeth. It was a day of judgement that he would inevitably regret, but it was necessary.

Eschewing his workaday black garb, the Secretary of State had opted for clothes that he felt befitted the momentous occasion, a smart doublet of silver-grey with padded sapphire breeches and a matching blue cloak, cut so it did much to conceal his hunched back. Nothing, however, could hide the rolling gait that always revealed the curse of his twisted form. He hated the way everyone at court stared at him as if he were weak in mind as well as body, someone to be pitied, when his wits were sharper than any of theirs.

Looking around, Cecil saw the familiar loathsome stares were there too. Five other members of the Privy Council had gathered by the great oak door of Bedlam for the day's business, a meagre feast of funereal garb and wintry expressions.

Glowering, the spymaster avoided his secretary's helpful hand, and strode over. 'Let us be brave in our decision,' he urged the waiting council members, 'and keep God in our hearts and minds at all times. It has been decided that an agreement by the six of us on the state of William Swyfte's mind will be accepted by the full council later.'

Nodding, the other men muttered their agreement. All of them had skittish, unsettled eyes at the prospect of setting foot in Bedlam.

Cecil's secretary, a pale, intense young man with the demeanour of a preacher, grabbed the iron ring on the door and pounded on it three times. A moment later, the Keeper appeared, bowing and fawning and then spitting in the palm of his hand and smearing it across his sleep-tufted hair to flatten it. Excited by the reverberations of the secretary's knock, the inmates of the Abraham Ward clamoured wildly.

'Ignore them, my lords. They'll quieten down soon,' the Keeper muttered, sweeping one chubby hand towards the newly whitewashed corridor that led to the ward.

'Let us be done with it, then,' the spymaster said, leading the procession of councillors behind the grubby man. 'We have important business when we are done with this distraction.'

By that important business he meant ensuring he quickly regained favour in the eyes of the Queen, and that swaggering jackanapes Essex was consigned immediately to the shadows of Nonsuch. The spymaster was sickened by how much advantage this whole affair had cost him. Her Majesty would barely meet his eye, and his rival's spies blustered around the palace as if they owned it.

Fresh straw had been scattered across the dirty floor of the Abraham Ward and bunches of newly cut purple lavender had been hung above every door. The sickly-sweet aroma did little to dispel the stink of the vault, but at least the Keeper had made some effort for his honoured guests, Cecil accepted grudgingly.

Their sweaty guide led the way to a locked door halfway along the gloomy ward. The spymaster hated losing an operative with the skills of Swyfte, but the spy was expendable, like all the men in the secret service. Yes, Cecil thought with a nod, the over-confident, smug, drunken, fornicating rake had certainly outlived his usefulness.

Selecting one large iron key from the huge ring he carried, the Keeper unlocked the cell door and swung it open. With another fawning bow, he raised an arm to direct the Privy Councillors inside.

Stepping across the threshold, the Little Elf took a moment for his eyes to adjust to the gloom. It was quiet, and he could just make out the dark shape of the spy lying on the floor near the far wall. The hunchbacked man was surprised. He had expected to be greeted by mockery, perhaps one of the caustic comments that he had tolerated for too long. Had the experiences in Bedlam been so terrible that the cell's occupant had been broken, his wits gone, like the other unfortunates who resided in that foul place?

'Master Swyfte,' the spymaster said in a firm voice.

There was no response.

Impatiently, Cecil beckoned to the Keeper, who passed a candle in a wax-encrusted holder. With one hand to protect the wavering flame, the small man held the light in front of him. 'Swyfte,' he barked.

Shadows danced across the wall. Still the spy did not move. Just as he had started to believe he had been spared the unpleasantness of ordering an execution, Cecil heard a weak groan emanating from the figure in front of him. As he leaned in to urge the spy to sit, the words died in his throat.

Black dots flecked the back of the spy's prone hand.

The spymaster's chest tightened. With trembling fingers, he moved the candle to his left to reveal a glistening, bloody pool of vomit trickling from the edge of Swyfte's mouth. Cecil's mind screamed at him to flee, but it was as if the candle was drawn inexorably along the body. The man's head was tilted at such an angle that the bare skin of his neck was revealed, and there, caught in the wavering light, was a purplish boil, and another just visible under the bloodstained ruff.

The spymaster recoiled as if he had been burned. 'The plague!' he cried, his voice breaking. 'He has the plague!'

The other Privy Councillors hurled themselves away from the cell door, one of them stumbling backwards on to the floor in his fear and haste. Blood draining from his face, the Keeper clutched both hands to his mouth.

Cecil all but ran from the cell, slamming the door behind him. 'This hospital is now under quarantine,' he shouted, hurrying towards the exit from the ward. 'Let no man enter or leave.'

The spymaster was afraid he was going to be sick from the terror sweeping through him, but the other Privy Councillors were all too distracted by their own inelegant scramble to escape from the plague-infested ward to notice Cecil. Cursing loudly, they jostled through the door and continued running into the yard where the carriages waited.

In the sun, the spymaster regained his composure. Turning to the blanched Keeper, he said, 'God has already passed His judgement on William Swyfte, and may the Almighty have mercy on his soul. This matter is now closed. I will inform the Privy Council this afternoon.'

'What . . . what do I do with him?' the frightened man whispered.

'When he passes, call for a watchman who will send the death-cart,' Cecil replied with a deep, juddering sigh. 'The labourers will take the body on its final journey to the plague pits, where it will be buried with the other poor souls.'

CHAPTER THIRTY-THREE

THE CELL DOOR GROUND OPEN. AFTER A MOMENT OF SILENCE, A low voice said, 'Stinks.'

'Stinks everywhere in here,' a gruff voice growled in reply. 'Stink and madness go together.'

'Looks dead.'

'Ah, he does.'

Lying face down in the filthy straw, Will couldn't see anything, but he guessed the two men were pulling cloths over their mouths and noses to keep out the noxious, infecting fumes of the plague. He sensed one kneel beside him, hovering for a moment before prodding him sharply in the back.

'He's done, all right. Not breathing. Cold,' the death-cart labourer muttered. 'Let's get him out of here.'

Will's head ached from where it had been pressed for hours against the chill flagstones. His limbs had ceased working within moments of taking the clear potion which Red Meg had left with him after she had applied the plague disguise over his exposed skin. He had found the sensation of his thoughts roaming freely within a seemingly dead body unsettling in the extreme at first, a foretaste of the grave, and, with his devil whispering in his ear, perhaps a flavour of hell too.

Inured by their daily dose of plague deaths, the labourers didn't even give the spy a cursory examination as they rolled him in a fresh linen shroud. As the two men pulled the material tightly over his face, Will was overcome with panic that even his barely perceptible breathing would be stifled. Might he die while faking death? he wondered, the irony not lost on him.

Rough hands gripped his ankles and under his arms and he was lifted amid grunts and curses. The cloth smelled of damp and mildew. His mouth was dry, his tongue fat and unmoving and heavy in his cheek.

Swaying, the spy was carried across the cell. At the door, his head cracked against the jamb, stars flashing before his closed eyes. His ankles clattered against the wood. But the discomfort cleared his thoughts a little, and when the shroud snagged on the splintered wood of the old cell door, he felt the linen tugged from his face enough to let in a little cool air.

Quarantined in their cells, the inmates were silent, but Will was convinced he could once again dimly hear Griffin Devereux's wild laughter rising up from the depths. *There is more madness in the governance of England than there is in this pitiful place*, the spy thought bitterly.

Cursing and wheezing behind their masks, the death-cart labourers carried Will's body through the Abraham Ward, along the corridor and into the entrance hall, battering his bruised limbs on every door they passed. And then he was out in the hot sun, which warmed him even through the linen. From the street, he could hear the rattle of wheels on ruts, the whinny of horses and the whistle of carters, the hailing of good friends and the shouts of the guards on the wall above the city gate. Despite his predicament, his spirits rose after the long days in the stinking gloom of Bedlam.

His toes twitched involuntarily. The potion was starting to wear off, as Red Meg had told him it would.

The two men came to a halt, and then began a slow swing. Gathering speed, Will was swept back and forth three times, until, with a loud grunt, the labourers let go of him. The dizzying sensation of flying made his head spin. Winded, he crashed on to what he knew must be the back of the death-cart, with his feet higher than his head. The shroud tore away from the upper half of his face and sunlight seared his eyes through his lids, painful after the ever-present gloom of his incarceration.

As the stink of human rot swept into his nose, the spy's stomach turned. Unmoving elbows and knees prodded his back, and with his limited vision he could make out four blackened fingers close to his face. The index finger was extended downwards as if pointing the way to the doom that awaited them all. Will felt a pang of fear that he might contract the plague, though he had heard that some physicians thought the dead were no longer infectious. If he had been a religious man, he would have prayed for that to be true.

Will could hear the death-cart labourers arguing nearby, but couldn't make out their words under the stamp of the horse's hooves and the breeze whistling around the hospital yard. After a moment, the two men climbed on to the cart's seat and with a crack of the whip they lurched off.

Shaken roughly, the spy watched the cobbles pass beyond the edge of the cart. The horse took a wide arc, trotting through the open gates into the flow of traffic on Bishopsgate Without. Conversations faded away the moment the grim burden was seen. Will felt a shadow as he passed under the city walls, and then the rough ride eased as the cart rolled on to the smooth limestone and flint paving of Bishopsgate Street. As life began to return to his limbs, the spy gave in to the gentle rocking and the sounds of the vibrant city.

Ahead lay the plague pit, his final resting place.

CHAPTER THIRTY-FOUR

'KEEP YOUR HEADS DOWN AND STOP YOUR BICKERING OR YOU will be the death of us,' Nathaniel hissed, a wide-brimmed hat pulled low on his face. Behind him, in the shadows of a court on the east of Bishopsgate Street, Grace glared at the woman they knew as Lady Shevington.

Smoothing down her crimson skirts, the Irish woman replied with a condescending smile, 'Bickering only happens among equals.'

The younger woman's tart response was drowned out by the loud honking of a flock of geese being driven south along Bishopsgate. With the traffic backed up in all directions, the carters and draymen yelled abuse, shaking their fists and their whips, but the drover marched along behind his birds, uncaring.

'Will they bring the death-cart through this crowd?' Nathaniel asked, concerned.

'You must trust me. They will want him in the pit and buried, and the business done with as soon as they can,' Red Meg replied. 'They would not wait until the evening for a man like our Will.'

'*Our Will*,' Grace snapped. 'You have spoken to him . . . what? Twice?'

'But I know a kindred spirit when I see one.'

Nathaniel thought his young friend was about to strike the auburn-haired woman. Grace's face was flushed, her left hand gripped into a tiny fist.

Shouting, whistling and beating his stick on the limestone roadway, the drover moved his flock of geese on. The traffic began to flow once more, most of it running south to the river or west to the market at Cheapside. Shielding his eyes against the sun, Nathaniel continued to look north along the row of large houses, past the great stone bulk of St Helen's Priory to the city walls. After a while, he saw a ripple pass through the merchants and servants bustling along the street's edge as head after head ducked down and turned towards the walls of the houses.

'It comes,' he whispered, waving a hand to catch the attention of the women behind him.

With silence in its wake, the death-cart trundled along Bishopsgate Street, its progress as steady and relentless as the plague. Nathaniel tried not to think what horrors his master must be experiencing.

At the crossroads, the death-cart drifted out into the centre of the street. The flow of drays and carts gradually drew to a halt, allowing the morbid carriage to turn right on to a cobbled way.

'Yes!' Nathaniel exclaimed quietly. 'We were right. They go to the Lombard Street plague pit.'

'It's the nearest one to Bedlam,' Red Meg said in a bored voice.

Filled with anxiety, Grace urged, 'We must hurry, before Will is thrown into the pit.'

'Do not hurry!' the Irish woman snapped. 'We must not draw attention to ourselves. We will have time to stop those slow-witted fools, even if we adopt the steady pace of servants off to market.'

Nathaniel set off first from the lea of the shadowy court, darting among the horses and carriages and into Lombard Street. Clutching his hand to his mouth, he smelled the stench of rot long before he reached the location of the mass grave. In the summer heat, droning clouds of black flies swarmed over-head. Bloated and lazy from feeding, they formed a thick cover on windows, blocking out the light.

Twisting up the brim of his hat, Nathaniel spotted the two labourers sitting on the edge of the street in the shade of a whitewashed house, mopping the sweat from their brows before the exertions that were to come. A roughly erected wooden fence with a gate in it led to a field of churned earth where the trees, shrubs and flowers had been rooted up. Rats scurried over each other in their feeding frenzy. The land was divided into plots. Five had already been used, the fresh earth heaped atop them. In the sixth plot lay a yawning hole. Crossing himself, Nathaniel couldn't help a shudder when he looked at it.

The two women arrived at his side a moment later. Grace's face was drained of blood, her gaze skittering across the graves and the contents of the cart, but Red Meg was unmoved. She primped her auburn hair, a seductive smile alighting easily on her lips.

'As agreed, we shall distract the labourers with light conver-sation and flirting,' the Irish woman said, flashing a glance at Grace. 'Are you capable of that?'

'Yes, of course,' the younger woman snapped.

'You must creep to the back of the cart and search for Master

Swyfte,' Red Meg instructed Nat. 'The effects of the death potion will not yet have faded, but your master should be able to walk a few steps with your support. Take him into that street to the north. We will meet you there.'

'And if I am seen?' Nathaniel replied.

'Then I will leave you here to your fate.'

Red Meg stepped into the street with an unsettled Grace close behind. But they had barely taken a pace when they caught sight of five men in black cloaks and tall black hats striding along the street from the west. Rapiers hung at their sides, and their grim features told of men about serious business.

Returning to Nathaniel's side, the Irish woman urged him into a small, shaded street to the south from where they could observe proceedings without being seen.

'Who are they?' Grace whispered.

'I think they are the men who pursued Will and me from St Paul's,' Nat said, peering at the faces of the new arrivals.

The five men surrounded the two puzzled labourers. One of them, clearly the leader of the group, leaned down to talk in low, fierce tones, ending his speech with a sharp sweep of his arm towards the death-cart.

With sullen faces, the two shabbily dressed men hauled themselves to their feet. Grabbing the first shroud-wrapped corpse, they carried it through the gate on to the cleared land, kicking out at the rats swarming around their feet. They tossed the body into the grave with all the bored disrespect of a woodman stacking logs for the winter.

Appalled at the sight, Grace cried out so loudly that Red Meg had to shake her furiously. 'You do not have the luxury of acting like a child any more,' the Irish woman snapped. 'You will be the death of us and of the man who clearly holds your heart.'

'But Will—'

'—has his life resting in our hands. Would you have it on your conscience that your own weakness killed him?'

Grace calmed, her face hardening. She glanced back to the mass grave, to which the two labourers were now carrying the second body under the vigilant watch of the five men. 'What do we do now?' she whispered.

'Once they have deposited these poor souls they will fetch more,' Nathaniel replied, his knuckles white where his fingers gripped the corner of the wall. 'There is a shortage of land for the pits. They fill each to the brim before they start another.'

Barely had he uttered the words than one of the labourers broke off from his work to collect shovels from the rear of the cart. He rammed them into the heap of black earth next to the grave and returned to dispose of the rest of the bodies.

Shaking his head, Nathaniel gasped, 'They are going to bury Will alive.'

CHAPTER THIRTY-FIVE

HIS HEART POUNDING, WILL SUCKED IN A MOUTHFUL OF AIR and fought to clear his sluggish head. Some life was returning to his limbs, but agonizingly slowly.

Black walls towered up on every side to a square of blue sky overhead, which seemed to him at that moment impossibly far away. Now that the linen had been torn clear of his face, he could see around the dank hole, half filled with mouldering corpses in shrouds stained with bodily fluids. The ones directly beneath him, where decomposition was well under way, were soft and yielding. His eyes watered and he gagged as the reek of escaping fumes seeped into his lungs.

At first the spy thought stones were being dropped into the grave, but as he rolled his eyes, he saw rats plummeting from the edge of the pit. Their movements had a feverish intensity. Many of the shrouds nearby had been gnawed through, and the rats ducked their heads into the gaps, their jaws working hungrily.

Will watched one rodent speed sinuously towards his exposed face, its jaws gaping wide in anticipation to reveal two rows of tiny white teeth. Snarling deep in his throat, he spat at the predator. The rat flipped over in shock and raced to easier prey. But the spy knew it was only a matter of time before the pack descended on him and ate him alive.

Hearing the grunts of the approaching labourers, he played dead again. A body crashed across him, pinning his arms.

'Can you now see your end?' the devil's voice echoed from some corner of the pit that the spy couldn't see. The rats continued their furious feeding, oblivious.

'Leave me be,' Will said under his breath. 'I have work to do.'

Mephistophilis' laugh was like a cold wind.

Bodies rained around the spy. But by the time the last one had crashed into the pit, he had almost regained enough movement in his arms to free himself.

Will wondered how much longer he had. He received his answer a moment later when the first shovelful of earth hit him full in the face. Spitting the soil from his mouth, he continued to press against the shroud, straining his unresponsive muscles, willing the potion to leave his body.

But the dirt fell in a black rain. Across his legs and torso, the rats scurried in a frenzy, snapping at the linen in their eagerness to feed before they were deluged. The square of blue sky seemed to recede. Will felt the earth cover his body, then his face, and his heart began to thunder.

Twisting his head, he found a pocket of air under a fallen corpse. Within moments the last of the light had winked out.

Stay calm, Will told himself. *If you panic, you die.*

He felt the weight upon him increase with each shovelful. With precise but painfully slow movements, the spy drew his leaden body out of the shroud, but he wasn't fast enough. He was lost to a dark, stiflingly hot world. Each breath was small and shallow and a band began to tighten across his chest.

Drenched in sweat, Will dug his fingers into the corpses and tried to haul himself up. The earth was alive all around him with the constant churning of the rats.

Yet the dirt crashed down faster than the spy could move, filling his mouth, his eyes, his nose. Dread began to shred his thoughts.

For Jenny, he told himself. *For Kit. For Grace and all the others relying on me.*

'But for yourself?' his private devil whispered in his ear. 'No, you have forsaken Will Swyfte in your embrace of death. And now it embraces you.'

'You will not distract me,' the spy hissed.

With the toes of his right foot, Will dragged the last of the shroud down, but the weight of the earth was now so great he could barely move his battered limbs. Making mole claws of his fingers, he began to drag soil from above him into the few spaces that lay below. Burrowing rats raked his flesh as they continued their own, more rapid journey back to the light.

'You will never find your Jenny,' Mephistophilis whispered again. 'While you die in slow, suffocating agony, you will reflect that you have wasted your life chasing an illusion. Days go by, years go by, and you cling on to one tiny thing, a discarded locket, that is your only evidence that she may still live. Hope exceeds reason.'

As the life returned to Will, so did the pain from his beatings in Bedlam. His limbs trembling from the exertion, he paused. Thin air wheezed into his lungs. Loam lined his mouth and caked his tongue.

Digging deep for the last of his reserves, Will renewed his efforts. Dragging handfuls of soil down, forcing himself upwards with his feet, searching for what little air remained to ease his struggling lungs, he inched on.

The black world appeared to be endless. He was unsure if he

was rising or sinking, or how near he was to the surface. But he could still feel the faint thud-thud-thud of soil falling from above. His exertions grew weaker again, the strength draining from his limbs. He could not go on.

All around him, the devil's laughter drifted. 'Beyond the sea your love lies, in the west, where the dead go. Under the full moon, in a golden city, she sleeps, and cries, and you will never feel her loving touch again.'

Breathing in the stink of the grave, and death, and hopelessness, Will pressed his face into the soil and closed his eyes.

CHAPTER THIRTY-SIX

SWEATING AND SCOWLING, THE TWO LABOURERS LEANED ON their shovels beside the sea of trampled earth now covering the plague pit. Nearby, at the fence, the five armed men smoked as they watched the sun sink past the chimneys of the surrounding houses. The job was done. Will Swyfte was dead and buried.

Clutching on to the brick wall in the small street across the way, Grace fought the urge to sob. She felt numb, as if a part of her had died with every shovelful of earth that fell into that black hole. She had wanted to run to the grave and attack the men with her bare hands, digging Will out herself if it was necessary. But she knew it was a foolish girl's dream that would only lead to harm for Nat, who would undoubtedly have rushed to help her.

And now, a grown woman, she had been forced to watch the man she loved die.

'You said they would break off from their digging. You said we would be able to help Will,' Nathaniel raged. His hands shook as he fought to control himself. 'Your plans have come to naught. You killed him.'

'If he had not died here, he would have died in the Tower. I gambled on a slim chance that we might be able to save him,'

Red Meg replied quietly, her hands clasped in front of her, her face emotionless. 'But it was not to be.'

'And that is all you can say?' Nat turned on her. 'William Swyfte is more than my master — he is my friend. He saved the life of my father, and he helped me when I needed it most, even at cost to himself.'

A crack appeared in the Irish woman's mask, and her green eyes flashed.

Grace confronted Nathaniel. 'Do not risk your life when the situation is hopeless,' she pleaded. 'Will would not want you to die needlessly.'

'Where there is life, there is hope. That is what the preachers say, is it not?' He glanced over his shoulder at the men standing around the plague pit in the ruddy light of the setting sun. 'I have Will's sword that we were due to give him after we . . .' The words caught in his throat. 'After we rescued him.'

'Nat, you are not a fighting man!' Grace said incredulously. 'You are as likely to fall over your sword as to kill with it. I would not lose you too.' She couldn't hold back the tears any longer.

'Nevertheless, I must do what I can.' Without another word, Nathaniel strode out into the street, keeping his head down but allowing one hand to fall on the rapier that hung incongruously at his side.

'Fool!' Red Meg snarled. Hesitating for a moment, she looked back along Lombard Street, weighing her decision. But just as Grace became convinced she had given up on them, the Irish woman stepped out after Nat, a broad, seductive grin leaping to her lips.

A better player than Kit ever had on the stage, Grace thought.

As Nathaniel closed on the burial site, the five men threw aside their clay pipes and turned to face the new arrival.

'Keep moving, stranger,' the steely-eyed leader of the group said.

'On whose authority?' Nat called, vaguely recognizing the man. Was he in the employ of Lord Derby?

'The Queen's.'

'You do not do the Queen's work.'

As she neared, Grace could see Nathaniel's hand shaking above the rapier hilt. The five armed men were sure to have spotted his inexperience and doubt.

'The papers I have from the Privy Council say otherwise,' the leader said with a faint sneer. He walked to the gate, his hand resting on his own rapier as a warning to Nathaniel.

'Boys! How handsome you all are.' Red Meg's rich voice rang out across the street. 'It makes my heart beat faster to see hard-working men sleeked in sweat.' She drew the attention of the five men with the swing of her hips and a flourish of her crimson skirt as she danced across the cobbles. Her right eyebrow was arched, her eyes and her broad smile promising much.

Four of the men turned their attention to the Irish woman, unable to prevent the hint of a leer reaching their lips. Sensing trouble, the leader remained grim, his eyes darting between Red Meg and Nathaniel.

'Step aside,' the young man called. 'I do not wish to find trouble here.'

'You will find it if you do not move on.' The leader's fingers clenched around the hilt of his sword.

'Let us have no fighting,' Red Meg trilled. 'We can put those passions to better use, I am sure. Come here and help a maid find her way about a strange city.'

'Away with you, doxy,' the steely-eyed man snapped.

Grace flinched at the slur, but the Irish woman appeared

unmoved. Drawing her bodice a little lower, she continued to advance on the burial site.

Her actions unnerved the leader. He drew his rapier and pointed it from Red Meg to Nathaniel. 'Away with you both, now,' he growled.

With a fumbling action, Nat unsheathed his own sword. It wavered as he brandished it at the five men.

The leader gave a humourless laugh.

'Stand aside!' Nathaniel shouted, stepping towards the gate. Still smiling seductively, Red Meg advanced too.

The leader's cheeks flushed with anger. Throwing open the gate, he levelled his blade.

By the plague pit, one of the labourers let out a fearful cry and pointed at the newly filled grave.

In the deepening twilight, Grace could not see what the labourer was indicating, but the two dirt-smeared men threw themselves backwards, shrieking. Stumbling and flailing, they scrambled out of the plot and away down the street.

Her breath catching in her throat, Grace hurried to the fence. The dying rays of the sun cast an infernal glow across the stinking waste. In the centre, the newly turned earth was churning like the gushing river water that flowed around the columns of London Bridge. Clods of soil shifted amid a wave of writhing brown fur as the rats rushed from the grave in all directions.

One filthy hand burst from the midst of the disturbed soil. It was followed by a second, and then a monstrous figure levered its way out of the plague pit, smeared black from head to toe, bright eyes ranging across the assembled group.

Hands flying to their gaping mouths, the five armed men stumbled backwards.

The resurrected figure grinned. 'And now,' it croaked, 'let all hell break loose.'

Grace felt giddy with the rush of emotion and made to call her love's name, but Nathaniel pushed by her. 'Your sword,' he called, tossing the rapier over the fence.

Though Grace could see he was close to exhaustion, Will snatched the glinting blade from the air and instantly found his balance. The steely-eyed man darted forward, thrusting his rapier towards the spy's chest.

Will hooked his bare toes under one of the scurrying rats and, with a flick, hurled it through the air. Writhing, the hungry rodent hit the attacker full in the face. Needle-sharp teeth tore into flesh. Blood spattered and hands clawed, to no avail.

'I made new friends,' the fearsome apparition said, 'and they are hungry.' As the man shrieked in pain, the spy ran his opponent through.

Stunned by the attack on their leader, the other four men advanced slowly, rapiers drawn. With a cry, Nathaniel barrelled into the nearest man, knocking him to the dried mud of the burial site. The next man turned on him, but Red Meg was already there, still swaying her hips, still grinning. Up from nowhere she brought a gleaming dagger, drawing a thin red line across her foe's neck. Blood spurted. Gurgling, the dying man fell to his knees and then pitched face down on the black earth.

The death caught the attention of the remaining two men. Lunging, Will drove his rapier through one. With a flamboyant twirl, Red Meg slammed her dagger into the eye of the last, pushing the blade deep into the man's brain. The final attacker died under Will's blade as he wrestled with a ferociously flailing Nathaniel.

259

Grace realized she wasn't breathing. Sucking in a huge gulp of evening air, she struggled to understand how so many deaths could happen in what seemed the blink of an eye. The swarming brown rats were already feasting on the blood-spattered bodies.

Caked in the filth of the grave, Will staggered as he stepped forward. He looked as if he could barely stand. Nat rushed to help him through the gate with Red Meg a step behind, her smile now wry, her brow knitted thoughtfully.

Grace made to speak, but her voice broke and tears stung her eyes.

'Hush,' the spy said with an affectionate smile, his voice hoarse. 'I survived. And I am stronger for it. It is remarkable the things you can learn when you are close to death, things that can turn your life in a different direction. And I have learned to embrace my devils.'

His smile, his bright eyes, his expression, were so enigmatic the young woman wanted to ask what he meant, but his legs buckled again and Nathaniel had to take his full weight.

As Will recovered, Grace recounted all that had transpired at Nonsuch while he rotted in Bedlam. When she had finished, he said, 'London is no place to be right now. It is only a matter of time before the Enemy will come looking for me again. My destiny lies beyond this city.'

'Where?' Grace asked with a disbelieving shake of her head.

'Our Enemy may think this war already won. It is not. A few good men can turn the tide. You and Nat have work to do at Nonsuch. John and Robert, should they have survived, have their own task. And there is one man who has always proved himself formidable in our struggle, and who is needed now more than ever: Dr John Dee.'

'Even in Ireland, I have heard tell of that powerful court

magician,' Red Meg said. 'Then I will accompany you. God help you, you will not walk ten paces on your own.'

'No. You cannot trust her,' Grace protested.

Will eyed the two men killed by the Irish woman. 'You may be right, but our friend has shown herself an effective ally.' He nodded. 'Very well. But I will watch you very closely, Mistress O'Shee.'

A high-pitched cry like that of a gull at dawn echoed across the rooftops. Yet there was another quality to that unsettling sound, a deep rumble as if two opposing voices were calling at once, that made it unlike any bird they had heard before.

A shadow fell across Red Meg's features. She looked around urgently until her attention lighted on a tall stone hall along the street to the west near where Lombard Street met Corn Hill. On one of the large chimney stacks, a figure was silhouetted against the darkening, star-sprinkled sky. It was unnaturally tall and thin with long slender limbs, but protruding from its head was what appeared to be a long, curved beak. As they watched, it put its head back and emitted that strange, troubling cry once more, and this time it was picked up by another, across the city to the south. More cries followed in quick succession.

'Who is that, up there so high? And why does he wear a mask?' Grace asked, disturbed, though not sure why.

'The Corvata,' the Irish woman said under her breath. She had grown pale, her features taut. 'Your survival has already been noted. There will be no rest now.'

261

CHAPTER THIRTY-SEVEN

ON THE FAR HORIZON, A SPECTRAL GLOW LIT UP THE BLACK waves washing into the horseshoe-shaped bay. Amid that pearly luminescence, the outline of a ghostly galleon rocking gently on the swell could just be discerned. A smaller craft made its way steadily towards the shore.

In villages along the Kent coast, candles would be extinguished as storm-hardened sailors and their wives turned away from the windows, whispering prayers against the haunted vessel, or denying its very existence.

The night was warm, the salty breeze licking the surf into a gentle symphony where it met the sand. Beyond the whisper of the waves, owls hooted in the trees that ran down to the shore, and the marram grass on the edge of the dunes rustled as if small things moved among it.

On the beach, looking out to sea, Deortha stood with one hand high on a staff carved with black runes that resembled no human writing. Braided with trinkets and the skulls of field animals and birds, his hair glinted gold and silver in the moonlight. Despite the heat, he wore thick grey-green robes, faintly marked with a gold design of the same symbols that were on his staff.

The Unseelie Court's magician fixed his attention on the approaching vessel, his contemplative nature set alight by satisfaction as a long-forming pattern fell into place.

An ending was coming.

Squatting, baleful and brooding like one of the gargoyles on the great cathedrals of Europe, Xanthus drew patterns in the sand with one long finger, occasionally laughing humourlessly to himself. On his shaved, pale head, the blue and black intersecting circles stood out starkly.

'The seasons turn slowly, but a change was always coming,' wise Deortha said, his gaze fixed ahead. 'The king-in-waiting arrives this night and nothing will be the same again.'

The squatting thing grunted in reply.

Beside the magician, waiting like a statue of cold alabaster, was the one who passed for Lord Derby, a minor member of the Privy Council who rarely raised his voice in opposition to more outspoken characters such as Cecil and Essex, but who was always heeded when he did speak. Dressed in a black gown, a black velvet cap on his head, the Scar-Crow Man had a long, grey beard that glowed in the moonlight.

Deortha paid him no attention. Nor did the other grey shapes flitting around the fringes of the beach like moon shadows.

The small craft sped across the chopping waves in complete silence; not even the constant, rhythmic splashing of the six oarsmen could be heard. A lantern swung from a pole at the stern. And at the prow stood Lethe of the High Family, hands pressed flat against his belly, unmoved by the undulations of the craft on the waves. A long, grey cloak swathed him, the hood pulled back to reveal his silver hair, black-streaked along the centre, and a fierce expression that was tinged with both triumph and the flush of violent passion. Around his feet, a small creature gambolled. Sophisticated London folk would have thought it like the little apes that the foreign merchants sold in the market on Cheapside, but it was hairless, its ears pointed and its golden eyes held a disturbing intelligence.

When the boat reached the shore, the oarsmen jumped out into the white-licked surf and hauled it a way up the sand. Lethe stepped out into the backwash and strode up the beach to Deortha, his pet rolling and tumbling in front of him.

'These mortals, this cattle swaying stupidly towards slaughter, have woken us.' The faint sibilance in the new arrival's voice echoed the sound of the sea. 'They have gained our attention. And that is a good thing, Deortha, for we had grown complacent. The human beasts do not know what they have done.'

The wise one nodded in response. 'We are close. England hangs by a thread. But there is one matter that demands our notice.'

Lethe's eyes narrowed. Deortha explained about the English spy, Will Swyfte, who had seen glimpses of what was unfolding – but far from all – and who was now abroad in England and beyond control.

'Beyond the watch of our Scar-Crows?' Lethe asked with a note of irritation. He cast a supercilious eye at the emotionless man who stood nearby.

'For now,' the Lord Derby figure replied.

'This spy is known to the High Family. But he is one man, as weak as the rest of them, and he cannot be expected to cause any interference with our work.' Deortha chose his words carefully. He was not concerned, but in his divinations he had often seen how the smallest and seemingly most inconsequential matter could drastically change the greater pattern. 'Still,' he began, 'he is resilient, and driven by demons that we would all understand. He will not rest until he has uncovered truths that he hopes will salve his secret dreads, and in so doing he may sow confusion or cause difficulties in the construction of our grand design. For all to be thrown awry at this late stage would be . . .' He tapped one finger on his lower lip in reflection. 'Unfortunate.'

'Then let us ensure this mortal is destroyed. I would see him struck down, his body torn open and his internal workings laid bare for the ravens to feast upon,' Lethe said. He held his left arm out for his pet to scramble up his body and nestle in the crook of his elbow. Its golden eyes fell upon the Scar-Crow Man and it bared its needle-sharp teeth and hissed. 'And it should be done in plain view, so all his own kind will see and learn.'

'We have played him in times past,' Deortha replied, looking beyond his master to the dark horizon, 'thinking he might be suitable to advance our plans. Like all mortals, he is riven with weakness, his strengths made ragged by emotions. Love, yearning, dashed hopes, despair. There may still be a part for him to play.'

'England falls before this summer turns. What need for him then?'

'Very well.' Deortha gave a faint bow of his head.

Lethe pressed the tips of his fingers together and turned his attention to Xanthus, who still squatted like a beast beside them. 'This spy killed your brother, a Hunter like yourself,' he said. 'He has troubled you too, I understand.'

The shaven-headed thing gave a low, contemptuous growl deep in his throat. Looking up at his master with hollow eyes, he nodded. 'I will find him.'

Lethe pursed his lips. 'Of course you will, for no quarry ever escapes you. Your brother could never be driven off course, pursuing his prey with the cold, relentless force of a winter storm. But you are better. This spy is already as good as dead. But I would have more.'

Deortha gave another slight bow and turned to Lord Derby. 'Let the word travel out to every corner of this land: William Swyfte is no longer England's greatest spy and garlanded hero of all Albion. He has betrayed his Queen, his country and his fellow men. This traitor is now an outlaw, who must be hunted down and given up to the authorities. His name, his reputation, mean nothing. All England now stands against him. Do you understand?'

The Scar-Crow Man nodded, emotion springing to his face – at first concern, then righteous fury as he searched for the correct response. 'I will return to Nonsuch this night and summon a meeting of the Privy Council for the morrow. The Queen will be advised forthwith. Will Swyfte will be shunned by all God-fearing Englishmen and brought to justice in no time at all. Traitor. Outlaw. His days are numbered.'

CHAPTER THIRTY-EIGHT

THE HOWL OF A HUNTING DOG DRIFTED ACROSS THE NIGHT-shrouded countryside, low and mournful in the stillness. It was joined by another, and then another, the baying of the hounds becoming one insistent, hungry voice.

Breathless from the chase, Will grabbed a leaning elm to halt his careering descent down the steep hillside. In the dark, exposed tree roots threatened to break his neck, tufting grass obscured sudden drops where the soil had slipped away in heavy rain, and rabbit holes peppering the slope promised to break ankles or tear ligaments.

The spy held out a helpful arm to the red-haired woman scrambling down the bank behind him. She clutched for branches to prevent a sudden fall and tore at her crimson skirts where they were caught on brambles. Dirt streaked her face and sweat glistened on her knitted brow.

'I do not need your aid,' Red Meg responded ferociously, as if he had offered to take her there and then.

'This is not a time for pride, my lady. Proclaim your independent spirit now, but it will only result in a noose round both our necks by dawn.'

The Irish woman let forth a stream of cursing the like of

267

which Will had heard only in the bustling shipyards along the Thames. 'Do not think me some weak and bloodless woman,' she snapped. 'I have fought your marauding countrymen with a sword, a dagger and an axe across the bogs and mountains of my home. And I have survived, alone, in the cities of Europe and Africa, where women are traded like goats and treated worse.'

'We have an entire village in pursuit and you would rather proclaim your independence? You will be the death of us.' With a shake of his head, the spy set off down the slope once more, skidding among the great old oaks and tangled hawthorns. Occasionally, he stopped to look back and saw Meg keeping pace, determination etched on her face. Grudgingly, he had to accept that her boasts were all true; few other women could have survived the privations they had experienced since escaping the hot, plague-ridden capital.

His heart racing, Will cast his mind back across the two weeks since the escape from London under a mound of dirty sackcloth in the back of a cart. When he had scrubbed the plague-pit filth from him, he had bought cheap clothes, and then he and Meg became Samuel Maycott, a draper, visiting family in the north with his wife Mary. He stole a dagger from a blacksmith and allowed his beard to grow unkempt. As they continued north, they were passed by riders distributing pamphlets. Under an engraving of his face, so crude as to be barely recognizable, was the legend: *England's Greatest Spy – Traitor.* And beneath it, *William Swyfte, hero of the perfidious invasion by the Spanish fleet, wanted for treason. By order of the Privy Council. A reward has been offered.*

The spy's thoughts burst back into the present as he careered from the foot of the hillside into a meadow, the long grass swaying like silvery water in the moonlight. Behind him, torches and lamps glimmered like fireflies among the trees. The baying of the hounds rolled down the hillside, closer now.

The two fugitives had been running since sundown when a field worker drinking his beer by the hedge had chanced to talk to them, and had grown suspicious. But Will was tiring now, he could feel it. His leaden legs shook and fire seared his chest, and he guessed Meg was in a worse state, though she never complained.

The spy heard the pounding of the Irish woman's feet in the undergrowth. Out of control, she burst from beneath an oak into the meadow straight into Will's arms. Strands of auburn hair fell across her face, and when she blew them back, the spy found himself looking deep into her emerald eyes. For all her forthright playfulness, her cheeks still flushed, and she was the one who pulled away.

'Master Swyfte,' she breathed with a hint of embarrassed laughter in her words, 'you are my saviour.'

'I will do my best to live up to that title, my lady. Though at the very least I can promise you an entertaining ride to the bitter end.'

'I heard you were an accomplished rider, sir. I would see it at first hand.' Her teasing smile faded as she glanced over her shoulder to the dark, wooded hillside.

An undulating cry rumbled behind the baying of the dogs and the increasingly loud shouts of the nearing villagers. Unnatural and unsettling, it throbbed into the very core of Will's being.

'Let us not tarry, Master Swyfte,' Meg said, a flicker of unease in her eyes.

They ran.

Halfway across the meadow, with their twin trails snaking out through the long grass behind them, Will glanced back.

The lights were now flickering along the tree-line, and he caught a whiff of pitch from the sizzling torches. The other-worldly cry was caught in the wind, setting his teeth on edge.

When they reached the far side of the meadow, Will realized their time had all but run out. Meg was slowing by the moment, and the pursuers and their dogs were gaining ground. Ahead lay only more meadows, a stream, no tree cover or anywhere they could hide.

'Stop,' he called, skidding to a halt.

The Irish woman whirled, her eyes blazing. 'I never give up!'

'Nor is that my plan.' He dropped to his knees and pulled his flint from his doublet.

His companion saw instantly what he was doing, but looking towards the bobbing lights she insisted, 'There is not enough time.'

'Let us pray that there is. For it is our only hope of escaping that rabble.' Will struck the flint once, twice, a third time. The crack of the stone was lost beneath the howl of the dogs and the jubilant cries of the villagers who saw their quarry had come to a halt.

His full attention focused on the flint, the spy struck it again. This time a spark caught on the yellowing grass along the hedgerow. It had not rained for nearly two weeks and under the hot summer sun the countryside had baked and the vegetation had grown tinder-dry. A cloud of fragrant white smoke swirled up. The grass crackled, the red spark licking into golden flames that spread along the foot of the hedgerow.

Will glanced back at the meadow. White faces now loomed out of the gloom beneath the lights of lantern and torch. The tone of the hounds' howling became uncertain as they scented the smoke, and the spy watched the pursuers slow. Flames

270

surged up the hedgerow with a sudden roar that carried far over the quiet landscape. Within moments, a wall of red, orange and gold rushed across the grassland. White smoke became grey, billowing in thick clouds that soon obscured the hesitant villagers.

Shielding his face against the heat, Will stepped away from the fire, coughing as the acrid fumes stung the back of his throat. 'Come,' he gasped. 'This should provide us some cover, at least for a while.'

Impressed, Red Meg nodded as she lifted her skirts and hurried away from the blaze. 'Your reputation is not unwarranted, Master Swyfte. But we are still in an ill pickle.'

Behind them, the dogs' frightened barks were drowned out by the long howl of the thing they feared more. A note of jubilation edged the cry. Whatever was there sensed its prey at hand.

All humour now gone, the Irish woman cast a troubled glance at Will. Neither of them spoke as they clambered over a stile and ran across the next meadow.

When they reached the other side, Meg said in a hesitant voice, 'What do you suggest?'

'You know as well as I there is little to gain by running. If the Enemy is at our backs in open countryside, it will not relent until it has us.'

'Stand and fight, then? But where? And do you have the strength to defeat one of those foul things?'

Will guessed his companion already knew the answer.

They reached a rutted lane, the edges lined with nettles. At the top of the stile, Will looked back to the thick fog drifting across the meadow. Dark smudges of villagers moved through it, more hesitant but refusing to give up. Yet the spy's attention was caught by a wilder activity away to his left. Something

271

bounded across the meadow, outpacing the men with the dogs. Will found it hard to discern its true nature; at times it moved on all fours, at others it rose to two feet, with a loping gait. It kept fast and low at all times.

Meg had seen it too. 'It will be on us in moments,' she said, drawing herself up. 'Unsheath your sword. I will use my dagger. If we are to die this night, let it be with blood on our blades.'

Spinning round, Will surveyed the dark countryside. One glint of moonlight stirred a hope.

'I am not ready to die yet.' He leapt from the stile to run along the lane.

As they moved away from the roaring of the fire, they could hear the tinkling of water falling across stones.

A change in the wind brought dense clouds of smoke sweeping all around the two fugitives. The keening cry of their now-hidden pursuer became louder. Will wondered if the thing at their backs was circling them, choosing its moment to strike.

The shouts of the hunting party had grown angrier. The hounds were baying again, and they too were drawing nearer.

Out of the smoke, an old stone bridge emerged, the worn and crumbling parapets dappled with lichen. As Meg ran to cross it, the spy caught an arm around her waist, forcing her off the dusty lane and down the grassy bank to the stream he had heard earlier. Will didn't slow their pace and they splashed into the cool, black water up to his calves.

Meg flashed a questioning look, but he only urged her into the dark beneath the bridge's single arch. Amid the smell of wet vegetation, they came to a halt against the chill stone, drawing the dank air into their burning chests. Through the other arch of the bridge, they could see grey tendrils of smoke floating past and the hellish glare of the fire burning across the meadow.

'Running water dulls the senses of the Enemy,' Will whispered. So Dr Dee had told him, and he hoped the alchemist was right.

Meg nodded.

But would the stream dull those senses enough to mask the presence of the quarry hiding beneath the bridge? the spy wondered.

The night was punctured by the shouts of the hunting party trying to decide which way to go along the lane. Will heard someone give an order to split into two groups. But then the strange, reedy cry echoed nearby and he felt Meg's body tense beside him.

They waited, listening to the distant crack of the fire and the splashing of the water. The cry came again, not far from the bridge, and then ended suddenly.

It knows we are here, Will thought.

Meg sensed it too. She held the spy's gaze, offering a silent prayer. He felt her body grow taut once more, and he was sure their hearts were beating so hard they could be heard beyond their bodies.

A soft tread rustled above their heads. It paused, began again. *Searching.*

Nails scraping on stone. Low, rasping breaths. A thump as the predator leapt on to the parapet of the bridge.

The Irish woman flinched, her mouth working against Will's hand. Pulling her close, he held her tight to prevent her crying out by accident.

'Can't see nothing down here!' a young man's voice rang out from further up the lane.

A growl rumbled out from deep in the throat of the thing

waiting above. The spy heard it leap from the parapet and scuttle down to the other side of the bridge. Hiding from the approaching men, he guessed.

Footsteps pounded along the dried mud of the lane to the edge of the bridge. Dogs snuffled in the undergrowth. Within a moment, however, the hounds began to whimper and then turned tail and ran back along the lane.

'What's wrong with 'em? They afeared a summat?' Will heard one man say.

'The fire. Beasts don't like it,' another replied.

''Ere. Let's have a look over the bridge,' a third said.

From the sound of the footsteps cresting the stone structure, the spy guessed that three was the total number of villagers in the group. The men tramped a little farther down the other side of the bridge and then stopped. Will imagined them looking out into the night.

'Back home?' the first began. His next word was drowned out by a terrible roaring. The three men shrieked as one.

Meg folded into the spy's body, glancing fearfully through the arch where the hellish fires blazed. The men scrambled backwards, their yells unintelligible beneath the deafening rage of their attacker. Will heard the thing race up the bridge, and then there was a sound like ripping silk again and again and again. The screams of the three men pierced the night.

Something fell into the stream with a loud splash. When the water settled, Will saw the dead eyes of one of the villagers staring back at him, the mouth wide in terror.

The cries became whimpers and gradually died away, but the crunch and spatter continued a while.

Then silence fell.

The spy realized he had stopped breathing. Meg was rigid too. Will tried to imagine the predator standing above his head, caught in the lamp of the moon, stained red from head to toe. Was it licking its lips? Was it looking hungrily to where the rest of the hunting party searched? Or was it listening slyly, waiting for Will to emerge from hiding?

Now he could hear the frightened, questioning voices of the other villagers following the screams of the dying men. The thing must have decided it had no further appetite for slaughter, for Will heard it turn and lope from the bridge along the lane in the opposite direction.

'We must be away from here before we are discovered,' the spy whispered.

His companion was loath to move and pressed her back against the stone of the arch, but Will grabbed her cold hand and gently eased her away. Within a moment they were splashing along the stream, scrambling over slippery rocks down the channel between the meadows.

Horrified shouts echoed through the dark behind them as the villagers found their fallen friends. 'God's wounds,' one man exclaimed. 'The Devil is abroad this night.'

And Will could not deny it.

CHAPTER THIRTY-NINE

'YOU CAN NEVER OUTRUN THE THING THAT THE UNSEELIE COURT has set on your trail,' Meg warned, her mood dark as she wrung out the hem of her bedraggled skirts. A boiling July sun was beating down on the barleyfields edging the stream where the Irish woman and Will were resting. They had sought the shade of an ash tree five miles away from the bloody bridge.

'Then I will stand and fight.' His legs weary from the long run, the spy watched the lonely countryside for any sign of movement.

'This is not just any foe,' the woman pressed. 'It is one of their hunters. I have seen them at their murderous work, pursuing my countrymen through the forests. They never stop until they have their prey.'

'I have killed their kind before,' Will said bluntly, 'and I can do so again.'

Meg snorted, dragging her fingers through her damp, tangled auburn hair. 'You are a stubborn man.'

'What do you suggest? That I roll over and die?'

After a moment's pause, the woman ventured, 'Come away with me to Europe. I have seen your worth. There is good pay to be had for men and women of our skills. Spies are always in demand at the courts of great nations. We can change our names, our appearances, and with England fallen, the Unseelie Court will not care about two poor, bedraggled mortals.' With studied, heavy-lidded eyes, she breathed into his ear, 'We could become rich. More than that, we could experience many delights in each other's company.'

'Your offer is tempting, Mistress O'Shee, but I will not abandon England.' Will could not tell his companion of the notion that truly set him afire: the one slip in his tormentor's subtle assault when death seemed close in the plague pit, the hint that Jenny still survived in a hot land across the sea.

Thank you, Kit, the spy thought, still astonished how hope could arise from something so dark and despairing.

'Ho! What have we here?'

Will leapt to his feet, on guard in an instant. He was looking straight into the barrel of a musket.

On top of the bank across the stream, four armed men and a woman in dirty, ragged clothes levelled their weapons. The men were old soldiers, morion helmets tied under their chins with red tape, their bodies encased in mud-splatted corselets with tassets to protect their thighs. Two carried matchlocks, the rest rapiers. Wearing filthy grey skirts and only a corset on top, the woman stood with one hand on her hip. From the knowing look in her eye and the brazen way she held herself, Will guessed she was a doxy.

'Have ye not heard,' the man at the front said with a sneering smile, ''tis not safe to travel along the byways of England. Rogues and ruffians wait at every turn. But for a small contribution, we can ensure safe passage for you through these dangerous fields.' His eyes narrowed. 'Unless, of course, ye be Will Swyfte, in which case there is more than a pretty penny to be had.'

Will sized up the soldier, noting the easy stance and the confident gleam in his eye, and the cheeks flayed by the elements that suggested he had been living rough for a long time. Was he one of the disenchanted soldiers returned from Sir Francis Drake's failed attack upon Portugal four years earlier? One of those who had caused such violent trouble in London during the Bartholomew Fair?

'Oh, please, sir, do not harm us,' Meg protested, instantly adopting a terrified expression. She skipped lightly across the stream to the side of the footpad.

'Leave now,' Will said in a calm voice, his eyes locked on his opponent's, 'and you will not be harmed.'

The man shook his head in incredulity while his companions fell about in mocking laughter. With a shrug, Will drew his rapier. The group fell silent, their faces darkening.

'Fool,' the outspoken footpad muttered. He went to strike his flint to ignite the fuse of his matchlock, but before a spark had flown Meg had knocked the musket from his hands, thrusting her dagger towards his neck. The doxy lunged for the Irish woman, but was brought down in a flash when a small fist rammed against her jaw.

Will bounded across the stream and drove the tip of his rapier into the wrist of the soldier fumbling with the other matchlock. As the footpad fell back, howling, the spy turned his blade on the remaining two men.

'Drop your weapons or I will kill your leader,' Meg spat, her face now hard, the edge of her dagger digging into the exposed throat of her opponent.

'Kill him, then,' one of the other men muttered, his eyes darting from Will's sword to his mate.

'Honour among thieves,' the spy said in an acid tone. 'Come on, then. Let us finish this now.'

278

Floating over the meadows came the rhythmic tinkling of bells and the sound of rich, deep voices singing in a strange language. 'Moon-Men,' one of the footpads whispered to his mate. 'They will cut out our hearts and eat them if they catch us here.'

Sheathing their swords, the two men scrambled up the bank and were soon racing away through the ripening barley. The dazed doxy and the other old soldiers followed close behind.

'What scared them so?' Meg mused as she watched the robbers disappear into the sun.

'Footpads are all cowards,' Will replied, plucking up the dropped matchlock. He held out a hand to his companion, who took it with a playful curtsey and they made their way back across the stream and up the bank.

'We make a good team, Master Swyfte. No enemy could stand against us,' the woman said. 'We would be rich in no time.'

'Or dead. For we both throw caution to the wind.'

The sound of the bells and the singing drew nearer. Just beyond the hedgerow a large crowd of people processed along a lane. Poised in thought, Will listened to the music as he watched the bobbing heads pass slowly by. Brilliant scarlets, golds and azure blues blazed among the greenery of the countryside. He saw an opportunity.

'Come,' he said, 'let us have some pleasant company and conversation.'

As they set off across the meadow, Will glanced back at the open countryside. He had the uncomfortable feeling of eyes upon him. Their pursuer had found them again, he was sure, and was biding its time until nightfall.

At the hedgerow, Meg slowed, growing contemptuous. 'Egyptians,' she hissed. 'Would you have us killed in the night,

279

or my virtue stolen before I am sold into slavery on the Barbary Coast?'

'You have a colourful imagination, my lady,' Will said. 'Though now you mention it, perhaps I can get a good penny for you. At least enough to buy me a hot ordinary in a tavern on the way.'

The Irish woman cursed loudly, but the spy only laughed.

The brightly dressed band of gypsies numbered at least forty, men, women and children, some mounted, others leading laden horses, though the beasts were poor, scrawny things. Many of the travellers had their faces painted yellow or crimson, embroidered turbans on their heads and silk scarves draping their necks. Their clothes were little more than rags stitched together, but the patches had been chosen artfully so the colours swirled across their bodies. The tinkling sound came from bells on small chains they wore around the ankles, and their feet were bare.

Will understood Meg's dislike, though he didn't share it. The Moon-Men were feared as thieves, black magicians, coney-catchers who tricked the gullible, and violent rogues who left for dead anyone who crossed their path. Villagers drove them on whenever they settled for a night. The Privy Council saw them as a threat to the stability of England and had passed more than one Act to control them. And so they continued their wandering across the length and breadth of Europe, playing up to the suspicions and earning a meagre living through begging, fortune-telling or giving displays of ventriloquism and puppetry at the fairs and taverns. Yes, and robbery too. But the spy knew greater truths were hidden among the rumours and gossip.

'What I have seen of the Enemy has made me slower to condemn my fellow men,' Will said as he helped the Irish woman over a stile. 'In London, the common man fears the blackamoors and lascars, yes, and the Spanish and Dutch too. The men of Kent loathe the men of Suffolk, for being strange in their ways, and in Bankside the men and women of one street eye with suspicion their neighbours on the next. The Unseelie Court see us all as barely more than beasts fighting anyone who dares stray on to our feeding ground, and sometimes I fear they are right.'

Meg cast a suspicious glance at him. 'Siding with the Unseelie Court?' she said. 'Some would find treason in your words. I would learn to bite your tongue, for those in other circles may not be as amenable to you as I.'

'Ah. You are amenable to me.'

Her cheeks flushed. 'I simply meant—'

Will held up a hand as the procession of gypsies slowed and a man in an ochre turban embroidered with black crescents and stars turned towards them. His dark eyes gave nothing away, but his hand slipped surreptitiously inside his robes, no doubt to grasp a hidden dagger.

'Tell me,' Will said to his companion, sweeping one hand towards the colourful throng, 'these Egyptians, as you call them, travel through the loneliest places in Europe, across the cold, dark moors and by lonely lakes, over mountaintops and by the sacred wells and pools and stones, all the places where the Unseelie Court are at their strongest. Yet they are here. They still live. Why have they not been slaughtered, or turned to straw, or lured underhill by haunting music to emerge old and broken years later?'

Meg's brow furrowed in thought.

The gypsy came over and gave a deep bow, as practised in pretence as any spy. 'We are but poor travellers, blown hither and yon in this world by the winds of need,' he said in a deep voice flavoured with an unidentifiable accent. His right hand still hidden in his robes, he held the left out, palm up. 'Spare a kindness to help us through this day and the dark night that follows.'

'I will do more than that,' the spy replied. He held out the matchlock. 'Take this firearm. It will earn you a pretty penny if you sell it at market, or you might find it offers you better protection along the dangerous roads of England.'

With one suspicious eye on Will, the man brought his hand out of his robes and took the musket, turning it over to inspect it. He nodded. 'A good piece. And in return . . . ?'

'You allow us to travel with you for a while.'

The gypsy shook his head. 'We do not allow strangers in our group.'

'I am not a stranger.' The spy placed a hand on his heart. '*Te'sorthene.*'

The man weighed the spy carefully. 'You speak our secret language,' he said with a hint of threat.

Will held the Moon-Man's gaze. 'In Krakow, three years gone, your people and I had a common enemy. The Fair Folk. We escaped by working together. I would hope we can do the same now.'

Nodding non-committally, the gypsy examined the musket again and returned to the caravan, where he engaged in whispered conversations with his fellows. After a few moments, he flashed a gap-toothed grin and said, 'We thank you for your gift and offer our hospitality on our journeys across this land. My name is Silvanus, my wife is Sabina. We have two boys. You are welcome to travel with my family and share our food.'

'Thank you. As we are among friends, my true name is Will Swyfte.'

'We do not discuss the Good Neighbours around our fire,

but as you raised the matter . . .' Silvanus whispered gravely, looking past the spy into the open countryside. 'Though it is summer, I feel the cold breath of winter on my neck. There has been peace in England for many years now, but this is a devil-haunted land once more.'

CHAPTER FORTY

'IF YOU WISH TO SAVE MY LIFE, WHY ARE YOU TRYING TO KILL me?' Edmund Shipwash sobbed. His heels scraped on the crumbling stone parapet surrounding the blue-tiled roof of St Paul's Cathedral, the rest of his body hanging out over the void, buffeted by the hot morning breeze. The winding, filthy streets of London throbbed with the working day's rhythms more than two hundred feet below.

'I am a man of contradictions,' the Earl of Launceston replied in his whispery voice, his fist caught in the front of Shipwash's emerald doublet. 'Answer the question.'

Shipwash whimpered as his body swayed from side to side. Swooping overhead, the gulls mocked him with their cries.

'Robert,' Carpenter cautioned, shielding his eyes from the glare of the snaking river to the south where the sails of the vast seagoing vessels billowed as they left the legal quays. The scarred spy could see his pale companion loosening his grip. The Earl was imagining what their captive would look like lying among the throng in the churchyard, his body broken and bleeding.

Launceston sighed and nodded.

'I have not seen Frizer or Skeres or Poley since Kit Marlowe

284

was killed,' Shipwash burbled. 'No one knows where they are. Not in London, no.'

As we had heard, Carpenter thought with irritation. The trail to the devil-masked killer was as cold as Launceston's heart. When they had escaped by the skin of their teeth from the supernatural forces haunting the woods to the south of Nonsuch, the two spies had plunged straight into London's underworld, beating and burning and cutting in search of the answers Will had demanded. But there was no sign of the man charged with the playwright's murder, nor his two accomplices.

'And what of Thomas Walsingham, Marlowe's patron?' the Earl demanded.

A black stain spread across Shipwash's breeches. 'N-no. Not seen. Nowhere.'

The rich cousin of the old spymaster had something to do with this business, Carpenter could feel it in his bones. But like the other three men, Walsingham had vanished. His fine home in Chislehurst stood deserted.

'Bring him in,' Carpenter spat.

Reluctantly, Launceston hauled their captive on to the baking roof. Shipwash fell to his hands and knees and vomited. The Earl sighed once more. 'Now what will the fine gentlemen and ladies think when they climb up here on Sunday morn for their weekly enjoyment of the view?'

Catching the scruff of the captive's jerkin, the Earl dragged the man lazily to where Carpenter leaned on one of the tower's buttresses. His sandy hair plastered to his head with sweat, Shipwash pressed his hands together as if he were praying to the bad-tempered man.

'I am no angel,' Carpenter said with a cruel wave of his hand. 'If I were, you might have a chance of escaping the fate that awaits you.'

'Please,' the terrified man begged. 'The Unseelie Court are hunting me? And I am to die, like Marlowe?'

'And Gavell and Clement and Makepiece,' Launceston sniffed, examining his nails. 'Yes, you are on the list.'

'I know nothing of any list!'

'It is a list of all spies who worked with Kit Marlowe at the behest of our old master Sir Francis Walsingham. Tell us what matter you were engaged in and there may still be some thin hope,' the scarred man growled.

'But you know our business! Oft-times we have no idea who else works with us.'

Carpenter feigned boredom. He looked past the pall of smoke hanging over the clutter of poor plague-ridden houses near the Tower towards the tenter grounds on either side of Moor Fields. Long strips of crimson and popinjay blue fluttered in the wind where the cloth finishers were drying and stretching their recently dyed textiles.

Shipwash began to cry. 'The Unseelie Court! I am a dead man.'

'How fragrant it could be up here above the foul-smelling streets with the wind bringing the scents of the fields to the north,' the Earl's nostrils flared, 'if not for the stink of piss and sick.'

The captive looked up. 'I . . . I kept records. I know that is grounds for treason. But I thought—'

'You thought you might blackmail someone, somewhere, with some secret or other you had gleaned along the way.' Carpenter shrugged. 'Well, we have all considered it at some time or other. Life is hard and a little coin helps it pass easier.'

'But why is this important?' Shipwash asked, standing shakily.

'If we find *why* the Unseelie Court wish those named in

the list dead, we may be able to discover *who* wields the knife,'
Launceston muttered. 'Or not.'

'You could protect me,' the frightened man said hopefully.

'No point.' The scar-faced spy turned up his nose at the
man's urine-stained breeches. 'The Enemy will simply find
another victim to help break down our hard-fought defences.'

'But if our devil-masked killer still thinks you are handy for
a little throat-slitting and flaying, we may yet draw him out
into the open,' the Earl said with a quiver of excitement.

Carpenter sighed and rolled his eyes.

'What? You seek to use me like cheese in a mousetrap?'
Horrified, Shipwash looked from one spy to the other.

'For the moment, we will keep you safe,' Carpenter snapped,
glaring at his companion. 'Now fetch your records.'

The two spies accompanied their anxious colleague down
the three hundred steps into the nave. Outside in the rumble
of cartwheels and the reek of dung, Carpenter pulled his cap
low and sidled up to where his love, Alice, waited with a pot
of New World paprika for the palace kitchens. 'Tell Swyfte's
assistant we have our man Shipwash,' he whispered. 'He may
yet have the information we need.'

'Can I kiss you?' the kitchen maid teased, her eyes sparkling.

'No!' The scar-faced man's cheeks flushed, though it was
more with excitement than embarrassment. 'Alice, I thank you
for what you do. But take no risks. I could not bear it if—'

'Hush,' she said. 'If I can help bring this terrible business to
an end and we can be together once again, then that is worth
any risk.'

Full of gratitude, Carpenter could only give a curt nod and
hurry back to his companion.

'You are a fool,' Launceston said with surprising emotion.
'You play games with her life.'

'Alice is her own woman. I have no more power to drive her away than I have with . . . you.'

The two spies held each other's gaze for a long moment. Behind them, heels suddenly clattered on the worn flagstones surrounding St Paul's. The men spun round to see Shipwash racing away through the crowds swarming into the nave in search of work.

'Damn him,' Carpenter cursed. The scarred man and the Earl plunged into the throng, hurling bodies out of their path. Past the bellowing preachers they ran, knocking over book-sellers and upending servant girls, elbowing merchants and kicking out at children. But by the time they reached the cart-clogged street, their former captive was nowhere to be seen.

'Ah,' Launceston said, placing a finger to his lips in reflection. 'That went well.'

CHAPTER FORTY-ONE

IN A FRENZY OF GLEAMING BLACK WING, THE CROWS FEASTED on the fine banquet of young Edward Tulse. Eyes gone, white bone shining through the tatters of his face, the kitchen boy was losing his identity one peck at a time. A day after his life had been taken, the lad still hung from the gallows at Nonsuch, and there he would remain until another victim was chosen to take his place.

And that will not be long, Grace thought.

Hurrying silently along the first-floor corridor, the lady-in-waiting tried to avert her eyes from the grisly sight, but the deteriorating corpse said too much about life in the palace. The boy, who struggled with some deformity of the mouth, had been as good-natured as anyone consigned to labour all day near the hot ovens during the summer. He could never have been a spy reporting back to his secret Catholic masters.

The young woman paused at the end of the corridor and listened. Outside the crows had been disturbed, taking wing as one, a shadow of black feather and bloody beak passing across the sun. So soon after dawn only the kitchen staff would be up preparing the morning meal, but she could not take any risks.

Everywhere she went someone was watching her with beady, suspicious eyes. And not just her.

Accusations were coming thick and fast to the Privy Council: of treason, atheism, unnatural acts, and any other crime that could be imagined. Men and women looked at their friends and acquaintances and wondered who was reporting on whom, and which person could be trusted, and who had most to gain by bringing another down.

'You are well?'

Grace stifled a cry of surprise. It was Nathaniel, who had crept up on her as stealthily as a cat.

'You said to be light of foot,' he muttered. He looked pale, with dark circles under his eyes.

'I did not say scare me into an early grave.'

'This creeping around takes its toll, 'tis true. I have not slept well since we parted company with Will. At every noise, I feel they are coming for me in my sleep.'

'What have you uncovered?'

'I whiled away an hour with Jane Northwood in the gardens yesterday evening,' he winced, 'and someone owes me a great debt for that. After listening to all the gossip of every dalliance and slight and rivalry in the entire court, I began to feel my life drain from me. But by the time the bats were flitting overhead, a lull in the conversation finally appeared and I could ask my question. She tells me Master Cockayne is away in London on some business.'

'Come, then,' Grace said, excited. 'We must search his chamber.'

Her friend's face grew grave. 'And if we are caught we will be hanging out there with Edward Tulse.'

'Now, Nat, before the palace awakes,' the young woman urged softly.

With a sigh, Nathaniel nodded. He led the way through the still corridors to Cockayne's chamber, three doors from the spymaster's own room. Grace listened at the door. No sound came from within, and after a moment she steeled herself and stepped inside.

The chamber was barely bigger than a box, with a trestle, a chair, two stools and mounds of parchments and books. The woman felt her heart sink as she surveyed the piles of papers, but she gave a weary nod to Nathaniel and they began to sift through them. Grace tried to picture Cecil's adviser at work in the room, a small man, ruddy-faced and grey-haired, hunched over these volumes deep in thought. Where would he hide the play?

The young man tossed parchments aside with seeming disregard. 'At least we will have some distraction from all this misery,' he muttered.

'Oh, what?'

'Jane Northwood told me there is to be a masque, to take the Queen's mind off the plague drawing closer to her palace. Costumes and music and dancing, with the most lavish scenery and devices and machines ever to grace Nonsuch. All paid for by the Earl of Essex.' Nathaniel flashed his friend a grin. 'If he cannot fawn enough, he will buy his way into the Queen's favour. They say he has even hired Sir Edmund Spenser to pen the words and verses. Perhaps not the best choice when his *Faerie Queen* antagonized Lord Burghley so.'

The sound of footsteps echoed outside the chamber.

Nathaniel quickly moved to a corner out of immediate sight from the entrance to the room, but Grace stood transfixed.

The door swung open to reveal a scowling Tobias Strangewayes, rapier drawn. 'What are you doing here?' he snarled in a low voice.

The woman flinched from the spy's gaze. Her blood growing cold, she approached the man, holding her hands before her. 'Please, Master Strangewayes, I beseech you. This is not how it appears.'

Every fibre of her being thrummed with awareness of Nat only feet away.

The spy began to look around the room. Grace snatched out a hand to touch his cheek. The shock of that contact almost threw them apart.

Keep your eyes upon me, the woman silently prayed.

She forced a flirtatious smile, like the ones she had seen Meg conjure so easily. Her fingers remained on the man's cheek, hot and tingling and so brazen it might have been an embrace. Uncomfortable, Grace thought, *I have never been so forward before.*

'It appears that you are one of the traitors at large within Nonsuch Palace.' His tone was harsh, and he began to look around the room again.

Panic made the woman's heart flutter. Forcing herself to overcome her resistance, she parted her lips and stepped so close to Strangewayes that her body brushed against his. She balanced on tiptoes, wavering, so that he knew she could easily fall forward and press her breasts against his chest. Her cheeks flushed with awkwardness, but she widened her smile to turn it into a colouring of passion.

Strangewayes swallowed, his brow furrowing. His gaze still wanted to dart.

Keep. Your. Eyes. On. Me.

'You are a brave and honourable defender of our Queen and I am but a lowly servant of Her Majesty, but we wish the same thing: her safety and security,' Grace breathed. 'I followed a hooded man to this part of the palace, but lost sight of him. Then I saw this door was ajar—'

The red-headed spy made to step into the chamber. Her heart beating faster, Grace leaned forward so her lips were close enough to kiss him.

'If I was seen . . . why, I fear for my safety. I have no strong protector here at court.' She held his wavering gaze until a faint smile leapt to his lips.

'You have one now,' he said gently. 'My master sent me to . . .' He hesitated. 'To request some information from Master Cockayne . . .' His voice tailed away.

At this time of day? Grace thought. It seemed that the Earl of Essex was taking advantage of Cockayne's absence to look into the business of his rival, Sir Robert Cecil.

'Would you walk with me awhile until I find peace?' the woman whispered.

Strangewayes nodded, eager to be away from the chamber now he had been caught out.

Her blood throbbing at the close call, Grace flashed a glance at a rigid Nathaniel as she left the chamber.

She knew she had earned only a brief reprieve. Before she had been all but invisible; now that Strangewayes had discovered her among Cockayne's things she had been noticed. One more false step would bring her immediately to the attention of the powers at Nonsuch, and then her life would truly hang by a thread.

CHAPTER FORTY-TWO

'SOMETHING FOLLOWS US STILL. DO YOU SEE?' SILVANUS POINTED down the rolling Staffordshire uplands to where the lush meadows fell against a dense strip of shadowy woodland. Will followed the line of the gypsy's finger. Squinting, he could glimpse a grey shape flitting among the trees, though under the slate-grey skies at the end of the day he could not be sure it was not a trick of the light.

'The same thing you have seen for the last three nights?' the spy asked.

The man bobbed his ochre turban in a grave nod. His face was painted scarlet from the festivities in the village they had just left, where the gypsies had played their roles as fortune-tellers, magicians and performers. They had been given enough scraps of food to last them three days. 'It draws closer with each day, sometimes appearing from the east, sometimes the west, searching for a break in our defences. It plans to attack if it can find a way in, or it would have left us alone long ago.'

The spy looked back at the children chasing each other alongside the laden horses of the caravan. What kind of man was he to show such callous disregard for the lives of the people who had protected him? Meg appeared to care little about the harsh decision they had taken for the greater good, but Will felt it weigh heavily on him every moment of the day.

The Moon-Man returned to his wife Sabina, who rode a horse with baskets hanging down its flanks. Their two boys, Goliath and Samuel, had taken a liking to Will, enjoying his tales of adventure. He felt another pang of self-loathing at their warm glances.

He looked back down the slope, but the shadow was gone. Whatever was out there would be back soon, though, he was sure of it.

He strode back to the slow-moving column where Red Meg played with the gypsy children. She had warmed to the Egyptians during the seven days the two spies had accompanied the caravan, sharing the travellers' food round their fires under starry skies, and listening to the lilting poetry of their strange, secret language. On their journey across the flat Midlands plain, Will had seen his Irish companion peel away layers of deception to reveal what he believed were her genuine feelings. At times, he had almost grown to trust her.

The sun broke through the clouds as the caravan made its way steadily upwards. It was hot and muggy with the threat of rain. The dusty air of the track across the lowlands gave way to the scent of fern and cool, damp vegetation. As a dark band of forest loomed ahead of them, Silvanus made his way back. He wore a relieved smile.

'We are nearing a safe place,' he said, dabbing at the sweat on his brow with a red kerchief. 'We have made camp here many times before. The tracks through these hills are always dangerous, with footpads and rogues roaming constantly. But there are many places nearby that the Good Neighbours call their own. When we move so close to their realm, we always take more care.'

Meg looked at the hillside and then down into the lowlands where the shadows of clouds scudded across the woods and meadows. 'This reminds me of home,' she said with a note of yearning. 'Where are we?'

The Egyptian pointed from the shimmering line of the River Dane in the green valley towards the nearest heavily wooded mountain beyond the hillside. 'That is the White Peak and this wood ahead is Back Forest. In there is our destination. Lud's Church.'

'A church?' Meg asked. 'You are God-fearing men, then?'

Silvanus grinned. 'This church has been here much longer than the ones you know. It was old before the Bible was written.'

'And who worships in that house of God?' Will enquired.

The Moon-Man only smiled.

When the caravan wound its way under the cool canopy of Back Forest, the singing of the Egyptians grew quieter. The children kept closer to their mothers, wide, bright eyes searching the shadows among the trees. They could hear birdsong and the movement of small woodland creatures in the verdant undergrowth, but they all felt an odd weight upon them, as if the forest was holding its breath, watching the strange beings wandering into its midst. Will found the sensation unsettling, but not threatening.

The two boys, Goliath and Samuel, stepped in close to the spy, taking his hands. 'Tell us a story, master,' Samuel, the older boy, whispered, trying to be brave. 'Tell us again how you fought the bear with your bare hands.'

Picking up Goliath, Will continued to hold the other boy's hand as he spoke again about his exploits. Meg rolled her eyes at her companion's heroic exaggerations and the weakness of his jokes, but she stayed by his side nonetheless, head down as she listened to his words. Glancing down at Samuel, Will had the strange feeling that he was looking at himself, on his way to hunt for birds' eggs with his friends in the Forest of Arden. He was surprised by a brief but powerful pang of loss.

The caravan wound through the ancient greenwood, the track wide enough only for one person at a time. Their low, rhythmic singing rolled out among the gnarled trees. Although the Moon-Men were moving up into the highlands, Will noticed the front of the column had started to dip down. Eventually he came to a set of uneven steps cut into the grey bedrock, so old and worn by generations of feet they might have been formed by nature. The steps led into a chasm that had been created by a great landslip, as wide as the height of two men, the bottom lost to the dark. The singing stopped as each man, woman and child began their descent. Shafts of evening sunlight slashed through the jumble of overhanging trees, illuminating areas of moss-covered sandstone on the sheer walls.

The chasm was even cooler than the dense wood. As his eyes adjusted to the half-light, Will saw it was thickly over-grown with fern, bracken and long grass. When they reached the gulley's stony foot, Meg looked up in awe at the patchwork of green leaf and blue sky as high overhead as the top of a stee-ple. 'It is indeed a church,' she whispered.

Silvanus turned back to Will and said, 'Only on the day of midsummer does the sun reach to the very bottom of this sacred place. They say that, in the time before the church-people came to England, men and women ventured here to bow their heads to old gods.'

'A good choice,' Will replied with a nod. 'It would not be difficult to defend this place against brigands.'

'There is more to this sanctuary than that,' the gypsy said, looking along the chasm to where his people were already pulling their bundles off the horses. 'Some places even the Good Neighbours must walk with care.'

Silvanus went to help his wife erect their shelter. Along the soaring sandstone walls, the men unfurled brightly coloured squares of linen, draping them over arrangements of poles, while the women folded sheets for bedding. When they were done, fires were lit in the gathering gloom, the sparks swirling upwards towards the slash of cerulean sky. Huddled around the flames, the garishly painted women prepared the stolen poultry and trapped rabbits for the evening meal, their faces even more grotesque in the red light.

Meg called Will over and they sat under a shelter, watching the flickering light throw looming shadows across the wall of the chasm. 'How does it feel – a tool of the English state, now on the run and allied with the very outsiders your government and people have hounded?' the Irish woman teased.

'Life surprises us with different roles when we least expect it.'

With a wistful expression, Meg watched the children at play.

'I hear there is little love for Englishmen in your homeland,' Will enquired from beneath the wide brim of his felt hat.

'Would you expect any different after the massacres your Earl of Essex inflicted on my people?' There was a crack of restrained anger in her voice. 'Our lands sold off so that wealthy Englishmen can settle their plantations in Munster? Our women raped by your adventurers? The Irish have long memories, Master Swyfte.'

'Yet here you are, helping the long-hated enemy. Apparently, life surprises us all with improbable roles.' Will pushed his hat back, letting the flickering flames illuminate his features. 'I wonder, do you truly help Henri of Navarre? Or do you

298

aid Hugh O'Neill, with his ambitions to rule Ulster without interference? Or do you stand with the Gaels who just want blood for blood?'

Meg jumped to her feet. 'You have been a spy so long that all you see is politics,' she snapped. 'There is more to life than that.' She marched off among the flapping shelters and disappeared into the dark at the end of the chasm.

Will was baffled by the woman's reaction. But when he made to follow her, he noticed an old gypsy staring at him. The man's long white beard had been stained green at the tip, and there were bells in his snowy hair. He pointed a wavering finger. 'There is a shadow with you,' the Moon-Man said in faltering English. 'It eats its way into your heart. If you do not rid yourself of it soon, you will die.'

'We all die, sooner or later,' Will retorted. But he was stung by the Egyptian's words, for they echoed his own fears that his devil was drawing closer. As if Mephistophilis sensed his thoughts, the spy heard a faint laugh close to his ear.

His mood now dark, Will made his way through the camp to where the elders prepared the nightly defences. Chanting quietly, one of the gypsies sprinkled salt and herbs at the foot of the stone steps. Silvanus was looking up to where a patch of night sky was visible among the overhanging trees. He appeared to be unnerved by a rustling in the undergrowth near the lip of the chasm.

'We will be safe?' Will enquired.

'As ever.'

'But you are worried.'

'I have never known the Good Neighbours to be so persistent. They like their mischief, but are easily bored and usually seek out other sport.' Silvanus watched the trembling in the undergrowth subside, then shook his head and turned

299

to the spy. 'I fear something terrible is about to happen. It is in the cards that the women read every night. In the visions the old men have.' He kneaded his hands together, glancing back up to the top of the chasm. 'This devil–haunted land . . . What is happening? Are any of us safe?'

Returning to the shelter, Will accepted chicken and a knob of stolen bread from Sabina, which he gnawed on deep in thought, his mood growing more unsettled by the moment. Silvanus could sense it; they all could. England was slipping back into the hands of the Unseelie Court.

After the food, amid the crackle of the fire and the contented chatter of those around him, his eyelids fluttered. In the centre of the camp someone was playing a fiddle. The women would be dancing, their coloured calico scarves flying around their bare shoulders, their black hair lashing the air, the bells at their ankles jangling in a frenzy.

As he slipped towards sleep, an odd thought struck him. The Egyptians had the same word for life and death: *merripen*. What did it mean?

Through the dark of his head, Mephistophilis drew closer, whispering truths that he didn't want to hear.

Will was roughly shaken from his deep slumber. The fires had died down to red ashes and a strong wind blustered with a hint of rain upon it.

'You must help us.' Silvanus' frightened face filled the whole of Will's vision. When the gypsy pulled back, the spy saw many others standing nearby, watching him uneasily. 'Samuel is missing, his bed empty. We have searched all of Lud's Church, but he is not here.' The Moon-Man glanced fearfully in the direction of the stone steps.

Clambering to his feet, Will shook the last of the wool from his head. Meg was away to one side, comforting the boy's

300

mother. 'He is a clever lad. He knows better than to wander off, especially at night, and in this place.'

Silvanus bowed his head, his voice falling to a whisper. 'Yet my son is not here.'

CHAPTER FORTY-THREE

LIGHTING A LANTERN, WILL STRODE TOWARDS THE UNEVEN stone steps, Silvanus beside him. The other Egyptians clustered back near the ruddy glow of the embers. Holding the lamp high, the spy glanced up into the impenetrable dark. Fat droplets of rain fell on his face, and he could hear nothing under the roar of the wind in the trees.

'There are two defences, yes?' he asked.

'One here at the foot, and one at the top,' the Moon-Man replied. 'We will be safe as long as we do not cross the final boundary.'

'Come, then.'

Emerging from the chasm first, Will searched his rain-lashed surroundings in the dancing lantern light. He held a firm hand out behind him to halt the gypsy's progress. 'There is no need for both of us here. Return to the bottom and I will shout down if I find Samuel.'

'I must help,' the Moon-Man protested, his dagger shaking in his hand.

'You would only hamper my search. I move quicker and faster alone, and too much noise would only draw the attention of what we both fear is out here.' Will held Silvanus' gaze until the gypsy nodded. As he descended, the man cast reluctant glances over his shoulder until he disappeared into the dark.

Once he was sure his friend was gone, the spy set the lantern on the woodland floor just beyond the top step. 'Let the boy go,' he said, just loud enough to be heard over the gale.

Beyond the circle of light, he thought he glimpsed a dark figure in the trees. He could feel its menacing presence acutely. Blood began to trickle from his nose.

With slow steps, the lurker emerged into the light.

'I know you,' Will said. Recalling vividly the horrific events of that snow-blanketed night in Cambridge when he first met Marlowe, he felt anger at the torment this thing must have caused Kit over the years.

'And I know you.' Will could see an equally deep loathing in the Hunter's eyes. In the crook of his arm, the Fay dragged Samuel, one sharp talon curled at the neck. The boy's eyes were dazed, his lips working silently.

'Name yourself,' Will demanded.

'Xanthus.' His lizard tongue flickered over his lips. 'Thrice-fold will your punishment be. For the shame you inflicted on me at our first meeting. For my brother, slain by your hand. And for Cavillex of the High Family, executed at your order. Thricefold the suffering for the misery you have caused.'

'And your despised breed have torn from my life the woman I love and my closest friend. All your misery does not even come close to a balance for those crimes. Not if I killed another hundred of your people. A thousand.' The spy drew his rapier and waved the point back and forth. 'Draw nearer, and I will do to you what I did to your brother.'

As the rain began to torrent, Xanthus dug his talon a shade deeper into the boy's neck. Samuel mewled weakly. 'You cannot hide behind that protective line. Give yourself up.

303

For the boy's life. Or stay there and have his death upon your conscience for ever. Either way, you will be destroyed.'

Will watched the dazed look fade from Samuel's eyes. As the lad glanced up at the bone-white face next to him, he was gripped with terror. Trembling, his gaze fell on Will and he cried, 'Master. Help me.'

'You will kill him anyway,' the spy laughed dismissively. The warm summer rain pelted his face, soaking him to the skin.

Xanthus shook the boy like a rag doll, eliciting howls of terror that stabbed into Will's heart. 'Your blind arrogance reaches new heights,' the Hunter raged. '*We* are always honourable. Your kind are the kings of deceit and trickery and betrayal.' His eyes fixed firmly on Will, the Fay lunged for Samuel's throat.

'Stop!' the spy called. 'Let him go.'

Lightning flashed overhead, and the roar of the wind in the trees sounded like a great beast circling the three figures.

The pale thing shook the wailing boy again.

'Very well. You bleed like any man,' Will called. 'Come turn my sword red.' Defiant, he stepped across the invisible line.

Xanthus dangled Samuel at arm's length, then let the lad drop to the wet turf. In a burst of white lightning, the young gypsy scrambled past the spy and threw himself down the rain-slick sandstone steps into Lud's Church. Will watched a victorious, yellow-toothed smile creep across the Fay's face. Dipping one hand into a pouch at his side, the Hunter tossed a handful of sparkling golden dust into the air, and as the wind swirled the glittering cloud around him, he disappeared.

The spy darted forward to where his enemy had stood, but

his blade cut only thin air. Whirling, he saw only swaying trees and driving rain and the black slash of the yawning chasm.

'Damn you,' Will cursed under his breath.

Continuing to turn, he glimpsed a flash of Xanthus crouched near the foot of a twisted oak. A moment later his opponent was moving closer from the opposite direction, once again vanishing in the blink of an eye.

The spy continually slashed his rapier in the hope that chance would aid him so he could carve a chunk out of his enemy. The thunder rumbled. Rain poured down his face and turned the ground beneath his feet to mud.

'Farewell,' the quiet voice rustled just behind his ear.

Jerking round, Will was caught in the lamps of loveless eyes, warm, meaty breath washing into his face. Silver glinted, a dagger, the hilt curved into the shape of a dragon's head, black symbols inscribed on the blade.

Instinctively, Will rolled away from Xanthus; too late. The dagger sprayed his blood into the driving rain. Throwing himself backwards, he skidded along the muddy turf, pain searing his chest. Yet, although the blade had ripped his flesh through his doublet, the wound was shallow.

As Will searched for his invisible attacker, a thought came to him. At the instant the Hunter struck, the spy had glimpsed blood trickling from the corners of his foe's eyes. Had the glittering dust taken a toll?

He breathed deeply and allowed the storm's fury to fade into the background. Locked in concentration, he turned slowly on the balls of his feet, each moment stretching, every detail magnified. Rain drifted down, flickering drops of white caught in the lantern light. Branches swayed, grass trembled.

And then he saw it: a splash in a puddle with no obvious cause; the kind of splash a foot would have made. His enemy was unseen, but still there, still corporeal, a fitting target for cold steel.

Will knew Xanthus would already have moved on. He had to be quicker. In a sheet of lightning, he glimpsed a shadow cast on the wet turf, and thrust his rapier into what seemed to be thin air.

A cry rang out.

The Hunter flashed into view, clutching a wound in his side. Snatching a small pouch from the folds of his cloak, Will flung a handful of the gypsy concoction of salt and herbs into the face of the writhing figure. There was a sound like lamb fat sizzling in a fire. Howls of agony spiralled up into the storm. Xanthus was on his feet in a moment, his face scarred and smoking, but he was lurching, off balance. *Weakening*, Will thought.

In his fury, the fading Hunter flung himself at the spy, stabbing wildly with the silver dagger. Each frenzied blow drove closer until the blade nicked Will's cheek. Recoiling, he stumbled, and in a flash Xanthus was upon him, pinning his arms to the ground.

The Fay raised his dagger over his head. 'For my brother. For Cavillex. For all the crimes committed against my people—'

Her sodden hair plastered against her brow, Meg loomed over the Hunter's shoulder. She plunged her own dagger down. The pale creature must have sensed her, the spy guessed, for at the last it twisted aside, the blade tearing into its shoulder. With all his strength, Will thrust Xanthus off him.

Scrambling to his feet, he caught the woman's hand. 'Get behind the line of defence,' he shouted over the storm. 'You should not have come to me.'

Before she could argue, he thrust Meg back towards the chasm. Determined to seize his chance to end the Hunter's life,

Will turned to see Xanthus hunched over a small silver casket with a death's-head carved on the front. As the box began to open of its own accord, Will was struck by a blast of icy air. In the shadows beneath the lid, he thought he glimpsed movement.

The Irish woman grabbed Will's shoulder. 'It is the Wish-Crux, containing the Hunter's *daemon*,' the Irish woman said. Afraid, she stared past Will's shoulder to the yawning dark inside the casket. 'All Hunters have their familiars.'

Swarming shapes were emerging from the box. Hunched over the Wish-Crux, Xanthus glowered at the two spies.

Tearing herself from the sight, Meg dragged Will towards the chasm and together they tumbled over the now-invisible line of defence left by the Egyptians on to the sandstone steps. Looking back, Will saw the Hunter had retreated beyond the circle of lamplight.

'I will never turn away, never stop.' Xanthus' growling voice rolled out of the dark. 'It would have been better for you if you had died here.'

In the next flash of lightning, Will saw his enemy had gone.

Turning back to Meg, puzzled, he said, 'You risked your life for me.'

'You risked your life for the boy.' Her eyes were pools of shadows, her face unreadable.

'I am in your debt.'

'I do not want your gratitude,' she said with a dismissive turn of her head. 'Do you think I would stand by and watch you die if I could help?'

Will couldn't answer without offending her. Courage of that kind was the last thing he had expected from someone so duplicitous, and he felt troubled that his ability to appraise her coolly was now in question. Was all that she said about helping him honest? Did she truly hold the affections at which she hinted? He bowed. 'I thank you, nonetheless.'

As they approached the foot of the steps, the lantern light revealed the gypsies waiting silently. In their faces, Will saw awe, and hope. He felt humbled.

When Samuel ran up and hugged his legs tightly, Will handed the lantern to Meg and lifted the lad on to his shoulders. 'I thank you,' Silvanus said, stepping forward. 'My wife thanks you. And all of my people are grateful to you. You owed us nothing, yet still you risked your life to save my son.'

'Any man would have done the same.'

'You know as well as I that is not true. My son now lives because of you and you alone. None of us here will forget that. In our travels across this world, we will always speak kindly of William Swyfte, and your name will pass rapidly among my kind. In future, when you need aid, the Moon-Men will answer the call.'

CHAPTER FORTY-FOUR

'I SHOULD WARN YOU,' WILL WHISPERED TO MEG AT THE DOOR of the Warden's chamber at Christ's College, 'Dr Dee is quite mad.'

The caravan had reached Manchester in the hot, muggy early evening of 15 July. As they crested the hills ringing the town, the brassy sun punched shafts of light through the grey cloud cover to illuminate brown-tiled roofs, workshops spouting plumes of white smoke, and the grey stone bulk of the churches and great halls amid the jumble of tiny streets. The St Swithin's Day celebrations were still under way, and Will and Meg had left the gypsies juggling and dancing as their women moved among the crowds, begging for food. A gap-toothed man had directed the couple to what he called 't'owd church', the college buildings to the north, quiet now that Evensong was done.

The spy hammered on the door with the hilt of his dagger. From within came the sound of loud, unholy curses, and the door was thrown open with such force Meg stepped back in shock, her hand at her mouth.

Though approaching seventy, the alchemist crackled with

the vitality of a man half his age. Will saw Meg was entranced by the magical symbols etched on his pale arms, disappearing into the depths of his ruby-coloured gown, and the small animal bones hanging from silver chains strung across his chest so that he rattled whenever he moved.

Dee's fierce grey eyes immediately peeled back the layers of the new arrivals. 'Swyfte!' he barked, scowling. 'My misery is complete. The one saving grace of my banishment to this dismal place was that I would never have to see your impertinent, conceited face, you grinning jackanapes.'

The spy gave a deep bow. 'Dr Dee. My life has been darker without you in it. May I introduce my companion, Mistress O'Shee?'

The Irish woman gave a seductive smile. 'I am honoured to be in the presence of such an exalted personage,' she breathed. 'You may call me Meg.'

Without a hint of embarrassment, the alchemist's eyes slid slowly over her frame and then a serpent tongue flicked out between his lips. Thrusting Will out of the way, Dee offered a hand to the red-headed woman and led her into his chamber. 'Your beauty brightens this dark, northern town,' he said with a lustful laugh.

Despite the summer heat, a fire blazed in the hearth. Dry rushes were scattered on the stone flags and there was an acidic reek of sweat in the air. The room was cluttered. A high-backed chair stood near the fire, alongside a pair of stools, a bench and a stained, chipped table, but almost every available space was taken up with stacks of books, charts and rolls of parchment. A faded tapestry marked with magical symbols hung on one wall. Circles of polished glass lay on the table, glinting in the candlelight.

'I apologize for the heat in my rooms,' the alchemist said as he guided Meg towards the bench. 'I find it impossible to get warm these days.'

As Dee hung over Meg, whispering comments at which she giggled in an uncharacteristic but practised manner, Will's attention was drawn to a circular mirror made of highly polished obsidian.

'What is this?' he asked, reaching for the object.

The magician leapt across the room to slap Will's hand away. 'Leave that!' Dee yelled, his eyes blazing.

The spy took a step back, concerned at the passion he saw in the elderly man's face.

The alchemist appeared to recognize he had overreacted and adopted a nonchalant manner. Waving a hand towards the mirror, he said, 'It comes from the New World, part of a haul of Spanish loot. An ancient magical item, it is said to have been treasured by the age-old race which inhabits that region, and was considered sacred to their god Tezcatlipoca, who protected rulers, warriors and sorcerers. Does that answer your question?' he added with a snap.

'And you use its undoubtedly great magical powers for communing with angels?' the spy asked, feigning innocence.

With a snort, Dee turned back to Red Meg. 'I fear I am a poor host,' he said, pressing his hands together. 'We should have sustenance. Wine, perhaps, and beef. These aged legs of mine are feeble, however, and can barely carry me across my chamber. Could you help an old man? Pray hurry to the chaplains and ask them to order the servants to deliver food and drink to my study.'

With a polite smile, the Irish woman rose from the bench. 'Of course,' she replied, and left.

'Old man?' Will snorted. 'You could strangle a blacksmith and still have the strength to torture a lawyer or two.'

Dee jabbed a finger angrily. 'Do not speak to me about games of deceit, *England's greatest spy*. Now, she will be gone for some time – the chaplains are away tending to the poor. Tell me – can she be trusted? Does she work for the Irish? I presume you have investigated her motives.'

Picking up a book, Will flicked through the creamy pages with a wry smile. 'I thought you had been enchanted by her smile and dazzled by her generous form.'

'I am no fool, Master Swyfte. You know that.' With irritation, the alchemist took the book and replaced it on the stack.

'I would not trust her entirely, though I have found no reason to doubt her.' The spy's tone darkened and he beckoned for the older man to take his chair near the fire. 'But that is neither here nor there. We have grave matters to address.'

Easing himself into the high-backed chair, the alchemist listened intently as Will related all he knew: of the Scar-Crow Men, and the plot to murder spies by the devil-masked man, of Marlowe's death, and his play with its hidden code, of Kit's secret spying work, and of Griffin Devereux. 'I would understand how all these questions connect, but more, I would know who killed my friend, Kit Marlowe, and for what reason. Then I will seek revenge.'

The candles in the room appeared to dim, as if even talk of the Unseelie Court had drawn a cold darkness to them. Dee stared into the depths of the fire for a long moment. Will had never seen him so grim. 'You require my help?' he asked in a quiet voice.

'I need you, Dr Dee. England and the Queen need you before the last of our defences fall. Yes, we are few. Yes, the forces ranged against us are overwhelming. But we are fearless, and bloody-minded, and a resistance group this small can be fleet of foot. It may already be too late, but if there is one chance we can strike back, we must take it.'

'The defences could fall at any time.' The alchemist's voice was almost lost beneath the crackle of the fire. 'The Enemy already has its puppets in place. Once they are secure, they will come for us first, you know, and our suffering will be worse than a thousand hells. You are mad to fight this. Run. Hide.'

One foot upon a stool, Will reached out his hands, imploring. 'There is hope, doctor. The Enemy has expended great effort in hiding whatever Kit Marlowe discovered. Why would they send a Hunter at my heels unless they feared I might discover one chink in their plot that could bring it all crashing down?'

Dee nodded thoughtfully, but was still unconvinced.

The spy saw his opportunity. 'I have travelled the length of England in the most perilous circumstances for one reason: to call upon the great and powerful Dr Dee. You are the terror of the Fay, the man who locked those foul creatures out of the land they had tormented for generations. I have risked all because with you on our side anything is possible. The Unseelie Court fear you, sir.'

Dee's eyes blazed. 'Those popinjays should never have dismissed me from the court. That grand betrayal after all I did for the Queen and England. This would never have happened if I had been there.'

Will smiled to himself.

'But where would we begin?' the alchemist mused, tugging at his beard. 'The defences will need to be repaired. But that takes weeks, perhaps months.'

The spy paced the room, feigning deep thought, although he had planned his strategy long ago. 'Who would be privy to Kit's secrets?' he muttered. 'Someone must have knowledge of that mysterious business of his.' He paused theatrically and raised one finger. 'Wait. Griffin Devereux spoke of a clandestine group . . . the school that meets at night, he called it. Have you heard of any such thing?'

In the gleam in the alchemist's eye, Will saw all he needed to know.

Dee weighed how much he should say, and then came to a conclusion, waving a cautionary finger at the spy. 'There is much you do not know about your friend, Master Swyfte. He lived another life far removed from the one he shared with you.'

'Kit did not want to endanger my life or taint my reputation, such as it is.'

The alchemist rose from his chair and cracked his knuckles. From a hook in one corner, he fetched his cloak of animal pelts, a grotesque assemblage that still retained the heads of the beasts. 'What would you say if I told you Master Marlowe was part of a conspiracy that threatened the very stability of England?'

'Kit was no traitor.'

'Oh, he was, Master Swyfte. As am I.' As Dee pulled on his cloak, he came to resemble some country poacher rather than one of the most feared men in all England.

'Do not play games with me,' the younger man cautioned, more sharply than he intended.

The magician spun round, his eyes narrowing at the implied threat. 'I speak the truth, you rump-fed pignut. Within England there is a group of men who oppose the government, yes, and the Queen herself.'

'You are Papists?'

Dee gave a mocking laugh.

'Those accusations were levelled at Kit.'

'Come now, Swyfte. You have played this game for a long time now. You know as well as I that when power speaks, it never says what it means.'

'The accusations of atheism the Privy Council made against Kit?' Will prowled the chamber, keeping one eye on the older man.

'You are closer to the truth with that, but only a little. Atheism covers many sins, and it is a suitable tool for the government to use to frame Master Marlowe as, shall we say, a certain kind of offender who carries no weight in the eyes of God-fearing folk.'

'A slur, then. The Privy Council tried to demean him. Make him appear worthless. And Kit was never worthless!' The spy grew angry.

'I know this: the Privy Council feared young Marlowe's ideas more than the Catholic plotters, more than the Spanish. Yes, more than the Unseelie Court.'

Will turned to Dee and glared. 'Are you suggesting it was not the Enemy who killed Kit? That his murder was at the bidding of the Queen, or Cecil, or one of those other bastards?'

The alchemist hesitated.

'If they did, I will have their blood.'

Dee eyed the younger man. 'Even the Queen's?' he asked in a quiet voice.

'We both gave our all to the powers that govern England, doctor, and we have not been repaid with kindness. In the end, you must ask who you really trust. Who matters most. Who decides what is right or wrong.'

'Why, Master Swyfte, I fear you are finally leaving callow youth behind,' the older man mocked. 'You are now entering a twilit world where there are no longer any easy choices. Are you up to the challenge?'

'We shall see. So, Dr Dee, can I count on your support in this suicidal endeavour?'

The alchemist returned to the obsidian mirror on the table and stared thoughtfully into its depths. 'How could I possibly resist?' he replied sourly. Becoming animated, he clapped his hands once, loudly, and then stabbed a finger into Will's face. 'If we are to halt the terrible events that are in motion, we must act quickly. The one who is killing the spies will follow a prescribed pattern. Time, place, the stars in the heavens – all part of the ritual. When he failed to slay you, he was forced to wait for the right moment for his next victim. I cannot know what path he follows. It is in the hands of the gods now, and all we do may already be futile. But we must try, eh, Swyfte, for that is who we are?'

'Throw caution to the wind, doctor, and let us strike fast and hard.' The spy's grin faded when he realized the alchemist was staring at him in a curious manner. 'What is wrong?' he asked.

'You have two shadows.'

The spy glanced back and saw that Dee was right. Stretching behind him was his own shadow, and, beside it, another, overlapping, but twisted, monstrous.

'What have you done?' the elderly man asked in a small, troubled voice.

'It appears I can never be afflicted with loneliness,' Will said, attempting to make light. When he saw Dee's expression remained unmoved, he added with a flamboyant sweep of his arm, *'Hell strives with grace for conquest in my breast. What shall I do to shun the snares of death?'*

'Well you may ask.' The alchemist circled the spy, examining him this way and that. 'You have been cursed.'

'My devilish companion was conjured during the performance of Marlowe's new play, a warning from Kit.' Will gave a shrug to show he was unmoved by the threat.

'Then in his aid your friend has damned you.' Will was surprised, and troubled, by the hint of pity in Dee's voice.

'This curse can be lifted?'

'By the one who set it. And he is dead. I wish it was within my power to provide a solution, but for all my subtle skills there is nothing I can do when such a thing has been raised by another.' For a long moment, the magician plucked at the sleeves of his gown in reflection, unable to meet the younger man's eye. 'The devil will burrow deeper into the heart of you until he destroys you from within, and there is nothing you can do about it. There is no way for me to sweeten this bitter pill, Swyfte, and I know you would not want me to. You are a strong man, and you have shouldered much suffering in your life, and I have no doubt you will face this with the valour I see in you. I would not have it this way, but there it is. You are doomed, and the end will not be pleasant.'

'Enough, doctor,' the spy interrupted. 'I have carried burdens before, and I am more concerned with surviving tomorrow, and the day after, than with what miseries may or may not await me in the future.' He gave a grim smile. 'Live for today, and let the devil take what may be.'

The alchemist appeared oddly touched by the young man's words. He moved rapidly to the clutter at the rear of the chamber, knocking over piles of books until he found a large wooden chest. 'A little help in the battle to come would not go amiss, eh?' From the depths of the chest, he pulled a wooden tube and a velvet pouch and offered them to the spy.

Will examined the object: the tube was hollow and the pouch contained small, sharp arrows.

'Our adventurers treat the New World men as savages, but

317

their knowledge is quite profound. That is a blowpipe. Tip those darts in poison, slip one in the end . . .' Dee mimed a blowing action. 'They travel far . . . farther now that I have improved the design.'

'Poison, you say?'

The alchemist drew several small cloth bags out of the chest. 'I have refined the potions over the years. The blue paste . . .' He grinned. 'Even those white-skinned bastards will recoil from that one.'

Will slipped the gifts into the secret pockets in his cloak.

'One final thing.' Dee held up another tube which appeared to be made of iron, but which the spy could see was much lighter. The elderly man pressed a hidden knob and four hooked arms snapped out.

'A grapnel,' Will exclaimed, taking the device. Attached to the bottom was a coil of rope that was thinner and lighter than any he had encountered before. 'This is no weight at all.'

'What wonders I could have provided for England's spies if only I had not been exiled to this cold, wet town,' the alchemist grumbled. 'But there you have it. Use the tools wisely and well. Now, let us find your friend. After staring at you, my eyes need some relief.'

Dee snuffed out the first of the three candles lighting the room.

'We must travel to meet our fellow conspirators, great men all, names that will surprise you, and they will have some of the answers you seek,' the alchemist said. 'If what you say is true and the old defences are falling, the journey will be dangerous. I can protect us a little, but even my vaunted abilities may not enable us to survive.'

'So be it.' Will snuffed out another candle. The shadows closed in around them, with only the flickering light of the

318

final candle and the dull red glow of the dying fire illuminating the room. Dee pulled his cloak around him and stepped towards the door.

'Where do we travel?' the spy asked.

The alchemist turned back to the younger man, his eyes sparkling. 'We go to see the Wizard Earl.'

Will snuffed out the final candle and the dark swept in.

CHAPTER FORTY-FIVE

THE QUEEN OF ENGLAND'S FACE RESEMBLED A DEATH-MASK beneath its frosting of white make-up. At Elizabeth's side, Elinor, her ever-present maid of honour, whispered words that no one else heard as she guided Her Majesty through the clutch of carpenters and artists at work on the scenery for the forthcoming masque. Cecil lurched in her wake, looking like a frightened dog, with the big mercenary Sinclair glowering over his shoulder, and trailing at the rear was Rowland, the record-keeper, distracted by the rolls of parchment tumbling from his arms.

Standing in a sunbeam where sawdust danced, Grace watched her mistress pass by with growing concern. New faces had appeared at the court over the last few days, men and women who answered to no one, but who seemed to have the Queen's ear. Who were they? What was their business?

When Nathaniel entered, Grace joined him out of sight behind a still-wet canvas painted to resemble the greenwood. 'It is becoming harder to meet,' the young woman whispered. 'Her Majesty has appointed another lady-in-waiting, a young girl by the name of Mary Wentworth. It appears her sole task is to follow me wherever I go.'

'The Privy Council has this morning agreed the execution of two more *traitors*. A stablehand and a butcher from Leadenhall who delivered pork for the kitchens,' the young man replied bitterly. 'The case against them was flimsy. Their deaths are solely to cause fear at court. If everyone is suspected, attention does not fall easily on the true culprits.'

'And Master Cockayne?'

'Since his return from London, he never seems to leave his chamber. I fear we have lost our best chance to recover Kit Marlowe's play,' Nat sighed.

'Among the women who sew together, there has been talk of mysterious lights at night in the fields around the palace, a ghost seen on the Grand Gallery, and voices heard in empty rooms,' Grace whispered, peering around the edge of the scenery. 'The portents are growing. And still no word from Will.'

'Why speak of Will? You have a suitor now.' The young man's tone was acidic as he nodded towards the door. Strangewayes was looking around the hall.

'Nat, you know my heart is for Will only,' Grace said unconvincingly. 'I spend time with Tobias' – she caught herself – 'Master Strangewayes for the information he can provide. He has eyes and ears all over Nonsuch.'

'And what if he is part of this plot, and he keeps an eye upon you while you are using him?' Nat leaned in and whispered, 'You are playing with fire, Grace. But both of us will be burned if you are wrong.'

When he walked away, Grace allowed the colour to fade from her cheeks. She was annoyed that her friend treated her like some little girl. At first Tobias Strangewayes had appeared no more than a braggart, swaggering around her and making no attempt to hide his lustful thoughts. She had found it surprisingly easy to manipulate him.

But on a hot early morn when she had been sent to collect flowers from the garden, she had found him standing among the yew trees, his head bowed in grief. 'I have received news that my brother, Stephen, is dead,' he had said in a hoarse voice. 'In Venice, though the circumstances remain to be explained.' He had tried to speak further, but the words would not come.

Grace had seen a man in the grip of loneliness and confusion. Her heart had gone out to him, and for the next hour they had spoken deeply and personally. She still did not know how she truly felt about the red-headed man, but she accepted that she no longer had contempt or scorn for him.

Beaming when he saw her, Strangewayes stepped over. 'Will you walk with me a while?' he asked. 'In the gardens?' His eyes darted around and his smile faded. 'There is something I must tell you.'

Puzzled, Grace followed him into the warm, lilac-scented garden.

'I feel in my heart I can trust you. Is that true?' he asked.

'Of course. What troubles you?'

Tobias ran a hand through his red hair. 'Sometimes I feel I am bound to be one of Bedlam's Abraham Men. My master employs a keeper of records, one Barnaby Goodrington, a clever fellow with a sharp wit. Whenever we discussed business, we got on well. But in recent days, he . . .' His words dried up.

'Has seemed like another man?' Grace continued. 'Acted oddly, perhaps?'

'Yes! Yesterday he began to cry when I told him a joke. And he is not the only one. Fulke Best, Christopher Norwood, Agnes Swetenham in the kitchens. They all seem like . . . echoes of the people I knew. Always distracted, sometimes addled even.' He paused, fighting against himself, and then said, 'I am loath to say it, but I wonder if Swyfte was right.'

322

'Help me,' Grace urged.

'Help *you*?'

'There *is* a plot here, I know it.' She steeled herself and decided to speak out. 'And I have been charged to uncover it. Before he was murdered, Kit Marlowe hid a cipher in one of his plays. It tells of the conspiracy. I need your help, Tobias. Master Cockayne is a part of this conspiracy and he has hidden the play in his chamber. If we are to stop the tragedy that will ensue, we must steal it back.'

Grace saw her companion look at her in a new, unsettled light. 'You are a woman. These are not matters for you.'

Grace flushed with anger. 'We have a queen who has proved herself the equal of any man—'

Strangewayes shook his head furiously. 'What you are talking about would be considered treason. Steal from an adviser to Sir Robert Cecil? How do I know you are not one of these plotters, trying to entice me into your web?'

The young woman watched the red-headed man's face harden and she knew she had lost him. 'Forget what I said, Tobias. I spoke out of turn.' As she stepped to the garden door, she could feel the spy's eyes heavy upon her back.

Had she made a terrible mistake?

CHAPTER FORTY-SIX

THE CRIMSON CROSS ETCHED ON THE DOOR SEEMED TO GLOW in the suffocating dark of the mud-baked street. Carpenter shuddered. It spoke to him of the transience of life, of those now mouldering in the earth and of the cold and bloody deaths yet to come. As he approached the cramped, timber-framed house in the shadow of the Tower, he wished he had a God who would offer him respite from the horrors of that life.

'Hrrm,' Launceston muttered as he glanced along the row of silent homes, 'the plague has taken its toll here.'

'And it will take another two victims if we do not hurry, you beef-witted foot-licker.' Carpenter tied the cloth tighter across his mouth and nose, but the apple-sweet stink of bodily rot still choked him.

Every door along the street had been marked with the sign of the plague. No candles glowed in any of the windows. No voices drifted out into the night, no husbands and wives arguing, or mothers singing their babies to sleep, or drunken apprentices winding their way home. There was only the warm July wind moaning under the eaves.

Now, Carpenter paused, resting his fingertips on the rough wood but not finding the courage to push it open. Each passing day, he wanted to be out of this morbid business a little more, to start afresh with Alice. He refused to accept that he was ruined for the mundane world, as the Earl insisted. He could still escape the shadows and the lies and the insidious threat of the things that came at midnight.

What you fight holds you in an embrace, Launceston had once said.

'Let us be done with this so we can all move on with our lives,' the scar-faced man growled, thrusting open the door.

Inside, the reek of rot was even stronger. Carpenter pressed his hand to his mouth to stop himself gagging. 'When we find Shipwash I will gut him myself for putting us through this,' he muttered.

'What better place to hide?' the Earl whispered, adding without a hint of irony, 'No one in their right mind would dare venture into a plague-house.'

'We left our own wits behind the moment we agreed to spy.' But Launceston was right. If one of the doxies from the Cross Keys had not seen Shipwash entering the house with bread, they would never have found him.

In the faint moonlight breaking through the dusty windows, Carpenter looked around the small room. It was a meagre place with a hard-packed mud floor and three stools before the empty grate. A bunch of dried lavender hung from the beams.

With a twirl of his finger, the scarred spy directed Launceston towards the stairs. As they crept across the room, a door at the rear of the house banged. Carpenter jumped, half drawing his rapier. The door banged again, and again.

Just the wind.

Careful not to wake the sleeping Shipwash, Launceston tested each step for creaks as he climbed the stairs. The scarred spy could only think how terrified of the Unseelie Court their fellow spy must be that he would risk a gruesome death among the victims of the sickness.

Crossing the room, Carpenter felt moisture fall on to the back of his hand. A droplet gleamed darkly in the moonlight on his pale flesh. Following its trail upwards, he saw a black stain spreading across the plaster between two beams, and more drips waiting to fall.

'God's wounds!' the spy cursed. 'Get up there, quickly.'

The Earl bounded up the wooden steps with the scarred man clattering at his heels. In the bedroom, they found a hellish scene. Shipwash, flayed to the waist, his eyes missing, lay in a pool of spreading crimson. Runic symbols had been drawn on the walls in some of the poor soul's blood.

Carpenter slumped against the door jamb. 'Damn him. If only he had stayed with us.' His heart sinking, he bowed his head.

Only two more victims.

And then the Unseelie Court would rule over all. England would burn, and the deaths from the plague would seem like nothing compared to the carnage that would follow.

Only two more victims.

And his dreams of a new life with Alice would be destroyed. Somehow, he felt that more acutely.

'We have to find Pennebrygg, whatever it takes,' he urged his companion. 'This must end here.'

Launceston appeared not to be listening. 'This is a fresh kill.' His whispery voice was tinged with a queasy glee.

After a moment's dislocation, the meaning of the Earl's words became clear. Of course it was fresh. The blood, still dripping.

Carpenter threw himself down the stairs and out through the back of the house into the hot night. The door banging. It had been the devil-masked killer, fleeing the scene of slaughter. He silently cursed himself at the thought of how close they had come to apprehending their prey.

An alley ran along the rear of the houses, filled with piles of rotting debris. The scar-faced man peered into the gloom one way, then the other, but as he had feared, nothing moved.

Returning to the bedroom, a morose Carpenter found the Earl kneeling in the blood next to the flayed corpse, hands dripping. His eyes gleamed with an inner light. 'There is a mark 'pon his back, as we saw with Gavell in the deadhouse.'

'Is that not what we expected?'

'It is. But consider: Marlowe was not slain in this manner. No skin removed, no eyes taken. He died from a simple stab wound to the brain.' Launceston gave a faint smile of satisfaction. ''Twas not the same killer.'

'You say the playwright's death was meaningless, as the inquest decided? But his name was upon the list in his lodgings.'

The Earl shook his head slowly. 'Marlowe is tied too closely to these matters for his passing to be an unhappy accident. But he was not a sacrifice to break down Dee's magical defences. He died for another reason.'

Carpenter waved a dismissive hand. 'Why should that trouble us now? We are sipping from the cup of failure, and all is turning dark around us.'

'Not so.' Launceston stood, casting one last loving glance at the sticky corpse. 'In Bedlam, Griffin Devereux told Will that through the nature of the killer we could divine the identity of the man. What is his nature?' His shoes made a sucking sound as he stepped out of the congealing pool. 'This night is not wasted, for we have learned something of the man we hunt which may help us in the future. See here.' He indicated black smudges on the glistening muscle. 'These same marks lay upon Gavell. They are important in some way I have not yet discovered. But that . . . that is the killer's nature.'

The Earl pointed to a bloody cross etched on the cracked plaster of one wall.

'At the Rose Theatre, he wore the mask of a devil but he took angel's wings to wear,' the Earl continued. 'He is a religious man at heart, perhaps a Catholic hiding among enemies, who feels he has been driven to do the devil's work for the sake of a greater good. A conflicted man, who does not want to lose sight of his God amid all the slaughter.'

'How do you know these things?' Carpenter looked at his companion suspiciously, as if, perhaps, Shipwash had spoken from beyond the vale.

Launceston raised a pale finger to his temple. 'I understand his mind,' he whispered, casting another warm look at the bloody remains. 'This is not the work of a butcher. He treats each victim with love and attention, as a man who understands that he deals with God's plan.' Waving one supple arm towards the dripping runic symbols, he added, 'From those artfully crafted signs we know that he is no yeoman, but a gentleman. One of us.'

'One of you,' Carpenter snapped, horrified at the assertion that there was anything linking himself with his tainted colleague. He stared at the symbols for a moment and decided that he could find no argument with what the Earl was saying. 'When the mask slipped at the Rose, Will said he thought he recognized the face he glimpsed behind it. Could . . . could our killer be a member of the court?'

CHAPTER FORTY-SEVEN

'RIDE! RIDE AS IF THE DEVIL WAS AT YOUR BACK!' DEE YELLED above the raging storm.

'He is,' Will called through gritted teeth. As he leaned low along the neck of his mount, the wind tore at the spy's hair and rain whipped his face. His black cloak thrashed the air behind him. Amid the inky darkness of the narrow track winding through the storm-torn forest, he feared his steed would slip in the churning mud or trip on the snaking roots, that it would all be over for him, for England, and all the days and nights of fleeing south, the constant threat from the resurgent Unseelie Court, the hiding, the creeping along byways and splashing across rivers, all would be for naught.

Gripping the reins tighter, he glanced back to where Meg was riding just behind. In a lightning flash that turned the night-world pure white, he saw her pale face was grimly determined, her red hair flying behind her like flames.

But then Will glimpsed the terrors that lay at their backs.

Fires burned in the preternatural dark, high up in the swaying branches, close to the ground, moving faster than the horses, flickering and insubstantial, dreamlike. Keeping pace, a white cloud billowed with a life of its own, stars sparkling in the folds as if something was forming within it. And glowing as though with an inner light, pale forms bounded among the sodden fern, as lithe and sinuous as foxes, but larger.

Xanthus the Hunter was no longer alone. His fury exacerbated by his failure in the encounter at Lud's Church, he had drawn to him the Unseelie Court's dark forces at loose in the wild countryside, the numbers growing the further south they progressed, until now it appeared there was an army of night at their backs.

'A plan would be good, doctor,' the spy yelled. But the thunder of hooves and the roar of the storm took his words away, and there was no response.

Wiping the stinging rain from his eyes, Will saw ahead a faint lightening of the forest's gloom. Within a moment the three riders burst out of the trees into the full force of the storm. Immediately they were galloping over rolling grassland with nowhere to hide and nothing to slow the relentless pursuit of the wild horde.

Dee waved frantically, slowing his horse to ride at the spy's side. 'Call upon it,' the alchemist yelled. 'Call upon your devil.'

Will was baffled.

'Your mortal soul is already lost. Your life is near over – but not this night! The devil torments you, but it is *yours*. It must bend to your will. That is why Marlowe sent it to you – protection and damnation in equal measure, but for now, in this world, protection.' The magician's voice cracked and broke from the strain of shouting. 'But take care – it will try to resist you at every turn. It wants misery and suffering and despair to sweeten your final agonies. Do it now!' Another lightning flash made the magician's eyes glow with white fire.

Will knew he had no choice. Whatever the price demanded of him, it would be worth paying.

The spy gave himself to the rhythm of the hooves and the bluster of the gale, his thoughts settling within him. 'Come to me now,' he whispered, 'come to me, my Mephistophilis, and let us see what sport we can have.'

Thunder cracked over the dark countryside, and another thunder echoed within him.

Will felt a weight pressing at his back and invisible talons digging into his shoulders. He smelled damp loam, reminding him of the plague pit, and of Marlowe's newly dug grave, and then a face slid next to his cheek, the smooth flesh as cold as snow. From the corner of his eye, he could just discern Jenny, the other Jenny, the lost, dead, soul-destroyed Jenny. The lank-haired, black-eyed thing kept its cheek pressed tight against Will's and threw its mottled arms around his chest in a mockery of an embrace.

'My love,' it sneered in his ear.

'Dee tells me you are my pet, to order as I please.'

The devil's arms grew tighter around him.

'But you do not deny it,' Will said. 'You speak just enough truth to flavour the greatest lie, you spin me round in circles so I cannot tell which is up or down, you do all you can to keep me from thinking clearly. Now you must obey me.'

'Take care,' the Jenny-thing breathed in his ear, 'for it would be best not to anger me. I can inflict much pain before the time comes when I take that smallest but most valuable part of you.'

'Do what I say!' the spy snapped.

'Of course, my love.' The mocking words were punctuated by a quiet laugh. 'But I would ask something of you. In return for my aid, you will give me something, and only for five minutes, no more, then I shall return it.'

'We have agreement,' Will shouted, his needs and those of his companions too pressing for argument. 'Do what you can to prevent those things reaching us.'

Another tinkling laugh was caught in the gale, and then the Jenny-thing unfurled her arms and slipped back, her cheek sliding past him, and back farther until she was gone. The spy had a vision of her laughing in the face of the storm as she flew backwards like a leaf in the wind, twisting and turning until she faced the Enemy. And what then? Would her face light up with the brightness of the moon, and her hair roil around her head like snakes, and would she raise her hands high, her expression filling with dark glee at the mischief she was about to unleash?

The storm whipped into a frenzy, screaming in Will's ears, the wind tearing him like knives, the rain blasting horizontally. His struggling horse half stumbled. The barrage of thunder ended with lightning striking so close behind them that the ground shook, and the horses reared up in terror, and the whole world turned white. One strike, then another, and another, blasting the earth and filling the air with the stink of scorched vegetation.

The three companions struggled on until it felt as if they had burst through the skin of a bubble. The wind fell, the rain stopped, and an unsettling peace lay across the countryside.

Will looked back to see the entire meadow was obscured in a fog of smoke and driving rain, and rhythmic blinding flashes. His devil had bought them a little time, no more.

'Ride on,' he shouted, 'and stop for no man.'

When the sun came up, the three companions dismounted and led their horses along the puddled, muddy tracks. Will deflected all Meg's questions; she didn't need to know about his devil. It was 24 July. The spy knew from the villages they had passed through that they must be somewhere in Oxfordshire, with London away to the east. They were close to their destination.

He could not criticize Dee. The alchemist had done everything in his power to hide them from the Unseelie Court on their long journey south from Manchester: charms carefully constructed from bones and pelts of animals that the magician had killed with his own hands, potions brewed from plants, herbs plucked from the wayside and mingled with salt stolen from inns along the way, were scattered around them every night to protect them while they slept, in rituals of chanting and gestures and processional paths that sometimes lasted for an hour.

To a degree, it had worked. One night Will had woken to glimpse the moonlit silhouette of something large with steaming breath roaming around them in the undergrowth. But despite its proximity, they had not been discovered. And on other occasions, he had seen figures in the distance picking over their trail, but roaming far and wide as if unable to identify the true direction.

But the Corvata, the things that Meg had named that evening by the Lombard Street plague pit, had been everywhere, silhouetted high on church steeples with the bats flapping all around them, or in the upper branches of towering beech trees, or on barn roofs. Their heads were always turning slowly, scanning the woods and meadows. Even Dee's magic could not hide the three fugitives completely from those endlessly searching eyes.

As they trudged onward wearily in the first light of a new day, the spy whispered to the alchemist, 'If there is more you know about my devil, I would appreciate no more surprises in the midst of a fight. Speak up now, and save my poor constitution any future shocks.'

'I was protecting you, you fool,' Dee growled. 'The more you make use of that thing, the more you speed your end. Leave it alone and let your life run its course.'

'But if I can use it—'

The magician rounded on Will, eyes blazing. 'You told me about Marlowe's new play. Did his words pass through your eyes and out of your arse? Men are consumed by arrogance – myself included. We always think we can bind these powers to our will. But the truth is, they corrupt by degrees. Their black disease infects the heart and the mind and soon you find yourself becoming the thing you fight. What then? A William Swyfte with a devil at his beck and call causing more suffering than the Enemy? A black-hearted rogue who sets himself above queens and kings? And God, too? Leave well alone, or you will bring about what you seek to prevent.'

Keeping away from the much-travelled tracks, they pushed through the centres of barleyfields and fought their way through dense woods. When night fell, distant thunder encouraged them to pick up their leaden legs and they were soon hurrying down a grassy slope to a grand stone house with two wings where candles burned in many windows.

'Who lives in this place,' Meg enquired, 'and why should we trust them?'

'It is Petworth House, currently the residence of Henry, Earl of Northumberland,' Dee said, striding ahead with the vitality of a man half his age, 'and you trust him because I say so.'

As they neared the house, they were confronted by a line of sticks on which were mounted the skulls of cows, sheep, badgers and deer. In front of each one, stones had been carefully placed in what appeared to be the letters of an unknown language. The grisly display disappeared into the dark on either side, but the spy had the impression that it continued around the entire house.

Pausing in front of the nearest skull, the alchemist bowed his head and muttered a few words. With a deep sigh of relief, he beckoned Will and Meg across the threshold.

'Henry Percy, the Wizard Earl, has strange tastes,' Will said, eyeing the alchemist. 'Most prefer quaint hedges of box and lines of perfumed lavender.'

Dee chuckled to himself.

At the door, the alchemist was greeted by a servant who appeared aware of the elderly man's identity. The three travelling companions were admitted into the stone-flagged hall while the servant hurried away to find his master.

'You will find surprises aplenty here,' Dee muttered, 'but whether it is all to your liking is another matter.'

The servant returned and ushered them into a chamber on the west side of the house. In the ruddy glow from the dying flames in the wide stone hearth, Will discerned the outline of chairs placed around the fire. Tapestries hung on the walls, the design lost to the dark, and a trestle stood near the window.

'Dee!' A black-gowned figure rose from his chair. 'This is a great surprise and I'll wager not a pleasant one.'

The man strode forward. He had not yet turned thirty, and was tall with brown hair and beard and dark, intense eyes. Will recognized Henry Percy, the eighth Earl of Northumberland, known at court as an elegant, studious man. They had spoken on a few occasions, but the peer kept a small circle of friends and was not known for making merry.

'And Master Swyfte,' Henry continued with a note of

335

surprise. 'You are much in demand, sir, though for once not for your adventurous exploits.' He appeared unmoved by the treasonous allegations made against the spy.

'My lord.' Will gave a deep bow. 'And may I introduce my companion, Mistress O'Shee.'

Northumberland bowed deeply too, extending his left arm behind him and taking the Irish woman's hand and brushing it with his lips. 'I am honoured.'

'These are dangerous times, and they call for extreme measures,' the alchemist said, roaming the room in a burst of wild activity. He peered into the corners, shaking his fist at things no one else could see. 'I am asking for your forgiveness, for I have broken the bonds of secrecy we agreed should surround our cabal. But Master Swyfte here needs the urgent help only we can give.'

'Not just I, my lord, but all of England,' Will said, taking up Dee's plea. 'A plot moves close to the Queen herself. Indeed, it may already be too late. Agents of our enemies now exert an influence within the Privy Council and may soon have full control of the government.'

Northumberland looked to the alchemist, who strode to the fire, running his hands frantically through his white hair. 'He speaks truly, Henry. The things we have long feared have come to pass and we can no longer afford to stand idly in the shadows.'

Tugging his beard, the Earl thought deeply for a moment and then said, 'Your wisdom has always been much in demand in our circle, Dr Dee, and if you vouch for Master Swyfte then I can do no more than trust him implicitly. Besides, Kit Marlowe always spoke highly of him.'

Will flinched at the mention of his friend. Henry beckoned, and as the spy stepped close to the fire he was surprised to see the chairs were all occupied, their owners silent and thoughtful. Looking round, he was shocked to recognize many of the faces he saw there.

'Welcome,' Northumberland said with a sweep of his arm, 'to the School of Night.'

CHAPTER FORTY-EIGHT

AT NORTHUMBERLAND'S COMMAND, THE SERVANT BROUGHT Will a goblet of good sack. Meg flashed him an irritated glance as she was ushered out to a bedchamber the Earl was having prepared for her.

The spy feigned a sympathetic nod, but he took some pleasure from the Irish woman's fury at her exclusion from a source of vital information. Once she had departed, he flopped into a chair next to the fire and for the first time was acutely aware of his exhaustion.

He eyed the great men sitting around him. There was George Chapman, the playwright and scholar, his bald pate glinting in the light of the candle that Northumberland now carried over to set beside the fire. He had just turned thirty and was an acquaintance of Marlowe through his patron, Sir Thomas Walsingham. Beside him sat Thomas Harriot, almost the same age as Chapman and a student of the stars and numbers. Dressed in a black gown with a white ruff, his hair receding, Harriot had a sensitive cast to his features. There were two other men Will did not know, but the spy was struck most by the final guest.

In his jewelled doublet of green and red, Sir Walter Raleigh cut a dashing figure, strong of jaw, dark-eyed, with a well-tended brown beard and moustache and curly hair. He studied Will with a wry smile, the heel of one Spanish leather boot resting on his knee.

'Master Swyfte, it has been a while since we met. But despite the threats currently emanating from London, I remember only the great things you have achieved . . . and, of course, those drunken nights in Liz Longshanks'. I would have you on one of my expeditions to the New World and soon,' he said in a strong, rich voice.

'Perhaps that can be arranged, if we survive the coming weeks.'

The spy knew Raleigh would not succumb to the lies issued by the Privy Council, for the soldier and explorer had been on the receiving end of them himself. Only a year ago, the Queen had appointed him Captain of the Yeomen of the Guard and rewarded him with houses and estates after the success of his expeditions to the New World. He had been Elizabeth's favourite. But then he fell from grace when the Queen discovered his secret marriage to one of her ladies-in-waiting, young Bess Throckmorton. Her Majesty's temper had been incandescent, Will recalled. Raleigh had been imprisoned and Bess dismissed from court. Though the adventurer was now a free man, he had still not been pardoned by the monarch.

'You will forgive me, but this is a strange and surprising collection of fellows,' the spy said, sipping his sack.

'Come now, Master Swyfte,' Northumberland laughed. 'As a spy you should know of many hidden connections that exist in modern life.'

'Still,' Will said, 'I would be hard-pressed to define what you all had in common.' He eyed Dee, who still ranged around the room, whispering to invisible companions. The alchemist had nothing in common with anyone.

'The School of Night,' Raleigh began, taking a goblet of sack from the Earl, 'is a name we use to hide our identity, though Marlowe always threatened to insert it into one of his plays.' He shook his head sadly. 'That will not now come to pass.'

'A secret society, then.' Will laughed. 'I sometimes wonder if there is a man in London who is not a member of some hidden clique or other. Perhaps we are all members of many and in the end we are working against ourselves unbeknown.' He shrugged and sipped his sack. 'Or perhaps this business of spying has made me a cynic.'

Dee prowled over to the fire and roared, 'You are a fool, Swyfte, but a wise one. Indeed we plot because everyone else plots. There are secret wars raging all the time in this world. Nothing is as simple as it seems at first glance.'

Raleigh leaned forward and said, 'In a world of lies it is easy to dismiss everyone, but I would say this to you: Kit Marlowe sided with us. Indeed, he was there at the very beginning.' He held the spy's gaze until he was sure his meaning had been understood. And it was: if Kit believed in this School of Night then it surely had value.

Will called for more sack, and then looked to the alchemist. 'Dr Dee suggested you plotted against the Queen and England itself. Can this be true?'

A chill had grown in the room despite the season and Northumberland tossed another log on the fire. A shower of gold sparks shot up the chimney. 'Not England. Never that,' he said. 'We do what we do *for* England.' Glancing around at his fellows for support, he added, 'But England is more than the Queen, more than the Privy Council. It is an idea.'

'That sounds very much like treason,' the spy said quietly.

'Which is why,' Dee snarled from the far corner of the room where he had cloaked himself in shadows, 'once Marlowe was suspected of being a member of our little group the charge of atheism was levelled at him.'

'The charge of atheism,' Raleigh continued, his voice dripping with contempt, 'that great scythe which cuts down all who stand before it. For who would speak out in favour of a man who sets himself in opposition to God? Who makes a jest of the scripture and calls Mary a whore and Jesus Christ a bastard justly persecuted by the Jews for his own foolishness? Who practises black magic and conjures devils? Atheism – easy to prove with fabricated letters and the statements of criminals, and hard to argue against. The Privy Council had finally decided to move against us, and Marlowe was to be the first. They thought they could get him in the Tower and then torture him to give up our names. But he was murdered before their plan could be put into effect.'

The spy looked to the dark where Dee stood. 'Then Kit's murder *was* the work of the Enemy. The Privy Council had other plans for him.' When he got no reply, he realized the corner of the room was empty. Unseen, the alchemist had sneaked out.

'We know of whom you speak – the Unseelie Court, the Fair Folk, the Good Neighbours,' Harriot said with a nod when he saw Will's surprise. 'We have known of them for a good many years.'

'We are aware only that Kit was slain,' Chapman added, steepling his fingers in front of him, 'but not by whose hand. There are plots upon plots here, and as we sit and look out, we feel no one can be trusted.'

'True enough,' Will said. Sick in his stomach at the thought

341

of his friend's death, he rose from his chair and sauntered to the window, looking out across the dark deer park. 'What is your purpose, then? Why are you opposed to the Queen and the Privy Council?'

'We are opposed to the Unseelie Court too,' Raleigh called gently across the room. 'Indeed they are the reason for our existence.'

Northumberland whispered to the two men Will didn't recognize and they nodded and quickly left. 'Our friends would prefer their identities to remain a secret,' he explained. 'Even from you. They have much to lose, and they are the closest to being uncovered.' He strode over to Will's side and continued, 'We are, if you will, a third way, between the Unseelie Court and the Crown. And we have found ourselves caught in the middle of this damnable world, hated by both sides, hunted, threatened, our lives at risk. But we seek only peace.'

'Peace?' Will snorted. 'There can be no peace with the Enemy.' He thought of Jenny and his devil gave him a painful tweak.

'That is an understandable first reaction,' the Earl replied. 'But hear what we know and your views may change.'

A glittering corona of light shimmered through the diamond-pane glass. It disappeared so quickly that the spy thought it must have been a reflection of the candle standing on the stool near the hearth. But then another came, and another, earth-bound stars twinkling among the dense, black row of trees running along the slope of the high ground beyond the deer park. The chilling familiarity of the sight drove Will's hand instinctively to his rapier.

'The Unseelie Court are here,' he said in a low, determined voice.

The other men rose from their seats and gathered behind him, peering out into the night. 'Do not concern yourself for now,' Raleigh declared. 'Our defences will suffice until dawn.'

'The skulls on the poles?' Will enquired, his eyes following the sweep of fires along the tree-line. An army waited. The house was under siege.

Chapman folded his hands behind his back and raised his chin in an attempt to show defiance, though the spy sensed uneasiness behind his movements. 'We draw from the growing knowledge of the natural sciences, and from studies of the occult. We have designed our defences with the help of the greatest minds and the most arcane knowledge. They are secure.'

'You stand between the light and the dark, between man and the Devil, and you expect to win?' Will said with barely hidden scorn. 'What conjured this madness in your heads?'

Raleigh rested a heavy hand on Will's shoulder. 'Let me tell you a tale of madness and horror. Of the part good Kit Marlowe played in the formation of our group. Then you will understand.'

While the fires blazed in the night, and cries rose up that sounded like no animal the spy knew, a hush fell across the room as Raleigh began to speak.

CHAPTER FORTY-NINE

15 JUNE 1587

The carriage thundered across the cobbles of the wharf at such a speed it almost turned on its side. The horse was sweat-slick and foaming at the mouth, the driver, Edmund Shipwash, thrashing his whip as if he were demented. When the coach careered to a halt beside the barrels of pitch and coils of oiled rope, Kit Marlowe hurled the door open and leapt out, followed closely by Jerome Pennebrygg, both of them wearing the tricorn hats and black gowns of the English College, the Catholic seminary at Reims.

From his rowboat, skimming the waves towards the quay, Sir Walter Raleigh could see the terror etched on the two men's faces in the lamplight.

What could have transpired to elicit such a reaction?

Four men on horseback galloped on to the wharf in a similar state of panic. Raleigh recognized Clement, Makepiece, Gavell and the slippery Robert Poley. Just as he wondered where the final spy was, a hunched, wild-eyed figure crawled out of the carriage and sat next to the wheel, looking around fearfully as if he expected God to strike him dead at any moment.

Good Lord, *the adventurer thought.* Could that really be Griffin Devereux, the cousin of the Earl of Essex?

Running to the edge of the quay, Marlowe peered out across the dusk-shrouded waves. When he saw the rowboat, he all but screamed, 'Hurry! For God's sake, man, hurry!'

Raleigh knew all the spies from their work in London and he could not imagine any of them so filled with dread. As his rowers steered his vessel into the quay at Saint-Pol-de-Léon, he eyed the gloom that cloaked the small town on the north-west coast of France, but could see no sign of what had frightened the men.

When the rowboat bobbed in against the wharf, Shipwash almost leapt from the stone steps into the vessel. 'Steady on,' the adventurer barked, but within a moment the other spies were all throwing themselves on to the wet boards among the unsettled crew.

'Wait!' Marlowe shouted, his voice cracking. 'We cannot abandon the thing we have brought, if England is to survive.'

Hesitating on the brink of the quay, Poley cursed and then ran back to the young playwright. They delved into the carriage and emerged, sweating and blowing, with a large wooden chest bound with chains which they dragged across the cobbles to the water's edge.

'What is in there?' Raleigh demanded. 'The body of one of your poor victims?'

Marlowe gave the adventurer such a haunted look that Raleigh dared not ask again. He ordered his men to haul the box on to the boat, and then watched as Marlowe helped Devereux on board. The crazed man sat in the prow, his arms hugged around his knees, his eyes darting.

Before he joined the others, Poley paused to set fire to the barrels of pitch with his flint and some scraps of sailcloth. Rearing up, the horses voiced their fear as the flames roared up into the night.

'Row, damn you to hell!' Shipwash shrieked once Poley was on board. 'Get us away from this devil-haunted country.'

As the vessel pulled away from the quay, Raleigh noticed a curious sight: the rowers nearest to the chest lost grip of their oars and reeled on their benches, each one glancing back towards the box as if whatever was within called to them in a voice only they could hear.

The rowboat ploughed through the waves towards the galleon at anchor in the deep water. As the smaller vessel neared the creaking ship, Raleigh glanced back to the wharf and in the red and gold glare of the flames thought he glimpsed figures lurching with an awkward gait to the water's edge.

The spies scrambled up the ropes as if consumed by madness. Once the rowboat and its strange cargo was hauled aboard, the adventurer strode the still-warm deck, his gaze continually and uneasily drawn to the quay, although it was impossible to see anything in the dark but the blazing barrels.

'Raise the anchor,' Gavell yelled.

'I am the captain here,' Raleigh bellowed. 'Get below deck or I will have you clapped in irons.'

As the crew slowly drew the anchor, the spymaster Sir Francis Walsingham emerged from the captain's cabin, his hands folded behind his back. Black-gowned, he stood erect, his dark gaze moving steadily across the men until it alighted on Marlowe, who sat by the rail with his head in his hands, staring at the chest. All the crew gave it a wide berth.

'It went well?' the saturnine spymaster enquired.

'No,' the young playwright responded, a sob bubbling under the word. 'We have looked upon hell and we are all changed. Especially . . . especially poor Devereux.'

'What did you see?' Raleigh asked, feeling a chill despite the warm night breeze.

Marlowe shook his head. 'I cannot speak of it. But it will haunt me for ever.'

'And the chest?' Walsingham said.

'Not here.' Marlowe nodded to the crew. 'Spare them.'

When the box had been dragged into the captain's cabin, the

adventurer helped Marlowe unlock the padlocks that held the chains tight. Raleigh dabbed at a dribble of blood at his nose. Closing his eyes, the playwright steadied himself before he hauled open the lid for the spymaster to peer inside.

The explorer recoiled before he had even seen the contents, a convulsive reaction felt at some level he didn't understand.

Chained in the box, knees against his stomach, was one of the Unseelie Court. His eyes burned into the three men who looked down upon him, and they all thought they would never forget what they saw in that glare until their dying day. He looked like a pool of ink in the bottom of the chest, dressed in black doublet and breeches, his hair black too. A piece of filthy cloth had been tied across his mouth.

'He is Fabian of the High Family,' Marlowe choked. 'The things he does . . .' He chewed the back of his hand, unable to complete his sentence.

Raleigh felt the atmosphere in the room grow more intense, as if a storm was about to break. None of them could bear the eyes upon them any longer, and the spymaster gave the order to close the chest.

'How did you capture him?' the explorer asked in disbelief. He was trembling, despite himself.

'It may well have cost me my soul,' the playwright replied in a small voice. 'But I had to! I had to!' He ranged about the cabin like a cornered beast, unable to draw his gaze away from the box. 'We must question him, at the Tower, and find out the truth of the monstrosities he performs. What do they mean? What terrible thing does the Unseelie Court plan for them? Why, it could be the end of all England! And then we have to return and seize the Corpus-Scythe—'

'No.' The voice boomed from the door. The three men turned to see one of the crew, a short man with grey whiskers and a ring in his ear.

'You dare speak to your betters?' the spymaster said with a cold fury.

347

'Hold your tongue,' Raleigh cautioned. 'Return to your post—'

'I was placed on board this ship by my master, Lord Burghley.' The sailor looked from one man to the other.

Walsingham glared with such intensity that the explorer thought he would take a dagger to the outspoken sailor. 'We spy on each other now?'

'Lord Burghley has greater plans that he cannot see disrupted,' the sailor said, offering a scroll sealed with red wax. 'He bid me give you this should such a situation arise.'

Walsingham tore open the scroll and scanned it. 'Leave now and do not speak to me again upon this voyage,' he said to the new arrival without once looking at him. When the sailor had gone, the spymaster crushed the parchment in his fist in anger. 'The fool,' he muttered, forcing a wan smile when he remembered Raleigh. 'It appears Lord Burghley does not want the presence of the Unseelie Court diminished in France. While the Enemy maintains a vital presence among our rivals, it weakens those who compete against us for gold and trade, and thereby strengthens England's position.'

'Politics? No, not here,' Marlowe hissed, tears of anger stinging his eyes. 'This matter is about more than our petty earthly rivalries. We must deliver this one to London for questioning about the Enemy's plans. The atrocities they undertake at Reims will have terrible repercussions for our countrymen. Do you not understand?'

'Silence,' the spymaster snapped. 'Do not question business that is beyond your understanding.'

'And this is beyond your understanding,' the playwright raged. 'You did not witness the horrors we experienced in the English College or you would never agree to this. Our only chance of survival is to act now, not play games.'

In his desperation, Marlowe was on the brink of damaging himself irreparably, Raleigh saw. As it was, Walsingham would not easily forgive such open questioning of his orders. 'England is in a struggle for survival on many levels,' the explorer said calmly, trying to soothe the spy's temper. 'There is no easy choice between right and wrong, and it is the role of the statesman to balance the many competing interests of a great nation attempting to survive in a harsh world.' Even as he spoke the words, Raleigh did not wholly agree with them. From the terrified state of the spies, he suspected this matter truly was greater than mere politics.

Marlowe looked broken. 'I do not agree,' he said in a small voice filled with power. 'It should be about right and wrong. That is all that matters.'

'You are naive,' the spymaster said.

'Leave now,' the explorer urged quietly. 'Spend some time in reflection, and then ask for your master's forgiveness.'

His head bowed in frustration, Marlowe trudged from the cabin. But as he opened the door, terrified cries resounded from the deck. When the playwright's face drained of blood, Raleigh realized the spy's worst fears had been confirmed. Drawing their rapiers, the two men raced towards the disturbance.

On deck, in the dying heat of the evening, the crew fought furiously along the starboard rail against a stream of shadowy figures attempting to board the galleon. Swords glinted in the light of the swinging lanterns. The explorer ran to join his men in the fight, only to come to a juddering halt when he saw their faces ragged with fear and incomprehension.

Raleigh's gaze was drawn inexorably to the nearest assailant and his breath caught in his throat.

Beneath a wide-brimmed felt hat, a face of straw.

Ivy eyes, hands of yew, teeth of blackthorn, a tattered jerkin and breeches stuffed with dried vegetation.

A constructed man. Yet with all the animation of a living being. It snarled and snapped, its human-like eyes glowing with a sickening intelligence.

With horror, the explorer watched the straw man lunge for the nearest sailor, gripping him with an unnatural strength and tearing out his throat. The man's scream turned to a wet gurgle. Blood splashed on to the deck.

'Do not yield! Do not treat them like barleyfield scarecrows,' Marlowe yelled as he ran along the line of struggling crewmen. 'They are bred for slaughter. Run them through. They can die like any man.'

As if to prove his point, the young playwright darted into the mêlée and thrust his rapier through the heart of a straw man. The lurching thing squealed with the voice of a baby, clutching at its chest.

Raleigh recoiled, pressing his hands to his ears to block out the hideous sound. It soared up to the rigging, growing ever louder, until not a man could bear it.

Blood seeped through scarecrow fingers. Sickened, the adventurer could not tell from where that life-essence came.

More straw men clambered over the rail, dripping wet with seawater, and attacked with a greater frenzy, as if the thing's dying shriek had driven them to greater extremes. Wildwood arms wrapped around a sailor and shattered his spine. Another man fell with a face torn in two. Across the deck, the scarecrows lurched towards anything living, silent until wounded when they joined in with the howling symphony of agony.

Marlowe, too, renewed his attack. His face fixed with determination, he slashed his rapier across straw throats and plunged it into overstuffed bodies. Raleigh flung himself into the fight alongside the playwright.

'These are just the start,' the younger man gasped, with tear-stung eyes. 'There is worse to come.'

'Clear room at the rail!'

The explorer recognized Walsingham's booming voice. Glancing back, he saw the spymaster standing alongside two white-faced sailors who had dragged the chained chest from the captain's cabin.

The straw men come for the one in the chest, *Raleigh realized.*

'Send him over the side,' Walsingham said coldly.

While the battle raged, the two gasping crewmen hauled the chest to the rail, lifted it with a grunt and a curse, and then rolled it over the edge.

The resounding splash was like a bell signalling the end of the battle. The scarecrows let men drop to the blood-soaked deck, unfurled wooden fingers from pulsing necks, and turned away from killing blows. One by one, they stumbled towards the rail and climbed over the side, following the siren song of their master.

The grim-faced crew staggered back, hands pressed to mouths, to a man trying to make sense of the horrors they had witnessed.

Raleigh ran to the rail and peered into the black water. 'What were they?' he asked.

Marlowe shook his head and turned away, a man on the edge of despair.

The adventurer caught the playwright's arm and asked, 'The one you brought here . . . Fabian. Will the Unseelie Court let us escape now he is dead?'

'They are hard to kill,' Marlowe said in a flat voice. 'I would not worry yourself unduly.'

Walsingham strode over, his expression unreadable. 'Set sail for Kent, Sir Walter,' he said. 'Master Swyfte waits for us, expecting news of a great victory. He will be disappointed.'

Marlowe rounded on his master. 'We will rue this day,' he raged. 'We had here a chance to stop the horrors that are moving steadily towards England. Playing games with politics has doomed us all.'

The spymaster's graven expression was a warning of the punishment that awaited the young playwright. 'When we return to the Palace of Whitehall, you will tell me all you know. But you will speak to no one else of what you discovered in Reims, do you understand?'

Dismally, Marlowe nodded. 'And what of poor Devereux? This last day has destroyed him.'

'Set him free,' Walsingham said, turning on his heels and striding towards the cabin. 'He has lost his wits. What harm can he do?'

CHAPTER FIFTY

'WHAT HORRORS DID KIT WITNESS AT THE SEMINARY IN REIMS?'
Will stared into the glowing embers in the hearth with visions
of bleeding straw men playing out across his mind.

Raleigh took a draught of sack to steady himself. 'Whatever
he told Walsingham, the old spymaster took it to the grave with
him. Marlowe certainly never discussed it with me, though we
talked long and hard on the journey home to Kent.'

*Where I welcomed Kit, without realizing the monstrous things he
had experienced in France, nor the nature of that work or the others
involved*, Will thought bleakly. So much suffering could have
been prevented if secrets had not been kept. All the strands of
recent events were drawn together in the story the explorer
had just related: Gavell, Shipwash, and the other names on the
list from Kit's boarding house were there, as was Poley, that
sly character who was in the small room where the playwright
was murdered. And what connection was there betwixt those
straw men who terrorized Raleigh's ship and the Scar-Crows
who could not be distinguished from living, breathing men?

'In that conversation between Sir Walter and Marlowe, the
seeds of the School of Night were sown,' the Wizard Earl stated
solemnly. Pacing to the window, he observed the distant lights

burning in the trees. 'A conspiracy, by any other name, that would no longer accept the brutal politics of empires, where risks are taken with the lives of good men and women for the sake of power and gain.'

'We agreed to set ourselves to a higher standard.' Raleigh drained his goblet and called for more. 'Artists, writers, philosophers, thinkers, men of physics, aye, and men of magic too, who could understand the ways of the Unseelie Court and the strange realm from where they originated. Men like our good Dr Dee and those in his occult circle. Indeed, Kit already dabbled in these things. While at Cambridge, shortly before you two first met, he attended a lecture by that High Priest of the Sun, the Italian Giordano Bruno, and borrowed a book of magics from him.'

'And that damnable volume brought to him the Fay that has haunted him these long years and made his life a misery at every turn,' Northumberland muttered from the window.

Will paused, his cup halfway to his lips. 'Xanthus the Hunter? That thing with rings of blue and black marked upon his head, which I fought during my first meeting with Kit, and which now pursues me through hell and high water?'

'The very same.'

In that moment, Will understood so much about the sad life of his long-suffering friend and the events that had transpired in recent weeks. 'I see patterns where I thought there were none,' the spy whispered to himself. Like his protagonist, Faustus, Kit had summoned his own devil through a search for secret knowledge and it had destroyed him by degrees. He was the architect of his own end. How that must have tormented him.

'Kit struggled hard to ensure you were not drawn into his circle of misery,' the explorer said with a sad smile. 'He was adamant in that. "Will is a good man and he should not suffer for my sins," he said to me on that journey back from France. Indeed, the School of Night has helped you many times over the years, though you have never seen it. Information reaching your ears at just the right moment. Aid arriving as if by magic in times of danger.'

'And the plotting of those bastards in the Privy Council, and of your new master, Cecil, diverted from your door,' the Wizard Earl said, turning to face the chamber.

'We are everywhere,' Raleigh added with a nod.

Will rose on weary legs. 'So now all is made clear. If I am to know what Kit discovered and what the Unseelie Court wish to keep hidden, I must retrace my friend's footsteps, to Reims and the English College. But one thing escapes me. You say Kit was keen to return to France to find this *Corpus-Scythe*. And Griffin Devereux spoke of it too. What is it?'

The adventurer shook his head. 'It was of the greatest importance to Kit, I can say that. He felt it was key in preventing whatever plot he feared was about to unfold.'

'Then I thank you for taking me into your confidence,' the spy said, 'but there is no time to lose. I must make arrangements to leave within the hour.'

'And the School of Night will do whatever it can to aid you,' Northumberland responded, 'as your good friend would have wished.'

Leaving the men to their discussions, Will made his way back to the entrance hall. The gale buffeted the door, but beyond it he thought he could hear the same shrieking, insane laughter that rang off the walls of Bedlam.

When the spy reached the first-floor gallery, he called Dee's name, but the only response was the rattling of the panes and the wind in the eaves. A corridor branched off ahead of him, panelled with wood and lit by a single candle at the far end. Bedchamber doors lay along the wall to his right. When he had investigated the first two rooms, he heard dim moans behind the third door.

The old man has injured himself, the spy thought with concern. Only when he reached towards the handle did he realize he was mistaken.

Those are moans of passion.

Will could hear the rhythmic thump of a bed and the sighs of lovemaking. The door was ajar. Unable to avert his eyes, he glimpsed Dee lying on the bed, his naked body pale and wrinkled and covered with faded blue symbols. Astride him was Meg, riding hard. Her head was thrown back, her mouth open in an O of ardour, her red hair flying. She ground her hips into Dee and drew her nails across his flesh.

Will was stunned. Stepping away from the door, he couldn't begin to understand what he had witnessed. The Irish woman had flirted with the alchemist ever since they had met in Manchester, but he could not believe this was pure attraction. Why was she taking him between her thighs on this very night, when threats lay all around?

But what troubled him most was the surprising twinge of jealousy he felt underneath it all. He told himself he felt nothing for Meg. He could see right through her manipulations and he didn't trust her one bit. But still the green emotion stung him.

Making his way downstairs, the spy found the kitchens, where he collected together some cold meat, cheese and bread for the coming journey, but he continued to ponder on the meaning of what he had seen.

When he had found a sack for the provisions, a loud crash reverberated through the house. He raced out to the entrance hall, where the door banged in the teeth of the gale. The other men had gathered to investigate.

'Do not concern yourself,' Raleigh shouted above the storm, 'none of our enemies can have traversed the line of defence. It is just the wind.'

As the explorer ran to close the door, Will caught his arm. 'When I ventured upstairs, it was shut tight. Wind cannot blow open a latch.' Pushing past Raleigh, he squinted against the hard rain driving into his face. He thought he heard a voice somewhere out in the tumultuous weather, but it was impossible to see anything beyond the small circle of light cast by the lantern above the door.

Pushing his way past the other men, the spy raced upstairs. The room where he had seen the alchemist and Meg in congress was now empty, the musky smell of lovemaking still hanging in the air.

Will searched the house and then plunged through the group of puzzled men into the rain-swept night. Along the tree-line the fires flared. He began to fear the worst. Thrown around by the howling wind, he ran up the grassy slope, his leather shoes slipping on the slick sward.

In the fading glare of a lightning flash, he glimpsed two dark shapes stumbling towards the line of skull-topped poles.

Red hair plastered to her head, Meg struggled up the slope with both arms wrapped about a limp, lolling Dee. Her pale, rain-slick face was set with determination. Twisting round, the Irish woman dumped the magician to the ground and drew her dagger from her skirts in one fluid movement. 'Stay away,' she hissed. 'Our business together is done.'

'Betrayal truly is in your nature.'

'You do not know me,' the woman snarled. 'You have no right to judge me.'

357

Pointing at the prone alchemist, the spy demanded, 'What have you done to him?'

'A minor potion administered while his blood was up—'

Will laughed without humour. 'During your seduction.'

'I do what I have to do.' Tears of anger flecked her eyes. 'Though I am sure you doubt every word I say, this life of mine is not an easy one. A woman in this business is forced to make hard choices. And you shall not judge me!'

'I have had enough of your deceit. Speak plain. Now.'

'The magician comes with me.' In another flash of lightning, Red Meg's eyes sparked. 'You cannot begin to understand what it is like in my homeland. You have been safe here behind Dee's defences. But in Ireland, entire villages are destroyed by the Unseelie Court as they hunt my countrymen for sport. Misery inflicted on families down the generations. Children torn from their parents and taken to that foul place the Fair Folk call home, and replaced in their cribs with mewling, spitting things that drink only blood. You cannot begin to know our heartbreak. You cannot plumb the lakes of tears my people have cried. You will never understand the suffocating blanket of terror that swathes every village, every home. Dee can save us! He knows the secret ways to enable us to defend ourselves.' The dagger wavered in her trembling hand. 'He could bring us back to the light. But you would never pass on his knowledge willingly. You have always treated Ireland as a larder to be raided whenever your bellies were empty, and our people as slaves to tend to your every whim.'

'And so you plotted to steal him from under my nose. You accepted Henry of Navarre's request to aid me so you could get close to me, and thereby close to Dee.'

The spy took a slow step around the Irish woman, waiting for her to lower her guard.

'Is it right that your country is protected and mine suffers so badly?' she cried above the desolate wind. 'You talk of the Brotherhood of Man, how we should all stand together against the Unseelie Court, ignoring our religious differences and our trivial human concerns. Yet you ensure England is safe and my home suffers. Is this fair? Is it right? Does it meet the moral standards you have set for yourself?'

The pounding rain stung the spy's face, but the woman's words struck just as hard.

'Let me take Dee.' Her voice softened. 'Show compassion. Do a great deed that will transform the lives of an entire people.'

Will wavered. He glanced down at the rain-soaked alchemist. The elderly man was beginning to stir.

'If you do not, then you and you alone condemn my people to suffering,' Meg pressed.

'And when you proposed that we should flee this business and live a high life in each other's arms across Europe – was it all lies, Mistress Meg? Trying to find a weakness in my heart just as the Unseelie Court seek to exploit the weaknesses in men for their own ends?'

A devastating look of painful, heartfelt emotion flared in her eyes. Like a cat, she sprang at him with the dagger. Shocked by the ferocity of her attack, the spy watched the blade drive towards his heart, only flinging up his left arm to knock her wrist away at the last.

'There is too much at stake to consider the emotions of two people. We are nothing here,' Meg hissed.

'Agreed.'

Under the lightning-torn sky, Meg twisted again, so that she appeared to be a part of the storm. Swooping under his outstretched arm, she thrust her blade through the spy's doublet and nicked the flesh over his ribs. Ignoring the burst of hot pain, Will dropped to his haunches, balancing on the tip of his left hand and swinging his right leg around in an arc. He hit Meg at the back of her knees, and her feet slipped from under her.

He pinned the Irish woman's wrists with his hands and squeezed until the dagger fell from her grasp. 'This is over,' he urged. 'Leave now and you can keep your life.'

Before Meg could respond, Will noticed the alchemist was lurching up the slope in a daze, unaware that just ahead lay the long, arcing row of skull-topped poles. Will propelled himself off the Irish woman and began to race towards the elderly man.

Dee stumbled into one of the poles, knocking it flat. The yellowing skull of a badger rolled across the turf.

Instantly, the wind dropped.

Along the tree-line, the fires winked out as one. A sound like a low exhalation rolled across the grassland.

Will dragged Dee back. His robes flying, the elderly man tumbled down the slope and slid on to his hands and knees.

The rain grew stronger. A crack of thunder rolled out and on in an unending drumroll, and sheets of white light flashed one after another. In between the strikes, the spy glimpsed ghostly grey shapes leaping like foxes, almost invisible in the downpour.

Grasping the rain-slick pole, Will rammed it back into the hole in the ground without disturbing the pattern of stones in front of it. Before he could replace the skull, Meg's shrill cry rang out through the booming thunder. He turned just quickly enough to avoid a grey figure bounding out of the pounding rain.

Unsheathing his rapier, Will glimpsed a corpse-like face that transformed before his eyes into vibrant, strong features. His attacker was a warrior, dressed in a leather buckler stained silver and marked on the front with a black pattern that resembled a tree in winter. Like a poacher's trap, his own blade flashed towards the spy's heart.

Will parried, deflecting the blade to his left. Without pausing for breath, the grey man renewed his attack with a sudden spin and a forceful upper slice of his steel. Will parried again, but he was driven a step back.

In an unorthodox, unpredictable fighting style that reminded Will of the wild dances he had witnessed in Muscovy, the Enemy swordsman whirled around, changing direction in the blink of an eye. Blinded by the rain, Will parried high, then low and to his right, barely blocking each strike.

Green fire burned in the eyes of the grey foe. His face was emotionless.

As he half slipped on the wet grass, the spy felt his foe's rapier tear through his cloak. Clamping his arm tight against the steel in the folds of the wet cloth, Will held it fast long enough to lunge with his own blade. The sharp tip stabbed the Enemy's shoulder. The pale face darkened.

Aware that other Fay warriors could overwhelm him at any moment, Will renewed his attack. But with elegance and strength, the pale-faced swordsman spun to the left, struck, spun back, struck again. The spy felt every bone in his body jarred each time the blades clashed.

In his opponent's icy, ebony eyes, the spy saw no hope of defeating this foe in an honest swordfight. The Enemy was too skilled with the rapier, too strong, too fast, and Will was worn down by the long, desperate pursuit across the country.

Avoiding another thrust, Will hurled his blade. Wrong-footed, the supernatural Enemy dropped his guard. Pulling out one of the pouches Dee had given him in Manchester, the spy unfurled it with a flick of his wrist.

When the blue paste splattered across the ghastly face, the Fay warrior lurched backwards, tearing at his cheeks in a frenzy. Black foam bubbled from between swollen lips, and blood dribbled from the corners of staring eyes. Gasps became unsettling, fractured cries, like the call of rooks on a winter's day, and then the poisoned thing turned and wound a wild path across the grassland until it disappeared into the driving rain. The keening cry continued for a moment longer and then ended suddenly.

Snatching up his rapier, Will turned towards the gap in the defences. His mind filled with a vision of a wave of ferocious bone-white things washing him away. Yet the skull was now back in place, an exhausted Dee clinging on to the pole. The alchemist's eyes were still hazy with the remnants of whatever potion Meg had used to steal his wits. ''Twill suffice, for now,' he muttered.

The spy helped Dee to his feet and supported him back down the slope to where the other men waited, rigid with apprehension, under the lamp by the door. Meg was long gone. Though Will knew it would not be long before she was spreading blood and mayhem in her trail once more, he was surprised by a dull ache of regret and a feeling of mounting loneliness.

CHAPTER FIFTY-ONE

HOLDING THE CANDLESTICK ALOFT, SIR WALTER RALEIGH LED the way down the dank stone steps into the dark cellars of Petworth House. 'Great danger waits ahead, Master Swyfte,' he warned, the green and red jewels of his doublet glimmering in the wavering light of the flame. 'By all the evidence we have, the Unseelie Court are near to the fulfilment of their plot. They will do anything to prevent victory slipping from their grasp. If you think you can pass beneath their gaze unnoticed, you are mistaken.'

'I am well aware of the threat that surrounds me at every turn, but do not underestimate my cunning,' Will's voice echoed in the chill, mildew-smelling air. 'All is not done here.'

'The Enemy certainly agrees,' Northumberland muttered as he took up the rear, 'or they would not have the house under siege.'

At the foot of the steps, the candlelight revealed vaulted cellars festooned with silvery cobwebs and pools of stagnant water glistening across worn flags. The Earl pointed into the shadows to their left and they continued on their way amid the echoes of their footsteps.

'Dr Dee appears to have suffered no lasting harm from the

potion the Irish witch used to seduce him,' Northumberland added. 'In no time at all, I foresee him once again contributing his wisdom and his magical skills to the fight we now have ahead. We may yet break this siege quickly.'

'Once they discover I am gone, as they will in no time, I am sure, they will leave you alone,' Will said. 'At least until their plot is complete. And then I would imagine the School of Night would be high on their list of problems to be excised with alacrity.' He gave a low laugh. 'I am impressed by your achievement, gentlemen. To be despised by both the Privy Council and the Unseelie Court is a remarkable thing.'

'We cannot be trapped in this war for all time, Master Swyfte.' As they came to the far wall of the cellar, Raleigh let the candlelight play along the slick stone. 'We have all been imprisoned in the dark for too long, caught between opposing forces that have only their own interests and survival at heart. It is time for a new age of enlightenment, when we can throw off this benighted existence and continue our journey upwards.'

'To walk with the gods themselves?' the spy asked wryly.

'Aye. Why not? There is godhood in all of us,' the explorer replied.

'I fear your stomach for blasphemy and treason will be the death of you.' Will pressed one hand on the wall. It felt solid enough.

'You are part of our conspiracy now, whether you like it or not.' The Earl smiled.

'You are not afraid that I will betray you, given the opportunity?'

'Kit Marlowe trusted you, and so do we. He held you to the highest standard, Master Swyfte, and you were not found wanting. He refused our entreaties to admit you to our circle only because he wished to protect you from the sword that hangs over all our heads.' Henry Percy turned back to the wall and began to feel along the edge of a column.

When he found the stone he was searching for, he put two hands on it and pressed. With a grinding noise, the stone slid into the column. A section of the wall shifted. The spy felt a blast of cold, stale air.

Raleigh raised a finger and one wry eyebrow. 'The fine thing about a secret society is that its members can hide in plain sight. Here in England, and across Europe. You will never be short of friends, Master Swyfte. And in your darkest hour you may find allies that you never knew existed.'

'That is reassuring, and I thank you both.' Will bowed.

'Take this.' Raleigh proffered the candlestick. 'This tunnel was built long ago, as a route for escape in times of trouble. Parts of it may not be safe. At the far end there is another secret door that leads into All Hallows church in Tillington, far beyond the forces of the Unseelie Court. It will buy you a little time.'

Taking the candlestick, Will stepped into the gap in the wall. Ahead of him lay a stone-lined passage with a roof so low he would have to stoop. An inch of dirty water covered the floor.

Northumberland leaned in. 'There is a cottage overlooking the churchyard, the home of Jerome Marsham, a good, hard-working man,' he said quietly, his voice still carrying deep into the dark. 'Tell him Henry Percy has asked for the loan of his horse, and that he will be well recompensed. Ride south to Portsmouth where you will find Captain Argentein and his ship and give him this.' He handed the spy a rolled-up parchment with a still-soft crimson wax seal. 'It will buy you free passage to France and the secrecy you need to hide your identity.'

Will slipped the parchment into a hidden pocket in his cloak. 'Then I leave England behind me. This country teeters on the brink of an abyss and I know not if it is within my power to prevent it,' he reflected darkly. 'It seems with each day this world turns further from the light. But I will not be swayed, whatever horrors lie ahead.'

The spy nodded to both men and made his way along the passage. Raleigh and Northumberland watched the golden light receding like a firefly disappearing into the dusk.

Soon only the dark remained.

CHAPTER FIFTY-TWO

IN THE BLACK, LONELY FORESTS, SPECTRAL LIGHTS FLOATED. Unfamiliar reflections stared back from streams and rivers, the flesh slowly melting from the skull beneath. At crossroads, crows sometimes appeared to speak in a shrieking, unrecognizable language. And in the silvery meadows underneath the full moon, dark figures danced with carnal abandon, while in nearby villages parents with tear-stained faces searched for their missing children.

From the moment he set foot on French soil, Will had sensed the haunted atmosphere that lay across the land. England had been slowly waking to the evil of ancient days as the defences fell. Here it was as if the land had long since passed into the hands of the Enemy. He had never felt the like before, even in places where the Unseelie Court walked freely.

It was 9 August. The spy's horse trotted towards Reims, where the great bulk of the three-hundred-year-old cathedral was silhouetted against the ruddy sunset. Beyond the walls of the small town, the jumble of narrow, winding streets was thrown into near-permanent shadow. It was, Will felt, a place that held its past close to its heart.

The glassy surface of the Vesle river burned with reds and

oranges as it wound past the town, the air heavy with the acrid smell of smoke from the workshops producing cloth for trade across Europe. It was a busy town. Even in such a time, Will could hear the competing cries of merchants and apprentices ringing out from the streets, the clatter of tools and the hiss of bellows. The face shown to the world was that of the honest artisan toiling fruitfully every day. But it was religion that truly ruled in Reims.

The spy's throat was dry from the dusty tracks he had followed through the vineyards scattered across the landscape. The sea journey from Portsmouth aboard Captain Argentein's carrack had allowed him to put aside thoughts of Meg's betrayal so he could concentrate on plans that required the greatest subterfuge. An Englishman abroad in France was no unusual sight with so many Catholic refugees fleeing Elizabeth's resolutely Protestant rule, but he knew it was only a matter of time before Xanthus would pick up his trail once more. Will knew his only hope was to find answers with the utmost speed and move on.

And if the spy had any doubt about the growing power of the Unseelie Court, he found confirmation in the lights far beneath the blue-green waves on the sea crossing, and in the booming noises, like thunder, that rose from the deeps.

Arriving in Cherbourg on a bright, windswept morning filled with the salty scent of the sea and the spices brought in by the Portuguese great ships, Will had bartered with the merchants overseeing the unloading of barrels along the quay. Among the harbour workers there were signs of the tension between Catholics and Protestants but no mention of a super-natural threat, though Will saw hints of fear in eyes darting towards the roads leading into the countryside. Surrounded by the constant slap of sailcloth and crack of rigging, he secured employment guarding three carts transporting barrels of sack to a warehouse to the north of Paris.

Once they had reached their destination, and with a pouch of Dee's trinkets for protection, he purchased a horse and travelled north-east by day, at night sleeping in taverns where there was at least some chance of safety from the powers that controlled the lonely countryside.

His beard and hair now unruly, his clothes travel-stained and worn so that few would identify him as a gentleman, he kept his head low as he rode into the darkening streets of Reims. The cathedral's twin towers loomed over the town, its creamy-yellow stone and ranks of weather-worn sculptures blackened by smoke. The dying sun turned the rose window on the west front into a glittering, multi-coloured eye, unflinching and unforgiving.

It was a Papist fortress, Will knew, and under the guidance of Rome had become one of the most dangerous places in Europe in the eyes of Queen Elizabeth and the Privy Council. He recalled the old spymaster Sir Francis Walsingham losing his normally impassive demeanour to fly into a rage when speaking of the threat originating from the town. Its source lay behind the walls of the Catholic seminary attached to the university that crouched in the cathedral's shadow. The elderly puritan had railed at *God's spies*, as the Papist bastards called them, the seminary's graduates, who were trained as much in insurrection as scripture and then delivered to England's towns to seek the overthrow of the Queen's rule.

Dismounting, Will led the horse over the cobbles on the last leg of his journey. Black-robed students walked in pairs, their tricorn hats lowered as the young men engaged in earnest conversation. Even in the street, the sweet smell of incense hung in the air.

369

From the shadows of an alley, the spy watched the comings and goings at the door to the English College. He knew it would not be difficult to infiltrate the seminary. In London, Marlowe had used to joke that there were more English spies studying the catechism in Reims than honest Catholics. Escaping with his life would be a different matter.

What terrible secrets had his old friend discovered here?

Tying up his horse, Will adopted an exhausted shuffle for the benefit of watchful eyes and made his way to the seminary.

The door was opened by a young priest, perhaps around twenty, with jet-black hair, a sallow complexion and a pointed nose that gave his features an unsettlingly avian cast.

'Forgive me for disturbing you at this hour when you are undoubtedly preparing for your evening meal,' the spy said with a bow. 'But I am just arrived in Reims after a long journey from my home.'

'From England?' the priest enquired, his English heavily accented with French.

Will nodded. 'My name is Francis Clavell. Like many of my countrymen, I am a victim of the bastard heretic Queen. Her persecution has driven my family from their home. My brother was slaughtered in a ditch, my sister forced to endure the most terrible depravities.' The spy lowered his head and covered his eyes, eliciting a comforting hand upon his shoulder.

'We have all heard tales of the atrocities inflicted on the Christian men and women of England,' the young man said gently. 'This will change, and soon. It is God's will.'

'In the depths of his grief, my father dispatched me here to enter the priesthood so I can return and do whatever is in my power to right these terrible wrongs.'

The priest hesitated. 'My friend, we are already hard-pressed with the flood of poor souls arriving at our door with stories

370

similar to your own. We have to turn many away, and the ones who are admitted are young and open to the teachings we deliver within these walls.'

From his cloak, Will pulled the pouch that Northumberland had given him before he set off for France. He held it up and jangled it. 'My father is a wealthy man, a merchant who provides timber for England's great and growing fleet. His heart is set upon my entering the priesthood. And he will pay well to wipe away the stain of misery that now lies upon my family.'

With a sweep of his arm, the young man stepped aside to admit Will into the well-lit hall. 'Father Mathias will be able to make a judgement upon your request,' he said warmly. 'Wait here and I will see if he is available.'

The scent of candle smoke mingled with the earthy aroma of the broth being prepared in the kitchens. Everywhere was silent. Will knew the offer of gold would buy his way into the seminary. He would have a few days' grace to conduct his business before the authorities began to ask questions about the non-arrival of more funds. He hoped it would be enough.

Within moments, the young priest returned to guide the spy into the chamber of Father Mathias, a portly man with a red face and currant eyes. The small room was panelled with aged oak that made it appear dark despite the two candles positioned on either side of the hearth. A gold cross gleamed on one wall.

Will explained his predicament again, but it was clear the older priest was barely listening. Only when the money pouch was deposited on the trestle did his features suggest interest. The man restrained a smile and in faltering English gave an offer of a few days' accommodation and an opportunity to observe the teachings in the seminary before any final decision was made.

Father Mathias ordered the young priest, who was introduced as Hugh, to look after Will and make sure the rules of the seminary were made clear. A small chamber, barely large enough for a bed, was made ready for the spy next to Hugh's room.

As they made their way to the evening meal, the young priest appeared excited at the prospect of fresh conversation, and gabbled brightly about his brothers and sisters who worked on the family farm not far from the border with Navarre. The spy said little, listening with one ear while observing the other priests as they waited to enter the great vaulted hall where trestles were set end to end in two long rows with benches on each side. Separate trestles were arranged at the upper end of the hall for the senior priests.

Heads bowed, the students stood for the blessing in the lush golden light of the candles burning in the two iron chandeliers overhead. They ate in silence, simple fare of root vegetables in broth, and water to drink. Will estimated there were about a hundred priests, some of them in their twenties, a handful older, but most in their teens. The spy imagined Kit sitting at this very table, thinking the same thoughts as he used his guile to gain the acceptance of his peers. The playwright had had the luxury of time in which to earn the trust that would make lips loose and bring secrets to the surface. As Will chewed on a knob of bread, the weight of his responsibilities pressed down upon him.

After the meal, Hugh helped the spy settle in his room. The young priest was likeable, with a quick wit and a pleasant humour. 'You will enjoy your time here, Francis,' he said as he lit a candle and placed it upon the ledge beneath the small, arched window, 'but the teachings you receive will change your life and the lives of all those you encounter.'

'That is my hope,' Will replied.

'But you will be worked hard. There is no time for rest. Our studies consist of two parts. Firstly, the *trivium* – grammar, in which you will learn to read, write and speak Latin, then rhetoric, where you will discover the powerful voice God gave you for drawing the masses into the heart of the Church. And then logic, by which you will understand how to deliver strong arguments. The other half of our studies consists of the *quadrivium* – music, arithmetic, astronomy and geometry. Through this you will understand the world God has created, and his plan for it.'

'I have spent my life attempting to understand God's plan for the world,' the spy responded truthfully, though he hid the irony.

'And there are, of course, prayers, and our study of the catechism, and reverent song and reflection. You will find meaning here, in a world that yearns for it.' Hugh gave a shy smile.

Stretching, Will said, 'I would take a walk through my new home before I lay my head down. It will help me sleep, and it would be good to get to know the school before my studies begin.'

Hugh's face fell. 'That is not possible. Very shortly the doors will be locked until first light. Under the orders of the old Cardinal, Louis de Guise, no priest is allowed to wander the halls of the seminary until first light.'

'I am to be a prisoner, then?' Will saw his plan failing before his eyes. He had imagined the night would be his best opportunity to explore the college and discover whatever Marlowe had found there. Any chances during daylight hours would be few and far between.

Hugh crossed himself. 'As God's agents upon this earth,

we are a prime target of the Adversary. Every day we must fight off subtle attacks upon our purity. Licentious thoughts. Uncharitable notions. But the night . . . that is the Devil's time. He is at his strongest. For long years, there have been rumours that our greatest enemy walks the quiet halls at dark, seeking lone priests to seduce or destroy.'

The spy pretended to examine the reflections of the candle flame in the window panes. The Church was riddled with devils from top to bottom, men consumed by desires for power or wealth who saw no wrong in manipulating believers to achieve worldly ends, he thought with bitter humour. Beside churchmen, even spies seemed honourable.

'And so we must stay in our chambers, and hold on to our purity, and stay safe until light returns to the world,' Hugh continued.

Will wondered if there was indeed a devil stepping silently through the seminary at night, but he doubted it was the one the younger man imagined. How clever, then, to keep prying eyes shut away. 'Then I will sleep soundly,' he said.

Once the young priest had left, the spy did lie on his hard bed, but he knew he would not sleep soundly, if at all. '*Time doth run with calm and silent foot, Shortening my days and thread of vital life*,' he muttered, once again recalling words from his friend's play. The echoes hung eerily in the air. It was almost as if Marlowe had foreseen everything that lay ahead.

Will struggled long and hard to find a solution to his new conundrum, but when his eyelids began to droop for a moment he was shocked alert by a weight pressing down upon him.

Jenny's pale, dead face lay cold and hard against his cheek, her arms around his chest, nails digging into his flesh. She felt like a bag of bones and smelled of the deep, dark earth. His limbs leaden, the spy did not have the strength to throw her off. Half turning his head, he saw her all-black eyes glinting in the light of the guttering candle flame.

'Let me out,' Mephistophilis whispered. Though the face of Will's love remained impassive, the devil's voice was filled with a hunger that Will had not heard before. 'Set me free and I will help.'

'And have the deaths of good if misguided men upon my conscience? Never.'

The devil's nails dug deeper. 'Set me free. I can cause such mayhem here in this house of goodly men. I can bring their deepest fears up hard against them, and perhaps, when they see the darkness that dwells just beyond their doors, it will reaffirm their faith in the light.'

The spy laughed at his tormentor's attempts at manipulation. 'Or perhaps it will destroy them. And then you will take joy in a blow struck against all that you oppose, and I will be the cause of it and it will haunt me to the end. Two birds, one stone.'

The not-Jenny licked Will's cheek slowly, a mockery of the creature's seductive pose. The tongue felt rough and chill. 'You do not know what I oppose, nor anything of my true nature. You hear the ruminations of small men and think them fact, when in truth you know nothing of the mysteries of life, of devils, of the Unseelie Court, of what you think magic, of anything that spins around your mundane existence. How could you – you are man, and men are like cattle locked up in the dark of a barn. When you try to make sense of the sounds from beyond the walls, you can only guess.'

'Fair guesses, though.' The spy tried to will strength into his arms, but he could not move them an inch. 'I know your nature is to cause harm. Whether you are one of the devils

375

the preachers warn us about, or something else entirely, I recognize evil.'

Mephistophilis gave a scornful laugh. 'There is no good nor evil in this world. There is only what you want and what you will do to achieve it. I want to be set free. You want to save the people of your homeland from the terrible harm that is about to be unleashed upon their heads. And you still say no?'

Will was struck hard by the dilemma the devil presented to him. He felt lost, cut adrift from the moral certainties he had once enjoyed, and now he found it a trial to see right from wrong. There was only what he wanted, and how far he would go to achieve it.

'You will disrupt the workings of the seminary, and allow me space to go about my business?' the spy asked.

'Yes.'

'But you must not kill.'

Silence.

'That is my only condition.'

The laughter began low in the devil's throat and rolled out to fill the chamber. 'There are worse things than death, indeed.'

CHAPTER FIFTY-THREE

IN THE SUFFOCATING HEAT OF THE NIGHT, THE SWEAT-SLICK MAN kneeled against the splintered post, whimpering. A large iron nail had been rammed through his left ear into the wood. Held fast, he was splattered with mud and dung from the crowd that had pelted him intermittently throughout the day for causing an affray in the nave of St Paul's. His tears had long since dried along with the blood that encrusted his swollen lobe, but he could still muster a curse through his dry, split lips. 'Damn you, Launceston. Carpenter, thou pig-swiver.'

From the shadows edging the cobbled square outside Newgate Market, the two spies watched Jerome Pennebrygg with weary eyes.

'How much longer must I sit here waiting for the plague to tug at my elbow?' Carpenter balanced his throwing knife on the tip of his index finger.

'Must I listen to your complaints all night, you mewling, idle-headed pumpion?' the Earl protested. 'Does the mouse throw itself upon the trap the moment the cheese has been set? These things demand patience.'

'That's easy for you to say, you yeasty puttock. You have nowhere better to be.'

'The woman,' the pale man said with a faint sneer.

'Yes, the woman. Alice and I are to meet and walk and talk and act like normal people for once, just for an evening, so we can pretend the world is not about to fall around our ears. Is that too much to ask?'

'Of course not,' Launceston replied archly. 'Take a wherry to Bankside. Watch a play. Dance at the Bull. Skip through the fields and pick wild flowers together.'

Carpenter cursed.

The Earl searched the dark around the market for any sign of movement. Though the stink of animal dung was still ripe in the warmth, the carts had long since departed, and the market-sellers had packed up the remnants of their corn and meal. In that busiest part of London, the few quiet hours were passing.

'What if the devil-masked killer does not come tonight?' Carpenter continued to grumble. 'Do we nail Pennebrygg's nose to the post tomorrow for a scuffle in Christ Church? And his other ear the day after, and so on until he looks like a pincushion?'

'If need be.'

'The killer may not come.'

'All of London now knows Pennebrygg is suffering here. A religious man will certainly have heard of the outrage perpetrated in the cathedral.'

'The murderer may have changed his plans. He might suspect a trap. He might not come for days, or weeks.' Carpenter slipped his knife back into its sheath. 'Meanwhile, we waste our time.'

Sighing, Launceston turned to his companion and levelled his unblinking gaze. 'The killer understands the movements of the heavens, like Dee, and works by the waxing and waning of that silver light,' he said, pointing at the moon peeking out

378

from behind a solitary cloud. His tone had the weary patience of an elderly teacher addressing a child. 'Consider: Clement and Makepiece disappeared, presumed murdered, before the end of May. Gavell was slaughtered on the cusp of June, Shipwash in July. We are not overrun by white-skinned night-gaunts so the last of our defences still hold. No other murder has been committed, and now we have passed Lammastide. The apples have been bobbed, the horses garlanded and the harvests of August begun. The killer will come, before the moon is full.'

Carpenter looked from the sky to the Earl, and then down to the cobbles, shrugging. 'He might not,' he mumbled.

For another hour, the two spies watched.

Carpenter saw the movement first. A shadow separated from the inky dark beneath the overhanging first floor of the grand house across the street, darting along the edge of the Great Conduit that supplied water to the city's homes. Launceston drew his dagger. Pressing himself against the wall, the scarred man held his breath and watched the moonlit area around the post where Pennebrygg was slumped. No one could reach the spy without being seen.

The figure crept to the edge of the cobbled square, the stark interplay of light and shadow gradually revealing a grotesque form, horned and angel-winged, floating in the dark. He moved so silently that Pennebrygg was not aware of his arrival.

As Carpenter stared, he realized that he was looking at a masked man wearing voluminous black robes and a cloak. A knife glinted.

'Ready?' Launceston asked.

Carpenter grew rigid. He saw another movement, this time on the other side of the square. A swirl of a cloak, a flourish of ivory skirts.

Alice.

379

The spy felt the blood drain from him. She had come look-ing for him, he was sure, and she was troubled. Her face was etched with concern, her movements insistent as she looked around the square.

Ice-cold, Carpenter's breath grew hard in his chest. He looked from his love to the devil-masked man, who had seen the new arrival and had come to a halt on the edge of the shadows. The knife caught the light as it turned. Was the murderer thinking to attack Alice, kill her and then continue with his sickening ritual? Was he waiting until she had departed?

Carpenter shuddered. What should he do?

'The fool,' Launceston spat. He turned from the woman to his companion and glared. 'See what you have done.'

The Unseelie Court's agent had stepped back into the dark. With his heart thundering, the scarred man tried to pierce the gloom around the circle of moonlight.

Casting half a glance at the muttering Pennebrygg, Alice stepped into the square and called softly, 'John?'

Carpenter made to step forward. The Earl flashed out an arm to hold his companion back. 'This may be our only chance,' he hissed. 'Would you sacrifice all England for your love?'

I would sacrifice all England and more, the scar-faced man thought.

Barely had the notion crossed his mind, when he glimpsed the flutter of angelic wings behind the woman's left shoulder. The fearful spy began to move forward as the murderer stalked towards Alice, his cruel blade ready to plunge into her back. Thrusting Launceston aside, Carpenter hurled himself out into the open, his rapier drawn.

His love began to smile when she saw him.

'Run!' Carpenter bellowed. He saw the woman's features grow taut, and feared he was too late.

Instinctively, Alice darted to one side. The knife skimmed her shoulder under her cloak. With a shriek, she half turned to see the monstrous devil-mask looming over her, then she pulled up her spreading skirts and ran.

The spy was flooded with relief, but only for a moment. Through the holes in the red mask, black eyes locked upon his. Carpenter saw understanding. Sickened, he knew exactly what was running through the cut-throat's mind as the devilish figure spun round and set off after his disappearing love.

I am his enemy, the one thing that may stop his plot.

He knows I love Alice.

He is going to kill her to punish me.

To destroy me.

Carpenter felt terror turn his thoughts to mulch. There was only the thunder of blood in his head and the sight of that billowing black cloak fading into the night as the killer closed on his woman. Distantly, he was aware of Launceston at his shoulder as he raced across the cobbles.

'Run, John. I am with you,' he heard as if through a veil.

As the two spies sped into the ankle-deep dung of Newgate Street, the moon slipped behind a cloud and the only light came from candles gleaming through bedchamber windows. Carpenter glimpsed the shadowy outline of three rogues lurking in an alley and then alighted on a doxy sitting on the step of a timber-framed house.

Before the man could question her, the woman gave a gap-toothed grin and pointed along the street. 'That way, lovey,' she laughed. Following her filthy finger, the scarred man saw a flurry of white disappear into an alley beside the Three Tuns inn, with the fluttering wings close behind.

Carpenter plunged into the pitch-black alley, dimly aware of fiddle music, laughter and raucous voices leaking from the tavern. In the yard at the back of the three-storey building, golden candlelight flooded out of an open door. Bursting into the sweaty, crowded back room of the inn, the scar-faced man noted men arguing over spilled ale, others shaking their fist or shouting, and two scowling women helping another to her feet.

Launceston pointed to a narrow set of wooden stairs. 'Up there.'

Frightened by the drawn rapiers, the angry customers threw themselves out of the way as the two spies barged through to the foot of the stairs. Carpenter took the steps two at a time, trying not to think what he would find.

Candlelight revealed a wooden landing with doxies framed in the doorways of three bedchambers. A cursing, red-faced man lurched out of one room, pulling up his breeches.

'Where are they?' Carpenter roared, waving his blade for good measure. One of the doxies pointed to the fourth door, which hung ajar. The red-faced man threw himself against the wall as Carpenter crashed by. The spy kicked open the door and dashed inside.

By the flame of a single candle, the desperate man saw that the sparsely furnished room was empty. The window hung open, the sticky scent of the hot night drifting inside. He felt a void within him. Fearing he would see Alice broken in the alley below, or worse, fearing he would not see her at all, he pushed his head out into the night.

'John?'

At the sound of the hesitant voice, the spy felt a heady rush that exceeded his most drunken night. He spun round to see Alice crawling out from beneath the bed, and within a moment he had her tight in his arms. 'Clever girl,' he whispered. 'You saved yourself.'

'Clever girl?' Launceston stood in the doorway, his pale face a cold mask. 'This foolish mare may well have damned us all.'

'Do not speak to her that way!' Carpenter thrust his blade towards his companion.

'I only came to warn you, John. The Privy Council have branded you . . . and Robert . . . traitors, as they did your friend Will. There is a price on your head. The whole of London will be looking for you soon.'

'It is too late now.' The Earl's unblinking stare lay heavy upon his companion.

'Say one more word about her and I will run you through,' Carpenter replied, his voice trembling. Turning to Alice, he exchanged a few quiet words of comfort and once he was sure she could return safely to Nonsuch, he saw her on her way.

Carpenter found Launceston waiting for him in the cobbled square next to the market. Pennebrygg was gone. The ragged remains of his ear was still nailed to the post.

His fists bunching, Carpenter stormed towards his companion. 'Do not criticize me. I did what I did out of love. You would never understand that.' He saw the familiar flare of blood lust in the Earl's eyes, but he could not hold back. 'Nothing matters to you apart from your own all-consuming urges.'

Somehow Launceston restrained himself.

Carpenter's shoulders sagged. 'You will never change – there will only be blood until they finally catch up with you and mount your head above Tower Bridge. I have ruined my life keeping your hunger contained, Robert, and it was all for nothing. It means nothing to you. I only wish to be free.'

The Earl looked towards the empty post as if he had not heard a word his companion had said. 'This play is almost over,' he whispered. 'The players are about to leave the stage. And when they are gone, there will be no applause. Only silence.'

CHAPTER FIFTY-FOUR

HIDING IN THE ALCOVE MIDWAY ALONG THE GRAND GALLERY, Tom Barclay watched the door to the throne room suspiciously. He was a bear of a lad, with muscles built from carrying sides of beef in the kitchens and shouldering barrels of ale in the cellars, but he had enough grace to creep along empty corridors without drawing attention to himself. Like everyone in Nonsuch, he had been caught up in the potent stew of mistrust and doubt that filled the palace from morning to night, and so when he glimpsed Elinor, the Queen's maid of honour, leading a hooded figure through the silent passages at first light, he had feared the worst.

A plot. Intrigue. Murder!

The kitchen ovens could do without him for a while, the young man decided. If he discovered something of import, he might be rewarded by the Privy Council, perhaps Her Majesty herself.

The throne-room door creaked open and Elinor slipped out alone. Tom thought there was something almost rat-like about her in the way she scurried, shoulders slightly hunched, casting sly glances all around. He imagined her with whiskers and tiny paws, two sharp front teeth protruding over her bottom lip. He had never liked her.

Once the woman had disappeared at the far end of the gallery, the kitchen lad eased out of the alcove and crept along the panelled wall to the door. It stood ajar. No sound came from within.

Peeking through the gap, Tom saw the hooded figure standing in front of the large, silver-framed mirror on the far wall. He could see now it was a woman, her head slightly bowed as if in deep thought. The rest of the chamber was empty apart from the low dais on which the Queen's throne sat. Determined to discover the identity of the mysterious woman, he dropped low and crept around the edge of the door.

After a moment, the woman let out a deep sigh which appeared to echo loudly in the stillness of the chamber. She raised her head and removed her hood.

The young lad was shocked to see it was the Queen. She wore her fiery red wig and had applied her white make-up, which he always found gave her an unsettling corpse-like appearance. She looked as tired as he had seen her on every occasion recently, her shoulders slightly hunched, her arms hanging limply at her side and her eyes containing a faraway look as if she were drifting in a daze.

Afraid that he would be seen, Tom began to creep out. But then he glimpsed something troubling.

The mirror.

At first, the young lad couldn't make sense of what he was seeing. The Queen's reflection stared back at her, but this Elizabeth held her head proudly, her eyes flashing, and a darkly knowing smile played on her lips. And she was not alone. In the looking glass, elegantly tall, pale-skinned figures stood around the monarch. Tom saw they wore doublets and bucklers and robes that harked back to a different time, and their eyes blazed with an unnatural light. The man who stood next to the Queen was slender, with long silver hair streaked black down the centre. The lad was terrified by the unaccountable cruelty he saw in that face. The figure clutched what Tom at first took to be an ape, but it was hairless and its eyes glowed golden in the early light.

Ghosts.

Tom felt a rush of dread as he recalled every terrifying story he had heard on dark nights by the hearth. But he was caught fast by that eerie sight.

The silver-haired man gave a small, victorious smile to the true Elizabeth, and mouthed the word, 'Soon.'

And then young Tom could bear it no more. He bolted from the room, only to run straight into a small crowd waiting just outside the door. Stuttering, he began to recount the terrifying thing he had seen, only for the words to die in his throat. Elinor was there, and Lord Derby of the Privy Council, and Roger Cockayne, the adviser to Sir Robert Cecil, and others he didn't recognize, but they were all as still as statues, their unblinking gazes fixed upon him.

'Please help me,' Tom whispered.

As one, the faces were torn by savagery. The waiting figures became snapping and snarling wild beasts, and they set upon the kitchen lad.

CHAPTER FIFTY-FIVE

'THE DEVIL!'

Fearful whispers clashed with cries of terror and then resolved into a tumult that tolled relentlessly throughout the echoing corridors of the English College.

'The Devil!'

'The Devil!'

'The Devil has come to Reims!'

Will threw himself from his hard bed and hammered upon the locked door of his chamber, calling to be set free. His shouts were picked up by the other young priests who had yet to be released from their night-prisons, and after a moment a key turned in the lock and the bolt was drawn. When the door was thrown open, an ashen-faced older priest held Will's gaze with a look of abject despair before he lurched on to the next chamber.

Turning in the direction of the loudest cries, the spy felt a hand on his arm. It was Hugh, his expression etched with concern. 'Perhaps it would be wise to remain in your chamber,' the young man suggested. 'You have not yet allowed God's great spirit inside you and so you may be vulnerable—'

'I am strong,' Will replied. 'Come.'

Following the throb of conversation, he raced ahead of Hugh past several praying priests to a small crowd gathered around the entrance to the Mary Chapel. Shouldering his way through the unsettled men, Will was greeted by a scene of devastation, pews upended, the altar shattered, candles smashed into shards of wax, iron candlesticks twisted in ways that would require an inhuman show of strength.

And at the end of the chapel the great gold cross had been turned on its head and rammed into the shattered flagstones.

In one corner squatted a young man wearing a priest's black robes, his arms gripping his knees. Will saw madness in the roaming eyes and the tight grin. The priest's scalp was bloody where he had clearly torn out handfuls of hair. One bleeding lock still hung from his fingers.

Hugh appeared at the spy's shoulder. 'Charles,' he whispered, crossing himself.

The priest in the corner began to claw at his cheeks with jagged fingernails. '*Caelitus mihi vires*,' he called, but the resonant voice was that of an old man. The other priests recoiled from the doorway with cries of horror.

My strength is from heaven, Will translated. The devil played his part well.

Stifling a pang of guilt that he was responsible for the priest's suffering, Will allowed Hugh to lead him back along the corridor where a clutch of grim-faced older priests were approaching from the opposite direction. At the front of the group lumbered the gout-ridden bulk of Father Mathias.

'Leave this place immediately,' the limping priest boomed. 'We shall cast the Devil out of our brother in this house of God and send the thing back to hell with his arse afire.'

As he pushed his way through the younger men to begin the exorcism, Father Mathias' suspicious eyes fell briefly on Will.

Soon it would be a time for accusations and interrogation to determine who had brought the Devil into the seminary. The spy guessed he had the better part of a day before they came for him.

'Come, Francis, pray with me for the soul of our brother Charles,' Hugh gently advised.

'You were right, my friend, and I should have heeded you. This business lies heavily on me. Allow me a while to reflect in solitude in my chamber. I must decide if I am capable of waging this war against the powers of evil.'

When the priest gave a sad, understanding nod and joined the flow of serious young men heading towards the cathedral for mass, Will moved quickly away from the hubbub.

'Damn you, Mephistophilis,' the spy muttered. 'When the time comes for you to drag me down to hell, I will fight you every step of the way.'

Despite his guilt, Will saw that his plan had worked perfectly. Fear lay heavy across the seminary. The priests saw the Devil in every shadow, and the day's lessons were soon abandoned as the men bustled in confusion, seeking solace from the older priests or rushing to prayer time and again. The spy used the chaos to his advantage, ranging back and forth across the length and breadth of the school in his search for anything that might have raised Marlowe's suspicions during his stay.

By late afternoon Will had cast a dispassionate eye on teaching chambers filled with stools, the deserted studies of the older priests, the silent library, gloomy chapels, the kitchens, the stores and every other space he could find.

Frustrated, he returned to the cloisters where he watched the lengthening shadows. Chanting floated across the square of grass, punctuated every now and then by curses and screams from poor Charles.

Kit would have followed a trail with the same meticulous attention to detail that he had used to plot his intricate stories. But what had been his first hint?

Will let his attention drift from the shadows plunging across the grassy centre of the sunlit cloister to the aged, carved columns along the walkway. He saw the light and the shade, the natural stone and its hand-worked state. He thought of angels and devils and where he stood 'twixt heaven and hell. And then he considered the two faces he – and all men – presented to the world.

Within a moment his footsteps were echoing off the walls like shots from a matchlock. He found Hugh kneeling at the rear of the cathedral. Barely able to contain his urgency, the spy waited for the younger man to finish his contemplation. When the priest stood, Will said in a tone of hazy confusion, 'Brother Hugh, I seek your help in my reflections.'

'I am your servant, Francis. I will do whatever I can to shine a light along the path to God.'

Urging the priest to walk with him, the spy said with one hand to his furrowed brow, 'Forgive my questions. They may make little sense to you, but my thoughts often lead me on a merry dance. I have been reflecting on this great seminary in which I find myself – this breeding ground of thought. It is very old, no?'

Hugh gave a shrug. 'Old? Is fifty years old? The Cardinal de Lorraine founded the school through Papal Bull—'

'Not the school, my friend,' Will interrupted with a regrettable snap of irritation. 'The stone and mortar and very fabric of this place. This part of Reims has been a centre of religious thought for many centuries.'

Hugh held open the door for the spy to pass through. 'Ah,' the priest said. 'Then hundreds of years. The cathedral, the basilica, the glorious buildings you see around . . . outside of Rome you will find no greater monument to Christianity.'

Leading the way back to the seminary, Will continued to feign bafflement. 'I have heard tell that the old masons who built these glorious structures often made hidden places below the ground, secret chambers to hide treasures in times of strife, or to keep safe the great teachings of God above.'

'I know why you ask these things.' The priest's voice dropped to a lower register as he spoke.

'You do?'

'I have heard the same stories. And more besides. They say it is the reason we are locked in our chambers by night . . . that there is a secret place beneath the cathedral and the seminary where the Devil lives, with a gate to hell itself. Our brothers fight a daily battle to keep the Adversary locked below ground, but there is always the danger he will break through. And so it has proved.' He rested a hand on Will's shoulder. 'I am sorry, Francis. I thought these tales had no more substance than the ones the old wives tell around their hearths. Nor did I wish to frighten you needlessly. Now we should all speak of them so that we remain on our guard.'

Nodding, Will's thoughts skipped several paces ahead. To lurk beneath the feet of godly men in one of the holiest places in Europe would suit the Unseelie Court's perverse outlook, the spy decided. The sacred and the profane, joined as one. 'And of course, no one knows the entrance to these hidden places, should they exist.'

'No,' Hugh said in a grim tone that suggested he did not want to discover such a thing.

'There are records here of the priests who studied?'

'Of course,' the younger man replied, curious at this strange question. 'And copies are sent to Rome.'

So that the Pope knows where his best spies are, Will thought. 'Take me to them, brother. I have questions about a former priest.'

Puzzled, Hugh led the way to a large chamber at the rear of the seminary, lined with shelves creaking under the weight of parchments and volumes. It was deserted, as Will had expected in the atmosphere of terror that Mephistophilis had brought to the place. The air was filled with the sweet smell of the ink the scribes used to keep their records. Dust motes floated in a shaft of sunlight falling through the small window high on the west wall, but the rest of the chamber was gloomy.

Lighting a candle with his flint, Will searched along the shelves while the young priest waited uneasily at the door. 'When Brother Cuthbert returns, I am sure he will tell you all you wish to know.'

'I am sure Brother Cuthbert has more important matters to concern him than my meanderings,' the spy muttered.

The candle flame illuminated a volume with the date 1587 inscribed on the spine. Removing it from the shelf, Will carried it to a cluttered trestle and flicked through the pages, each one headed by a name, followed by an account of their residence and studies at the seminary. He paused when he came to the name *Christofer Marley*. Tracing a finger along the flourishing script, he found the location of the playwright's former chamber and then turned to the priest.

'I need your help once more, my friend.' The spy cast a concerned eye at the slant of the sunbeam. The hour was drawing late.

From the silence that had fallen across the seminary, Will knew the rite of exorcism had ended and Father Mathias and his fellow priests would be resting. But not for long.

Like all the other chambers of the young priests, Marlowe's old room contained a single small window, a bed and a stool. Will's eyes fell upon the item that held all his hopes, a Bible, well thumbed, the leather spine splitting. Placing the heavy volume on the bed, he turned the pages, scanning each one with a studied eye. The black print fell into a background blur. It was the white space between the lines that drew his attention. And there, in Genesis, he found what he had hoped for, and expected, from a spy as clever and diligent as Kit Marlowe: a single dot above the letter B of *beginning*.

'Brother Hugh, I would thank you for the kindness you have shown me since I entered this place. You are a credit to your faith. I apologize now for any misery I may have brought into your house, but needs must when the devil drives.' A wry smile flickered on to the spy's lips.

'You speak as if we will never meet again?'

'This world is filled with mysteries, my friend, and I would not dare to predict what may happen even one hour hence. But for now I must be left alone with the word of God, to mull over the meaning hidden within.'

'The meaning is plain, Francis,' the priest said with a bow.

'Indeed it is, if one has eyes to see.' Will stood beside the door, waiting for the other man to leave.

'I will pray for you, my friend.'

'Pray for yourself, brother. I already have friends in low places.'

When a confused Hugh departed, the spy returned to the Bible. He doubted Marlowe would have used an obscure keyword for his favourite cipher. The message had been left for any spy who followed in his tracks, and who would need to uncover his secrets.

And there, on the very first page, on the very first line, was the sign: *In the beginning God created heaven and earth.* The word *earth* had been underlined.

Good Kit, shunning heaven as always, Will thought.

Once he had located a quill and some ink, the spy knew he could decipher the message in no time. He felt a bittersweet sensation of loss and warmth. His old friend continued to speak to him from beyond the grave, and sometimes, if he allowed himself, Will could almost imagine that Kit had never left.

The thought was quickly drowned by his sense of urgency. Soon Father Mathias would come for him. Soon night would be falling and whatever walked the halls of the seminary after dark would be abroad.

The sands of time were running rapidly through the glass, and he still needed to find the gateway to the underworld so he could begin his descent into hell.

CHAPTER FIFTY-SIX

ONCE THE SHOUTS OF THE SEARCHING PRIESTS DIED DOWN, silence fell across the seminary. In the shadows, high up in the vaulted roof of the hall where the priests ate their meals, Will lounged on a broad oak beam with his hands behind his head. The collapsible grapnel Dee had given him in Manchester lay farther along the beam, ready for his descent.

With feline grace, the spy eased himself to his feet and strode along the rafter. In the atmosphere of candle smoke and the fading aroma of the hurried evening meal – a vegetable stew, he surmised – he listened to the distant music of locks turning and bolts being secured as the students were sealed in their chambers. He imagined them all praying desperately by their beds for God to keep them safe through the night, their hearts beating fast at the thought of the Devil loose in their home.

Steadying himself with one hand against the rough ceiling plaster, he gazed down the dizzying drop to the stone floor far below where he had earlier watched the students searching for him in the candlelight. Father Mathias' barked orders had reverberated throughout the entire building – 'Find Francis! Bring him to me! He must answer questions about the Devil!'

– and they had grown angrier as his charges failed in the search. Eventually, in a conversation conducted directly beneath him, they had concluded he must have fled the school.

Squatting, he waited for the last footsteps to fade away and the final business of the day to still, and then he hooked the grapnel on the edge of the beam and prepared to lower the rope.

Away in the depths of the seminary, the spy caught the sound of a door opening. Cursing, Will hesitated. A straggler on the way to bed, or perhaps a watchman doing his rounds? The spy grew tense as he heard the soft tread of several people coming his way.

Even though it would take a sharp pair of eyes to see him in the dark ceiling vault, the spy lay along the beam and peered over the edge. The tread grew louder as it neared, and now Will could hear it was not the shuffle of the priests but a step that was purposeful, strong.

Through the door into the hall, ten figures passed, looking around as they entered. With the confidence of masters in their own territory, the Unseelie Court's representatives in Reims prowled beneath the spy, their eyes glimmering with an inner fire as the candlelight caught them. Their features, though pale, appeared to glow with a faint golden light. Moving with grace and strength, like the most proficient swordsmen, they all wore their hair to their shoulders and their cheekbones were high and sharp, their eyes almond-shaped. Their colour-leached clothes had that familiar ageless quality, and although they harked back to ancient times in their material and cut – leather bucklers, silk sleeves, tight, hard-wearing breeches – they seemed in some way thoroughly modern. But all the garments appeared to glisten with silvery mildew, as if they had been stored in dank cellars. The fragrance of sandalwood and lime and some nameless spice wafted upwards. Each member of the group was armed, their swords rattling to the rhythm of their strides.

Will's attention fell on one at the centre of the knot, who was distinguished by a gentler, almost doleful face. His hair was black, and his eyes too, as were his doublet and breeches which shimmered like a pool of ink among those of his fellows. The way the group gathered round him suggested he was important, perhaps the leader. The spy wondered if this was Fabian of the High Family, whom Raleigh had described at Petworth House. Had the Fay survived his dunking in the ocean?

As they passed beneath him, the spy felt their presence as if they burned with an intense but cold fire. A deep foreboding descended upon him.

Once the pale figures had left the hall, Will attached the grapnel to the beam and lowered the rope. Swinging out over the edge of his roost, he threw his legs around the strong line, sliding down silently to the stone floor. A flick of the wrist brought the grapnel down, and he collapsed it, wrapped the rope tightly around it and hid it in one of the pockets in his cloak.

Offering silent thanks to Dr Dee, the spy raced soundlessly across the hall, pausing briefly at the door to listen before slipping out into the corridor. Most of the candles had been snuffed out for the night, but a few still remained lit here and there. In the faint golden illumination, he followed the ten Fay through the seminary to the point where Kit's secret message had told him they would finally arrive: a silky white alabaster statue of the Virgin and Child in an alcove on the corridor leading to the Mary Chapel.

Peering round a corner, the spy watched the black-clad

being stand before the statue and bow his head slightly. His actions were hidden by the clutch of figures around him, but a moment later the statue pivoted and the ten Unseelie Court representatives filed into a space behind it. Once the last had passed through, the statue spun silently back into place.

Without Marlowe's guidance Will knew he would have been at a loss. He followed his friend's instructions to the letter, pulling forward on the Virgin's left arm, and out to the right at the same time. There was a barely audible click and the statue pivoted freely. Drawing his rapier, the spy stepped into the chill dark. On the air currents, he smelled dank, deep earth, and heard distant, muffled sounds as though of a blacksmith's hammer at the anvil. Behind the steady beat he caught occasional high-pitched notes that could have been screams cut off mid-cry.

In the tunnel, Will sensed the oppressive atmosphere that always seemed to surround the Unseelie Court; it was as though a storm was about to break on a baking hot day. As the statue swung back, closing the way behind him, his eyes adjusted to a thin light reaching him from far along the tunnel.

Keep low for ten paces, then step to your left. Listen for the whisper, then step right. Marlowe's instructions had been precise.

Crouching, Will stepped forward, counting his paces. On the fifth step, he heard a metallic ringing from the wall and he felt motion above his head. Whatever had passed clanged back into the stone again. The Unseelie Court liked their traps and their alarms to catch unwary mortals trespassing on their territory.

At the tenth pace, Will stepped left. From the corner of his eye, he glimpsed glinting metal swinging down from above, passing through the place where he had been standing. When it returned to its fitting he caught a whisper of escaping air.

The spy leapt to his right, just as another blade fell from above. He sensed it miss him by a hand's-breadth.

'Thank you, my friend,' he whispered.

With the muffled booming drowning out any potential warning sounds, Will crept cautiously towards a hissing torch affixed to the wall at the end of the passage. Another tunnel branched to the right. Crouching, the spy peered around the corner. A grey-cloaked sentry waited with his back turned. Sheathing his sword, the spy pulled out his dagger and darted forward. Though he made no sound, the sentry appeared to sense him, for the pale figure began to turn, his hand going to his own blade. Will was on the Fay in an instant, grasping his long hair with his left hand and whisking the dagger along the guard's throat with his right. He continued to drag the head back as the lifeblood pumped out. And then, dropping his dagger, he clamped his free hand over the dying foe's mouth to stifle the gargles.

'For Kit,' the spy whispered, but he felt no sense of elation, no triumph, only a flat bitterness, for he knew every kill destroyed another part of him.

Once the sentry was still, Will laid the body down and reclaimed his dagger. The steady beat of metal upon metal growing louder by the moment, he ran along the passage until he came to a flight of steep stone steps.

As the spy descended, he felt it grow colder, the worked-stone walls eventually giving way to a rough hewing into the natural bedrock. Acrid wisps of smoke wafted up, followed by more unpleasant smells: burned meat, excrement, the sweet-apple stink of rot.

Unable to hear himself think above the thunderous metallic beat, Will drew his sword once more and slowed his step. He allowed a calm to settle upon him. He felt no emotion, no fear.

Ready to react in an instant, his eyes continually probed the dark between the intermittent torches.

The steps ended at a long, low-ceilinged stone chamber lit by a brazier at the far end. In the dim red light, he discerned dark squares on the walls marking other rooms opening out on either side. Chains ending in lethal-looking hooks hung from the ceiling. Swinging gently, a human-shaped cage was suspended to his left. Filthy, matted iron tools of unknown use leaned in a line against the opposite wall. Channels had been set into the floor so that the chamber could be sluiced clean.

Will felt a dismal mood press down upon him, a feeling that he recalled experiencing in only one other place: the torture chamber beneath the Tower of London, where all of England's traitors eventually ended their days.

'Hell, indeed,' the spy whispered. His devil would have enjoyed that oppressive place, but Mephistophilis was undoubtedly still finding sport among the priests in the seminary.

Stepping close to the wall, Will edged forward, eyes darting right and left.

Thoom. Thoom. The beat echoed through the very stone.

Where was the Enemy?

Reaching a broad stone arch, the spy peered round the edge. In the far distance, more braziers glowed like summer fireflies. The shifting air currents told him what he already suspected: the place was vast, chamber after chamber reaching out for unknown distances in the shadows. How long would it take him to conduct a search?

A woman's anguished cry tore through the dark space.

Will's heart thundered in response. The cry was human, he was sure, and infused with fear; one of the Unseelie Court's many victims.

Rushing forward, the spy accepted that helping the

mysterious woman was his immediate priority. His head rang from the hammer-and-anvil beat, so loud he could no longer tell if his running feet made any sound on the flags.

As he neared one of the smoky braziers, Will saw the silhouette of the woman in the ruddy glare. Running wildly from another chamber, she glanced back in what must have been terror. She tripped and fell, crying out once again in shock.

Before Will could react, figures separated from the dark ahead of him, unseen till now and unheard in the ringing din. Hoping they had not seen him, he attempted to step back into the shadows, but two pairs of strong hands caught him from behind, wrestling his rapier free and pinning his arms to his side. He was thrust forward and thrown on to the flags in front of the woman.

The light from the brazier lit her tousled hair red, though her face fell into shadow still.

'Be strong,' the spy whispered to her, 'all is not yet lost.'

Will realized the woman was staring at him in what he guessed was shock. *No*, he thought, *recognition*.

She turned her head slightly so that the glow illuminated her face for the first time, and then it was Will's turn to gape.

'Grace?' he gasped.

CHAPTER FIFTY-SEVEN

IN THE RUDDY LIGHT OF THE SETTING SUN, GRACE HURRIED along the Grand Gallery from the Queen's chambers at the end of her day's labours. With his black cloak wrapped around him and his red hair hidden beneath a felt cap, Strangewayes waited in the shadows to intercept her. He thought how beautiful she looked with her chestnut hair tied back with a blue ribbon, and a bodice the colour of forget-me-nots emphasizing her slim waist. From the moment the Earl of Essex's spy had first laid eyes upon her, he had not been short of lascivious thoughts, imagining the body beneath the skirts, the young breasts, the pleasure of throwing her breathless with passion upon his bed.

But from that day in the garden when she had offered him only sympathy and care after he had heard the news of his brother's death, Strangewayes had been shocked by deeper feelings, each slow emergence changing how he felt about himself and how he saw the world.

'Grace.' He stepped out into the gallery.

'Hello, Tobias.' The young woman showed no surprise.

Strangewayes was stung by the lack of warmth in Grace's face, but it had been that way for days. 'I do not want it to be this cold between us. You have ignored me for too long—'

'I have work to do, Tobias. The Queen needs my full attention.'

'I spoke harshly that day we stood outside the garden door. You had concerns. I was wrong to brush them aside as if they . . . as if you did not matter.'

The woman gave the spy a practised smile and made to push by him.

'Grace, you are the only person to have shown me any warmth in many a year,' Strangewayes said, the desperation forming a hard weight in his chest. 'I want us to be friends again.'

In a moment of madness, the young man grabbed Grace's shoulders and pulled her to him. He expected her to resist in her usual high-spirited way, but she folded compliantly into his arms and he pressed his mouth upon her. The spy was disturbed to find her unresponsive lips had a texture like fish-skin, and when he opened his eyes, she was staring at him, unblinking and emotionless, as if he had merely enquired about her health. Ruffled, the red-headed man broke the embrace.

'What will it take to win you back?' Tobias stuttered.

Ignoring the question, the young lady-in-waiting gave another chill smile and walked away. The spy felt crushed.

'I will do what you asked of me,' Strangewayes called. 'I will prove to you that I am deserving of your affection.'

Grace continued on her way without looking back.

The spy wanted to hate the young woman for making him feel such a fool. He had always mocked the lovelorn, and yet there he was, in the midst of great danger, facing a plot that could sweep away the Queen and important affairs of state, and all he could think of were his own petty feelings.

Clenching his fists, Tobias swept through the deserted palace corridors. The Privy Council was meeting late and all of the advisers and record-keepers and snivelling hangers-on would be gathered in the Banqueting House, waiting for their masters to emerge from their discussions with Her Majesty. He had a brief opportunity.

The sun had set by the time he reached the quiet rooms of the Secretary of State. None of the candles had yet been lit and he realized he would have to complete his business in the dark. Kneeling in front of Cockayne's door, he took out his velvet pouch of tools and set to work.

While probing the brass tumblers, he wondered if his loathing of Swyfte had been fired by the gossip that Grace mooned over his rival like a little girl, or if it had been because *England's greatest spy* received all the adulation that he so deserved. When Essex had recruited him into his nascent spy network, the red-headed man had dreamed of fortune, adventure and acclaim. He had learned to loathe the less flamboyant spies of Cecil's network – the killers, the thieves, the liars and torturers – and all the choices, and his future, had appeared clearly delineated. When had it all changed?

The tumblers turned with a dull clunk. Strangewayes slipped into the chamber. Through the single window, the moon cast a silvery light over the jumbled piles of parchments, charts and books.

After a few moments, the spy realized it would take him all night to sift through every paper in that cluttered chamber. He had to think clearly. Stepping back to the door, he looked around the sparse furniture and the towers of dusty volumes. There was nowhere to hide something of importance.

Moving around the chamber walls, Tobias gently rapped each wooden panel. When none sounded false, he turned back to the room in frustration. In that moment, his gaze alighted on the honey-coloured Kentish ragstone of the hearth.

Grinning, Strangewayes bounded across the chamber. During the hot summer, there had been no need to light the fires in the palace and the grey ashes in the rusty iron grate were long undisturbed. Reaching one hand up the chimney, he felt around, wrinkling his nose at the shower of sticky black soot. His fingers closed on rough sackcloth blocking the flue.

In jubilation, the spy tore down the sack, coughing at the black cloud he raised. Inside was a sheaf of papers with Marlowe's scrawled signature clear on the front.

'Who are you? What are you doing in my chamber?'

Strangewayes started at the harsh voice. Spinning round, he saw that Cockayne had entered silently. In his black robe, the adviser was a pool of shadow by the door with only his ruddy face and shock of grey hair visible.

Tobias reeled from the terrible consequences of being discovered in the chamber of an adviser to the Secretary of State. 'I . . . I was just—' he stuttered.

'Thief!' Cockayne called, turning to the door. 'I am robbed!'

The younger man threw himself across the room. Clamping one hand across Cockayne's mouth, the spy wrestled his opponent into the door with a crash.

'Hush, I mean you no harm,' Strangewayes hissed. But suddenly he could see no way out of his predicament. His reputation, and Grace, had been lost.

The struggling adviser clamped his teeth on the spy's fingers. When the younger man snatched his hand away with a cry of pain, Cockayne called out, 'Traitor!' and in that instant Strangewayes realized he had lost his life too.

'No!' the spy barked, tears of desperation stinging his eyes. Furiously, he flung the older man across the room. Books and papers flew everywhere. The chair was upended, and Cockayne crashed into the wood panelling next to the fireplace. Strangewayes was on him in an instant.

'Traitor!' the adviser barked.

Tobias was consumed with fear. He drove his fist into the older man's face. The nose burst underneath his knuckles. 'Be quiet,' the spy hissed. 'I have no wish to harm you. Be quiet.'

Yet Cockayne continued to struggle. 'Essex's man,' he muttered through split lips.

Half sobbing, Strangewayes made a decision. He pulled out his dagger and thrust it into the adviser's chest. Recoiling, he snorted through hot tears of angry frustration, 'I never meant for this.'

Sucking in a juddering gasp of air to calm himself, the red-headed man tried to think clearly. There was still a chance the adviser might have returned early and no one had overheard the struggle. Forcing aside the thought that he might have killed an innocent man, he plucked up the sooty sack and leapt to the door.

The spy allowed himself one glance back at the body of his victim – and was rooted in horror.

It was no longer Cockayne.

In disbelief, Strangewayes stepped forward to see more clearly. His eyes widened, his wits whirled and he thought he would go mad.

Gripping the dirty sack to his chest, the spy bolted from the chamber.

CHAPTER FIFTY-EIGHT

'WHERE IS GRACE?' WILL ROARED.

His throat was raw. He felt blood dripping from a gash on his forehead and a searing ache in his ribs from the beating dealt out by his Unseelie Court captors. Pulling himself up the damp stone wall, he stood in the corner of the low-ceilinged chamber and faced the pale figures who watched him dispassionately. Choking on the fumes from the brazier in the far corner, Will tried to see by the dull red glow of the coals. He sensed the brooding presence of more Enemies in the shadows.

'Your friend is safe. For now.' Dressed all in black, Fabian appeared to be floating in the greater darkness, his sad face bloodless.

'Why is she here?'

'Answering questions, providing information that will help us in the days to come. You are the spy, yes? Swyfte?'

'And you are Fabian.'

With a touch of surprise, the Fay nodded. 'I am one of the High Family. In this place, I carry out my great and terrible responsibilities to my brothers and sisters, and thereby to my people.' Stepping forward, he looked Will up and down.

Will suppressed the concern for Grace that was gnawing in his chest. He had expected to see only contempt in his foe's face. Instead, the looming, black-clad figure showed only a deep concern and, perhaps, pity. Unsettled by the revelation, Will reassessed his approach. 'What is your business here?' he asked.

'Here I learn what it means to be human,' Fabian replied in a quiet voice.

From somewhere deep in that cavernous place, a man's cry echoed and was cut short. The pale figure's breath caught in his throat. Snapping his head around, he listened to the silence that followed the scream with a note of dismay. 'You are an intriguing race. Inspiring in many ways. Your lives are so short, your suffering so great, and yet you find joy in the smallest things. You create beauty. You love. You care. Your bodies are tiny vessels, so fragile, seemingly too small to contain the vast oceans of emotion that shift within you. You are, all of you, miracles.' He shook his head in awe.

Will ignored the gentle words. With mounting revulsion, he was beginning to sense what truly transpired in the dark beneath the seminary. 'What do you do here?' he asked, each word a thrown stone.

'I break wondrous things.'

The bald statement was so at odds with the poetry of what his captor had been saying that Will at first thought he had misheard. But then he pieced together all the sounds, smells and sights he had experienced since his descent into the Unseelie Court's realm and he recognized the truth. 'Torture.'

Fabian started as if he had been stung. 'Nothing so crude. We know a myriad ways to extract information from your kind. Torture requires no skill. No, there is an artistry to what I achieve here. I have a unique ability, a talent perhaps, that also destroys me by degrees. But that is my curse. We must all live with the things that destroy us.' Tapping one slender index finger on his lips, he prowled the dark in reflection. 'We must know our enemy if we are truly to defeat them,' he continued. 'We must know the inner workings of your mind, and your body. What makes you, you. The very essence of what it is to be human. You are like us in many ways, and so different in others.'

Will was sickened by the visions flashing through his mind. 'You butcher us, then. Like cattle being prepared for table.'

'No,' the supernatural being cried. He bounded back to the spy and reached out a hand tenderly to frame Will's face. 'In my work, as I search for the secrets buried deep within you, I treat all of your kind with respect and tenderness.'

'You dress it up in pretty words but you bring death, like all of your ilk,' Will spat.

'Death is not the end.' Stepping back, Fabian looked askance, a curious gleam in his eye. 'There are many secrets you have yet to discover.' He turned away as if he had said too much and strode towards his fellows. 'Over the years, I have worked tirelessly here. The mysteries always appeared elusive. But in recent years we have made a discovery.' His breath caught with excitement. 'It changed everything. All our plans, our very thoughts about what we should and could achieve.'

'And what did you learn?' the spy asked with contempt. 'That we are more than the sum of our parts?'

'That is understood.' Fabian bowed. 'The physical world can be altered by the great powers that surround us. Through ritual and potion, words of power, we can weave great things out of the lights of the world. The great and wise Deortha has been invaluable in these matters. You know him?'

With a nod, Will recalled the mystic's appearance on misty Dartmoor all those years earlier.

'With Deortha's help, and the discoveries made in these silent chambers, we learned how to shape your mortal clay, and imbue a spark of life within it, some semblance of being.' He waved a hand towards something hidden in the dark.

From the shadows stepped a lanky young man of perhaps twenty, a puzzled smile upon his smooth-cheeked face. Wearing a plain brown doublet, too large for him, and worn black breeches, he looked too innocent to survive in that awful place. And so it proved.

Whisking out his dagger, Fabian plunged it into the man's heart.

'No!' When Will lunged, the Unseelie Court's silent watchers hurled him back into the corner, drawing their rapiers to underscore their unspoken threat.

Almost comically baffled, the young man looked down at the blood pumping from his chest and then fell to the flags, dead.

'Some semblance,' Fabian continued as if nothing untoward had happened, 'but not perfection.'

'Devil,' the spy growled.

'These are straw men. Scar-Crow Men. They look like you, and speak, and think to a degree, but they cannot truly feel.' Fabian wiped his dagger on the young man's doublet and returned it to its sheath. 'They do not understand emotions. And so they are useless as complete replacements for your people. But they can keep up appearances for a while, enough to adopt a position of power, and shepherd, and twist, and urge, and in that way achieve our aims, not yours.'

With a wave of his hand, the Fay directed his prisoner's attention to the body. It was no longer the young man. Sprawled on the stone floor, leaking bodily fluids, was a rotting corpse, of the same size, shape and sex as the puzzled figure the spy had seen, but much older. Yet what caught Will's eye were the blackened swellings on the grey body that revealed the presence of the plague.

The spy's thoughts spun as he tried to make sense of what he was seeing. Running one hand through his black hair, he gasped, 'You build these Scar-Crow Men from the remains of the poor souls who die from the sickness.'

Fabian nodded slowly.

'They are dead . . . yet alive.'

'They make a play of being alive, and give as good a performance as many of the players who walk your stages.' The pale-skinned being waved his hand and two of his fellows grabbed the remains by the arms and dragged it away. A wet trail gleamed blackly in the ruddy half-light. 'But their inability to comprehend emotions, that is what betrays them,' he continued. 'And that is proof that they are not truly human, for it is the acuity of feelings that makes a man.'

Will felt sickened by what he had heard, but he was already beginning to grasp the plot the Unseelie Court were weaving out of this frightfulness. 'And with the plague in London you have no shortage of the raw materials you need to build your Scar-Crow Men.'

'We brought the plague to London.'

The spy was stung by Fabian's bald statement. In that moment all he could think of were the plague pits and the bodies discarded in them like so much cordwood. Innocents who had died needlessly. The blood throbbed in his temple.

'But it is not a simple task to construct our agents. It takes time, and effort.' Looming over him, Fabian studied Will with a note of curiosity, as if he had found a new breed of beast.

'Slowly, though, we are replacing the ones who have influence at the heart of your government. Those who are close to power, but not so close that their failings will be revealed easily. The quiet people. The whisperers. Advisers, who stand in the shadows, ignored until their guidance is needed. Soon, though, we will replace more and more, until we rule your land completely without ever being seen by the common herd.'

'And Grace. She too has been replaced?'

'She holds a position close to your Queen, Elizabeth. We have influence there already, but one more is needed to achieve our aims.'

'I thought you wanted to smite us all dead and burn the bodies. That was always the stated intent of the Unseelie Court.'

'There will be some pain. There has to be vengeance for your grand betrayal, and the capture and imprisonment of our Queen,' Fabian continued. 'Once she is free . . . once our agent has destroyed the final defences that keep us from her . . . she will emerge from her prison like a tempest, furious and proud and terrible, blasting all that lies before her.' A fleeting smile leapt to his lips. 'But once her anger has abated, there is hope for your people. They will survive under the rule of our Scar-Crow Men . . . and our Scar-Crow Queen.'

'While you make the puppets dance from behind the scenes.'

'There can never be rebellion if a country does not know it has been conquered.'

Will began to grasp the Unseelie Court's plan, but there was one aspect he did not understand. 'Why rule England from behind the veil? You have your own land, wherever it may lie, beneath hill or lake.'

Absently, Fabian strode to the fuming brazier and began to prod the glowing coals with an iron poker. 'My people have been as unchanging as the seasons since the beginning of the world, but in recent days our thoughts have shifted greatly. And you have played a part in that.'

'I?'

His face transformed into a grotesque mask by the ruddy light, the black-clad being looked at Will. 'When you oversaw the murder of Cavillex of the High Family a vast shudder ran through the Unseelie Court,' he said with a note of pity. 'A mortal, killing one of our greatest! It was unheard of. And in that instant everything altered. We could no longer retreat to our home and pretend we were still the same.'

The spy felt a weight upon him. Since the war with the Unseelie Court began, every action had unforeseen consequences, one atrocity leading to a greater monstrousness. Where would it end? With the destruction of both races? And now he was responsible for the amplification of the Fay's ambitions, and for the misery they would heap on his own people. He began to understand that the School of Night – and Marlowe – were right. There had to be another way. 'Then what do you plan once you have seized control of England?' he asked.

Fabian thrust the poker into the heart of the burning coals, sending up a shower of golden sparks. 'We can no longer choose to ignore your world. We must engage with it. We must control it, and control you, mortals, who once were mere sport to us when we failed to understand your wondrous capabilities, and who now may well be a threat, not only to us but to all there is. Your capacity for destruction, betrayal, inflicting pain, slaughtering your own . . .' He placed one hand on his forehead in disbelief. 'You think you are the hero in this business, Master Swyfte. You are not. Humankind is a sickness, like the plague that rots your own bodies, and it must be cured.'

'You wish to eradicate us, all of us, wherever we roam.' Will saw the future unfold grimly before his mind's eye. Once the Unseelie Court controlled England they would have a foothold upon the world, a fortress from which they could exert their influence, and yet no one would ever know they were there. The Scar-Crow Men would put the orders of their hidden masters into effect, and all England would obey, blindly.

'Eradication, yes, if we have to. But for now we will be satisfied with containment.' Fabian strode back across the chamber and stood before the spy, one hand resting on the hilt of his rapier. 'I did not wish this path. I would celebrate you, not destroy you, and now I am forced to take actions that destroy me. But you brought it upon yourselves.'

Will imagined Marlowe overcome by the horrors he witnessed in this place, and fleeing back to England to inform Sir Francis Walsingham. And the spymaster, in his usual way, would have taken note, and reflected, and filed away, not realizing that the seeds of his own death had already been planted.

'And so you set out to cover your tracks,' the spy said, 'until you were ready to act. As the sacrificial victims required to enable the removal of our defences, you chose the spies who would know that you had unlocked the secret of creating life here in Reims, and who might piece together your great scheme. Two birds, one stone. Walsingham murdered first, then Clement, Makepiece, Gavell and the rest. And I was placed on your list because I met Kit Marlowe on his return to England, and you could not risk that he had told me of his nightmarish experience here beneath the seminary.'

But Kit sought to spare me, as he always did.

Fabian appeared truly sympathetic. 'I would not have wished this pain upon you, but there it is. Now we have won. Our

Scar-Crow Men are in position, with only your Queen yet to be replaced. One single death yet remains, and then all your defences will crumble. And our force waits in Paris, ready to sail to your shores once our own Queen has been freed from her imprisonment. Your time has passed. England is gone. The dawn of the Unseelie Court in your world now rises.'

Will ignored the Fay's chilling words. Something had been troubling him, and now he thought he had it. 'And yet I feel there is something missing from your words,' he said. 'Your decision to pursue our spies so ruthlessly tells me Kit Marlowe discovered more here than just the beginnings of your plot.'

Fabian nodded. 'That is true. The discovery of the plot alone would not have been enough to stop us. But when your friend witnessed the creation of our Scar-Crow Men, he also saw the means by which we may destroy them.'

'Because, if events turned sour, the soulless things could be a threat even to the great Unseelie Court.'

'Every weapon cuts both ways.'

'And what is this means of destruction?' the spy pressed. 'I would imagine 'twould need to be something that could extinguish the spark of life in your creations in one fell swoop, like the snuffing out of a candle flame. What would that be?'

The Corpus-Scythe, he thought. *And I suspect that too lies in Paris.*

Will waited for his captor to respond, but Fabian appeared distracted. With furrowed brow, the Fay half turned, cocking his head to one side as if listening to something beyond the reach of human hearing.

And then, echoing through the night-dark chambers, the spy heard the clamour of human voices drawing nearer.

CHAPTER FIFTY-NINE

WITH HIS CAPTORS DISTRACTED BY THE CACOPHONY OF VOICES,
Will rolled across the dusty stone flags to where he had seen
his rapier and dagger tossed earlier. The spy felt around in the
gloom until his fingers closed on cold steel. In the dim, ruddy
light, he glimpsed three of the Fay turn towards him, drawing
their own swords.

'Put down your arms,' Fabian demanded with a regretful
note.

'To relinquish them before I have used them would be a
waste,' Will responded.

Ferocious and fast, the three Fay moved like wolves, but
the spy was ahead of them. With a heave of his leather shoe,
he propelled the brazier forwards. Hot coals cascaded over the
nearest foe. Piercing screams rang out, a column of flames
lighting up the chamber. The air filled with the stink of seared
flesh.

Shielding his eyes from the blinding light, Will darted out of
the chamber. In the dense dark, he was lost in the disorienting
din of the metallic booming and the nearing shouts. 'Grace!'
he yelled. He just caught his friend's shrill response under the
clamour.

The spy found Grace pressed against a wall, her eyes burning with determination. Her Fay guard waited in front of her, rapier already drawn, eyes narrowed. When the supernatural being lunged, Grace hurled herself on to his back with a cry, tearing at his face with her nails. Seizing his moment, Will thrust his blade into his reeling foe's heart. As the pale figure fell, Grace leapt free and rushed to her saviour's side.

The spy was surprised to see such fierce emotion in her usually placid face. 'Why, Grace,' he said, 'I will need you by my side in the next Bankside brawl.'

'I have been battered and beaten and questioned and imprisoned and I have had my fill!' she snapped. 'Now get me out of here, Will, or so help me I will turn my fury 'pon you.' Despite her resolve, the spy saw tears of fear flecking the corners of her eyes. Her trial had taken its toll on her.

Grabbing her hand, Will ran through the chambers towards the clamour. Not far from the stone steps leading down from the seminary, he confronted a mob of about twenty black-robed priests, their faces etched with terror. One near the front held a torch, others grasped golden crosses taken from the chambers of the senior priests. Their wide eyes searched the dark as they shouted encouragement to each other. Some muttered prayers. The spy saw Mathias at the centre of the crowd, Hugh on the edge, trembling with fear.

'You wish to scar my conscience before you claim my soul, is that it, devil?' Will hissed to the invisible Mephistophilis. 'You have drawn these men to their slaughter.'

'Who do you speak to?' Grace asked.

The spy ignored her. A throaty chuckle crackled in his ear.

Distracted by their search for demons, the priests paid no heed to the two new arrivals. Will grabbed Hugh and pulled him aside. 'You must leave this place, now,' he urged.

'Francis? Is it true, then? You brought the Devil into our midst?'

'More than devils lurk down here. The evil loose in the seminary has brought you to your deaths. *Flee!*'

Seven of the Unseelie Court emerged from the dark at the far end of the chamber, rapiers drawn. With their grim, pallid faces and silvery-mildewed clothes, they looked like ghosts. The priests recoiled immediately.

A shadow crossed Grace's face. 'What are they? Since I was taken in Nonsuch, my days have passed like a dream from the potion I was given. I thought my captors were Spanish agents, but now—'

'Later, Grace,' Will snapped, drawing her attention from the supernatural figures. He would need to talk with her, but only when they were away from that place. He shook Hugh forcefully. 'You must compel your companions to flee. Those creatures will fall upon you like wolves,' he barked.

The young priest finally understood. Running back to the other men, he raised the alarm. Hauling Grace behind him, Will led the race back to the stone steps. Glancing back, he saw the gout-ridden Mathias had fallen behind, as had three of the elderly priests. Mouth torn wide, the lumbering father looked behind him, knowing what was coming. Out of the gloom swept the Unseelie Court, impassive, brutal. Their swords carved through the straggling priests with such ferocity the victims had no time to cry out. In a cascade of blood, Mathias went down. His killer barely paused.

Thrusting Grace up the steps with a promise that he would join her, Will waited, urging the remaining men behind the woman. With his rapier levelled in his right hand, he snatched the torch from the final passing priest and backed on to the steps.

Sensing the threat ahead, the Fay swordsmen slowed when they saw him. Waving the sizzling torch in front of him, Will edged up one step at a time. There was no room for more than one of his foes to strike at him.

As the spy crept upwards, the nearest opponent lunged. Parrying the thrust easily from his higher position, the spy jabbed the torch into his foe's face. The Fay screamed, clutching at his ruined face as he tumbled backwards on to his companions. Turning heel, Will raced up the steps.

When he reached the long tunnel, he could see the priests had left open the alabaster statue of the Virgin and Child. The bodies of six men littered the stone floor, victims of the Unseelie Court's traps. Avoiding the swinging blades, Will plunged out into the seminary and swung the statue shut behind him.

While the other priests fled, Hugh waited with Grace. 'Where now?' she gasped.

'Where now, indeed?' Will replied. 'If I could take you straight to England, I would. But it is Paris that calls me, a city I now fear is in the grip of our greatest enemy.' Sheathing his rapier, he turned to the young priest. 'You are a good man, Hugh, and do not deserve to be wrapped up in this terrible affair,' he said. 'I have little love for priests who plot the end of my Queen, but warn your fellows to stay away from the spaces beneath the seminary. I do not think the forces that lurk there can remain now they have been uncovered, but it would be best not to take any risks.'

'Who are you?' Hugh asked, awed.

Will gave a deep bow. 'Why, I am England's greatest spy, my friend. I have been on a long journey to hell, but now I am back and determined to take some of damnation's fire to my enemies.'

CHAPTER SIXTY

RECLAIMING HIS HORSE FROM THE SEMINARY STABLES, WILL WAS soon galloping through the narrow streets of Reims, with Grace clinging to his back. At the walls, a sleepy guard in a padded leather doublet opened the gates for them. As much as the spy hated passing through the lonely vineyards and meadows by night, he knew he could not remain in the town until daybreak. Fabian's warped compassion for the human race would be tested to the limit in the coming hours.

'Were you harmed?' he asked. 'You spoke of being battered and—'

'It is nothing. I am well,' the woman replied with a brusque tone that surprised him. He felt that he had offended her in some way.

For a while, he questioned Grace on the circumstances of her capture at Nonsuch and how she was brought to Reims, but her memory was addled by potions. He was, however, concerned to hear of the mounting fear and repression at the palace. But when Grace noted that she feared for Nathaniel, he added, 'Nat has survived far worse. I would trust him to win through in any situation.'

'Then you should tell him,' she snapped, 'instead of criticizing him at every turn.'

'Grace, if there is something wrong—'

'Nothing is wrong.' The woman gripped the spy's back as tightly as his devil.

Will rode on in silence. But as the dusty track passed from the vineyards into the woods, he noticed a light glimmering away in the trees. Two more appeared as he trotted on. Had Xanthus found him at last? The spy frowned. Reining in his steed, he considered riding back to the vineyards.

In silence, two musketeers stepped out from the trees and trained their weapons upon him. Their moustaches and beards waxed and pointed, they wore felt hats, short leather jerkins and bandoliers. From the well-tended weapons and clothes, the spy could see they were not roadside bandits.

In French, Will tried to explain that he and Grace were simply poor travellers who could not afford to pay for a night at an inn in Reims. The men's cold eyes didn't waver. With a thrust of their weapons they silently ordered the two travellers to dismount.

The spy could not risk injury to Grace. His anger simmering, he allowed the two of them to be marched through the trees.

On the other side of the small wood, canvas flapped in the breeze. Moths performed intricate dances in the pools of light thrown by lanterns at the entrances to a huddle of grey tents. The smell of roast pork still hung in the warm air around a crackling camp fire, and Will could hear horses snorting and stamping their hooves nearby. From the men sitting around in groups holding quiet conversations, he guessed it was a small fighting force.

As they neared the largest of the tents, a tall, balding man stepped out to greet them. His beard flecked with white, he wore a black gown, but he carried himself with the strength and grace of a fighting man. 'My name is Maximilien de Béthune, duc de Sully. Follow me,' he said in English, his voice deep.

'There is some mistake. I am just a lonely traveller,' Will began.

Maximilien gave a knowing smile. 'No, you are not. You are England's greatest spy, William Swyfte.'

For once, Will was silenced.

'We are not fools here, sir. Our spies are as proficient as your own,' the gowned man continued, holding open the tent flap for them to enter. 'You have been under observation since you disembarked at Cherbourg.'

'Then I apologize for my deceit,' Will replied, stooping to enter the warm golden glow of the lamplit interior. 'I doff my cap to fellow practitioners of the great art.'

Behind his wry exterior, the spy was instantly on his guard, his eyes darting around in search of any threat. A trestle stood to one side covered with charts, a flask and a half-eaten knob of bread with a knife stuck in it. But his attention was drawn to a tall, tanned man standing with his hands folded behind his back. He was expensively outfitted in a gleaming sapphire doublet, the buttons jewelled, the ruff extravagantly folded. His beard was well tended, his smiling face suggesting a man of good humour.

'The King,' Maximilien boomed.

'Your Majesty.' Will gave a deep bow. Grace curtsied at his side, her gaze fixed shyly on the ground. Henri let his eyes linger on her for a moment, his smile becoming playful.

'The King indeed,' he said in heavily accented English. 'The word is still strange to my ears after this long, hard struggle.

There were times when I thought I would always remain Henri de Navarre.'

'The Catholic League now support your claim to the throne?' the spy asked, puzzled.

Henri chuckled. 'Why, I am a Catholic these days, Master Swyfte. Had you not heard? On the twenty-fifth of July I renounced my old faith completely. Now I am a committed Papist,' he tweaked his waxed moustache, his eyes gleaming, 'the resistance in Paris will eventually crumble and I will finally be allowed to ride into my capital city. And so, all things fall into place.'

The spy recalled Cecil's suspicions at the Rose Theatre almost three months earlier. 'And the Huguenots?' he enquired.

'After the bitter religious strife that has torn this country apart for so long, they are understandably distressed that I appear to have crossed to the other side. But they will come around. What other choice do they have?'

'I imagine my Queen is not best pleased that you have renounced her faith.' It was an understatement. Will imagined Elizabeth flying into one of her incandescent rages when the news was delivered to her.

'Once I am crowned in Chartres, she will understand that I am still the same Henri.' The King strode to the trestle and took a sip from his flask of wine. 'Perhaps I will even be more useful to her. I see myself as a bridge, Master Swyfte, like the one I plan to build across the Seine when I am finally allowed into Paris, to unite the right and left banks. There will be peace in Europe only when our two religions can live side by side. When we achieve that, then we can join together against our common Enemy.' His eyes flickered from Grace to Will, and he nodded to indicate that he would not elucidate while the woman was present. 'For now,' he continued, 'Paris remains beyond my control.'

The spy inwardly winced. It would be difficult enough to spend time in the Unseelie Court's midst without also having to deal with a city that had only recently survived Henri's siege and would suspect any stranger of being one of the King's spies.

'There are other matters afoot, of which we will speak more in a short while.' Draining his flask, the King smacked his mouth.

The tent flaps were furiously thrown open and in a flurry of skirts a woman stormed in.

'You!' Grace exclaimed.

Red Meg O'Shee cast only a fleeting glance at her. 'I hear the buzzing of a fly,' she sniffed.

Grace fumed, but the Irish woman had already turned her attention to Will, a cold fire in her green eyes.

With a hand to his high forehead, the King exclaimed, 'Mistress, if Gabrielle finds you here—'

'Do not worry, Your Majesty. Your *true love*' – the red-headed woman gave the words a sardonic twist, her gaze still fixed on the spy – 'will not be made aware of such an outrage.'

In Meg's disrespectful attitude towards the monarch, Will saw the deep currents that run between old lovers.

'Did you not find my blade sharp enough the last time, Master Swyfte?' she asked scornfully.

'About as sharp as your tongue, Mistress O'Shee, which is very sharp indeed.'

Meg turned to the King and said, 'Send him away. He will never help our cause.'

Looking from the Irish woman to the spy, Henri gave another knowing smile. 'Your passions are aroused, my sweet. Master Swyfte must have struck you a stinging blow to anger you so.' He waved a hand, playfully dismissing the tension in the tent. 'But enough of petty emotions. Mistress Meg, our friend here has been helping my cause for long weeks, unbeknown to himself. And so have you.'

The redhead's eyes narrowed. 'What web have you been weaving, Henri? If you have been playing me for a fool you will regret it.'

'You threaten a king?' Henri feigned astonishment, then laughed. 'Ah, but that is why we all love you! You would shake your fist at the gods themselves.' He turned to Will and said, 'I would have a word, in private, about our common business.'

Understanding, the spy asked Grace if she would wait outside. Flashing a searing glance at Meg, she strode out.

After the monarch had called for Maximilien to pour them all flasks of wine, he said, 'A drink then, to an alliance of all the nations against our mutual Enemy. And to give thanks for the aid you have given France in these dark times.'

Sipping his wine, Will studied the French king with growing respect. He wondered how far the royal's clever scheming extended.

'Once England antagonized the Unseelie Court they preyed less upon my countrymen. Though they would never admit it, I believe they feared resistance on more than one front,' Henri continued. 'Yet they were still a threat. Of course they were. Life in France was one of constant balance. We always waited for the sword to drop.'

'Aye. Bastards all,' Maximilien growled, throwing his wine down his throat.

'And then, as I campaigned for the throne, a representative of the High Family asked me for my aid.'

'An alliance?' the spy asked.

The King snorted. 'Do the Unseelie Court ever truly ally? They take what they want and spit out the rest. I had to tread cautiously – I could not risk alienating them.'

'Your plans to win France would have been over in the blink of an eye,' Meg observed, 'and you would have been found stuffed with straw, with button eyes, a puppet with his strings cut.'

'That is true,' Henri said with a nod. 'A wise king lives in this world and not in his head. They wished to use France as a staging post for their invasion of England, and Paris in particular. In the city they could mass their forces, and conjure up whatever dark magics would help them achieve their aims.'

'I would wager that with Paris controlled by Catholics calling for your blood that decision did not trouble you for long,' Will noted wryly.

Returning his flask to the trestle, Henri gave a quick smile. 'I care for all my subjects equally, Master Swyfte. But, yes, I gave them Paris. I could not refuse. But I also knew that, once taken, they would not give it up again easily, if at all. You know they now seek to take this world for their own, sir?'

'I do.' Will mulled over his wine for a moment. 'So, while acceding to their request for the use of your capital, you also had to put into effect a scheme that would ensure their plans failed.'

The King clapped his hands with glee. 'You are a cunning fellow. I could find much employment for a man like yourself.'

'His Majesty played his part convincingly,' Maximilien said, pouring himself more wine. 'Trusting that he secretly loathed England as much as they, the High Family let slip aspects of their plan that we could use to our advantage.'

'I knew of their foul work beneath the seminary in Reims,

and of their Scar-Crow Men.' Henri's smile darkened. 'Those damnable things . . .'

'And you used me to save him,' Meg pointed at Will, 'so you could entice both of us into your web.'

'And who better to use, my sweet?' Henri smiled, teasing. 'You fit in so well everywhere. And you refuse to fail, even when faced with the most daunting odds.' He eyed Will. 'And England's greatest spy. How could such a man turn his back on this plot once he became aware of it? Why, he might even pursue my enemies into the heart of France itself, and undermine the foul works being carried out at Reims that were beyond my ability to influence. He might even – could this be – unseat the High Family themselves – a clan, I am told, that he has had some success against before.'

'You should have told me your plan,' Meg blazed. Will thought she was about to throw her flask at the King.

'You are always more effective when you are left to your own devices, my sweet.' Henri winked at Maximilien, who replied with a conspiratorial smile.

The Irish woman set her jaw. 'And in what other way did you play me? Tell me now, for if I find out for myself later my temper will know no bounds.'

'And your temper is a fearsome thing to behold. Then let me speak truly. As deep as my affection is for you, my sweet, I would not trust you with alms for the poor.' The monarch waved a finger when he saw Meg clench her fists. 'And I know you well. How could I not?' he said, softening his harsh assessment with a tender note. 'You love your country, and your people, and I knew you could not resist trying to steal Dr Dee away from under English noses. Which is why I had my own men waiting to steal the good doctor away from you.'

'I thought those men at Petworth were there to save me,' the woman exclaimed. Will held a hand out to restrain her. She glared at him.

Henri gave a dismissive shrug. 'Sadly, Master Swyfte thwarted that part of my plan. I half expected that would be the case. But Dr Dee is a prize that all the countries of Europe desire.' He bowed to Will. 'Yet he is not truly valued in his own land. That is always the way. Keep a hold of him, Master Swyfte, or else your defences will become someone else's.'

Meg rounded on the spy. 'You have been the King of France's performing ape,' she blazed. 'Where is your anger? He has had you dancing to his tune, tumbling and falling and fooling. And you have cleaned up his dirty business in Reims with your own life at stake.'

Will shrugged. 'Though it pains me to say it, I have had worse jobs in my time.'

Meg gaped, incredulous.

'Master Swyfte understands this business well, Mistress Meg,' Henri noted. 'He now has the soon to-be-crowned King of France in his debt. That is a good card to hold in your hand in any game. So, what now, sir?'

'Now we head to Paris, Your Majesty, and if you can find a way to get me past the city walls and into the very heart of the Unseelie Court's forces, that would go some small way to repaying me for the work I have done on your behalf.' Will gave a deep, ironic bow.

'I think I can help you there, Master Swyfte. Yes, indeed.'

'I am joining you,' Meg snapped.

'So you can thrust a dagger between my shoulder blades when I least expect it?'

'I would not resist her request, sir.' Henri laughed louder.

'Very well,' Will sighed. 'Perhaps I can throw you to the Unseelie Court as a distraction.' The spy could see the Irish woman was restraining herself, yet despite her betrayal at Petworth he was surprised at how appealing he still found her company.

'Good,' the redhead replied. 'Then I will go and make my preparations.' She flounced out, ignoring Grace, who stood outside the tent's entrance and stuck out her tongue as the Irish woman passed.

Will's tone darkened. 'The Unseelie Court have something which could destroy the Scar-Crow Men in the blink of an eye. It is the key to ending this business.'

The monarch looked to Maximilien, whose expression became grim. 'They gather at the Cathedral of Notre Dame. It stands on an island in the river and will be nigh on impregnable with so many of those bastards swarming around. You journey into hell, Master Swyfte.'

'That place holds no surprises for me.' The spy knew the immensity of the threat that awaited him, but he felt no fear for himself. All men died – it was a matter only of when, and how. 'But we must set out immediately. The High Family know my intentions and will do all in their power to prevent me reaching Paris.'

'Very well. Maximilien, give the men their orders,' Henri said.

After the adviser had left, Will added, 'If I can make good, I will need a ship to take me to England. It may already be too late if matters at home have taken an unfortunate turn. Speed is of the essence.'

'That too can be arranged. I have a galleon moored upon the mouth of the Seine at Le Havre-de-Grâce.'

Lowering his voice, Will said, 'I ask one further thing.'

'Go on.'

'If I am not to survive, look after my friend Grace. She is an

430

innocent in these matters and she has suffered greatly. England may not be safe for her if we fail.'

The King gave a concerned smile. 'I will care for her as if she were a member of my own family. But I warn you, Master Swyfte, if we fail there may be no safe place anywhere.'

When he stepped out of the tent, Will paused briefly to look at the stars in the vast vault of the heavens. He felt oddly at peace.

When she returned from the camp fire, Grace saw it too. 'You seem changed,' she said, peering curiously into his face. 'That black mood that has gripped you for so long has lifted.'

And Will was surprised to realize she spoke the truth. Although death was closer than it had ever been, he had rediscovered the urge to live. He would have laughed if it would not have unsettled the young woman.

Thunder rolled out across the warm landscape, and the horizon flashed white with lightning.

'Oh,' Grace said, puzzled. 'The weather has turned. How odd.'

The spy watched the black clouds rolling with unnatural speed across the hills. He knew what came with the storm.

CHAPTER SIXTY-ONE

STANDING ON THE HILLTOP IN THE BUFFETING WIND, WILL looked down at the twinkling lights of Paris and felt the stress of the last nine days' hard travel begin to ease. The running could stop; now the fighting would begin.

A sparkling island in the night-dark sea, the city was alight with lamps on all the municipal buildings and candles glimmering in the windows of the houses that faced the streets. Contained in its old walls, Paris squatted on the plain of the river that flowed through its heart. The spy had first considered the river to be the best route into the capital, but Maximilien, the King's adviser, had warned him that the Unseelie Court had 'set things roaming there to slaughter the unwary'.

'And so we reach the end of the road,' Meg said, brushing back a strand of her damp red hair. She loosely held the reins of her horse. The animal frothed at the mouth from its exertions.

'Not in more ways than one, I hope,' the spy muttered.

Grinning, the King strode over and clapped his hands. Will was impressed by the monarch's seemingly inhuman good nature in the face of the last few days' hardships. 'Hup-hup, no time to rest! You have nations to save. And, of course, lives to risk.'

'I thank you for reminding me,' Will replied. He was distracted by the bulk of the great cathedral rising up from the island in the centre of the river. His gaze followed the walls around the city's perimeter, but he could see no way of slipping into Paris unnoticed. Waiting until dawn and hiding in the back of some cart was not an option. Xanthus was an hour behind, possibly less.

The spy glanced back at all that remained of the King's men. They were exhausted and scared. Night after night soldiers had stayed behind to try to slow the Hunter's progress, and now, Will guessed, their bodies littered the countryside all the way back to Reims.

At least Grace was safe and on her way to the waiting galleon, with two of Henri's most trusted men for company.

With thunder rumbling like distant cannon-fire and spitting rain caught in the wind, they rode down the hillside to the city. Moving along winding, dusty tracks, the riders came to the remnants of an abandoned quarry not far from the city walls, where yellow grass and lichen covered mounds of extracted rock. Dismounting, Maximilien ordered the King's men to guard the path and then led Henri, Will and Meg through the quarry to a ragged black hole in the hillside.

'Paris sits on the edge of an abyss,' the monarch explained, peering into the dark. 'Quarriers have dug mines here for three hundred years, perhaps more. Most of the stone was removed outside the city walls, and few know of the old tunnels that stretch deep under the city.' He turned to Will and grinned. 'I promised you safe passage and here it is.'

'Keep to the left in the first cavern and the tunnel will present itself to you,' Maximilien growled. 'Were it more spacious it would have been of use during our siege, but only one man may pass through it at a time.'

433

The spy glanced up at the black clouds rolling overhead. 'No time to lose. Your dancing ape thanks you for your aid, Your Majesty, and I hope we will meet again in this life.' He bowed deeply.

Meg allowed the King to kiss her hand while feigning a lack of interest. 'Enjoy the arms of your love, but remember the times when your passion reached its true heights,' she told him.

Maximilien handed Will one of the torches he had brought from the cart containing the tents. The spy lit it with his flint, and as the rain began to pound he led the Irish woman into the dark cave. Before they disappeared into the underworld, he glanced back. For the first time since they had met, the King's face was grim.

Through the dusty-dry atmosphere, the spy and his companion moved into low-ceilinged caverns supported by columns of stone left by the long-departed quarrymen. The rasp of the two cautious travellers' feet made whispering echoes rustle around the edges of the vast space.

'Keep four paces to my right and one pace ahead,' Will said, holding the hissing torch in front of him. 'Where I can see you.'

'I walk where I choose,' the Irish woman snapped. 'And fear not, I have no wish to be by your side.'

'Then I presume you will keep your mind on the task at hand, especially as there are no men down here to distract you.'

'Says the one who has bedded every woman in London, if the stories are to be believed.'

'Do I hear the merest hint of jealousy? Or is it simply regret?' he asked.

'Only in your dreams.' Meg threw her red hair back, refusing to give Will even cursory notice.

The spy skirted the left-hand wall of the cavern until he found a tunnel carved into the rock, so small he had to stoop to enter. It gave way to rough-hacked caves and tiny rooms before continuing like an arrow into the heart of Paris. Will imagined passing beneath the old city walls, under the cobbled streets and the rough, filth-strewn lanes, the pale-faced men and women cowering indoors, away from the Enemy that now existed among them.

When Will heard a change in the quality of their echoing footsteps, he knew their underground journey was coming to an end. The golden glare of the torch dappled the timber that barred their way. Gently rapping on the wood, Will considered the hollow response and then glanced back at Meg. Her face looked serious and determined, her eyes glinting in the dancing flames.

'I would step back. I may have to kick this down,' the spy said.

'Pray use your head and keep the damage to a minimum.'

Once she had retreated a few paces, Will gave two sharp kicks and the timber burst into a dark cellar. Raising one hand, he listened for a moment and then stepped into the cool space.

The torchlight revealed barrels and glinting bottles in a vaulted stone chamber, the air thick with the aroma of sour wine. Once he had satisfied himself that no one was coming to investigate, Will led the way up stone steps to an arched door that opened on to a wood-panelled corridor. Extinguishing the torch, he darted through the still house, the swishing of Meg's skirts close behind.

The spy led them out on to a small cobbled street glistening in the rain. Water sluiced from the roofs into black puddles where the reflected candlelight from the windows sparkled and swam.

Meg followed Will's gaze up to the roiling black clouds

overhead. 'The Hunter's manipulation of the elements grows more intense with his frustration. Let us hope these magics drain him.' The Irish woman paused. 'Though I fear his hatred for you is now so great he would risk everything to see you destroyed.'

'That is less of an unusual occurrence than you might think.'

Slipping in and out of the shadows close to the walls of the houses, Will tried to get his bearings. At the corner of a broad thoroughfare, he smelled the foetid river and glimpsed the silhouette of the great cathedral rising up against the sky. He brought up an arm to hold Meg back.

'Hide.'

Ducking back around the corner, they pressed themselves against the wet wall. A faint light washed over the houses on the other side of the broad street. Within a moment, a bone-white carriage drawn by two colourless horses splashed through the pools of black water. Both beasts and vehicle emitted the ghostly light. It was soundless, a ghost-carriage, though clearly it had substance. There was no driver, but Will glimpsed two of the Unseelie Court through the window, a male in a broad-brimmed hat and a woman with hair piled high on her head, both equally leached of colour.

'They travel so openly,' the Irish woman hissed once the carriage had disappeared from sight.

'It is their city now. I hope your former lover sleeps peacefully.' The spy looked around at the streets devoid of human life, and the houses where nothing moved. Paris was not as populous as London, but it still contained almost two hundred thousand people, even without the many who had died of starvation during Henri's siege. Many more refugees had fled to the city from the fighting in the countryside. Did they now all quake in fear beneath their beds?

'Henri must make choices where there is no easy answer, oft-times no winners, and only the extent of each side's losses is the deciding factor,' Meg replied, adding sharply, 'and that is why he is king and you are not.'

'I would think birth and blood had some part to play in it, but be it as you will.' Once he was sure the street was empty, Will ran in the direction of the cathedral.

As they neared the river, the two spies ducked into an alley. Another Fay man rode past on a grey horse, his silver-mildewed doublet almost matching the tone of his bloodless face. Four other pale figures stalked by before Will and the Irish woman could leave their hiding place, and then they were running as fast as they could through the driving rain to the edge of the vast, stone-arched bridge that led to the island in the flow.

As they crouched out of sight, their attention was caught by a spectral glow from the river downstream. Peering over the small stone wall, the spy felt a chill. On the grey, choppy water, a fleet was moored, more galleons than Will could count, disappearing into the rain and night. They strained at anchor, their sails furled, no colours flying on their masts, but they needed none, for that eerie luminescence told him all he needed to know of ownership. There was no movement on deck that he could see, no frantic activity as the crews prepared to sail, and that gave him some comfort. But here, without doubt, was the Enemy's invasion force, ready for England whenever the order was given.

From the hills above the city, the ships had been invisible, hidden by the Fay's magics. And he felt no need to question how seagoing vessels could sail in the shallows of a summer river, nor how they could navigate the impassable sections of the Seine upstream. The Unseelie Court made their own rules.

Seeing the scale of the fleet, feeling the icy power that

washed off it, Will was fearful of what lay ahead. If those ships were free to sail upon England, all would be lost.

Turning his attention back to the bridge, the spy saw that like London Bridge across the Thames in London, Pont Notre-Dame was lined on both sides by tall stone and brick houses, their pitched roofs topped with orange-brown tiles. In the daylight, at any other time, it would be bustling with merchants, the road across the centre of the span packed with carts and livestock. Now it was deserted apart from three pale figures waiting in the rain-drenched gloom halfway across.

'There is no way past them,' Meg whispered.

'There is always a way.'

Studying the bridge, the spy saw only one perilous route open to him. Turning to the Irish woman, he whispered, 'Despite my doubts about your loyalty, I acceded to your request to accompany me on this dangerous mission. But you must now wait here—'

'I am no weak and cowardly woman. Do not treat me like your bloodless, flower-loving Grace. I will not be dismissed, abandoned, discarded. Ever.' Her anger simmered.

Softening his tone, Will said, 'Mistress Meg, you have proved yourself to have the heart of a lion and the skills and ferocity of any man. I would be proud to have you at my side in any battle. Although,' he added with a tight smile, 'not at my back. But this work now requires the stealth that can only be accomplished by one alone. You know this business well. See it with the eyes of a spy.'

Her anger faded, but she still surveyed him with hard eyes. 'Very well then. But I will watch for your return. Do not try to leave me here.'

'Though I am loath to say this, I need you.'

Her brow furrowed, her gaze becoming uncertain.

'If I die here, I need you to take up this fight.'

Meg nodded. 'If you die, I will carry the fight back to them. So do I now vow.'

Swinging one leg over the low wall, the spy paused again and, turning quickly, stole a kiss.

The Irish woman recoiled in surprise.

Will gave a rakish grin. 'If I go to my grave, I would do so with a happy memory.'

And then he threw himself over the edge of the wall and was gone.

CHAPTER SIXTY-TWO

RUSHING TO THE WALL, MEG FEARED WILL HAD PLUMMETED into the churning grey water below. Plucking her wind-whipped hair from her eyes, she peered into the dark. She could just discern the spy edging along a rain-slick ledge barely as wide as the span of a hand with only a cornice at head-height for support. Beneath him, the river eddied around the stone columns of the arches, calling for him to plunge into its lethal currents.

'You are a fool, Will Swyfte,' she breathed, with a grudging respect for her companion's courage.

As she watched him disappearing into the gloom, an unsettling confusion of feelings washed through her. Ever since she was a child standing over the bloodied bodies of her elder brothers, she had felt she knew herself, and that she understood the strict rules of life. Survival was paramount. Freed of weak emotions, she had learned her trade well. She had needed for nothing. There were small joys to be had, here and there. And she had aided her countrymen well in the bitter wars they had fought, among themselves, against the English and, in secret rebellion, against the Unseelie Court. The loneliness that had crept up on her like an assassin in the night had troubled her only intermittently and she had succeeded in keeping it at bay through the diamond-hard edge of her will.

She had been able to maintain her life of red blades, and joyless coupling, and heart-rending deception, with the conviction that only one solitary path was open to her, and that no one else could ever understand her oceanic depths. But now she realized everything had changed.

Hammering one small but strong fist upon the stone wall, Meg let out her unfocused rage for one moment and then tore her gaze away from the bridge. Swyfte was lost to the night.

The wind blasted along the river, stinging her pale skin with stone-hard rain. Her skirts and bodice were soaked through and she was filled with a bone-deep chill that belied the summer warmth. The storm was getting stronger. Lightning flickered around the hills as if the gods were circling the city.

Further along the road that bounded the river, she glimpsed movement, pale figures flitting here and there. At a distance the Unseelie Court had all the substance of moon shadows. It was only up close that they took on the lethal presence of hunting beasts.

Eyeing their comings and goings, she decided there was not enough cover there at the edge of the river and she turned and ran back to the shelter of the tall merchants' houses on the other side of the street. Though candles still gleamed in the windows, she saw no comfort anywhere. The Enemy were all over Paris, wherever she looked: carriages rolling silently along the street on the far side of the Seine, the spectral fleet bobbing on the choppy waves, riders emerging from the winding, narrow streets on to the large riverside thoroughfare and groups locked in conversation here and there, oblivious to the downpour. Secure in their control of the city, the Unseelie Court were not looking out for enemies. Perhaps there was hope the two spies could escape France with their lives.

But as Meg eased into the shadowy depths of a rat-infested alley, lightning flashed and she saw the silhouette of a figure on the roof of the first house on the Pont Notre-Dame. It was Xanthus, hunched on the edge of the house like a gargoyle, peering down into the street.

He had seen her.

Her heart thumping, Meg gripped her dagger tightly though she knew it would be useless.

Seemingly untouched by the tearing winds, the ghostly stalker raised himself up, balancing on the balls of his feet. As the Irish woman prepared herself for his descent, he turned and bounded like a wolf up the orange tiles and away across the connecting roofs of the houses on the bridge.

The Hunter wanted only Will Swyfte.

CHAPTER SIXTY-THREE

LASHED BY THE STORM, WILL CLUNG ON TO THE CORNICE WITH
aching fingers, edging forward one fumbling step at a time.
Beneath him, the grey waters of the Seine churned around the
base of the Pont Notre-Dame's stone footings. One slip and he
would be lost to the currents, never to surface again.

'It would be easier to let go.'

Snapping his head round at the voice, the spy looked into
glistening black eyes. Jenny clung to the ledge behind him,
her mottled skin now tinged with broken veins as if she were
decomposing a little more each time he saw her. Her rain-
soaked hair hung lank, her skirts clinging to her too-thin
frame.

'Get thee away from me, devil,' the spy growled. 'I am not
in the mood for your trickery.'

Jenny pressed her blue lips close to his ear and whispered,
'You have betrayed me. Where is that deep love that you pro-
fessed so strongly? A love that would never die, that would
survive the vast gulfs of time and space between us, my sweet?
It tripped off your tongue so easily. Were you lying to me?
Were you lying to yourself?'

'I love you still, as deeply as ever.' Keeping his head turned away from that haunting face, Will focused all his attention on the gloom shrouding the end of the bridge. 'Love is more complex than you would imagine in your narrow world of misery. And we are all pulled by currents we cannot fathom.'

Refusing to acknowledge any more of the whispered lies and threats and low, mocking laughter, he edged forward. When he passed the bridge's midway point, he realized he could no longer sense the presence at his back, but the weight he felt upon his shoulders did not lift.

With cold, painful fingers, the spy pulled himself up the cornice at the far end and eased his head above the parapet. The towering bulk of the cathedral loomed over the rain-lashed island. He thought how the tall windows on the twin towers resembled the eyes of a judgemental god looking down upon him.

A warren of dark, deserted buildings sprawled away from the wall. Pulling himself over the parapet, Will hurried through the narrow alleys until he overlooked a small cobbled square in front of the cathedral. The stained glass was afire, candlelight flooding out of the open doors.

Three pale figures moved on to the bridge and were lost among the towering merchants' houses, while others drifted out of the cathedral, pausing to exchange brief words with their fellows. Watching the ebb and flow for long moments, Will decided there were only two guards who patrolled the fringes of the square.

The spy huddled in the shadows close to the wall, wrapping his black cloak around him, and waited for his moment.

Thunder pealed overhead, and lightning lit up the front of the church. When the glare faded, only the guards remained. One walked near to where Will hid, the other stood by the cathedral door, attention fixed on the bright interior.

Drawing Dee's blowpipe from the hidden pocket in his cloak, the spy dipped a dart in the lethal blue paste and inserted it in the end of the tube. A pool of black ink in the deeper shadow, he waited with the pipe to his lips until the pale figure was only feet away. Will blew into the tube. The Enemy clutched at his face. The spy was moving before the guard crumpled to the wet cobbles.

His footsteps masked by the torrent of rainwater gushing off the cathedral roof, he slipped into the shadows next to the wall, unseen. Whisking out his dagger, he crept forward, sliding the blade across the sentry's neck in a flash. He dumped the body out of sight just around the corner of the building.

The relentless pounding of the rain matched the beating of the spy's heart. Peering in through the open door, he was relieved to see no further Enemies waited just inside the church. Notre Dame was flooded with golden light from the ranks of candles running along the nave. The Unseelie Court swarmed like ants in the far depths of the cathedral, studying charts, locked in discussions, or at work on tasks beyond Will's ability to comprehend. Some appeared to be maintaining weapons of unknown use, while others chanted in low voices as they inscribed symbols on the stone flags.

Keeping low, Will slipped along the rear wall of the cathedral to what appeared to be a small storeroom. He slid inside, unseen. Crouching in the shadows, he continued to observe the activity in the cathedral through a narrow slit in the door.

A tall mirror in a gilt frame stood incongruously in the centre of the nave, surrounded by a circle of squat candles. As Will watched, the glass became opaque, attracting the attention of the Fay near to it. One of them hurried away, returning a moment later with a grotesquely obese figure, naked to the waist, his sweating, shaven head gleaming in the candlelight.

Wheezing from the exertion, he shuffled into the circle and peered into the looking glass with his porcine eyes. The milky haze cleared to reveal Fabian's doleful reflection. He was standing in a dark place, perhaps still in the catacombs beneath the Reims seminary. For long moments, the two figures engaged in conversation. Although he couldn't overhear what was said, Will suspected he was the subject of their debate. He began to formulate a plan.

Scrabbling through the contents of the storeroom, the spy uncovered a dirty sheet. He returned to the door, from where he watched the corpulent figure begin to lose his temper in a language the spy didn't understand. The other pale figures crowded around the mirror to listen to the argument.

When one of the Fay passed near the door, the spy fired another poisonous dart. Leaping from the storeroom, Will flung the sheet over the convulsing being and tossed one of Dee's powder-packages after it. The chemicals ignited in a flash of searing light. Ablaze, the being careered down the side aisle of the cathedral, his screams ringing off the walls.

Will threw himself behind the back row of heavy wooden pews and crawled to the other side of the church. While the Unseelie Court flocked to stifle the flames on the body of their dying fellow, the spy kept his attention on the bald-headed mound of shivering flesh. Just as he had hoped, the grotesque figure called out in his wavering, sibilant voice and directed four of the Fay towards the altar.

From his hiding place, the spy noticed a knee-high sculpture of human bones topped with a skull. Standing in another circle of squat candles, it glowed with a faint emerald light.

The Corpus-Scythe, Will guessed.

With alacrity, the four pale figures lifted it into a wooden chest with rope handles on either end, and carried it along the central aisle. *Trying to protect it at all costs.* Keeping below the Enemy's line of sight, the spy slipped out into the storm-blasted night.

In front of the cathedral, the small cobbled area already lay under an inch of water. Will could barely see more than a few feet through the torrential rain, but that would help him. Crouching in the shadows along the wall, he took out the blowpipe and darts and waited.

The four Fay emerged with the wooden chest a moment later. Cloaked by the night and the gale, Will was invisible to them. His first dart struck the nearest Fay on the hand. As the pale figure began to convulse, the spy loaded a second poison-tipped dart and propelled it into the neck of one of the Enemy at the rear.

The chest splashed into the deepening pool of rainwater.

As the remaining two pale figures drew their rapiers, Will ghosted along the wall behind them and thrust his dagger under the ribcage of his third foe. When the final Fay began to turn, the spy plunged his blade into his opponent's throat.

Sheathing his weapon, Will grasped the chest by both handles. It was lighter than he anticipated. But he had only splashed four steps across the cobbles when a warning cry rang out. A bedraggled Meg stood in the nearest alley. Her eyes were wide with terror and with a trembling hand she was pointing above him.

Will spun round. Above the main doorway ran a long gallery of statues of the kings of Israel. One of them was moving.

Lightning illuminated the graven relief. Crawling across the carvings like a giant spider was Xanthus, his shaven, symbol-etched head turned towards the spy.

Mouth torn wide in a bestial roar, the Hunter leapt.

CHAPTER SIXTY-FOUR

THROWING HIMSELF OUT OF THE PATH OF THE WHITE-FACED Hunter, Will heard the chest shatter. The spy rolled back to his feet only to see the Corpus-Scythe lying exposed in the deepening pool of rainwater and Xanthus crouching over it. Will felt a pang of bitter regret. He'd come so close to escaping with his prize, but a face-to-face fight at that moment was a battle he was unlikely to win.

Meg had already fled. He sprinted away from the square towards a narrow street on the northern side of the cathedral. The way ahead was long and straight with no alleys in which he could lose himself.

At his back, the spy heard splashing as the Hunter bounded across the cobbles.

A door to the cathedral hung ajar to his right. Will dived into the dark space and drew the heavy iron bolts, although he knew it would buy him only a few moments. He raced up a flight of broad stone steps two at a time, a plan already forming in his mind. Ignoring the door to what he guessed was the grand gallery connecting the two towers, he continued climbing until his breath burned in his chest.

From far below, the clang of the bolt being drawn back echoed up the well of shadows.

The steps ended atop one of the cathedral's two towers. From the window space, he had a view across storm-buffeted Paris. Thousands of stars of candlelight flickered in inky space. On the grey Seine, the Unseelie Court fleet glowed with a ghostly luminescence.

Xanthus would think him trapped, the spy thought. That gave him an advantage.

Pulling the grapnel from his cloak's pocket, Will hooked it on the coping and threw the attached rope out of the window. He had no time to test if it would hold. Hanging out into the tearing wind, the spy grasped the rope and slid down.

He was hurled around wildly by the gale and blinded by the downpour. Smashed against the stone of the tower, he held on with shaking hands, then kicked away from the wall to continue his descent. As he swung, he glimpsed a face in one of the open arched windows along the gallery between the towers. He was sure it had been Meg. Was it she who had left the tower door ajar?

Will felt a wrench and the grapnel gave way. Arms whirling, he fell, the rope tumbling around him.

Slamming into the rain-slick cathedral roof, the spy felt his breath driven from his lungs. He had no time to recover. Numb from the impact, he careered down the steep pitch on his back.

When he glanced down, he saw the edge of the roof racing towards him.

Will curled his hand around the tangled rope and yanked hard. The grapnel flew through the air and crashed ahead of him; jerking his arm up, he caught the cold iron of the hook with his free hand as he sped by. With his stomach flipping, he shot over the edge.

Overcome by the dizzying sensation of falling, the spy felt every bone in his body jar when the grapnel caught on the coping at the edge of the roof. He slammed against the stone wall once more. His fingers slipped, then held tight.

He didn't look down, but he could feel the drop pulling beneath his feet. On straining arms, he hauled himself up, grabbed the edge of the coping with his right hand and pulled himself back on to the roof.

Will kneeled on the brink of the abyss and caught his breath. He felt the furious gale tear at him, threatening to pitch him over the side, and he knew he had to move on. But when he looked up, he saw he was not alone. Near the north tower, Xanthus now balanced on the edge of the roof, seemingly oblivious to the wind and the rain. Illuminated by the white light of a lightning flash, the predator stretched out his arms and closed his eyes in beatific supplication to the heavens.

'Across your world I have pursued you, for the vengeance demanded by my brother and my people,' the Hunter roared above the howling gale. 'But this ends now. Your time has come, spy.'

Your time has come, Will's devil whispered in his ear.

Returning the grapnel to the pocket in his cloak, the spy saw there was still a chance that he could follow his original plan. In the shadow of the soaring spire where the transepts crossed, a white stone arm reached towards the Seine. Will identified numerous places where he could descend – if he could but reach the roof of the southern transept before Xanthus caught him.

But the spy was gripped by a puzzling sight. Stooping on

the edge of the roof, the Hunter was removing an object from the sack he had strapped to his back. Silver gleamed.

The Wish-Crux.

The box the Enemy had attempted to use that rainswept night at Lud's Church.

Transfixed, Will watched the hunched figure set the gleaming chest on the coping and open the lid with a careful, almost awed motion. Will thought the dark within the box seemed to suck as powerfully as the void beside him.

After a moment, he saw movement in the black depths. Small shapes emerged into the driving rain and began to skitter along the edge of the roof towards him. Overcome by a grim foreboding, Will turned and lurched into the buffeting wind along the edge of the abyss. His shoes slipped on the wet stone. Arms outstretched to steady himself, he fought to maintain his balance.

Above the south transept, the spy glanced back. In the hunch of the Hunter's slowly loping form, Will saw weakness, perhaps exhaustion. Could it be that the predator's strength had been drained by his control of the elements during their long pursuit?

The spy's gaze was drawn back to that black trail of scurrying forms, each one almost as big as the palm of his hand.

Spiders?

Certainly like no spiders he had ever seen before.

On the south transept roof, Will was held fast by the crashing waves of wind. Bowing his head, he pressed on, one agonizing step at a time. Blinded by the driving rain, the thunder rolling out above and lightning crashing down in jagged forks, Will felt his world was in turmoil.

Turning, the spy saw the spiders had caught up with him.

Although they looked insignificant, he was sure some dark power lurked within them.

Death is close, his devil whispered with a throaty laugh.

'Damn you! Leave me be!' the spy raged.

Hammering one shoe down upon the nearest spider, he sensed the black shape burst under his leather sole. It felt like crushing a hen's egg. Black ichor oozed out from beneath his foot and was washed away by the rain.

Just as he began to think that the skittering things were too easily destroyed, one arachnid propelled itself on to his hose and scurried up his body. He felt each leg like a hot needle stabbing into his flesh. Too fast to be brushed off, it swept down his arm to the back of his hand. With a shiver, the creature sank its fangs into Will and tore away a chunk of flesh.

The spy yelled in pain, blood spraying from his hand. Tearing the spider free, he crushed it in his palm. The black ichor steamed as it gushed between his fingers, and he hurled the squashed remains away. By then the other spiders were swarming across his body, tearing and biting.

Fearful that his thrashing would pitch him over the edge, the spy battled towards a small spire at the end of the transept where there was a patch of shelter. Whenever the snapping jaws bit through his clothes, he felt like he was being burned by hot pokers. Blood ran freely down his arms and legs, and however much he tore the spiders away, others replaced them. Unopposed, they could strip a body in a matter of moments, he realized.

The sands of time run out finally, and hell awaits, the devil growled in his ear.

His hands slick with blood, Will gripped on to the spire for support. Through the sheet of rain, he could see the pale, hunched shape of Xanthus creeping towards him. The Hunter had drawn his rapier ready for the killing blow.

The spy ripped the spiders away with gore-drenched hands. He hurled his body repeatedly against the spire to crush more. Yet he felt his strength ebbing with each gout of blood he lost, and he didn't know how much longer he could endure.

Then his pale foe stood before him, swordpoint twirling in line with Will's heart. 'You have led me a merry chase,' Xanthus said, 'but finally my brother can rest peacefully, and the High Family will know that Cavillex has been avenged. When your Queen's head sits on a spike at Nonsuch Palace, yours will rest beside her.'

'Your brother died as he lived, a coward,' the spy snarled, drawing his own rapier. 'I ran him through as if I were spearing fish in the pond on Whittington Green, and thought even less about it.'

Raging, the Hunter lunged wildly. With a flick of his wrist, Will parried the thrust easily, the force of his response almost unbalancing his opponent. Steadying himself on the edge of the giddy drop, Xanthus saw what the spy intended. He calmed himself, his eyes narrowing.

'You appear weaker,' Will said, pulling a snapping spider from his bloody left cheek and tossing it away. 'You have allowed your hatred for me to get the better of you.'

'I have strength enough for you.'

The Hunter thrust again, his sword-stroke more refined this time, and faster. Will clashed his blade against his foe's, and returned the thrust. Xanthus deflected it with a twirl of his rapier.

They were only testing each other, the spy saw. Both of them had been weakened and each wanted to see the limits of the other's resolve.

As the spiders swarmed across his chest, Will's clothes were being eaten away. Through the tatters, he glimpsed bloody bites on his pale, wet flesh. He could feel his time on earth leaking away.

He thrust his rapier towards the Hunter's heart, followed up with a slash towards the neck and then struck low, driving the pale figure back along the edge of the roof. Lost to the storm and the burning bites, Will sensed his world retreat to the small circle of his vision, and to Xanthus' fierce face. Their swords clashed to the rhythm of the thunder.

The spy's foot slipped on the wet stone and for one moment he thought he was about to plunge over the edge. For an instant, he teetered. The Hunter swung his sword in an arc, the steel shimmering in the fading glare of a lightning strike.

At the last, Will dropped to his knees, gripping the coping while he regained his spinning senses. His Enemy's sword flashed over his head.

Seizing his moment, the spy thrust his rapier upwards into Xanthus' exposed stomach.

Crying out, the Hunter fell back, clutching at his wound. As he lay, half hanging over the edge, Will tore off the last few spiders with shaking hands. In the corner of his eye, he spied pale figures moving in both the cathedral's towers: the Unseelie Court had found him.

Retrieving the grapnel, Will affixed it to the mass of decorative carvings that cascaded from the small spire. As he wound the rope around his left wrist, he saw Xanthus was back on his feet, holding one hand over the blood-pumping wound.

'If I am to die this night, I will take you with me,' the Fay spat.

His strength draining from him by the moment, Will knew he had but a slim chance to survive another fight. Propelling himself up the pitch of the roof, he turned to swing towards his foe.

And in that instant the world went black.

So it ends, Mephistophilis laughed.

The spy's thoughts rushed through his head in that frozen moment, and he knew exactly what had happened. During the flight to Petworth House, Mephistophilis had demanded a payment in return for his aid.

You will give me something, and only for five minutes, no more, then I shall return it.

His sight.

The devil had chosen his moment well.

Unseeing, Will felt his feet sliding on the slick tiles. He would continue down the slope, directly on to the end of Xanthus' blade, and thus Mephistophilis would have claimed what he set out to achieve those long weeks ago in the Rose Theatre.

One last gamble, he thought. *For Jenny, for Kit.*

Yanking the rope taut, the spy leapt with all the force he could muster. His head spun as he flew.

In the dark of his head, Will felt the wild wind in his hair, rain drenching his face. His feet crashed into a solid mass, what could only be the Hunter. Pain seared his side. His foe's blade, tearing his flesh.

A cry rang out, and then spiralled away from him.

In his mind's eye, Will pictured Xanthus propelled over the edge of the roof, blood trailing from his stomach wound, his face contorted in impotent rage. And that pale figure falling away, down into the dark, and death.

Will continued to fly, off the roof and out into the void. When he reached the limits of the rope, his arm almost tore from its socket. Tumbling back, he crashed against the stone of the cathedral wall for the third time. His wits near knocked out of his head, he hung, too weak to descend. Every fibre of his being burned, and he could feel hot blood slicking his torso.

'I die on my own terms, devil,' he croaked.

With the Hunter's passing, the rain slowly stopped and the thunder rolled away. In the silence that followed, Will could hear familiar chilling music and smell the syrupy scent of honeysuckle caught on the wind. The Unseelie Court were making their way across the cathedral roof.

He considered letting go of the rope and plunging to his death, rather than letting himself fall into the hands of those foul creatures. Yet even then, at the end, he found it impossible to relinquish life.

'And are ye going to keep hanging there like a slab of meat in a butcher's?'

'Meg?' The spy pictured the red-headed woman leaning over the edge of the roof. 'My sight has been stolen from me, for now. I cannot climb down, but there is a way.'

There was silence for a moment and then she hissed, 'Our Good Neighbours will be with us soon. You must trust me.'

Will laughed.

'You must trust me,' the woman repeated. 'I will climb down. Take your hand off the rope and wrap your arms around me.'

'So you can fling me into the void and be done with me?'

Ignoring him, she replied, 'I am stronger than you think and I have a head for heights like no other. I can support your weight for a little while.'

Fading in and out on the breeze, the music of fiddle and pipes drew nearer.

'Trust me,' she whispered.

'Very well,' he heard himself saying.

As Meg grasped the rope, Will felt her breath on his ear. 'This is the moment when everything changes,' she whispered.

CHAPTER SIXTY-FIVE

SIR ROBERT CECIL PACED ANXIOUSLY OUTSIDE THE COUNCIL chamber, his hunchbacked form throwing off his gait so that it appeared he was on the deck of a seagoing galleon. Hands clasped behind his back, his face set, he looked the model of brooding contemplation. Nearby, the mercenary Sinclair and his shadow, Rowland the record-keeper, waited.

The Secretary of State's concentration was broken by echoing, urgent footsteps and he glanced up to see Robert Devereux, Earl of Essex, striding into the gloomy antechamber, blinding in white doublet with gold embroidery, white breeches and white cloak.

'You,' the Earl said, jabbing a finger at the black-gowned secretary. 'What are you doing here?'

'The same as your good self, I would wager,' Cecil replied with a false smile. 'Summoned to appear before Her Majesty, who has been ensconced for this past hour with the Privy Council.'

The flamboyant man blanched. 'The council? Meeting without either of us in attendance?'

The secretary noted cruelly that his rival's face and clothes now merged into one single pool of insipidity. 'Perhaps we are both on our way to the Tower. It appears your cunning manipulations – some would say deceit – have not earned you the advantages you so fervently desired.'

The door to the Council Chamber swung open and Cecil shuffled in. Essex hastened to catch up, ensuring that he arrived in the Queen's presence at the same time as his rival.

The throne stood with a row of arched windows behind it so that Elizabeth was always perceived in a halo of light. Even so, she looked old and withered, her chin falling to her breast, her white make-up and red wig serving only to exacerbate the cadaverous quality of her hollow cheeks and eye sockets.

The secretary was immediately struck by the presence of Her Majesty's maid of honour, Elinor, erect and beady-eyed at the Queen's left arm. *A woman? Here?* he thought, forgetting the gender of his monarch in a manner that would have made Elizabeth proud, were she aware of his thoughts.

But the Queen seemed unaware of almost everything in the room. Her lids hung heavily as though she were on the brink of sleep, her stare deadened.

Behind her, the Privy Council stood, black robes, grey beards, sallow skin, their expressions too emotionless for Cecil to read the intent of the gathering.

'Robert. And Robert,' the Queen drawled. 'In these dark times, I find your rivalry . . . tiresome.'

Essex shuffled uneasily and then gave a deep bow. 'Your Majesty, may I offer my profound apologies.'

Cecil tried not to show his contempt.

'You must put aside your differences, for there is a matter so pressing it demands all your abilities,' the monarch continued. 'It has been brought to my attention that the traitor William Swyfte is returning to England, from France, even as we speak.'

How has it been brought to your attention? the secretary thought, casting a sideways glance at his rival's baffled face. *The two masters of all England's spies are here before you, and we are both unaware of this development.* He saw no advantage in raising this question and instead gave a studied, thoughtful nod.

'Our disgraced spy sails on a merchant's vessel from Le Havre-de-Grâce and will dock at the legal quays between the Old Bridge and the Tower on the morrow.' With an unblinking stare, Elizabeth shifted her gaze between the two men in front of her. 'Swyfte plans my death, and the overthrow of this government. He must be prevented from reaching Nonsuch at all costs. *You* must prevent him reaching here. From this moment on, my two favoured councillors, you must work together. Use all the spies at your disposal, united in intent for the first time, and seize Swyfte the moment he sets foot on English soil. Then bring him before me, alive if possible, dead if necessary.'

Cecil flashed a quick glance at Essex's slow-moving face and seized the moment to make his own deep bow.

'Of course, Your Majesty,' the Little Elf said in a confident tone. 'I have a plan forming already.'

CHAPTER SIXTY-SIX

'WHAT DO YOU WANT AT THIS TIME OF NIGHT?' HOLDING A candle high, Nathaniel scrutinized the face of Tobias Strangewayes in the flickering flame. The young man was shocked by what he saw. His late caller looked so pale and drawn it seemed he had suffered a terrible bereavement.

'I would speak with you a while,' Strangewayes muttered hoarsely.

Feeling a pang of compassion, Nat beckoned his visitor inside his chamber. The last thing he wanted was an interruption at such a late hour. After failing to find any way to gain access to Cockayne's chamber to search for the play, he had heard news that Cecil's adviser had left Nonsuch for parts unknown. Hastily, Nat had concocted a last, desperate plan: to lower himself from the roof and break into the sealed room through the window. He would probably break his neck, or be arrested the moment he set foot inside the chamber, but he could think of no other option.

'I have not seen you around the court for many a day.' Nathaniel waved a hand towards a stool, but Strangewayes ignored the offer and went straight to the trestle by the window. He dumped a sooty sack upon it and then turned to face his host. Nathaniel saw the man's hand was shaking.

'Let us not waste time with small talk,' Strangewayes said. 'For days now I have wrestled with my problem alone in my chamber and I can see no way out.'

'The Bishop of Winchester has cautioned against lonely wrestling in chambers.'

'I know you and your master have only contempt for me. You think I am not worthy of the part I play—'

'I neither know nor care about your business.' Nathaniel placed the candle on the table next to the sooty sack. 'I know you have mocked and reviled Will publicly, and you despise the work carried out by Sir Robert Cecil's men.'

Strangewayes shrugged. 'We play rough and tumble in this business. I ask only that you hear me out with an open mind.'

The spy looked so troubled, Nat could only sigh and wave him to continue.

'I have developed . . . an affection for Grace Seldon. You may know this. I understand she is like a sister to you.' Strangewayes' eyes flickered with a touch of guilt. 'I wish for her only the very best, though you might think otherwise. But she trusts me, and she trusts me deeply, for she told me of a work by Christopher Marlowe that was in the hands of Sir Robert's adviser.'

Nathaniel flinched and turned away, pretending to search for a new candle.

'She never mentioned your name,' Strangewayes continued, 'but I can see that my suspicions were correct. You know of the play, and of the cipher it contains, I wager. It is vital in opposing the plot that now grips all of Nonsuch, yes?'

'I know nothing of this.' Nathaniel found the candle and proceeded to tease out the wick with intense concentration.

'I am but a lowly assistant, not privy to the great affairs of England's spies.'

The red-headed man grasped the end of the sack and tipped out a thick slab of papers. Nathaniel saw the familiar signature of Kit Marlowe on the stained and dog-eared frontispiece.

'Here is the play. *The Tragical History of Doctor Faustus.*' Strangewayes all but choked on the words as if he had uncovered the skull of a friend. 'I sought it out to win Grace's heart.'

Unable to contain himself, Nathaniel grasped the sheaf of papers and flicked through the pages to check it was the thing he had sought for so long. 'You stole this from Master Cockayne's chamber?'

'What I discovered in there was . . .' The spy paused and swallowed. 'It convinced me this was not a matter for Grace . . . nor for any woman. I could not deliver the play to her for fear it would draw her further into this monstrous affair.' Growing even paler as he reflected, he pressed the back of his hand to his mouth. 'For days I thought it would drive me mad. I slipped into a dark pit and was sure I would never be able to claw my way out. And yet . . . I did.' Strangewayes sounded amazed that he had survived his ordeal.

'What did you discover?' Nathaniel asked, unnerved. Memories of pale faces burst briefly in his mind, and he struggled to recall something that remained frustratingly elusive.

'I would not wish that knowledge upon you. A month ago, perhaps. But I am a different man now. There is no going back from what I saw.' The spy collapsed on to a stool, his head in his hands. 'Yet, the play is here. Can you break the cipher?'

'I can. But you should know, Grace is stronger than you think. Stronger than most men, though she acts at times in a reckless manner. She will not forgive you if you keep this from her.'

Strangewayes looked up with a haunted expression. 'Tell me, what should I do? I no longer know myself.'

Pulling up a stool, Nathaniel examined the play in the circle of light from the candle. 'You do not need to tell her what you found in that chamber. But we owe it to her to reveal we have this prize.'

Reluctantly, the spy nodded. 'Very well. Break the cipher. Then I will do whatever is necessary to oppose this plot. I have a stain upon my mind that I can only expunge with honest toil, and if it costs me my life, so be it.'

The young man studied the older, and felt a wave of compassion. Never would he have imagined seeing the arrogant, unpleasant spy brought so low. He was interrupted by a knock at the door.

'Grace,' Nathaniel said, answering the door to find his friend waiting there. 'We were just talking about you.'

The young woman stepped in and looked from one man to the other. 'I confess, I saw Master Strangewayes making his way here. How are you, Tobias? I have missed you.'

The red-headed man looked surprised by her comment, but forced a weak smile. 'It is good to see you too, Grace.'

Nathaniel closed the door and ushered the woman to the table. 'You will not believe this. We have the play. Finally. Master Strangewayes recovered it from Master Cockayne's chamber.'

Grace gave a strange smile.

The door swung open. Nathaniel spun round. 'We are uncovered.'

The spy leapt to his feet, drawing his rapier.

In stepped Grace, another Grace, her face flushed, her brow knitted. 'Now we shall have a reckoning,' she hissed.

Before the two men could move, the newly arrived Grace

465

strode across the chamber and grabbed her counterpart, throwing her against the wall. Snatching a candlestick from the mantelpiece, the furious young woman swung it with force at the temple of her rival. The first Grace slumped to the rushes, unconscious.

Nathaniel and Strangewayes gaped. Before either of them could make sense of what they had witnessed, another figure slipped into the room and closed the door.

'What a merry dance,' Red Meg O'Shee said with a sly smile. 'There have been fools aplenty in these fun and games, but now we start to peel away the masks.'

CHAPTER SIXTY-SEVEN

'I WANT TO SEE WILL SWYFTE'S BLOOD WASHING ACROSS THE quayside and into the filthy Thames,' Robert Devereux, Earl of Essex, announced from his commanding view over the legal quays. Dressed in his favourite white and gold doublet, he stood on the roof of a carriage surrounded by fifteen spies, one hand on his rapier. 'By this day's end, the man who was once England's greatest spy will be dead.'

The air was thick with the stink of pitch from the barrels along the quayside, but behind it floated the sharp smell of cloves and the sticky aroma of cinnamon from the spice ships. Shielding his eyes against the morning sun glinting off the glassy, slow-moving river, Devereux surveyed the forest of masts that obscured the north bank. Only the grey Kentish stone bulk of the Tower of London loomed above the long queue of ocean-going vessels waiting for a free berth. Almost a hundred stretched prow to stern, from the shadow of London Bridge past St Katharine's, bobbing in the gentle breeze.

Though London was still subdued under the yoke of the plague, the legal quays were throbbing with the yells and shanties of seamen and dockworkers, the slap of sailcloth and the creak of rigging, and the hammer of wooden mallets where hasty repairs were being carried out. Customs men buzzed back and forth assessing the cargo that had been landed from the foreign ships.

Swyfte had chosen his arrival point well, the Earl thought with a nod. In that hive of busyness, the spy could lose himself in the throng of sea-dogs shuffling towards the crowded ale-houses on the river bank, or in the jam of merchants' carts, or the groups of cat-calling doxies seeking trade.

Devereux smiled to himself. Swyfte thought himself clever, but this time he had met his match.

Leeman, a plump, red-faced spy with a missing eye, clambered on to the seat of the carriage, wheezing. 'All the cut-throats are where they need to be. I told 'em, not a penny until they brought Swyfte to us. Dead. You are still certain of that, sir?'

'We take no chances, Master Leeman. Swyfte has proved himself a cunning dog. You would not want his sword between your shoulder blades, no?'

'No, sir.'

'Then dead it is.'

The Earl brushed a stray lock of hair from his forehead, reflecting on the curious change that had come over his Queen. A passing thing, he was sure. He watched the barrels being unloaded along the wharf while the ship carrying Swyfte prepared to moor. Pedalling furiously, a man sat inside a large wheel contained within a cabin raised on poles. A rope ran from the wheel, over a pulley, along a jib and over another pulley, where it dangled to the deck of a carrack. There, three seamen attached a barrel to the rope with hooks.

Devereux allowed his gaze to wander to the carefully positioned carts and stacks of barrels along the wharf where Swyfte's caravel was about to dock. One by one he picked out the rogues they had rounded up, all of them in place, pretending to be dockworkers in felt hats moving barrels, or smartly cloaked merchants overseeing the unloading of cargo, or bare-chested seamen resting after hard labour. Ten strong-armed men, each carrying a musket. No chances.

'Master Leeman, give the order to get ready.'

With a nod, the one-eyed man lurched to the cobbles, hurrying among the flow of sweaty labourers to whisper to each agent in passing. Essex watched hands go to muskets hidden in the bales of straw or under sailcloth or timber.

The caravel came in. Straining, grizzled sea-dogs tied up the creaking ropes and the gangplank clattered on to the wharf. Essex studied the men moving around on deck. Where was Swyfte?

Mopping his brow, Leeman climbed back on to the carriage seat. 'All set, sir. He will be the first to disembark?'

'The arrangements have been made, Master Leeman.'

With nods and sly glances, the cut-throats abandoned their false tasks and picked up their muskets. Keeping their heads down, they gathered by twin rows of carts and other obstacles that flanked the gangplank and which would funnel their intended victim towards the pitch-filled barrels. The matchlocks were primed, flints ready to ignite the fuses.

Calm, patient, the Earl folded his hands behind his back, puffing out his chest. Leeman shaded his one good eye. 'There,' the ruddy-faced man announced, pointing towards the caravel.

In his black cape and cap, Will Swyfte stepped on to the gangplank and hurried down, eager to lose himself in the wharfside crowd.

The ten men stepped into the mouth of the funnel and levelled their weapons. Flints sparked. Devereux saw the flare of fear in the spy's face. At the foot of the gangplank, Swyfte skidded to a halt, caught in the grip of the terrible sight confronting him, and then he turned, preparing to bound back to the ship.

Ten barrels flamed. The cracks rang across the legal quay, sending the gulls shrieking up into the blue sky. Flung up the gangplank by the force of the shots, the black-clad spy convulsed and then grew still, one arm hanging down towards the black water.

Essex hammered a fist into the palm of his hand in jubilation and leapt from the carriage, thrusting his way through the curious dockworkers and seamen. The cut-throats milled around the body, avoiding the crimson pool gathering at the foot of the gangplank.

'Stand back,' the Earl ordered. 'Master Leeman.'

The one-eyed man lumbered forward and turned over Will's body. Essex's grin became fixed, slowly turning into a snarl of rage. 'That is not Swyfte,' he exclaimed. 'It is our agent on board this vessel.'

The dead man was about the spy's age, but his face was pockmarked and the cap hid a bald patch. Beneath the cloak, his hands were bound behind his back and he had a kerchief shoved into his mouth to prevent him calling out.

'Find Swyfte!' the Earl barked, whirling round. He felt a pang of fear. Though Will presented a dashing front to the world, Devereux knew the spy had no reservations about killing his enemies, whatever their status in life.

A gush of crimson splattered across the cobbles at the end of the funnel of carts and barrels. One of the rogues, a big-boned slab of meat, stumbled forward, clutching his throat, his life's blood pumping between his fingers.

The moment he collapsed, the cut-throats and spies erupted

470

in cries of panic. Rapiers and daggers flashed. The men circled, looking this way and that.

'Double the pay for the man who brings me Swyfte's head,' Essex shouted. As the rogues overcame their fear and fanned out across the wharf, the Earl beckoned to Leeman, whispering, 'Gather our men and retreat to the carriage. There is no point risking our own lives when we have these low men to do our business for us.'

As Leeman gathered the spies, Devereux edged along the carts, eyes darting around. Too many curious men clustered around for him to get any sight of the spy.

If Swyfte has sense, he will be long gone by now, he thought.

The flurry of a black cloak on a pile of barrels drew the Earl's attention, gone by the time he turned. But a rope tied loosely in a noose fell around the neck of one of the stalking cut-throats. It was yanked tight and the poor soul flew up, feet kicking, before his breaking neck cracked like a musket shot across the wharf.

While Devereux's gaze was on the corpse falling back to the cobbles, more blood gushed away to his left. One rogue dropped to his knees, hands pressed tightly against his stomach, a second grasped at his slit throat, and a third was already face down in a growing pool when Essex's gaze fell upon him.

''Swounds,' the Earl muttered in horrified awe. Throwing aside caution, he ran towards the carriage, the spies bolting all around him. By the time he reached the safety of the coach roof, three more bodies littered the wharf.

Across the quays, sailors, merchants, doxies and labourers crowded, cheering. Through the bobbing heads and raised arms, Devereux glimpsed a whirling shadow and the flash of steel. He felt a chill run through him. Another dying scream rang up to the screeching gulls.

Pale-faced, Leeman clambered on to the seat. The spies gathered all around, fearfully glancing at Essex in case he sent them into the fray. But the Earl was caught fast by the unfolding drama. Through a gap in the bodies, he saw Swyfte thrust his rapier through the heart of the final cut-throat, and then the spy leapt on to the back of a barrel-laden cart. He gave a flamboyant bow to his audience, his right arm thrown wide.

'This is not some stage,' Essex stammered, barely able to contain his outrage.

A roar went up from the assembled throng and hats were thrown high.

'Why are they cheering him? He is a traitor. The word has gone out to all parts of our nation,' the Earl gasped. 'Master Leeman, Swyfte must not escape or the Queen will have all our heads. Find him.'

Torn between two potential deaths, the one-eyed spy lurched away with three chosen men, but he returned in a few moments with a gap-toothed boy wriggling in his grasp. Leeman gave the youth a rough shake and barked, 'Tell your betters what you saw.'

Snarling like an animal, the youth wrenched himself free. 'For a penny!'

'Pay the boy, Leeman,' Essex said through clenched lips.

Once the exchange had been made, the boy calmed and said, 'Sir, the man in black stole a horse and rode away.'

Closing his eyes, Devereux threw a hand to his forehead. 'To Nonsuch,' he muttered.

'No, sir,' the boy said. 'I heard 'im say to his mount, "Away, to Tilbury."'

Essex stared at the youth, his thoughts racing. 'Tilbury?' The blood draining from his face, he turned to the one-eyed spy and gasped, 'Bloody John Courtenay is an old friend of

Swyfte's and he is captain of the *Tempest*, the fastest, most heavily armed galleon in all of Christendom. The *Tempest* is moored at Tilbury. If Swyfte gets hold of it, he can wreak untold havoc all around the coast of England. Master Leeman, gather our men. We ride for the docks.'

CHAPTER SIXTY-EIGHT

'I DID WHAT YOU TOLD ME, SIR,' THE GAP-TOOTHED BOY SAID, holding out a filthy hand.

Will slipped a penny into the youth's palm. 'Money well spent. You did the country a great service, lad.'

'The country? Bugger that. You are Will Swyfte, England's greatest spy. My father read me all your stories from the pamphlets.' The boy's eyes were bright with awe as he clasped the penny and bolted into the dispersing crowd of seamen and merchants.

The thunder of hooves and the rattle of carriage wheels echoed across the wharf. The spy allowed himself a smile at the fulfilment of his plan before slipping away to find a horse. Essex and the bulk of his local spies would spend the next day or two at Tilbury trying to prevent a plot that would never happen. That would make Will's monumental task at Nonsuch a little easier, with fewer swords to get in his way.

Within half an hour, the spy was merging into the flow of heavily laden merchants' carts trailing out of the legal quays towards London Bridge or routes to the south. His mind drifted back across the long, exhausting journey. After he had climbed down the vertiginous walls of Notre Dame in the dying storm his sight finally returned with a euphoric rush on the banks of the Seine. Stealing a small boat, they made their way to the coast. Meg had remained at his side throughout, but never once did they mention their feelings, though he was sure it was on both their minds.

At Le Havre-de-Grâce, Meg joined Grace aboard Henri's galleon and sailed first to make arrangements back in England. Will meanwhile sought out an English merchant, a tall, serious-faced man by the name of Carrington, whom Raleigh had identified as a 'close associate' of the School of Night. The spy was surprised how quickly he was provided with safe passage on a ship bound for England, and more, how easily Carrington had acceded to Will's strange request – a ship-to-ship transfer midway across the Channel to thwart the plans of Cecil or Essex, who, Will knew, would have spies watching for him in France. They would be waiting for one caravel, while the spy arrived a little earlier on another.

And when Will had discovered one of the Earl's spies aboard the first vessel, the crew had been quick to follow his directions, which had resulted in the poor soul's death at the legal quays.

Yet for all the help he had received, he was troubled by the influence of the School of Night. Their power and reach were greater than he had ever imagined, and Will wondered if they had hidden aims, perhaps great ones, beyond what he had heard at Petworth. But that was a matter for another day.

Following the lane east along the river, he came to a thick bank of oak and elm, directly opposite the grey stone mass of the Tower, just visible through the masts of the ships queuing for the legal quays. Dismounting, he led his horse under the cool canopy of the trees to an apple orchard. Beyond it were meadows, pools and gardens and beyond those lay Bermondsey

House, where the Queen had accepted hospitality on many an occasion. The grand hall had been constructed from the stones of the Benedictine abbey, knocked down under the orders of Old Henry, and it was in the abbey grounds he now stood.

As Will searched among the trees, a piercing whistle drew his attention. Carpenter beckoned him over to where a seductively smiling Meg waited with the grim-faced Earl, Launceston, and four horses. One other was there: Essex's man. Strangewayes.

Meg saw Will's face darken and she stepped forward to block the spy's path. 'Leave him be, my sweet,' the Irish woman said. 'Master Strangewayes has suffered enough in recent days. The lash of your tongue is one punishment too many.'

Eyes cast down, the red-headed man looked deflated.

'You can be trusted?' Will demanded. 'Or will you go running back to your master at the first opportunity?'

'I stand with you,' Tobias said flatly.

Carpenter cast a sideways glance at their new companion and whispered, 'He has had a brush with dark forces. Not the Unseelie Court, yet, but he will need to be inducted into our understanding of their ways soon, or his wits will be at risk.'

Will felt a note of compassion for Strangewayes. He had seen more than one spy destroyed by the realization that the world was a truly terrifying place. 'Very well. We will not turn away a strong sword-arm. And how goes the search for our killer of spies?'

'We have failed to find him,' Launceston replied in his whispery voice. 'The last name on the list was crossed out, despite our best efforts.' Carpenter looked away, his cheeks flushed.

'And yet the defences of England still stand,' Will mused. 'He searches for one more victim, then. An unknown.' He looked around the group. 'It may be one of us here who will fulfil his task, and unleash all hell upon this land. We must be on our guard.'

'And now?' Meg asked, already knowing the answer.

Will swung himself into the saddle and proclaimed, 'And now to Nonsuch, and blood, and vengeance.'

CHAPTER SIXTY-NINE

'PRAY DRAW NEAR, GENTLEFOLK, FOR THIS SPECTACLE BEGINS. Witness now, a tale told, in homely verse and music plain, of England now and England then, when knights in silver were compelled to brave the perils of the night.' The player boomed his speech with a flamboyant sweep of his right arm. His mask was plain white save for two eyeholes topped with a mane of peacock feathers, his cloak, doublet and hose all crimson. Prowling in front of the painted backdrop of a moonlit grove, he levelled one pointed finger at the audience with an air of menace. 'See now two faces, and two worlds, and ponder which is true. Sun or moon, or man or maid, the mirror or its reflection. For hidden in these paltry words lies the secret of your existence.'

Will stepped into the back of the Great Hall at Nonsuch Palace as the player's introductory words died away. His hood pulled up to preserve a sense of mystery, he wore a full-face black mask with gold around the eyeholes and the grinning mouth. He kept one hand upon his rapier but the audience paid him no heed, entranced by the first haunting chords of the music played on viol, hautboy and spinet.

The spy had been informed that the Earl of Essex had

funded this lavish masque, but it had been left to the poet Sir Edmund Spenser to devise its themes and story. He had named his work *The Maske of Heart's Desire*, a title that Will found oddly unsettling.

Yet he could not deny that Sir Edmund had created the most breathtaking masque that any royal palace had ever seen. The painted scenery, which stretched from floor to high in the shadows of the vaulted roof, covered every wall of the Great Hall so that each member of the court felt part of the unfolding spectacle. The silvery moonlight limning the ancient oaks of the greenwood and the starry sky sweeping like blue velvet above was so delicately painted that it created the illusion that the entire masque was taking place outdoors. Adding to that perception, there were trees standing throughout the hall, with wooden trunks and branches and paper leaves.

Looking around, Will guessed all the members of the court and royal household were there, everyone wearing a mask that they had laboured over for days, adding pointed noses or painting them with humorous or frightening visages. So colourful were their fine cloaks, doublets, skirts and bodices that in the candlelight the hall appeared to shimmer as if filled with rubies, emeralds, sapphires, opals and amethyst.

The Queen watched the proceedings from her throne, a large ruff of white and silver framing her powdered face, her skirts and bodice ivory so that she resembled one of the snow-people the children made on Cheapside. Will thought how ill she looked, her eyes heavy-lidded, her head drooping down into her shoulders. He saw none of the vivacity that she had always displayed in public.

After a few moments, the spy was joined by Meg, Launceston, Carpenter and Strangewayes, all wearing the masks that Grace had prepared for them. They had changed in Will's old chamber after Grace had distracted the guards so they could slip through the palace gates.

'How many here are Scar-Crow Men, their masks hiding yet further masks behind which is nothing but death?' the spy mused. 'Their plot is in its final hours. They will be alert to any threat, and so we must be on our guard.'

'Then let us not delay,' Meg murmured. Shaped to resemble the face of a doll, her mask was scarlet, as were her hood and cloak and skirts so that she resembled a pool of blood, a threat and a promise.

A shorter man sidled up, unruly brown hair topping a mask that had been so quickly and crudely completed it was impossible to tell if it was the face of a cat or a dog. 'Will? 'Tis you?'

'Nat, you would recognize me if I were disguised as a tree in a forest.' The spy felt a surge of warmth at seeing his young assistant again.

'Perhaps it is the whiff of recklessness that I smell.' The younger man paused and then added less caustically, 'It is good to see you, Will. When you survive such odds, even I may start to believe you truly are England's greatest spy.'

'Steady, Nat. That came dangerously close to a compliment. But enough pleasantries. I have work for you – to keep Grace safe and away from any trouble that may ensue.' Will phrased his words blandly, but behind them was a deep worry that Nathaniel and Grace might encounter the Unseelie Court. He had seen the wits of strong men shattered by meeting the supernatural foe. Though his memory had created a callus, Nat still bore the scars deep inside him of his own brush with the Fay, the spy knew, and those deadened thoughts must never be stirred into life. Grace was a different case. After her experiences under the Reims seminary, she appeared more resilient, although the spy was sure Fabian had shielded her from much of the Unseelie Court's malign influence. Will could not bear to think of harm coming to either of them.

'That is like herding cats,' Nathaniel grumbled, 'but there is a more pressing matter.' He leaned in and whispered urgently, 'I have spent these past hours deciphering Kit Marlowe's hidden message in his work, as you showed me. You must read it now.'

'Well done, Nat,' the spy exclaimed. 'You have done me proud. Hurry to your chamber. I will meet you there.'

Will could imagine Nathaniel grinning with pride behind his mask. But before the young assistant left, Launceston lunged forward to grab his wrist. The Earl, his ghastly features hidden behind a placid yellow mask with a black stripe down the centre, turned over the hand of the younger man and studied the palm and fingers.

'What is it, Robert?' Will asked.

'A notion,' the Earl muttered. 'I must think.'

Unsettled, Nathaniel dragged his hand free and hurried away. Carpenter, who wore a sapphire mask with black circles around the eyes, gave a questioning glance at his companion. Launceston ignored the gaze.

'We all have a part to play here,' Will said, looking around the group. 'John, Robert . . . you have been diligent in your pursuit of the one who murders our associates. I believe he will be here, somewhere, searching for his final victim. Do what you can to find him, but take care lest you become the sacrificial lamb that brings England's defences down.'

Nodding, the Earl and the scar-faced man melted into the audience.

The black-masked spy leaned into Meg and Strangewayes and whispered, 'Should we fail in our tasks here, the Unseelie Court will sweep in like a storm. There will be hell upon this earth in the blink of an eye. We must be prepared to fight to the last.'

'I am ready,' Tobias muttered. 'If I die this day, so be it. No great loss.' His mask was a deep forest green with gold tracings of leaves all over it.

'You have suffered a blow, my friend,' Will said. 'You have been offered a perspective on life that no man should have if he wishes to sleep peacefully again. But I can see you have a resilience that matches your arrogance, and so is great indeed. These feelings will pass and you will be strong again.'

Strangewayes seemed surprisingly touched by these words.

'Our job is to find the Corpus-Scythe that will destroy the Scar-Crow Men. It will be in the hands of our hated Enemy, and I feel that at this late stage in their plot they will be closer than we dare imagine,' Will continued. 'While the last of the defences still hold by a thread, they will not be able to walk freely among us, or draw near to our Queen. Yet they have found a nest somewhere at hand where they make ready. It is my hope that Kit Marlowe's cipher may guide us to it.'

The haunting music of the introductory passage transformed into an exuberant swirl of fiddle and pipe. Laughing, excited, the audience lined up along both sides of the Great Hall, dividing into couples ready to dance the pavane.

'We will begin our search,' Meg said to Will, holding out her hand for the spy to kiss. With her emotions hidden behind her red mask, the spy found the nod of her head enigmatic. 'Come, Master Strangewayes,' she said, waving one finger at the emerald-masked man. 'You have the look of the Irish about you. Let us see if you have the heart.'

CHAPTER SEVENTY

BOUNDING UP THE ECHOING STONE STEPS TOWARDS NATHANIEL'S chamber, Will drew to a sharp halt at the first window. Sparks of red and gold light glimmered through the diamond panes. The spy felt uneasy as he undid the latch and threw the window open to the warm, fragrant evening.

Barely a sliver of red sun lit the horizon and the shadows now reached across the still hunting grounds which surrounded Nonsuch Palace. In the black line of trees beyond the grassland, bursts of fire came and went. No longer cowed by England's fierce resistance, the Unseelie Court waited. Leaning out, Will followed the trail of flickering lights in the growing gloom. More than he had ever seen before, they reached around the palace on both sides. An army was there, waiting to sweep in once the final defence fell.

Running on, Will arrived at his assistant's door and knocked lightly before pushing his way in. Caught in the light of the candle on the trestle, Grace stood with her back to Nathaniel, her arms folded, her chin stuck out defiantly. She glared at the spy. 'You told Nat to look after me?'

'I did.'

'I will not be kept locked up like a child because you fear I will knock my elbows or my knees.'

'It is your neck I am concerned about.' Will tried to dampen the annoyed frustration he felt. He had little patience for his friend's temper at this time. 'You will do as you are told, Grace. When it comes to saving your life, I will act as I see fit and I will brook no arguments from you.'

The woman turned on him, her small hands bunching into little fists of rage. 'How much have you kept from me these long years?'

Will felt a cold, hard stone form in his chest. Was this the moment he had long feared? For years he had wrestled with the dilemma of how to keep Grace and Nathaniel close so that he might protect them from the threat of the Unseelie Court, yet how to shield them from the knowledge of the same when the supernatural forces swirled around him like a storm? His two friends deserved to live normal lives, but he had always known that sooner or later the pressures would tear apart his carefully constructed façade. 'This is not the time,' he said flatly.

'I cannot believe that mewling, laughing thing that we have locked away and fed on scraps was accepted as Grace,' Nathaniel muttered. Will could see the same suspicion in his young assistant's eyes that Grace took no pains to hide. They both felt betrayed. ''Tis the Devil's work.'

'There are devils and there are devils, Nat,' the woman said. 'In Reims, I saw and heard terrible things, but the ones who held me . . . they are as shadows in my mind.'

With concern, Will glanced at his assistant, whose features darkened as he tried to recall old fears mercifully locked in his mind.

'Though I can barely recall my captors, you knew them,' Grace continued, jabbing a finger towards Will. 'You have been keeping secrets from both of us, thinking that they would frighten us out of our wits. And, I would wager, secrets that involve the disappearance of my sister Jenny.' Will was stung by what he saw in her cold eyes.

'I am a spy. It is my business to keep secrets. There are many things that I do not tell either of you. And that is how it will remain.'

'Very well then. So you set yourself against me, after all this time.' The woman turned her back and marched into the shadows in the corner of the chamber. 'I am not a child any more. It is not for you to decide what is right for me. From this moment on, I will do all in my power to find out the truths that you know, and I will accept the consequences of my actions, for good or ill.'

Putting aside his worry, Will turned to his assistant. 'Nat, I need to see your good works with Kit's cipher. Time is short, and this entire conversation may be moot before the night is out. But you should both be careful what you wish for.'

Nodding in understanding, Nathaniel gave a placatory smile and beckoned Will to the trestle where the dog-eared play sat at the edge of the candlelight. There was a quill and a pot of ink, and a single sheaf marked with the assistant's precise handwriting. The black ink had splashed across the table and Nathaniel plucked a rag to wipe it up before attempting to clean his stained fingers.

Pulling up a stool, the spy studied what Nathaniel had written.

'There is one last section I have not yet deciphered,' the young man said. 'But I will do that forthwith.' He leaned over his master's shoulder and added, 'I know not what help it will be. It makes no sense to me.'

The spy read aloud: 'As defences fall, the Enemy makes a nest in plain sight of the Queen. Take heed. They hide in mirrors. Four candles will mark the way, at the rose and cardinal, a full fathom deep. Beware.'

The magnitude of Marlowe's message dawned on Will, and he sat back and repeated in an awed whisper, 'They hide in mirrors.'

CHAPTER SEVENTY-ONE

'WHAT DO YOU KNOW? DO NOT KEEP IT TO YOURSELF, DAMN you,' the sapphire-masked Carpenter growled to Launceston as they eased through the shadows on the edges of the Great Hall. The audience's attention was gripped by a beautiful blonde-haired young woman sleeping on a bed of red roses and blue forget-me-nots while masked children dressed as elves gambolled around her. Among the gnarled trees, a tall man in a black cape and a white beak-nosed mask watched the sleeping maiden with an air of menace. Low, tremulous notes from a pipe-player added to the scene's unsettling feel.

'When I have something to say, I will say it,' the Earl replied, thoughtfully looking up at the staring eye of a pale moon constructed out of candles, mirrors and white gauze.

'Over these past years I have learned all your deep currents. You saw something on Swyfte's man. What was it?'

'In good time. These thoughts must settle on me like the morning dew on the meadows. Only then will I know if there is any value to them.'

Riddled with impatience, Carpenter cursed under his breath.

The Earl looked across the sea of bizarre masks until his

gaze fell upon the short, hunchbacked figure of Cecil standing alone, familiar even in disguise. His black robes were topped by the face of a grinning ape.

'Where is Sinclair?' the sallow-faced spy mused.

'That slab of beef? Probably roughing up some poor soul for a handful of pennies.'

Pausing beneath an unfurled banner of silver stars against a midnight-blue background, Launceston slowly searched the audience.

Carpenter snorted derisively. 'You are a strange little man. Those beady eyes, always watching, watching, worming your way inside heads to chew on brains.'

The Earl gently touched the forehead of his yellow mask. 'Because all men are governed by those deep currents you claim to see in me. Some are beyond my understanding, however much I strive to know them. Young lovers. The fathers and mothers of children. The men I understand see little value in compassion. They do not comprehend love, or faith, or the softer emotions. They are hollowed out. Or mares, ridden by devils.'

Carpenter watched the Irish woman and that red-headed clot-pole Strangewayes slip out of the Great Hall, having completed one circuit. Off to search the deserted palace, he presumed. When he noticed his companion was still gazing intently around the hall, he snapped, 'What are you looking for?'

'Patience, thou flap-mouthed ninny. Let us consider what we have learned. The killer of spies is a man who perceives his victims as less than human, for who could commit such atrocities if the victims were seen as father, brother, son?'

Carpenter felt unsettled by his companion's perception. He knew the mind of the butcher too well. 'Yes, a God-fearing

Catholic perhaps, who has let his beliefs drive reason from his mind. Who believes he is doing God's work.'

'Hence the angel's wings.' Through the eyeholes, Launceston's eyes flashed. 'A Catholic who has been forced to deny his faith. Who lives a secret life.'

'Many do.'

The yellow-masked spy continued to look purposefully around the entranced audience. *Searching for someone in particular,* the scarred man thought. 'In the wrong man, these things build, like barrels filled with still-fermenting beer that blows the lids right off. Why, to contain such heartfelt beliefs can drive a man mad. And where, in all of England, would such a man most have to hide his beliefs?'

'Here, in the heart of government.'

Launceston nodded. 'Amid the very persecutors of his faith. Such a person would show the world the visage he saw on those he hated.'

'A devil's mask.'

'A man who pretends to be a devil, but thinks himself an angel.'

The play paused for the moment with the maiden awoken by her menacing suitor, the elves scattering in fear. With the excitement deferred, the musicians teased the members of the court with another lively dance. The fiddles began, the haut-boy rang out.

'But who would be capable of such things?' the scar-faced man asked.

'Who, indeed?'

While the Earl studied the lines of men and women forming on both sides of the hall, Carpenter noticed a woman in pale yellow skirts and bodice waving from the doorway leading out of the Great Hall. Even in her mask and in the half-light, he recognized his love, Alice Dalingridge. She had clearly seen through his disguise too. Yet something in her frantic waving alarmed him. The sapphire-masked spy thrust his way through the throng. When he reached the door, he was troubled to discover Alice was no longer there.

Stepping outside the hall, he heard the scuffle of footsteps in the stillness ahead. He ran through the antechamber and up the four steps into the long corridor. Anxious, he noticed all the candles had been snuffed out. At the far end of the corridor, the scarred man glimpsed a ghost, a whirl of pale yellow skirts, gone in an instant.

'Alice?' Carpenter called. His voice rustled along the walls and disappeared into the dark.

He felt his skin prickle with apprehension.

His chest tightening, the scarred man raced along the inky corridor to where he had seen the pale form. He skidded to a halt next to the steps down to the kitchens, smelling the spicy aromas of that evening's pork.

Grasping a candle in its iron holder, Carpenter lit it with his flint. Apprehensively, he watched the flame dance as he held it in front of the draughts rising up from below. He could hear no sound. Drawing his rapier, he descended.

He wanted to call Alice's name, but resisted. Better to go stealthily, he thought. Refusing to think about what might be ahead, he settled into his five senses, the grip of cold steel in his hand, the echoes of his footsteps, the dancing shadows, the rising scents of baked bread and strawberry wine, and the taste . . . the iron taste of fear in his mouth. But not for himself.

In the caverns of his mind, her name rang out: *Alice . . . Alice* . . . and the echoes of promises made in the dark.

Waves of heat from the crackling ovens washed up the stairs. With sweat beading his brow, the spy eased into the echoing kitchens, looking all around. Shadows drifted across the brick-vaulted ceiling. A row of trestles ran down the middle of the chamber, still streaked where they had been wiped down by the kitchen workers after the meal. Sacks of flour lined one wall. Fragrant cured hams hung from hooks overhead. One swung gently from side to side.

At first the spy refused to accept what his eyes told him. 'Let her go,' he whispered. Tossing the candle to one side, he tore off his blue mask and set it on the end of the trestle.

In front of the ovens, the black-cloaked man in the devil mask held Alice with one arm around her waist, the other holding a dagger to her neck. His angel wings cast a grotesque shadow on the orange bricks behind him. Alice's mask had fallen away, and she stared at the spy with wide, terrified eyes.

'It is me you want,' Carpenter urged. 'You have used Alice to draw me out, and now you have me. Set her free so you can complete your vile business and loose all hell upon this place.'

'No, John!' the woman cried, tears burning her cheeks.

His head spinning from fear for his love, the spy forced himself to remain calm. Making a show of it, he sheathed his rapier, but inside his cloak his left hand closed on his dagger unseen. 'See, I am unarmed,' he said. 'Set her free.'

Carpenter's eyes locked intently on Alice's.

Keeping the dagger pricking the woman's neck, the devil-masked man unfurled his other arm and beckoned for the spy to step forward. With a shudder, Carpenter saw a droplet of blood appear on his love's pale skin.

The scar-faced man stepped forward, presenting his chest for the blade. 'One final time: set her free now, or so help me I will carve you like those hams above.'

'John, go now,' Alice cried. 'If you die, I do not want to live.'

'Hush. Your life has more value than mine.' Carpenter fixed his gaze on the slits in the devil mask. The eyes within were tinged with madness.

Sobbing, Alice was barely able to catch her breath.

For one long moment, two pairs of eyes were locked in concert. Then, fluidly, the devil-masked man hurled the woman aside, thrusting his dagger towards the spy's chest.

Alice screamed.

Lurching away, Carpenter sought to bring his own blade out from beneath his cloak, but he was an instant too slow. He sensed death's cold breath on his neck.

And then the spy felt Alice's hands thrust him aside.

Stumbling to one knee, Carpenter jerked his head up to witness the devil-masked man's blade plunge into Alice's heart. The black stain spread too fast across her pale yellow dress. For one moment that seemed eternal, Carpenter was locked in hell.

Alice had given her life for his.

His love's startled eyes fell on the spy, and a final, sad smile sprang to her lips. As she slipped to the floor, pulling the dagger from the hands of her murderer, the spy caught her and cradled her in his arms. Tears seared his eyes.

Seeing his advantage was gone, the devil-masked man ran, the crack of his footsteps echoing off the brick walls.

In the silence that followed, Carpenter thought the world had tumbled into darkness. His heart felt like it was going to burst. Tears burning his cheeks, he held Alice while the last of her life drifted away and then his body was racked with sobs.

After a while his wits returned and he looked up to see Launceston watching him with an unsettlingly placid expression. The Earl held his mask in his left hand and his head was half-cocked, as if he was trying to grasp something beyond his comprehension.

'You can never understand!' Carpenter raged. 'You feel nothing! And, God help me, I wish I was like you!'

Screwing his eyes tight shut, Carpenter allowed his head to drop to his chest, so broken he was sure he would never heal again.

And when he looked up, Launceston was gone.

CHAPTER SEVENTY-TWO

HOLDING ALOFT ONE LIT CANDLE, WILL SLIPPED INTO THE
darkened throne room, closing the door quietly behind him.
Shadows flew away from the dancing flame. His footsteps
echoing in the large, deserted space, he strode across the
wooden floor towards the grand high-backed chair topped by
gilt curlicues. The spy turned to his right and was confronted
by a threatening figure, its shadowed features distorted by
a harsh, glimmering light. For a moment, he stared back at
his reflection in the large, silver-framed mirror. Gooseflesh
prickled his arms.

What watched there, hidden behind the faces of all who
looked into the glass?

Faint strains of lyrical music drifted up from the masque.
The sound of laughter. A cheer of excitement. Applause. But
in the spy's head, the drum beat relentlessly.

At the mirror, Will turned to face the darkened room and
took six measured paces. He pictured in his mind's eye a
compass rose lying at his toe and around it an invisible circle.
Orienting himself, he imagined the north road running
from the palace gates and set down the lit candle. The flame
flickered sharply although there was no breeze, and from one

corner he thought he heard a rustle as though of a giant serpent uncoiling.

The black-masked man collected three more candles and placed them at the remaining cardinal points around his imaginary circle. He lit the one to the south with his flint. When the chamber grew a shade colder, the spy recalled the chill in Griffin Devereux's cell beneath Bedlam.

The candle to the east flickered into life. Will's throat became dry with apprehension.

Hesitating for only a moment, he lit the final candle, to the west, where the dead go. All four flames bent away from the mirror and then returned to upright. His breath clouded.

Will felt a knot form in his stomach. Turning to the looking glass, he studied his brooding reflection and the four points of light at his feet. Despite the unsettling atmosphere that had developed in the room, he couldn't see that anything had changed.

'Go on,' Mephistophilis urged in the spy's ear, the first time his private devil had spoken to him since its near-lethal ploy in Paris had failed. It was a sign, Will knew, that danger was close.

'Quiet, now,' he said firmly. At the mirror, he levelled his left hand, slowly moving it forward until the tips of his fingers brushed the surface . . . and then continued on. The cool glass flowed around his hand like quicksilver. Shocked, he yanked his arm back.

Mephistophilis gave a low, throaty laugh.

Drawing his rapier, Will stepped forward, passing through the looking glass with a sensation that felt like light summer rain. He found himself in the same empty throne room, but here the candles on the floor were extinguished and the only light came from the silvery rays of the moon breaking through the window.

Where was he?

The spy felt oddly disorientated; the proportions in the chamber seemed slightly wrong, the lines of the walls, floor and ceiling distorted, but not enough for him to find it possible to pinpoint exactly where the sensation originated.

In the cool chamber, the sharp scent of limes hung in the air. Although Will could hear disquieting pipe and fiddle music fading in and out, the mirror-palace seemed still.

Opening the door a crack, the spy listened until he was convinced no one waited in the corridor beyond, and then he slipped out. No candles were lit, but as he moved along the corridor he found he could see by the light of the brightest moon he had ever experienced.

The Enemy, so close all this time and yet we never knew it.

When Dee's defences began to crumble, the Unseelie Court must have moved into their *nest*, as Marlowe had put it, still unable to storm through the chambers of Nonsuch but close enough to extract the people they needed to replace – like Grace – and to set their Scar-Crow Men in motion.

Will's skin crept at how the mirror-Nonsuch resembled the real palace in almost every aspect: but he saw no sign of life, no light, no warmth. He felt like he was looking at a stone-and-timber version of the Scar-Crow Men, an illusion of the human world but with something terrible lurking behind the façade.

The spy glided down the stone steps towards the ground floor. Somewhere in that dark palace the Corpus-Scythe was being held, he was sure, close enough to the Scar-Crow Men to be used if it were needed.

Where the steps emptied on to the long corridor, he spied a grey-cloaked, silver-haired figure marching towards the Great

Hall. Will followed at a distance. When the hall door opened, he glimpsed a silent crowd of the Unseelie Court facing the far wall where the masque was being performed in the real Nonsuch.

What would happen if the devil-masked killer was allowed to make his final sacrifice? Will saw how the Fay army would sweep across the hunting grounds to storm Nonsuch, while the High Family stepped through the mirror to take control of England, with their Scar-Crows as puppets. The horrors that would follow seared through his mind.

His breath hard in his chest, the spy peered into the room. In eerie silence, almost a hundred and fifty members of the Unseelie Court stood mesmerized before a tall, slender male of such imposing presence that he could only be a member of the High Family, Will guessed. The Fay's hair was silver-streaked with black along the centre, his expression fierce. As he communicated soundlessly, the Fay traced patterns in the air with elegant movements of his hand. A small creature resembling a hairless ape crawled around his body, its eyes gleaming with a golden light.

Another hooded figure stood just behind the silver-haired leader, a woman. As Will watched, the Fay waved a hand towards her and she removed her hood. It was his Queen, Elizabeth, the same powdered face, the same red wig, but filled with more vibrancy than the monarch he had seen at the masque in the real Nonsuch. *A Scar-Crow*, he thought. The final piece in their plan. The Unseelie Court would replace the real Elizabeth with this simulacrum and rule unquestioned, with complete obedience from the entire population.

Straining, Will peered around the door to see more of the hall. One sound, one too-sudden movement, and he knew he would be torn apart in the blink of an eye.

From the rear wall of the vast chamber to the first line of Fay was a space of about five men lying head to toe, and in it, on a dais like the font in a church, was the artefact of human bone topped with a skull glowing with a faint green light. The Corpus-Scythe.

Will saw his great opportunity, but to move so close to the Enemy and hope not to be seen was a madness that would have done his former Bedlam mates proud.

His breath tight in his chest, he slipped into the gloomy Great Hall and dropped to a crouch, balancing on the tips of his fingers and toes. He cast one eye towards the ranks of the Unseelie Court.

At the far end of the hall, the silver-haired leader held the attention of the Fay. Shrouded in his black cloak, Will crept forward, every movement slow and precise.

Time seemed to stop. The spy felt his hated Enemy so close that he could almost reach out and touch them. One glance back, one slight turn of the head and he would be seen. Barely breathing, Will's muscles burned with the effort of control.

When he reached the dais, he kneeled, one hand on each side of the Corpus-Scythe. The door seemed a world away.

As the spy raised himself up a little more to grasp his prize, a series of high-pitched shrieks and squeals ripped through the silence. Will's heart thundered.

At the far end of the hall, the hairless ape-creature was bounding up and down on the shoulder of its master, waving its arms in his direction. Its cries of alarm rang up to the rafters.

As one, the Unseelie Court turned.

Will was overwhelmed by row upon row of searing eyes and fierce, cadaverous faces.

As one, the Unseelie Court moved.

Grabbing the Corpus-Scythe, the spy bounded towards the

498

door in a billow of black cloak. He threw the door open with a resounding crash and raced into the corridor, his own footsteps drowned out by the thunder of an army of boots at his back.

Flashing one glance behind him, Will saw the Fay only a hand's-breadth away from his cloak, their eyes filled with hatred, their mouths snarling with fury, their silence only making them more terrifying.

To his left, the shadowy entrance to the narrow stairs loomed up in the moonlight. Will threw himself into the opening, taking the steps two at a time. The clatter of hundreds of boots rang off the walls behind him. His Enemies were closing.

Halfway up the steps, the spy tucked the Corpus-Scythe under his left arm and drew his rapier, whirling and thrusting in one movement. The tip of his blade drove into the neck of the nearest Fay. Amid a spurt of crimson, the foe grasped the wound and pitched backwards into his fellows. Will followed through with a stroke up and to his left, ripping open the face of another Enemy, and then he thrust once more into the heart of a third.

As the wounded and dying Fay fell, they blocked the steps and slowed the pursuit of the Court's army. Spinning, the spy bounded up the remaining steps. At the corridor, he heard his Enemies drawing nearer again. Blood thundered through his head. Grimly determined, he ran as fast as his feet would carry him, crashing through the door into the throne room.

He was met by a terrible sight. Reflected in the great mirror, a swarm of white-faced, corpse-like things raced, grasping hands outstretched, mere inches from his back. He could almost feel their icy breath upon his neck.

Sprinting the final distance, Will leapt directly at the mirror. Those bony fingers tore the air a hair's-breadth from his cloak. Passing through the shimmering reflection, he landed in the real throne room. In one fluid movement, he slid the Corpus-Scythe along the boards, upending and extinguishing two of the candles.

Turning, the spy slammed the hilt of his rapier into the mirror. The glass shattered, a thousand shards raining down to the floor. Will threw himself backwards, his eyes locked on the empty frame, still not believing.

After a moment, his rapid breathing began to subside. He was safe, for now. But there was no time to waste.

Snatching up the Corpus-Scythe, Will ran to the window and flung it open on to the warm late August night. The flickering fires of the Unseelie Court army were drawing ever closer.

CHAPTER SEVENTY-THREE

'SEAL THE DOORS. NOW,' LAUNCESTON BARKED ACROSS THE echoing entrance hall. From the hidden pocket in his cloak, he pulled the pouches of herbs and salt that all Cecil's spies carried and tossed them to Meg and Strangewayes. 'Pour the concoction along the thresholds of doors and windows, anywhere where it is possible to gain access to the palace.'

'This mixture will hold them only for a short time. The Enemy is determined. They will find a way inside.' The Irish woman removed her mask and poured the carefully prepared grains along the foot of the door.

'What is out there?' Tobias stammered. 'I . . . I saw lights, fires in the trees . . .'

'If we live through this night you will learn everything you need to know. And if we do not live, the answer will be made plain to you in the most terrible way imaginable. Now, to work.' As the sallow-faced Earl turned to leave, a thunderous hammering boomed at the door.

The red-headed woman leapt back in shock. Peering through the leaded window to the circle of torchlight around the entrance, her fearful expression turned to one of bemusement.

Swinging open the door, Meg called, 'Quickly. The Enemy draws near.'

'Do you think I am blind?' Dr Dee roared as he strode inside. Raleigh followed, and two men Launceston didn't recognize. 'We rode through hell to be here. Only my skill and experience enabled us to break through the Enemy's ranks,' the alchemist bragged, casting a lascivious glance at the Irish woman. She gave a flirtatious smile in return. 'And you,' the magician added, 'are forgiven.'

Meg curtsied.

'Why are you here?' the Earl demanded.

'Because you need me now more than ever,' Dee snapped, his searing gaze a stark contrast to the hollow eyes of the dead creatures stitched into his cloak. 'It was my intention to see you all fester in your own juices, until my associates pointed out that I would be festering alongside ye.'

'Then do whatever you must, doctor,' Launceston urged. 'Begin the work of rebuilding your defences. I have a more pressing matter to attend to.'

'What can be more pressing?' the alchemist sneered.

'Blood.'

The Earl strode away without giving the new arrivals a second glance. His thoughts were like the pristine winter snows, and a bitter wind blew through the ringing vaults of his mind. Returning to the Great Hall, he surveyed the members of the court and the palace workers, all entranced by the poetry of the masque. Launceston saw only meat upon bone.

At the front of the hall, in the centre of the twilit grove, a sturdy man in a peasant's shabby jerkin was professing his love to the maiden on the bed of scarlet roses and blue forget-me-nots. Their words were an unknown language, their movements like the empty lumbering of the beasts in the field.

Making one rapid circuit of the hall, the ghastly-faced man saw no sign of the devil-masked killer, in either of his identities. The Earl knew the truth now. He understood the mind of his opponent, and the placid detachment it took to dismantle bodies, and the precision and the attention to detail. Launceston saw as the killer saw, and vice versa. They were of a kind. It was a simple enough observation, one that he could have made at any time in his frozen existence, and yet, in the clean, white world inside his head, he felt a troubling disturbance, a blemish, perhaps, or a crack.

As surely as the Earl put one foot in front of the other, events fell into place before him. There was only one path, one outcome.

Striding from the Great Hall, the pale spy ghosted through the gloomy, still palace to the chambers that had been set apart for Cecil and his work as secretary. The first room he tried was deserted. Without knocking, he removed his yellow mask and marched into the secretary's own chamber.

His head in his hands as if he was afflicted by a terrible pain, the short, hunchbacked man stood at the window, looking out at the approaching fires. His crumpled face riven with sadness, the black-robed Robert Rowland stood by the cold, empty hearth watching his master. The record-keeper, his hands clasped behind his back, resembled a mourner at a funeral.

'Leave us,' Launceston said calmly, pointing his dagger.

Cecil whirled and looked down the length of cold steel in fury. 'What is the meaning of entering my chamber unannounced?'

'Urgency requires that convention is discarded. I am here to save one life and end another.' The Earl's empty, unblinking stare held the secretary's gaze for a long moment, until, uncomfortable, the Queen's Little Elf looked away.

'I am your master. Leave now,' Cecil demanded.

'I have been cut adrift from the rules and regulations of the life I knew. At this moment, in this place, I answer to no man.'

'To God, then?' Rowland interjected, peering into the Earl's face without understanding.

Launceston shook his head slowly.

'You cannot make demands in my own chamber,' the secretary insisted.

'Then let us all stay together.' The Earl looked from one man to the other. 'Though know that you must live with the consequences of what you witness here. It will be inscribed in hellfire in the depths of your mind for all time.'

A shudder ran through the secretary. 'You work for me no longer. You have always been a dangerous proposition, Launceston, but now you have crossed this line you have become a liability. And *you* must suffer the consequences.'

The Earl tested the tip of his dagger with his finger. A droplet of blood emerged and he studied it curiously for a moment. 'So be it. There is a greater calling in life,' he said, distracted. 'There is a vast space within me that you have all filled with the minutiae of your lives. I do not claim to know or understand you. But now I hear a single voice ringing through that endless cavern. It is a new experience, and a troubling one, and I wonder if this is what it is like to be you.' The sallow spy hummed for a moment, looking at the speck of blood this way and that. 'To pass each day in the pain of emotion? How terrible that must be. I understand your actions a little now, and I fear for myself. For the first time in my cold life.'

'What is this higher calling, if not God's work?' Rowland asked.

'Why, friendship.' Launceston looked up from the prick of blood and eyed the record-keeper. 'Chill winds blow through this world, and I see no sign of God anywhere. Yet in the midst of all this misery, one man can still extend a hand of friendship to others, and lift them out of suffering, and offer them his strength, though they be strange and unfamiliar. Is that not the equal of any miracle?'

'Blasphemy,' Rowland hissed.

The Earl gave a humourless smile.

Cecil began to edge towards the door, his eyes flickering with uncertainty.

Launceston pointed the dagger at the secretary again. 'Call the guards before I am finished with my business and I will take my ire out on you.'

The hunchbacked man came to a halt, unused to being ordered about in his own chamber, but knowing the Earl's reputation too well to resist.

The spy turned to the record-keeper, raising one finger. 'The work of the killer of spies has been much on my mind of late, Master Rowland. I imagine a bitter Catholic, trapped among his enemies, loathing the slow erosion of his religion, hating the state that inflicts such a cruel policy. And hating more the agents who carry out that state's design. Am I correct?'

Rowland glared. His right arm twitched, his hands still clasped behind his back.

'And then my considerations turned to the initial plan to slay the spies involved in a secret mission to the seminary in Reims, who may or may not carry with them information that could destroy the wider plot.' Tracing his index finger along his right eyebrow, the Earl sauntered towards the hearth. 'Who could possibly know the identities of those spies? Why, Sir Francis Walsingham, of course. But Sir Francis is dead. His records? They are missing. Who could have stolen them?

Who would have access to them? Who would know their content?'

'The record-keeper,' the secretary exclaimed.

From behind his back, Rowland brought the curved ritual knife and waved it towards the Earl.

Launceston was unmoved. 'But there was also the matter of the black marks upon the bodies of the murdered spies. The final piece of the puzzle. And then, this evening, I saw the ink upon the fingers of Will Swyfte's young assistant and I began to wonder: what kind of man would have fingers stained with ink that he could smear, by accident, upon the bodies of his victims? A man engaged in constant scribbling. In accounting. In the keeping of records.'

'You would be wise not to threaten me,' Rowland growled, stepping back.

'If I were wise, I would not be a spy.' The Earl glanced towards the secretary, but still spoke to his prey. 'You failed this night to murder my friend, and instead slew his love, but not in any ritual way that would serve your purpose. And you ran, and as you did, you imagined a new plan, did you not? You thought, who would make the greatest sacrifice, if this pattern were to be concluded? Why, the greatest spy of all. The master of spies.'

Cecil blanched.

'You murdered my friend's love at a time when he had discovered a spark of hope in his dismal, troubled life. You shattered his heart into a thousand pieces.' A single tear trickled from the corner of the Earl's eye. He touched it with his bloodstained finger, the two liquids mixing. He examined it with wonder. His first tear. 'My friend!'

Launceston's dispassionate face exploded into terrifying fury. Transformed into a storm of emotion as if all the lost feelings of an entire life had rushed back into him, he threw aside the trestle and thundered towards Rowland. A whirl of papers flew through the air. The blood drained from the record-keeper's fear-torn face.

But then a glimmer of the devil-masked killer flared in his mad eyes and he lunged forward, driving his knife into the Earl's arm. Launceston did not flinch. He gave no sign that he felt any pain. And with the blade still protruding from his flesh, he advanced.

With one fluid sweep from left to right, the sallow spy slashed open the neck of his victim. Blood gushing from his wound, Rowland fell to his knees, clasping his hands in prayer.

The Earl did not stop there.

Launceston hacked and chopped and sliced and thrust and slit until he was slick with gore and what lay in front of him was barely recognizable. And with each blow, a little of the rage left him until his usual dispassionate expression returned.

The Earl took a long, deep breath.

Cocking his head to one side, he examined the mess at his feet as if he was considering from where it came and what it might have been.

'May God have mercy on your soul,' Cecil croaked, clutching on to the wall for support.

Launceston pulled the knife from his arm and threw it. The blade spun, glinting in the candlelight, until it rammed into the panelling, singing for a moment before falling still.

'I have no soul,' the Earl said.

CHAPTER SEVENTY-FOUR

'THE SCAR-CROW MEN ARE SURROUNDING THE QUEEN,' Strangewayes hissed from the door to the Great Hall, his hood pulled up around his forest-green mask. 'At least, I think they are those monstrous constructions. Who can tell?'

Will Swyfte pulled the young spy aside and peered into the vast chamber. Centre-stage, the figure menacing the maiden tore off his mask to reveal another beneath, this one a hideous concoction of animal fur and leaves. A cry rose up from the audience, and many of the women turned away, their hands covering their eyes.

'I will protect you from yon fiend,' the peasant called out, drawing a wooden sword.

While most of the court and the palace workers were held rapt by the players, a few circled away from the crowd, moving from different directions towards the Queen. On her throne, Elizabeth's eyes fluttered and her head sagged. She seemed oblivious to the masque playing out for her benefit. Beside her, Elinor whispered gently in the monarch's ear.

'We must defend Her Majesty. Quickly, now.' Will turned back to the antechamber where the other spies waited with Dee and Raleigh. Although he had replaced his yellow mask,

508

Launceston looked a nightmarish sight, his grey cloak, doublet and breeches sodden and black, and a bloody trail across the flagstones behind him. Beside the Earl, Carpenter stood in his sapphire mask, despair and determination fighting for supremacy.

'You may leave us,' Will said to Meg, who looked disconcertingly innocent in her doll's mask. 'You will find it too much of a conflict to protect a monarch so reviled by some of your countrymen.'

'You mean you cannot be sure which way my blade will turn.' The Irish woman pulled her scarlet hood over her red hair. 'But I will play my part.'

From under his cloak, Will drew the Corpus-Scythe and thrust it into the alchemist's hands. 'Here, doctor. Do what you can with this. Its magics appear mysterious to me, but the Unseelie Court believe it can withdraw the spark of life that animates the Scar-Crow Men.'

Dee's eyes glowed with an insane glee. His cloak of animal pelts swirling, the magician clutched the bone artefact to his chest and ran into a shadowy corner of the antechamber.

'Now we make our stand.' Will swung open the door into the Great Hall. 'But take care where you point your rapiers,' he added, casting an eye towards Launceston. 'We shall not be thanked for skewering good, upstanding members of the court.'

'How do we tell who is friend and who is foe, then?' Carpenter snapped.

'We have no friends, John. Only those who will harm us, and those who merely despise us. Let them make the first move and then act accordingly.'

Immaterial but oppressive, Mephistophilis settled on Will's back, hooking his invisible talons into flesh. The spy sensed the devil's disappointment at the repeated failures to oversee a horrible death. Perhaps this was the time, finally.

Will pushed his way into the throng in the Great Hall with the others close behind. Those he presumed to be Scar-Crow Men were approaching the Queen slowly, so as not to draw attention to themselves.

Mournful pipe music floated through the trees under the fake moon. The players had frozen into a tableau, the peasant disarmed, the unmasked beast-man looming over the maiden. The audience applauded.

Darting around the edge of the hall, the spies reached the Queen before the Scar-Crow Men. With a serpent-like hiss, Elinor dipped a hand into the folds of her skirts.

Red Meg, who was nearest to the maid of honour, struck like a viper, grabbing the woman's hair and yanking back her head so that her own dagger could flash across the exposed throat. The female spy contemptuously dumped the dying Scar-Crow behind the throne, its skin growing mottled and black with the marks of the plague.

For one long, ringing moment, horrified silence fell across the court. When the furious cries erupted, Will and the other spies had already surrounded the stupefied monarch, their rapiers drawn and ready to repel any attackers.

'Treason!'

'Murder!'

'A plot!'

'They seek to kill the Queen!'

The voices were drowned by the ringing of cold steel. All around the circle of spies, the men of the court raised their swords to protect their monarch. Will surveyed the array of freakish masks – dogs, pigs, harlequins, wolves, glittering ensembles of jewels and gold – and realized it was impossible to tell the Scar-Crow Men from their human counterparts.

'Should they come as one we will be overwhelmed,' Tobias whispered aside.

Will was impressed by the resolve he heard in his former rival's voice. 'The great and good of the court are used to acting only in their own interests, Master Strangewayes. Each one here will first seek glory before they learn the advantages of humble teamwork.'

The words had barely left the spy's lips when a man in a black and white embroidered doublet and a cherub mask lunged with his rapier. Will parried easily, but within a moment his blade was flashing in a blur to prevent three attacks at once.

The din of steel upon steel surged all around.

'Can they not see we have our backs to the Queen and we are defending her?' Carpenter snarled above the clash.

'Their blood is up, and like any virgin boy in his first stew it has driven out their wits,' Will called.

Distracted by one opponent, Strangewayes failed to parry a second and the rapier tore through the sleeve of his left upper arm, raising blood. He cursed loudly, but did not flinch from the fight.

Will parried low to his right, whipped up his sword to deflect a lunge from the cherub-masked man in front of him, and continued through to parry another thrust from a swordsman to his left. Barely had his steel stopped ringing when he returned once more to the first. On the next pass-through, he circled his rapier around the blade of his cherub-masked opponent and with a flick of the wrist disarmed him. The sword flew through the air, the women of the court scattering amid shrieks.

For long moments, Will saw only flashing steel and looming, garish masks. He heard only clash after clash until his ears rang. But then, rising above the clamour, came a high-pitched noise like a bow being drawn across a fiddle, the sound continuing on and on until his teeth were set on edge.

A man in a ram's mask staggered, his hand fluttering to his forehead. Lurching back and forth like a drunkard, he pitched across the flagstones. The three swordsmen in front of Will hesitated and drew back a step, glancing at the prone figure.

Another man fell nearby, and a woman. Within a moment some twenty bodies were scattered across the hall floor. Dee had worked his magic. As the Scar-Crows dissolved into corpses, the masks hid the worst of the putrefaction but the exposed flesh of the hands and the rising stench sparked panic.

'The plague!' a woman screamed.

Will tore off his black mask and shouted, 'Stay calm, good gentlefolk. Heed the words of Will Swyfte. I stand here as a loyal defender of our Queen. This is no mark of the plague, but a plot, now exposed.'

'You have been charged with treason,' a man called. 'Why should we believe you?'

'Swyfte speaks truly.' A still-shaken Cecil lurched across the room towards the throne. As he eyed Will, the spy could see his master's sharp mind turning, sieving, weighing, seeking out the advantage in this situation. A flicker of a smile crossed the Little Elf's lips. Turning to the gathered court, he called, 'Where is the Earl of Essex? Is he not here to protect Her Majesty in this direst moment?' He shook his head in dismay, sweeping an arm to the gathered spies. 'Then thank God for my trusty men. For they each suffered hardship and false accusations to see this plot exposed. Master Swyfte is a hero, as we all know. Could anyone here believe him traitor?'

Launceston sidled up to Will and muttered, 'I could slit his throat before he reaches his chamber.'

'We will keep that option in reserve for now, Robert, but thank you for your kindness. Sir Robert Cecil is here to test me and make me a better man.'

The other spies stripped off their masks. Will saw the relief in each face, apart from Carpenter's. The scarred spy looked as if he would never smile again. The secretary called for the ladies-in-waiting to help the Queen back to her chambers to recover, and then beckoned to the man who was once again England's greatest spy.

While the bodies were dragged away, the spies rested, exhaustion clear in every face. Cecil beckoned for Will to follow him.

'This is a time for forgiveness and understanding,' the hunchbacked man said as he led the way through the ante-chamber and up the steps to the first floor. 'We have had our differences, you and I, but much of that was undoubtedly caused by the wilful mischief spun by the Enemy's agents.'

Will knew Cecil would betray him in an instant, if there was some personal gain in it. It mattered little. That was the game, and they both knew the rules.

'I am sure any differences that remain can be smoothed over, for a small monetary fee and an extended period of recupera-tion in Liz Longshanks' Bankside stew.'

'Enjoy your time, Master Swyfte, for I will have need of you shortly. The Earl of Essex will no doubt remain a buzzing fly in my ear, and I must show Her Majesty that my network of spies is worth more than his.' The secretary came to a halt at a window overlooking the hunting grounds. 'I have half a mind to recruit his man Strangewayes. It would annoy the Earl no end.'

'I would advise against that, Sir Robert. Tobias Strange-wayes is a hothead, unreliable, inexperienced—'

'And I am sure that under your training, Master Swyfte, he will blossom into an exemplary spy.'

Knowing there was no point in arguing, Will curbed his irritation. He peered out into the night and saw the ghostly flames melt away. 'It is over,' he said.

'For now. But we have much work to do to rebuild our defences. The Unseelie Court may strike again, quickly, while we are in disarray. We must never let down our guard.' Cecil eyed Will askance. 'I know you dislike me, Master Swyfte, and you feel I am a poor substitute for Sir Francis Walsingham, but I will never allow England to lose this war. We shall defeat the Enemy, whatever it takes.'

Will saw that Cecil believed his own words, but the spy had other things on his mind. He asked baldly, 'Did you, or the Privy Council, have Christopher Marlowe killed?'

'Your friend was a threat to England. He had blasphemous views, and treasonous ones too. He had grown apart from the policies of Her Majesty's government and we could not allow such a famed playwright to express those views publicly.'

Long-suppressed anger surged in Will. He gripped the hilt of his dagger, ready to thrust it into Cecil's heart.

But the hunchbacked man shook his head and held the spy's gaze. 'It was the Privy Council's intention to have Marlowe sent to the Tower, that is true. But no murder was sanctioned. When news of his death reached us, we were as surprised as you.'

Will couldn't deny what he saw in the spymaster's eyes. 'Kit was not slain by Rowland. The manner of death was different . . . no ritual marks or cuts. So who killed him?'

Cecil held his hands wide. 'Marlowe moved on the edges of

514

our society, among thieves and cut-throats, and though he was sent as a spy, he began to enjoy the life of those circles. Death comes quickly and easily there. It may well be that his ending was as meaningless as the circumstances suggest. An argument, over a few pennies.'

'I cannot believe that.'

The secretary shrugged; there was nothing more he could say.

'I will not rest until I discover the truth,' Will stressed. 'Somewhere, Kit has a hidden enemy.' The spy turned and strode down the stairs, blood pumping in his head. He had answered every question that had plagued him since the business began, except the one that mattered most.

In the antechamber, Meg waited, a splash of scarlet in the candlelight. She came over to Will and kissed him gently on the cheek. 'So, you trusted me to stand next to your Queen and not put a knife in her back. What has happened to you, Will Swyfte?' she asked wryly, her green eyes gleaming.

The spy didn't know the answer. Everywhere he looked, the world was changing, and few of his old certainties remained. 'A flask of sack will put the world aright,' he replied. 'Will you join me?'

'Are ye asking me to step out with you, then?'

'I have a love, Red Meg. She has taken my heart and I cannot offer it elsewhere.'

Will expected the Irish woman to be offended, but she only laughed. 'Men are such simple folk, and you expect the world and feelings to be just as simple. The heart is harder to navigate than the high seas, Master Swyfte.'

'What game are you playing now, Meg?'

The woman laughed again, catching herself with a hand to her mouth. 'We have trust between us now, yes?' she asked.

The spy thought for a moment, and nodded.

'Then that is enough for now, and I will ask no more. Let us see where the winds blow us.'

'I will not abandon Jenny. Do not waste your time hoping.'

The Irish woman gave only an enigmatic smile.

Before he could question the woman further, Nathaniel hurried up, clutching the sheaf of papers that was Marlowe's play. 'Will,' he began breathlessly, 'I have deciphered the final section of Kit's hidden message. It is as obscure to me as that business with roses and fathoms, but you may make sense of it.' The assistant handed his master an ink-spattered parchment.

Will read the final part of the playwright's secret communication. The meaning was indeed curious, but one word leapt out at him: *Wykenham*, the ghost village, where devil-haunted Griffin Devereux had slaughtered the entire population in his search for hidden knowledge.

CHAPTER SEVENTY-FIVE

THE FULL MOON TURNED THE MEADOWS OF NORTH NORFOLK into silver pools and limned the oaks and elms lining the winding lane. Guiding his horse at a steady trot, Will searched the lonely countryside for any sign of danger. The hooves beat a steady rhythm on the hard-baked mud. Dusty and tired from the road, he could smell the tang of the nearby sea in the salt marshes and thought he could hear the dim crash of the waves. An owl hooted, low and mournful, in the dark slash of wood to his right. A russet fox loped across the nearest field, pausing briefly to look in the spy's direction. There was no sign of human life.

It had been a slow journey north from Norwich along poor tracks and through areas roaming with footpads ready to rob the unwary traveller. Will had broken his trek at an inn where he had been warned repeatedly not to venture anywhere near Wykenham. Haunted, the locals said. The ground still wet with blood. The cries of the dying heard in the quiet of the night.

But Will had to know the meaning of the final cryptic comment hidden in his friend's play. *You will find the truth in Wykenham.*

Was Griffin Devereux, Bedlam's most terrible resident, responsible for Kit Marlowe's murder? Was that death linked to the scores who had been slaughtered in Wykenham, or to the devil that the poor, mad soul appeared to have conjured?

Nothing good could surely come of a journey to that haunted village, but he had to know the truth to put Kit to rest in his heart.

Will felt the spectre of his old friend creep back into his mind, as it had repeatedly since that evening at Nonsuch when the Unseelie Court had been forced into retreat. In the thin grey light of the following morn, the spy had stood over Marlowe's grave in Deptford Green listening to the wind from the river singing in the branches of the churchyard yews. Memories had surfaced, of drunken nights and intense debates about God and politics, but mostly Will had thought about the mysteries that had been threaded through the playwright's life. Though they had been the best of friends, there was so much that the spy had never seen in Kit. In truth, Will wondered, had he been a poor companion? Had he been obsessed by his own troubles and ignorant of the deep currents that had swept Marlowe into the arms of the School of Night?

And was that why the playwright had cursed Will with a devil that tormented his thoughts and drove him towards an early grave? The spy had thought it an aid, but as Mephistophilis gripped him tighter by the day, he began to wonder otherwise. It would not be long until an end came, he was sure, and his soul would be damned.

Even if that were the case, Will missed his old friend deeply, missed the kindnesses, missed the only man who had understood his life. He could never blame Kit.

As the spy followed the rutted lane around a bend, he saw the silhouette of a church steeple against the starry sky and the low outlines of what appeared to be houses. All was dark.

His horse trotted on.

The trees thinned out as he neared Wykenham, but on one great gnarled oak on the outskirts the spy noticed that a piece of timber had been roughly nailed. Dismounting, Will led his steed over and struck a flint to a handful of dry grass and twigs. The flames fanned up, the orange glow illuminating his brooding face as he leaned towards the timber and read what had been marked there in pitch.

Keep out. The devil is here.

As the spy climbed back on his horse and rode the last length of lane into the village, his skin began to prickle. He felt unseen eyes upon him and an unsettling atmosphere, like the tension before a storm. On the soft night breeze, what sounded to Will like whispers were caught and distorted, but it might have been just the wind in the eaves. A door banged. The shriek of the hunting owl floated across the still street from the yews in the churchyard.

Where to begin the search for clues? The spy tied up his horse and strode into the middle of the street, turning slowly. Long, yellowing grass grew against the timber and daub walls. Panes were shattered and doors hung ragged.

Investigating the nearest home, Will smelled damp and mildew. Pieces of furniture remained in place, stools, benches, a trestle spattered with bird and rat droppings, and flasks and knives stood ready for a meal never to be completed.

Only ghosts lived in Wykenham.

Moving from silent house to silent house, he neared the church where rumour said the greatest atrocity had been committed. The wind moaned through the yews as if to welcome him.

Standing at the lychgate, Will was caught by a movement on the edge of his vision back along the moonlit street. Whirling round, he searched the shadows. All was still. Yet he was sure he had seen someone dash across the way, keeping low.

A door banged, and again, and again, the rhythm matching the beat of the spy's heart.

At the far end of the village, near where he had left his horse, a shadow bobbed from an open door and was gone in the blink of an eye. Another appeared at the edge of a house on the opposite side of the street. Now he was seeing movement everywhere, as if the dead of Wykenham were gradually waking.

Drawing his rapier, the spy counted at least seven figures slipping in and out of the shadows along the street, all of them converging upon him.

Will's blood thundered in his head as the shapes crept nearer. He was ready for a fight. Looking around for a place to make a stand, he sensed someone behind him. Turning, he was confronted by another shadow stepping free from the gloom beneath the lychgate.

The last thing the spy heard was a low voice saying, 'You have found hell.'

CHAPTER SEVENTY-SIX

WILL CAME ROUND ON HIS KNEES IN THE DARKENED NAVE OF the church, amid the faint scent of old incense and with the moonlight breaking through the stained-glass windows. His wrists ached from where he had unconsciously chafed them against the ropes binding him to a roughly constructed timber cross-frame. His head throbbed, more with anger that he had allowed himself to be taken like a novice than from whatever potion had been used to still his senses. And that failure would undoubtedly cost him his life, for Marlowe's killer – or killers – would never allow him to walk free. He yanked hard at the bonds and rattled the frame furiously, but they held tight.

When the spy looked down, he saw a circle had been inscribed around him with some kind of pigment the colour of blood. Magical symbols were scrawled on the outside and four stubby, unlit candles had been placed at what he presumed were the cardinal points.

Peering into the dark, he thought he glimpsed movement. 'Reveal yourself,' he shouted, his voice laced with cold rage.

Footsteps echoed off the flagstones. A figure emerged into a moonbeam, the familiar face dappled by the reds, greens and blues of the stained glass. Dressed in a black half-compass cloak over a fine black doublet embroidered with silver crosses, Thomas Walsingham, second cousin to the old spymaster, Sir Francis, bowed. When he rose, he tugged at the tip of his beard and gave a lop-sided grin. Will had not seen him since they had stood together beside Kit's grave on the day of the funeral in Deptford Green.

'You are a long way from your grand new home in Chislehurst,' the spy noted.

'Needs must when the devil drives.'

Will could contain his anger no longer. 'You were Kit's friend,' he spat.

'Yes, I was. And patron too, as you well know.' In the flicker in Walsingham's eyes, Will saw the hint that this rich, elegant man had been more than a friend.

'Do ye still need us?' a voice called from somewhere near the font. Three figures emerged from the gloom. After the patron's appearance, the spy was not surprised to see any of them.

Sullen-faced and grey of hair, Ingram Frizer would not meet Will's eye, as he had refused to do in that warm room when he made his claim of self-defence at the inquest into Marlowe's murder. Beside Frizer were the other two key players in that mockery of an investigation: the moneylender Nicholas Skeres in a shabby brown doublet, and Robert Poley, the spy and cunning deceiver. Poley wore an old black cloak that hung down to his ankles.

'Take yourselves back to your business. This matter is near an end.' The patron dismissed the three men with a flutter of his hand.

'There are too many spies,' Will muttered, unable to hide his bitterness.

Walsingham nodded. 'We are good at our deceits. Some-

522

times so good we can even forget what is real and what is a lie.' A shadow crossed his face.

'So, a conspiracy, then.' Will strained at his bonds.

'A conspiracy indeed. There is no other way to describe the School of Night.'

'You are one of them?'

Tugging his beard once more in thought, the patron replied, 'We are many. Though we are not all known to each other, so there are mysteries and secrets among us, too. Raleigh and the others at Petworth had no idea of our involvement in this matter. It had to be that way. We could not risk word of our plans leaking out.'

'I see that clearly. They would be less than pleased to know you had murdered one of their own.'

Walsingham gave a sad smile. 'You think poorly of me. Understandable under the circumstances, but it still stings. I always admired you, Master Swyfte. You were a good friend to Kit. You made his life richer and provided a light to guide him through the darkness. For that, I thank you.'

Will was stung by the incongruous tenderness in the patron's voice. There was love, certainly, a confirmation of what the spy had seen in the man's eyes earlier.

Clapping his hands together, Thomas gave a silent laugh at the spy's expression. 'You have questions. Of course you do. But they are not for me to answer.' He gave another bow accompanied by a flamboyant sweep of his arm. 'Perhaps we will meet again, Master Swyfte, in another place.'

'In hell?' the spy growled.

'Hell is all around us. I aspire to somewhere greater.' And with that, Walsingham swept down the nave and disappeared into the dark.

The spy returned to his attempts to break his bonds, but they

523

were tied too tightly. Gasping for breath after his exertions, he did not hear another figure approach.

'Hello, Will.'

He was so shocked by the gentle voice that he was convinced his heart would stop. In front of him stood a ghost. Wrapped in a hard-wearing cloak, Christopher Marlowe sported the same sad smile that Will recalled from the last time they had met. His brown hair was a little longer, but the fuzz on his chin still resembled that of a youth. The spy gaped, trying to find words that could express his whirlpool of emotions and thoughts.

The playwright held up a hand, his face darkening. 'I have been a poor friend to you. I put you through great suffering, but it was all necessary, if you will only let me explain—'

'I saw your body.'

'You saw *a* body.' Kit sat on the edge of a splintered pew. 'A poor soul, a seaman, beaten to death outside an inn on the river and transported to Mrs Bull's house by my good friend Thomas Walsingham and his associates. The sailor had the great misfortune to resemble me in size and shape if not in features. But once his brains had become a caul across his face, none was the wiser.'

Will flashed back to the hot room on that June morning, remembered glancing at the body on the floor when the blanket was thrown aside to reveal the wound to the jury. His grief had prevented him from lingering upon the gruesome sight, and who else in that place would have paid it more than cursory attention? None of them knew Marlowe personally. They might have seen rough engravings in pamphlets, perhaps, but who would remember the features? In the end, it had come down to Frizer, Skeres, Poley and Mrs Bull to confirm the identity of the victim.

The spy grinned. 'It *was* a conspiracy.'

Marlowe's features lit up as he saw the warmth in his friend's face. 'It was. A conspiracy to save my life. And what better place to hide than here, in haunted Wykenham, desecrated by my good friend Griffin Devereux, where no man dare set foot.'

'To escape the death planned by your enemies.'

'The Unseelie Court had placed me on their list for the killer of spies. I had seen and knew too much of their plot to live. And the Privy Council had decided I was a threat to the very stability of the nation and had to be removed forthwith. Execution was only a matter of time. I have always been skilful at making enemies, less so at conjuring friends. But then the ones I have are worth more than any man could want.'

Will shook his bonds, grinning. 'Set me free. I would knock you on your arse, and then drink your good health.'

With clear sadness, the playwright shook his head. 'I cannot do that.'

'Why not? Set me free, you coxcomb.'

Marlowe leaned forward so he could look his friend full in the face. 'The consequences of my actions must play out. There is no going back from here. If your presence in Wykenham tells me the Unseelie Court have been defeated, as I hoped once I had alerted you to the plot, then well and good. But the Privy Council, and Cecil in particular, will not rest until I am dead and gone.'

'I will not let him harm you. I will petition the Queen—'

Shaking his head, the playwright smiled dolefully. 'My only hope for peace is to leave my old life behind.'

Will thought for a moment. 'A new identity?'

Marlowe nodded.

'Kit, what about your reputation?'

'My reputation.' Laughing, the playwright jumped to his

feet, declaiming like one of his players, 'That is like the air. But my writing, Will, that means the world to me. If I could not write, I could not live.' Bending down, he held out a hand passionately towards the spy. 'But I have made plans, coz. I have a friend, a good man, a playwright of some talent. We will collaborate on many great plays, and though they will be published and performed in his name, I will still have had a part in that grand creation and that is enough for me.' Spinning around on his private stage, he glanced over his shoulder and smiled shyly. 'Look out for them, Will. You will know them when you see them, wise and cultured friend that you are. And I will hide in them many clues and messages in wordplay and in code. And I will even give mention to my saviours and the future salvation of this nation, the School of Night. See if I don't.'

His arms aching, the spy settled back against the wooden cross-frame. 'Then you will tell me where you live, under what name, and we can meet on dark nights, and drink, and—'

'No, Will.' Serious-faced, Marlowe squatted on his haunches so he could look his friend in the eye once more. 'Cecil knows of our friendship. If there is even a hint I am still alive, he will get to me through you. Or he will, at the very least, punish you . . . torture you . . . for knowing my whereabouts. I will not see you suffer.' He swallowed. 'Suffer more.'

'The devil.'

'Believe me, Will, I would not have inflicted such a terrible thing 'pon you if it had not been the last recourse. To risk your very soul . . . what kind of monster am I?' In the grip of self-loathing, the playwright wrapped his arms around his head.

'Kit . . .'

'But I knew your name was on that self-same list, and that the killer of spies would claim your life soon.' Marlowe looked up, his eyes rimmed with tears. 'If I had got to you first, I could have explained everything. But there is no doubt I would have been murdered in the process by that foul Hunter that has stalked me half my life. No, I had one gamble and I had to risk all. Griffin and I had talked about the conjuring of devils, and I knew that through that spawn of hell I could both warn you and protect you, if only for a short while. The devil was your servant as well as your curse, was he not?'

Will nodded, stung by the pain his friend was feeling.

'Good, good.' The playwright wiped his tears away with the back of his hand and put on a bright grin, though his eyes still told the spy another story. 'And here you are! Alive and well!'

'And damned. But I have survived to see you again——'

'And you will continue to live, free of your curse.' Marlowe jumped to his feet and pulled out his flint, lighting each one of the four candles in turn. 'I conjured the devil and I can free you from him.'

The spy laughed heartily. 'Then all's well that end's well.'

Marlowe paused behind Will's back, his voice growing hollow. 'But no devil will return to hell without a prize.'

Straining to look round, the spy asked, 'What do you mean?'

'I must take your devil upon myself. 'Twas always my plan.'

Will felt a chill reach to the very heart of him. 'It will force you to an early grave and drag your soul to hell. You cannot!'

'I must.' Marlowe danced back in front of the spy. He looked as if a weight had lifted from his shoulders. 'This is my gift to you. A free life, and a long one, if any spy may have such a thing. And a chance to make your own mistakes, not carry the burden of mine.'

'No, Kit. I shall not allow it,' Will shouted.

'In this, you have no say.' The playwright cast one sad,

sideways glance at his friend and then walked along the nave
into the shadows.

Will raged and cursed, and in the spaces between his oaths
he heard Marlowe muttering some incantation, his voice rising
and falling in a rhythmic cadence. The world spun around him
and he thought he glimpsed angels and demons swooping out
of the darkness, and heard the haunting music of a pipe player.
Smells came and went – strawberries, rose petals and then
the suffocating stench of brimstone. Choking and coughing,
his skin prickling, he felt a burden drop from his back, and
his heart sang. He was free. A shadow moved beyond the red
circle.

His face drained of blood, Marlowe stumbled back up the
nave weakly, but he was smiling.

'Damn you, Kit,' Will croaked.

They both laughed at that, despite themselves.

'Tell me,' the playwright asked, 'did you see your Jenny?'

The spy nodded.

'The devil takes the form of a heart's desire that we consider unattainable. And in this way it inflicts the greatest pain.'
Though the shadow appeared insubstantial to the spy, Kit was
smiling at it, tears stinging his eyes once more.

'What do you see?' Will whispered.

Marlowe looked from the shadow to Will, but his smile
did not alter. 'I see my heart's desire,' he replied quietly, 'but
as unattainable as ever.' Throwing his arms wide, he waited.
The shadow crossed Will's vision, and his friend gave a deep
shudder.

'Kit, why did you do this thing?' the spy croaked.

''Tis no sacrifice, my good friend. I see you well. And that
is all the reward I would ever need.' The playwright walked
around his friend one final time, snuffing out each candle in

turn. The darkness swept back in. It felt colder, though Will knew it was only his heart.

'Then this is where we say goodbye. For all time?'

'Who knows? Fate plays strange games.' Marlowe walked to the edge of the moonbeam falling through the stained-glass window. For a moment, he was jewelled. 'But you know I live. And I know you live. And though we may never speak again, our friendship crosses the gulf in our dreams.'

'Do not go, Kit. Let us find another solution.'

Marlowe stepped beyond the moonbeam. Now he was grey, a ghost once more. 'Make the most of this world, Will, for life is fleeting, and the jewels you see around you disappear in a twinkling.'

Will felt waves of emotion rushing through him until he thought he would drown. There was joy that his friend was alive, and at the powerful bond they shared. And there was a terrible ache at the suffering Marlowe had taken upon himself so that Will could be free. Will felt the depth of that sacrifice burn into his heart.

The dark swallowed Kit up.

''Tis unseemly to quote oneself, but there is a time and place for all things,' the playwright said from the shadows, his voice laced with playful humour borne of relief that this dark game was over.

> *'Thinkest thou heaven is such a glorious thing?*
> *I tell thee, 'tis not half so fair as thou,*
> *Or any man that breathes on earth.*

'Goodbye, my friend, and live well.'

And then Christopher Marlowe was gone.

CHAPTER SEVENTY-SEVEN

THE BELLS RANG OUT ACROSS ALL LONDON.

Riding home, Will Swyfte enjoyed the feeling of release conjured by the musical peals rolling across the rooftops. The plague had passed, for now. But like the Unseelie Court it would come back, probably sooner than anyone knew.

Now that the Lord Mayor and the Aldermen had agreed it was time for life to return to normal, the markets would overflow once more, streams of merchants and rogues, rich visitors and labourers in search of work all flooding back to the thronging, noisy streets from the countryside, and from across Europe. The inns and the stews and the bear-baiting pits would be back in rude health, and so too would the theatres, where the common man would once again stand in ranks to hear words crafted by brilliant young men.

Like Christopher Marlowe.

On the long, hard journey from East Anglia, Will had had plenty of time to reflect on his old friend and the sacrifice the playwright had made. But he found comfort in the knowledge that Kit's days would be happier, whatever waited for him at the end of the road.

Life was about small victories. No one ever won the war.

The spy understood that now more than ever.

And you took your joys where you could.

But even in the middle of those lambent thoughts, Will began formulating hard plans, and ones that would take him far away from all he knew, to distant shores and hot climes, as hot perhaps as hell, where a devil told him Jenny was held.

In the warm, rosy light of the late afternoon, Will arrived at Nonsuch to be met by Nathaniel. 'Did you find an answer to the mystery?' the young assistant asked, his eyes gleaming with excitement.

'One mystery was solved, Nat, but we can never divine the mysteries of the human heart,' the spy replied as he dismounted in the inner ward.

The young man rolled his eyes. 'You have been drinking and dallying in a stew, have you not? It is only wine and women that draw the poetry out of you.'

'One day, Nat, I will teach you the value of poetry and that not all questions need answers.'

With a snort, Nathaniel took the reins of the horse.

'Where is Grace?' the spy asked. 'I would have thought she would be here to greet me. Is she engaged with the Queen?'

In the flutter of his assistant's eyes, Will received much of his answer. Nathaniel led the way to the garden door, pointing past the clouds of midges dancing in the sunbeams to where Grace walked with Tobias Strangewayes. Her head was bowed and a smile played on her lips, but it was in the flash of her eyes and her easy laughter that Will saw the truth.

'Grace deserves happiness,' Nathaniel suggested, a little uncomfortable as if he recognized that he was overreaching himself. 'She will never find it with you. You have said as much yourself.'

'I wish her well, Nat,' Will said with a reassuring grin, yet

531

he was surprised to feel a faint regret. To be loved so strongly and defiantly, as Grace had loved him, had been a source of hope and comfort, he recognized now, but it would be cruel of him to continue receiving her affection when there was no hope of him ever returning that love. But he would miss her, as he missed Marlowe.

'The court has taken note of its losses,' the young man began, pretending to study the swallows swooping in the blue sky. 'Men and women are missing, the ones who had been replaced. Are they alive somewhere, waiting to be freed, or were they slaughtered the moment they were taken? I have asked Master Carpenter to explain events, and Robert of Launceston, but all I receive are curses and abuse.'

'It is a great mystery,' Will parried.

'Will you tell me what happened here in these recent weeks?' the assistant asked hopefully.

'No, Nat, I will not.'

Nathaniel made a strangled cry of frustration in his throat.

'These are grave affairs of state, and suitable only for the ears of great men such as myself,' the spy gently taunted.

'Tell me at the least, was it the Devil's work?'

'We are all devils, Nat, and angels too, and hell and heaven is made by our own hands.'

Nathaniel slapped one hand on his forehead. 'A direct answer. One day. And my life will be complete.'

The spy smiled to himself.

The two men returned inside. Will intended to see Meg, for she had been much on his mind too on his journey home, along with thoughts of wine and food and lusty conversation. Though Jenny would always be his love, he was intrigued by the Irish woman and confused by the strange emotions she ignited within him. But as the spy climbed to his chamber to wash and change, the sound of two pairs of running feet disturbed him.

Carpenter and Launceston met him at the top of the steps. 'Our master demands our attendance,' the Earl said. 'There is trouble afoot.'

Sighing, Will waved a weary hand.

'Cecil has already seen you,' the scarred spy cautioned. 'There is no denying him.'

As the three companions marched along the Grand Gallery, Will sneaked a sideways glance at Carpenter. Something was broken in his face. Will thought his friend looked as if all the anger had drained from him, along with all the hope that had slowly built since his first meeting with Alice. Will had seen that look before, in the mirror, in the long days after Jenny's disappearance and he knew what lay within was even worse. He hoped it would pass.

'I am sorry to say, John, I fear you will be kept very busy in the coming days. No time for rest or private thought,' he said, trying to appear blithe. 'In my rush to get to Norfolk, I have not yet discussed matters with Sir Robert, but I learned some troubling news during my time in France.'

When he caught Launceston looking at him, the ghost of a smile appeared to be playing on the man's pale lips. Puzzled, Will presumed he must be mistaken.

'The Unseelie Court are in the process of unveiling an even greater plot than the one we defeated this past summer. It is no longer their aim simply to punish England for our transgressions. Their ambition now extends to all the countries of the world.'

Carpenter brought the other two men to a halt and grasped Will's arm. 'Is this true? We are on the brink of a war that could destroy all of human endeavour?'

'I am sorry to say it is, John. The Fay are like the hydra in the stories Kit Marlowe liked to spin. Cut off a head and two more grow. We have seen them extend their influence into Spain and France. Now they plot to move on many fronts, to control their puppets on thrones, to manipulate others, to seize control wherever they look.'

The scarred spy's grieving expression was replaced by one of righteous anger. 'Alice is dead because of their hand. Nothing will stop me from fighting those bastards wherever they might raise their heads. From now on, that is my purpose in life.'

Pumping one fist into an open palm, Carpenter marched ahead, filled now with fresh incentive. Launceston held Will's gaze for a long moment, but the spy could not read whatever moved behind the Earl's eyes. The sallow man gave a curt nod, of thanks, perhaps, and moved on.

Cecil was not in his own chamber. The three spies found their master in the room that had belonged to Robert Rowland, a hand pressed to his forehead. Instead of the heaps of records that had belonged to the killer of spies, there were now charts of the night skies, great volumes, their creaking leather bindings inscribed with magical symbols, small glass bottles, powders and potions, all of which Will guessed had been transported from Dee's old library in Mortlake.

'What matter is so pressing that a man cannot change his doublet?' Will asked.

The secretary pointed a wavering hand to the boards where the rushes had been brushed aside to reveal a magical circle marked out in pitch – or half marked, for the line trailed away next to a dripping brush. Around it were scattered shards of glass from smashed potion bottles and a book with the pages torn by an errant shoe.

'Dee has been taken,' Cecil raged, shaking a fist at the gods, 'before he could complete our magical defences.'

'How do you know the old man didn't stagger away in one of his rages?' Carpenter sneered as he looked around the chamber. 'Or that he is not pursuing one of the maids, as is his wont?'

'Because one of those very maids saw him lurch from this room and collapse outside the door, his eyes rolling back in his head,' the hunchbacked man said bitterly, prowling around the cramped room. 'And when that maid returned with help, the alchemist was gone.'

'And the defences were not yet repaired, you say? How much work had he done?' Will asked.

Cecil fixed a gimlet eye on the spy. 'Enough to stop the Queen being stolen from under our noses, I would wager. But we will see more incursions from the Enemy. More Englishmen tormented, murdered in their homes, corrupted. This must not stand!'

Launceston stroked a long finger down his chin, staring into the middle distance. 'But what enemy could get into Nonsuch and take the alchemist from his very chamber? Have we no guards 'pon the gates?'

Without another word, Will walked out of the door, and once he was out of sight of the other men he ran to his own room, a slow anger burning in his chest. On the trestle, by the open window, lay a scroll tied with a red ribbon. With feverish hands, he tore it open and read what had been written in a florid script.

My sweet,
By the time you read this, there will be miles between us. It pains me to leave you so, without at least a kiss, but

I fear you would demand more of me than I can give before you would let me depart!

This is a fine and valuable prize indeed. The hinges need oil for it creaks and groans, but I am certain it will serve its purpose and keep all manner of things. I imagine you must miss it dearly. Why, if I did not know better, I would be looking over my shoulder night and day.

Until we meet again, think kindly of me.

Your Meg

Will laid the parchment on the trestle and tapped it with the tip of his index finger in thought. A smile sprang to his lips, despite himself. The letter's intention was clear to him: part taunt, part tease, a kiss blown before the candle was snuffed out, but most importantly an encouragement to follow.

And that was undoubtedly what Cecil would want too. Will could almost hear the spymaster's barked orders to bring Dee home and lay waste to any who stood in the way. There was so much at stake – England's defences, the safety of the nation's men and women.

But what of the spy's own plans?

Red Meg had played her final hand well. She had gained the prize she sought so dearly to protect her countrymen, and she had left Will with a dilemma. Knowing full well he was determined to sail in search of Jenny, she had laid her trail to entice him into her own arms.

Will tapped the parchment once, twice, a third time, and on the final beat he had decided his course of action.

FINIS

ACKNOWLEDGEMENTS

My editor Simon Taylor for first-rate guidance; Carole Ambrose for codes and ciphers; my good friend David Devereux, gourmet, author and exorcist, for allowing me to steal his family name.

Note

The version of *The Tragical History of Doctor Faustus* by Christopher Marlowe used in this book is the quarto of 1616.

The roistering and dangerous adventures of Will Swyfte
continue in the next chapter of Mark Chadbourn's
swashbuckling 'Swords of Albion' sequence . . .

THE DEVIL'S LOOKING-GLASS

Go, Soul, the body's guest,
Upon a thankless errand;
Fear not to touch the best;
The truth shall be thy warrant:
Go, since I needs must die,
And give the world the lie.

The Lie ~ Sir Walter Raleigh

PROLOGUE

THE MERCILESS SUN BOILED IN A SILVER SKY. WAVES OF HEAT shimmered across the seething main deck of the becalmed galleon where the seven sailors knelt, heads bowed. As blood dripped from their noses on to their sweat-sodden undershirts, they muttered prayers in Spanish, their strained voices struggling to rise above the creaking of the hull timbers flexing against the green swell. Harsh light glinted off the long, curved blades pressed against each of their necks.

At the sailors' backs, the grey men waited in silence. Ghosts, they seemed at times, not there but there, their bone-white faces wreathed in shadow despite the unremitting glare. Oblivious to the sweltering heat, they wore grey leather bucklers, thick woollen breeches and boots, silver-mildewed and reeking of rot. As still as statues, they were, drawing out the agonies of the whimpering men before the swords would sweep down.

Captain Juan Martinez de Serrano knelt on the forecastle, watching the row of seamen from under heavy brows. Even now he could not bring himself to look into the terrible faces of the ones who had boarded his vessel. At the aft, the grey sails of the other galleon billowed and the rigging cracked,

541

although there was no wind and had not been for three days. Serrano lowered his head in desolation. How foolish they had been. Though they knew the devils of the Unseelie Court were like wolves, the lure of gold was too great. The captain cast his mind back to that night ten days gone when his men had staggered out of the forest with their stolen hoard. Barely could they believe they had escaped with their lives, and their laughter had rang out across the waves as they filled the hold and dreamed of the glory that would be lavished upon them by King Philip in Madrid. They had set sail with fair wind and all had seemed well, until the grey sails appeared on the horizon, drawing closer by the hour.

The steel bit into his neck and he winced. They should have known better. Now the remainder of his crew's blood soaked into the boards of the quarter deck where they lay, each one of them slaughtered within moments though they were among the fiercest fighters upon the Spanish Main.

A rhythmic rattling stirred him. Raising his eyes once more, he watched a strange figure cross the main deck. The sound came from trinkets and the skulls of mice and birds braided into his long gold and silver-streaked hair. Hollow cheeks and dark rings under his eyes transformed his features into a death's-head. He wore grey-green robes covered with unrecognizable symbols outlined in a tracing of gold that glistered in the mid-day sun, like one of the gypsy conjurers who performed at the fair in Seville. Sweeping out his right arm, he said in a voice like cracking ice, 'You are honoured. Our King.'

Serrano swallowed. He sensed the new arrival before he saw him, in a weight building behind his eyes and a queasy churn in his stomach. He closed his eyes. How long would this torment continue? A steady tread crossed the main deck and came to a halt in front of him. Silence followed.

When he had mouthed a prayer, the captain squinted. A pair of grey boots fell into view, and the fur-lined edge of a shimmering white cloak. He heaved his shaking head up, following that pristine cloth until he reached the head of the one who looked down on him. But the brutal sun hung behind the figure and the features were lost. He felt relieved at that.

'I am Mandraxas, of the High Family, and until my sister is brought back to the land of peace, I hold the Golden Throne.' The voice sang like the wind in the high branches. Serrano could not believe it was the voice of a cruel man, until he remembered that this was not a man at all, with no understanding of compassion or gentleness or the kindnesses that tied mortals together. 'Who are you?' the King demanded.

The captain muttered his response, his mouth so dry he could barely form words.

'Your name means nothing,' the monarch replied. 'Who are you, who dares to trespass on our land and steal our gold? Who thinks you are our equal?' When Serrano failed to reply, Mandraxas continued, 'You were damned the moment you insulted us with your arrogance. Let Deortha show you what you truly are to us.' The King waved a languid hand towards the main deck where the robed intruder waited. The one who appeared to be a conjurer nodded, the skulls clacking in his hair, and the nearest swordsman whipped his blade into the air and plunged it into the sailor who knelt in front of him.

Serrano cried out as the seaman pitched forward across the sandy boards. Deortha knelt beside the unmoving form, his lips and hands moving in harmony. Whatever he said and did, the captain could not comprehend, but a moment later the slain sailor twitched, jerked and with a long shudder clawed his way upright. He swayed as if the ship rolled in a stormy sea, his dead eyes staring.

'Por Dios,' Serrano exclaimed, sickened.

'Meat and bones,' Mandraxas said. 'No wits remain, and so these juddering things are of little use to us apart from performing the most mundane tasks.' He waved a fluttering hand towards Deortha. 'Over the side with it,' he called. 'Let it spend eternity beneath the waves.'

The captain screwed up his eyes at the splash, silently cursing the terrible judgement that had doomed them all. 'Let this be done,' he growled in his own language.

Mandraxas appeared to understand. 'There will be no ending for any of you here,' he said in a voice laced with cold humour. 'You, all of you, will join your companion with the fishes, never sleeping, never dreaming, seeing only endless blue but never understanding.' His words rang out so that all his fellows heard him. 'But for the rest of your kind, that ending is almost upon them. Listen. Can you hear the beat of us marching to war? Listen.'

A sword plunged down; a body crashed upon the deck. And another, and another, the steady rhythm moving inexorably towards Serrano. He sobbed. Too late for him, too late for all mankind if the cold fury of these fiends was finally unleashed.

'In England now, the final act unfolds,' Mandraxas said above the beat of falling bodies. 'And so your world winds down to dust.'

Serrano looked up as the shadow fell across him.

CHAPTER ONE

BEDLAM RULED IN THE EIGHT BELLS INN. TRANQUILITY WAS FOR the men of the land who sat by warm firesides in winter and took to their beds early, not for those who braved seas as high and as hard as the Tower's stone walls. Here was life like the ocean, fierce and loud and dangerous. Delirious with drink, two wild-bearded sailors lurched across the rushes, thrashing mad music from fiddle and pipe. With shrieks of laughter, the pock-marked girls from the rooms upstairs whirled around in each other's arms, their breasts hanging out of their threadbare dresses. The rolling sea-song crashed against the barks of the drunken men clustered into the shadowy room. In hazy candlelight, they hunched over wine-stained tables or squatted against whitewashed walls, swearing and fighting and gambling at cards. Ale sloshed from wooden cups on to the boards, and the air reeked of tallow and candle-smoke, sweat and sour beer. The raucous voices sounded lustful, but underneath the discourse odd, melancholic notes seemed to suggest men clinging on to life before they returned to the harsh seas.

When the door rattled open to admit a blast of salty night air, the din never stilled and no eyes turned towards the stranger.

He was wrapped in a grey woollen cloak, his features hidden beneath the wide brim of a felt hat. Behind him, across the gleaming cobbles of the Liverpool quayside, a carrack strained at its moorings, ready for sail at dawn. The creak of the rigging merged with the lapping of the tide.

The new arrival closed the door behind him and demanded a cup of ale from the inn-keeper's trestle. A seat in one of the shadowy corners called to him, away from the candlelight where he could watch and listen, unnoticed. If they had not been addled by drink, some of the seamen may have recognized the strong face from the pamphlets, the close-clipped beard and black hair curling to the nape of the neck, the dark eyes filled with a rapier's steel.

Will Swyfte was a spy, *England's greatest spy*, so those very same pamphlets called him, *the bane of the Spanish dogs*. Only the highest in the land knew his reputation was a superficial construct for a country in need of heroes to keep the sleep of goodly men and women free from nightmares of Spanish invaders and Catholic plotters, and other, darker things too. Swyfte cared little. He did his dark work for Queen and country without complaint, but kept his own machinations close.

He sipped his ale and waited. As the reel of the sea-song ebbed and flowed, he caught snatches of slurred conversation. Tall tales of haunted galleons and the clutching hands of dead seamen. Of cities of gold hidden in the lush forests of the New World. Of a misty island that comes and goes as if it were alive. Of golden lights glimmering far out across the waves and far down in the black deeps. Through the eyes of the sailors, the world was a far stranger place than their land-locked fellows believed; and Will Swyfte knew the sea-dogs were correct. They had sailed to the dark shores of life, where the truth lived, and had paid a price for their wisdom. The spy noted the missing eyes, the leather patches, the lost legs and hands, the scars that drew maps of the world across their skin. He felt a kinship. They were all marooned from the peace and order that most experienced, but his own wounds were not so easily seen.

He thought back more than a week to Nonsuch Palace, a day's ride to the south west from London's foetid streets. While the Queen recovered her strength in her bed, under the observance of the Royal Physician, turmoil reigned throughout the grand building. Servants scoured the chambers and searched the grounds. The Privy Council had been cloistered in the meeting room for more than an hour when the knock had come at Will's chamber door.

His assistant, Nathaniel Colt, waited on the threshold, flushed from running through corridors warmed by the late autumn sun. His dark-green doublet was stained with sweat under the armpits and his brown hair lay slick against his head. 'Sir Robert sent word from the Privy Council meeting to summon you to his chambers,' he gasped. There was fear in his eyes, and his voice wavered. 'Is this it, then, Will? Invasion? Our enemies are marching towards us?'

The spy hid his true thoughts with a grin. 'Nat, you worry like an old maid. Do you see me rushing to arms?' Enemies, yes, but not the ones Nat feared. Not the Spanish, nor Catholic agitators. The true Enemy, who lived by night, and saw men as men saw cattle.

'I do not see you rushing to a flask of sack, and that worries me more.'

Will rested a reassuring hand on the young man's shoulder. 'England lurches from crisis to crisis, as always, but we stand firm and we abide. This will pass.'

His words seemed to reassure Nat a little. Will left him resting by the open window as he made his way across the noisy palace. Lucky Nat, who slept well at night. He saw only glimpses of the greater war. Will sheltered him from the worst horrors for the sake of his wits; and the spy would continue to do so while there was breath left in him.

The spymaster's door was hanging open when Will arrived. Fresh from the Privy Council meeting, Sir Robert Cecil fired orders at a clutch of scribes and assistants as he marched around the chamber. The Queen always called him her *Little Elf* because of his small stature and his hunched back, but his sharp wits and cunning were more than a match for any other man at Court. He had a feel for the games of high office, and his ruthlessness made him feared and powerful.

When the black-gowned Secretary saw Will, he dismissed the bustling aides and closed the door. 'Gather your men,' he snapped, feigning calm with a lazy wave of his hand. 'You ride north today in search of Dr Dee.'

'You know his whereabouts?'

'A carriage was seen travelling along the great north road. I received word back this morning that it has taken a turn towards Liverpool.'

'You are sure?'

'Yes.' Unable to contain the apprehension he felt, his eyes blazed. The spymaster turned away to calm himself. 'Dr Dee was seen in the company of that Irish whore, Red Meg O'Shee. They must be stopped before she spirits him away to her homeland. If they reach that land of bogs and mists, we will never see Dee again. And then . . .'

England will fall, Will completed the unspoken thought. Dee was the architect of the country's defences. He worked his magicks to keep at bay the supernatural forces that had tormented England for as long as men had walked the green fields, and the Irish chieftains had long-envied that protection; they had suffered long and hard under the torments of the Fair Folk. But whatever wall Dee had constructed around England with his ancient words of power and candles and circles had been crumbling. Dee was the only man who could repair those defences. Without him, the night would sweep in.

'The threat is greater than you know.' Cecil bowed his head for a moment, choosing his words carefully. 'The mad alchemist has in his possession an object of great power. For years he denied all knowledge of it. But shortly before he was spirited away, he confided in me that he had used it to commune with angels.'

'Angels?' Will laughed. 'I have heard those tales, but Dee is most definitely on the other side.'

'This is a grave matter,' the spymaster roared, a twitching hand leaping to his flushed brow. 'Should this object fall into the hands of our enemies, there will be no laughter.'

Will poured himself a cup of Romney from a jug on the chart-littered trestle. 'Then tell me the nature of this threat.'

'It is a looking glass.'

The spy peered over the rim of his cup, saying nothing.

'No ordinary glass, this. An obsidian mirror, shaped by the mighty sorcerers of an age-old race who once inhabited the impenetrable forests of the New World.'

Will furrowed his brow. He remembered Dee showing him this mundane-looking mirror at his chamber in Manchester. 'Brought back to Europe in a Spanish hoard?'

Cecil's eyes narrowed. 'Legend says it could set the world afire, if one only knew how to unlock its secrets.'

The spy drained his cup. 'Very well. I will take John

Carpenter, the Earl of Launceston and Tobias Strangewayes. We will ride hard, but Red Meg has several hours on us.'

The spymaster narrowed his eyes. 'You allowed Mistress O'Shee into your circle. You trusted her, though you knew she was a spy—'

'I would not use that word. Tolerated, perhaps. I understood her nature, sir, and I am no fool.'

'Is that correct? I heard that you were more than associates. I need assurances that this woman has not bewitched your heart or your cock. If that were so, I would dispatch another to bring her back.'

'There is no one better.'

'You have never been shy in trumpeting your own achievements, Master Swyfte,' Sir Robert said with pursed lips. 'Nevertheless, I would rather send a lesser man I can trust to succeed in this most important . . . nay, utterly vital . . . work than one who will be led by the nose to a disaster that will damn us all to hell.'

'I am no fool,' Will stressed, setting aside his own uncertainty regarding his feelings for the Irish spy. 'There is too much at stake here for such distractions.'

'I am pleased to hear you say it.' The spymaster ran the gold-ringed fingers of his right hand through his brown hair. 'If Dee leaves our protected shores, he will be prey for the Unseelie Court, and the repercussions of that are something I dare not countenance.'

Will left the cold chamber with fire in his heart. Within the hour, he and his men were riding north as hard as their steeds could bear. Red Meg would expect him to be on her trail – she was as sly a vixen as he had ever known – and she would not make it easy to recover Dee. He had seen her kill without conscience. Even the affection she felt for him would not stand in her way of stealing that great prize back to her homeland.

Time passed, and Will's thoughts returned to the Eight Bells. The musicians had put away their instruments and were swigging Malmsey wine in such gulps they walked as if they were on the deck of a storm-tossed ship. The girls flopped into laps or draped themselves over shoulders in search of the night's earnings. Arguments sparked. Punches were thrown.

Dee was dangerous and needed to be returned to London at all costs, that was certain. But the alchemist revelled in misdirection and illusion, the spy knew. Was this mirror truly the threat Cecil feared? Or in this time of uncertainty and threat had the spymaster simply given in to superstition and fear? Will shrugged. The world was filled with worries, and the truth would present itself sooner or later.

Once he had drained his ale, he settled on his subject, a balding seaman with wind-chapped cheeks and a scrub of white hairs across his chin. Nursing a cup, the man leaned against the wall next to the stone hearth, eyeing the flames with the wistful hunger of someone who knew the sight would not be seen again for long weeks. He looked drunk enough that his guard would be low, but not so inebriated that he could not provide useful information. Keeping the brim of his hat low, the spy demanded another drink and walked over.

Will rested one Spanish leather shoe on the hearth and watched the fire for a moment before he said, 'I have never met a seaman who was not interested in adding to his purse. Are you that rare creature?'

'Depends what you need doing,' the man slurred.

'All I require are words.'

The sailor's gaze flickered over Will. He seemed untroubled by what he saw. 'Ask your questions.'

'I seek news of two new arrivals in Liverpool who may be requiring passage to Ireland. A woman with hair as fiery as her nature and a tongue that cuts sharper than any dagger. And a man . . .' The spy paused. How to describe Dr Dee in a way that would do the magician justice? '. . . white-haired, blazing eyes, a fierce temper, and a slippery grip on the world we all enjoy. He may have been wearing a coat of animal pelts.'

'I have heard tell of them, an Abraham Man, mad as a starved dog, accompanied by his daughter. The woman cut off the ear of Black Jack Larch, so I was told. His only crime was to lay a hand upon her arm and ask for a piece of the comfort she promised.'

'That would be Red Meg.'

The seaman smacked his lips, watching Will's hand. The spy unfolded his fingers to reveal a palmful of pennies. Snatching the coins the man said, 'They bought passage to Ireland on the Rapier, sailing at dawn. Wait at the quayside and you will see them.'

'I would prefer to surprise them before sunrise. Where do they stay?'

'The woman took Black Jack's shell outside Moll Higgins' rooming house. You would do worse than to seek them there.'

'You have earned yourself another drink. Go lightly on the waves.' Will gave a faint bow of the head and turned towards the door. He found his way blocked by three men, hands hanging close to their weapons.

'What have we 'ere, then? A Customs Man come to spy on us?' the one at the centre growled. His left eye was milky, a jagged scar running from the corner of the lid to his jaw. He wore an emerald cap and had the bark of authority in his voice, a first mate, perhaps, Will thought.

'Why, you are good honest seamen. I could find no rogues

or smugglers here,' Will replied, his sardonic tone as sharp as his gaze. 'Step aside. My business here is done and I will disturb your drinking no more.' He knew any sign of weakness would only encourage the drunken men further.

The seaman's one good eye flickered from left to right, and in an instant strong hands gripped Will's arms. Someone tore off his hat. The sailor whisked a dagger from the folds of his dirty linen shirt, and pressed the tip under the spy's chin, forcing his head up. A blast of ale-sour breath washed over Will as the man searched his features. Silence fell across the rest of the inn. The other drinkers crowded around.

One of the women leaned in, her eyes narrowing. 'I know 'im,' she said in a broad country accent. 'That's Will Swyfte, that is. England's greatest spy.' A lascivious smile sprang to her lips. 'I would see the length of your sword, chuck.'

'Later, in the privacy of your chamber, perhaps. Let us not point up how dull are the blades of these fine men.' He held her gaze and her smile broadened.

'The great Will Swyfte,' the seaman mocked. 'The dewy-eyed women and the witless fieldworkers might be easily dazzled by your exploits, but here you are just another sharp nose poking into our business.'

'Your business concerns me less than the contents of your privy. I am troubled by greater matters, the security of this realm.'

'Stick 'im now. We'll dump him in the drink and no one'll be the wiser,' another seaman said. 'Let 'im walk out and we'll be swarming with tax collectors like rats on the bilge-deck.'

Will's dark eyes flickered over the grizzled faces pressing all around him. He had been here before, too many times, and whether he was looking into the eyes of Spanish pikemen or

Kentish cut-throats, he knew the signs; there was no point in further talk.

Wrenching his shoulders back, he unbalanced the two men gripping his arms. With one sharp thrust, he planted a shoe in the gut of the sailor wielding the knife. The milky-eyed seaman doubled over with a forced exhalation. Will saw the drunken sailors were taken by surprise by the suddenness of his movement, and he smiled. Sober, they would be a formidable army of cut-throats. Soaked in ale, they wheeled around like small children.

Tearing his arms free, the spy lashed one toe under a three-legged stool and propelled it into the face of his former captor. Bone shattered, blood sprayed. A tumultuous roar rang up to the beams. Squealing whores ran for the rickety stairs at the back of the inn. Glinting lights cut through the shadows as the seamen drew daggers and hooks, each one catching a candle-flame. The men surged forward.

Will felt the familiar heart-rush. He whipped out his rapier, enjoying its trusty weight in his hand. With one bound, he leapt from a bench to the innkeeper's cluttered trestle. Cups flew. Coin jangled on to the boards.

'Who is the first to feel the bite of my blade?' he called, kicking the barrel. The wooden tap burst free, the honey-coloured ale gushing out. The keg spun off the table and into the path of the onrushing seamen.

The spy felt no desire to kill these rogues; he saved his steel for more deserving blood. But they swarmed around him like angry bees, eager to sting him to death. Yet as he searched for a route past them, the boards began to vibrate as though the trestle was being dragged over cobbles. The seamen came to a sharp halt, eyeing each other with unease. Across the inn, the candle flames wavered as one. Shadows swooped. Breath clouded as a winter chill descended, and one by one the sailors put away their weapons, casting uneasy glances all around.

Through the small, square window panes, distorted candle-light danced in an unnatural manner on board the carrack and in the wildly-swinging lanterns along the dockside. A moment later, the door crashed open. The master of the quay lurched into the space, his felt hat askew, his face drained of blood. 'Take up your weapons and any light you can find,' he croaked. 'The Devil has come with the fog.'

Mark Chadbourn's *The Devil's Looking-Glass*
— available from Bantam Press

Don't miss the first of the *Swords of Albion*
adventure . . .

THE SWORD OF ALBION
Mark Chadbourn

1588. As the Spanish Armada prepares to sail, rumours
abound of a doomsday device that, were it to fall into
enemy hands, could destroy England and her
bastard queen once and for all.

Enter Will Swyfte. He is one of Walsingham's new breed of
spy and his swashbuckling exploits have made him famous.
However Swyfte's public image is a façade, created to give
the people of England a hero in their hour of need – and
to deflect attention from his real role: fighting a secret war
against a foe infinitely more devilish than Spain . . .

For millennia this unseen enemy has preyed upon
humankind, treating honest folk as playthings to be hunted,
taken and tormented. But now England is fighting back.
Armed with little more than courage, their wits and an array
of cunning gadgets created by sorcerer Dr Dee, Will and
his colleagues must secure this mysterious device before it is
too late. Theirs is a shadowy world of plot and counterplot,
deception and betrayal, where no one – and nothing – is
quite what they seem. At stake is the very survival
of queen and country . . .

'Smart, fun, at times surprisingly moving, and occasionally
downright shocking . . . impossible to put down'
REALMS OF FANTASY

QUEEN OF KINGS
Maria Dahvana Headley

Once there was a queen of Egypt . . . a queen who
became through magic something else . . .

In 30BC, as Octavian Ceasar and his legions marched into
Alexandria, Cleopatra, Queen of Egypt, learned that her
beloved Mark Antony had taken his own life. Desperate
to save her kingdom, her husband and all she held dear,
Cleopatra turned to the gods for help. She summoned
Sekhmet, goddess of death and destruction, and struck a
mortal bargain. And not even the wisest scholar
could have foretold what would follow . . .

For saving Antony's soul Sekhmet demands something in
return: Cleopatra herself. Transfored into a shape-shifting,
not-quite-human manifestation of a deity who seeks to
destroy the world, Cleopatra follows Octavian back
to Rome. She desires revenge, she yearns for her
children . . . and she craves human blood.

'So magical, so dark . . . stalking the murky, dangerous
territory between Anne Rice's *Queen of the Damned*
and Robert Graves's *I, Claudius*'
NEIL GAIMAN